THE MADRIGAL

We gratefully acknowledge the support of the Canada Council for the Arts and the Ontario Arts Council for our publishing program. We also acknowledge the financial support of the Government of Canada.

Cover Design: Carter Pryor, Photograph: Katherine Knight.

The Madrigal is a work of fiction. All the characters and situations portrayed in this book are fictitious and any resemblance to persons living or dead is purely coincidental.

Library and Archives Canada Cataloguing in Publication

Day, Dian, author
The Madrigal / Dian Day.

(Inanna poetry & fiction series)
Issued in print and electronic formats.
ISBN 978-1-77133-493-8 (softcover).-- ISBN 978-1-77133-495-2 (Kindle).--
ISBN 978-1-77133-496-9 (pdf).-- ISBN 978-1-77133-494-5 (epub)

I. Title. II. Series: Inanna poetry and fiction series

PS8607.A98M33 2018 C813'.6 C2018-901525-X
C2018-901526-8-

Printed and bound in Canada

Inanna Publications and Education Inc.
210 Founders College, York University
4700 Keele Street, Toronto, Ontario, Canada M3J 1P3
Telephone: (416) 736-5356 Fax: (416) 736-5765
Email: inanna.publications@inanna.ca Website: www.inanna.ca

MIX
Paper from responsible sources
FSC® C004071

THE MADRIGAL

a novel

DIAN DAY

INANNA PUBLICATIONS AND EDUCATION INC.
TORONTO, CANADA

for Andrea
my best

Four arms, two necks, one wreathing,
Two pairs of lips, one breathing.
Fa la la la la, Fa la la la la,
Fa la la la la la la la.

—Thomas Weelkes, 1608

I WAS THE ABERRATION IN MY FAMILY: a single child. My mother had three sets of identical twins, and then me. Two boys, two boys, two boys. At least if I had been a girl it would have been some consolation for all of us. But I was not; I was the seventh boy, as unremarkable as anyone's child, born without my other half.

My mother favoured three-syllable names that could be shortened to one sharp sound:

Nicholas
Nathaniel

Samuel
Salvador

Abraham
Alistair

Frederick

On summer evenings, she would stand on our broken front step at dusk and yell down the street, in a steady rhythm like a metronome set precisely at ninety-two: Nick-Nat-Sam-Sal-Abe-Al-Fred! My brothers would run like hungry wolf cubs for the promise of meat—my mother learned early that the only way to lure them in for bath and bed was with food. She held off supper until it was almost dark. Once they were all inside I crawled out from behind the scraggly elderberry bush, where I'd been sitting for hours, picking the scabs from my insect bites and listening to the robins defend their territories with song.

I don't like people to call me Fred.

When I was a child my Winchester cousins—before they emigrated to Australia with *their* worn-out mother—called me Fred Mad. They never tried this with any of my brothers; teasing a team was a lot riskier than tormenting a singleton.

I never knew my Madrigal cousins, or even if there were any in existence. I knew nothing at all about my father's family, since my father left my mother just after I was born, and my mother was not inclined towards storytelling. I was left to draw my own conclusions, and I grew up believing that my father, too, found it unacceptable that I was born a lone child.

A MADRIGAL IS A MUSICAL SETTING of secular text for four or six voices, unaccompanied by instruments. Secular, *not* religious. Four or six, *not* seven. With a last name like Madrigal, you have to be precise about music.

When people I don't know very well learn about my involvement in music, they always ask, jokingly, about my instrument. It still makes me blush, though luckily the Madrigals are all dark-complexioned. Women, in particular, ask this question with a hint of sexual energy that suggests they have no idea this joke was overplayed by the time I was fifteen, let alone now, twenty-one years later. I blush for their sakes rather than my own, and I try to answer seriously, as if they were genuinely interested: I play piano, lute, harp, harpsichord, recorder, flute, and the *viola d'amore*—which, interestingly, has seven strings above the fingerboard and seven below.

I rarely mention that voice is my instrument of choice.

OF COURSE, MY FAMILY DREW A LOT OF ATTENTION. Three

sets of identical twins out of the same mother is a very rare thing. It's fraternal twins, apparently, that tend to run in families. After the SSs were born, it was bad enough. People stopped my mother in the street and in the grocery store, some of them to coo and others in simple shock at the reckless multiplying of the lower classes. But after AA came along, there was almost constant attention from the university. Nearly every week, graduate students would call my mother asking if the twins could participate in some research study or other. She always said yes—for a fee. Until they themselves were old enough to say no, my six brothers advanced the causes of biology and psychology considerably. They were taken to laboratories where every alphabetical part of them was tested and measured: CAT, IQ, and TED, along with any number of versions of Rorschach inkblots. You can read whole paragraphs about them in any of the books on twins that occupy the shelves of more serious bookstores. One myopic student, Courtney Glass, even wrote an entire dissertation on The Madrigal Twins, but she accidentally drowned in Lake Ontario a week before her defence date. The university let my mother have a copy of the draft; it sat curling on the kitchen shelf—a place of honour—with the chipped imitation-Doulton figurine, the shell from Adelaide sent by her sister Clara, and the good luck penny she'd found the day she met our father.

When my mother was pregnant with me, the Ns told me that a reporter from the *National Enquirer* camped out in the empty lot across the street for pretty much the whole duration of her third trimester. When my parents came home from the hospital with one meagre child tucked under one of my father's arms, the reporter packed up and went home to Boca Raton, Florida. Since I was born in an unseasonably cold November, he was probably doubly unimpressed.

AFTER I WAS BORN, we did not have a living room or a dining room in our house. We did not have anything except a cramped kitchen with a sagging floor, a bathroom, and multiple bedrooms. My mother—and my father, while he was still there—started out in one of the small upstairs bedrooms, and Nicholas and Nathaniel got another to share when they were born. Samuel and Salvador got the third, and then, of course, they were all used up. After Abraham and Alistair came, the living room was blocked off from the dining room with a thin sheet of dark panelling, and converted into another bedroom; as soon as they were weaned my mother moved downstairs and put all her children thus far on the second floor. And me, I got the dining room, which, after its separation from the front of the house, had no windows, and a big open archway without a door. There was an old red curtain tacked up in the doorway at first, but the SS kept ripping it down to use as a Superman cape—it was so long that they shared it, one at each end. In her own doorway, my mother had rigged up a giant piece of flattened cardboard that the neighbour's new fridge had come in; my brothers took it down over and over again to make a big game hunter's tent in the African jungle. After a short while, my mother gave up. In a house with so many twins, no one thought privacy was important. Sharing was just the accepted *modus operandi*. No one saw the difference between sharing with the other half of yourself, and being a constant victim of the unwanted attentions of double personalities. My brothers either never left me alone, or left me alone all the time. I was, perpetually, either completely overwhelmed or profoundly lonely. I imagine it was the same for my mother.

We ate in the small kitchen in shifts. There were only six chairs. My six brothers ate first, like raucous pack animals—my mother standing by the table, cajoling and snapping and snarling over the top of their considerable noise. When they had run like a herd from the watering hole, with full stomachs and unbound energy, my mother and I ate their leftovers in a dead quiet kitchen. I see now that she was too exhausted to speak to me. At the time, I believed she had nothing to say.

The kitchen may have been silent, but other noises came to us like faint music. I could hear the electric clock ticking in the front hall, and the occasional pounding of my brothers' feet on the uncarpeted stairs, and often—despite my mother's best efforts to keep them inside—the slamming of the front door. I could hear the rhythmic beat of their tennis balls against the brick back of the house, high and hollow, and their cries, *agitato*, like birds of prey. The scolding of Mrs. Bern next door came like the crashing of cymbals in the *sturm und drang*.

Alone in the kitchen with my spent mother, I heard my first symphonies.

Very early, I began to imagine myself a conductor. Three thumps on the stairs, *presto*, the syncopated tennis balls, *prestissimo* and *spiccato*, Mrs. Bern yelling, *spiritoso*. I stood on the wire-strung wooden chair in the sloping yellow kitchen. My arms waved in the air a split-second behind the sounds. Even when I knocked the overcooked Brussel sprouts off the table with the wooden spoon I used as a baton, my mother hardly noticed, except to look down at the green-grey balls rolling on the filthy linoleum and wish longingly and inexplicably for a dog.

But as the symphony conductor, I could imagine myself in control of the noises. And the space between the noises, normally called silence, was for me where the heart of music lay.

I spent a lot of my childhood standing liltingly on chairs.

THERE'S A SAYING ATTRIBUTED TO JESUS, recorded by Thomas, the twin. Whose twin, nobody knows. It's in the Gnostic Gospels, writings on the life of Jesus that were suppressed by the early Christian church. The Gnostic Gospels are the bits left on the cutting room floor in the making of the New Testament. Somebody gathered up all those out-takes and hid them in a cave in Egypt, in the third and fourth centuries, where they remained untouched until discovered by two brothers in 1945.

This is what Thomas wrote: "If you bring forth what is in you, what you bring forth will save you. If you do not bring forth what is in you, what you do not bring forth will destroy you."

Some people think the out-takes are better than the movie. Myself, I rather thought that what was in me should stay buried as deeply as possible.

IF PEOPLE THINK THEY ARE BEING ORIGINAL when they make instrument jokes, they think they're beyond brilliant when they call me the Singing Postman—even though none of them would ever have heard me sing. But enough people downtown know me; they know I teach voice and direct choir, and they know I deliver their mail. They can't help themselves; they put the two things together.

This morning it was Steve Packer, standing outside his electronics shop, dragging on the end of a cigarette like he had sworn to quit right after lunch. Everything in the window behind him was dusty. "Hey, how's the Singing Postman?" he asked, blowing smoke from the side of his mouth. I handed him his meagre pile of mail—bills mostly.

"Dead," I said. It's what I always say, though I don't know why. It just keeps the whole thing going. Most people don't really know anything about the Singing Postman, except the stage name. I should remember to reply with a remark about the weather.

"Say what?"

"Dead, he's dead. And I have better teeth." By this time I was on my way into the next shop, the used clothing place the university students frequent, but I turned and showed him my perfect teeth before I went in. The bell tinkled on the door, *ostinato*.

MOST DAYS AFTER WORK I WALK DOWN to the lake and along the bike path to the river, and then double back along Rideau Street to my house. Sometimes I make an extra loop and walk by the row house where I grew up. After standing empty for many years, it was finally bought and gutted by a young couple with a baby, and the first thing they did was replace the rotten front step. Sometimes when I see them outside, caulking windows or sweeping the leaves off the sidewalk, I think about stopping and asking if I can go in and have a look around—but I never do.

You would think I get enough walking with my day job, but there is something about the way the river looks that helps me shift from mail to music. At this time of year, the tree tips are blushed orange with dead leaves, and even in mid-afternoon their shadows stretch across the bike path like a bar code for God.

I could deliver the morning mail with my eyes closed, and tell you which shop door I'm opening by the sound of the bells hanging on the door. Luckily, it's a small city with a vibrant downtown, I guess because of the students at the university. Princess Street is still lined with shops with real tinkling bells rather than electronic ones—though there are a few and growing number of exceptions. Lately, I have begun to think about composing a piece that circles around the music of opening and closing doors.

My voice students are scheduled in the late afternoons and early evenings, after I finish the mail. I teach out of a music shop downtown. It's funny, because the shop I teach in is on my mail route. So, every weekday morning at about ten o'clock I go into The Whole Note and hand the mail over, and I say "Hi, Ed," and Ed says "Hi, Frederick," and for some reason we mostly pretend we don't know each other much. Especially if there are customers in the "Trade two for one" CD aisles, or fingering the guitars hanging along the wall. But, of course, I know he'd much rather be called Ed than Edward, and he knows very well I don't care to be called Fred.

No one wants to come into the house of a single man for music lessons anymore. Mothers would never trust me with their children in my living room. I guess I can't blame them, really. There are a lot of crazy people in the world these days. Besides, I'm not sure what Ed would do without me. I wouldn't want him to think that the soundproofed room was an unnecessary investment: a new sail for a sinking ship.

Sometimes I give Ed mail in the morning that he hands back to me in the afternoon: people sending in cheques for their music lessons, or occasionally non-profit groups asking me to bring the choir to sing at a benefit concert. Ed told me once that I should just keep the mail addressed to me, but I said no. I like to keep things separate. You never know what would happen if the different parts of your life got mixed up.

THE HOUSE I OWN NOW is long and skinny and semi-detached, and there's only a very narrow lane between the house and the one beside it. There's a place to park a small car, but I don't own one at the moment. It seems silly to keep a car just to move large instruments around once every few months, at most, especially since Jiro has a van on account of all those kids, and the seats are removable, and he is always quite willing to pick me up. I have a very tiny yard in the back, bounded by a wooden "privacy fence"—so said the brochure—but it would only provide privacy for very small children, being all of three and a half feet high. The yard is overhung by my new neighbour Maya's giant maple tree; its furrowed trunk has a significant lean, and I fully expect that one day I will wake up with the privacy fence flattened and the useless mast of a giant ship lying across my yard. Until then, it's a convenient arrangement for her, since I have to rake up most of the yellow leaves. When the branches are almost bare, as now, the bundled squirrels' nest hangs like a ruffled brown globe outside my bedroom window. The nest is inhabited by two grey squirrels who can jump from their branch tip to the shelf I attached to my window ledge. If I forget to put out peanuts, they wake me early in the morning by scratching on the window glass with their tiny nails, *dolente*. I think of them as twins—they both cross their paws the same way over the same white markings on their downy bellies—though I expect they are really mates. Nonetheless, they are twin-named: Free-for-all and Fly-by-night. I can tell them apart because Fly-by-night has a small tear in his right ear.

Sometimes it seems that I am surrounded by two of everything.

MAYA WAS OUTSIDE WHEN I GOT HOME, trying to light her barbeque with her blow torch. I came home from teaching, went right through the house, and stepped out my back door—it was such a fine evening—and that's when I saw her, over the privacy fence.

"Maya! No!" I called out to her between flicks of the switch on the torch, so she could hear me. Fly-by-Night was in the middle of her yard, burying a nut, but he scuttled up the leaning tree when I yelled. I had my hand on the fence post. I was squinting and ready to duck. Maya keeps her barbeque along the opposite fence line, but you never know how far these things could blow.

"It's all good, Frederick," she called back affably.

"You're going to blow yourself up!" I yelled. I don't know why I don't stop while I am ahead. What is it with me?

At that moment the gas caught uneventfully with an understated *puugh*, and she turned the flame down some. She straightened up then and turned to face me, still flicking the trigger of her torch so the blue flame shot to the sky. I thought she might burn the tree down, and save me from having to pay for its removal after it had fallen, though I couldn't speak to what the flying sparks would do to my roof. She was in the trademark orange coveralls she wore for work, with a wide black leather belt. There was an appliqued orange on the front of her coveralls over her heart, and at the back—I knew, though I couldn't read it then—were the words: CITRUS PLUMBING: A New Twist for Old Pipes. She looked like a new-wave flame-throwing comic book superhero. She took a breath and opened her mouth, but before she could start with the friendly sarcasm I said, "Right then, you've got it lit. Great." And I ducked back into my house and shut both doors behind me. I could hear her voice coming after me, but at least I couldn't hear the words. I went into the living room, sat at the piano, and played some jazz riffs, just waiting until she'd finished cooking her veggie burgers before I went back in the kitchen to make my supper.

Waste of time, anyway, firing up a barbeque for a hunk of soy protein.

ONCE, I ASKED MY MOTHER what she would have named my twin. I was still very small. I can remember looking up at her from a great distance, my small arms wound around her thigh; the top of my head was perhaps level with the loose elastic waistband of her full cotton skirt.

She looked down at me, her coal-haired singleton, as if surprised to find me tangled in her clothing.

"You don't have a twin," she said. Even then, I could tell that there was accusation in her voice, as well as relief.

"*If* I did," I insisted.

"Filander," she said, absently, and turned away towards the sound of glass breaking in the kitchen. I was dislodged, and tumbled on the worn pine boards. I stretched my scarred hands out and felt the draft under the front door.

"Fil?" I asked, but her back was already all I could see, her skirt swaying down the long dark hallway.

I lay on the floor a long time, until my fingers were stiff from the gusts coming under the doorstep. I believe it must have been winter outside. The thin white lines along the outside of each of my palms turned blue in the cold and stood up like zippers running from my wrists to the bottom of my baby fingers. I lay there, pretending to unzip my hands, as more glass shattered in the kitchen and the SS sobbed and howled distantly.

If only I could get my hands open, unzipped, I thought, I would find the rest of Filander. I knew when he emerged he would only have four fingers on each hand, four toes on each foot. The Ns told me that I'd come home from the hospital with six digits at the end of each limb; the doctors had spent a year trying to convince my mother to agree to the removal of the extras. Around my first birthday she finally acquiesced, tired of the ignorant public attention that made me a different kind of freak than my six twin brothers.

All I had had of Filander had been surgically eliminated by bone excise and plastic surgery.

WE HAD A LOT OF BOOKS ABOUT TWINS in our house; they were the only books we had. It seemed that they came in by the box-load: classmates, neighbours, friends, and relations brought or sent them gaily wrapped on my brothers' birthdays and at Christmastime. Most of them had photographs of beaming look-alike faces, and over-used phrases like "special bond" and "close connection." I'm not sure why anyone thought that, after living every day as a twin among twins, my brothers would have any interest in reading about it—even supposing they had any interest in the quiet and sedentary pursuit of *reading*. They *were* the phenomena; even the occasional book with a photograph of the six of them held no more than momentary interest. For them, it would have been like reading about breathing or sleeping soundly or eating something dull, like meatloaf. Two-ness just *was*.

I was the only one who read those books, or rather, since I couldn't yet read when I discovered them, I looked at the pictures in the kind quietude—since even AA was in school by the time I was born—between *fine*, breakfast time, and the noisy *overture* of supper.

The morning sun came slanting in silently, gracing every surface with dust motes. I lay on my belly in the upstairs hall, where our house's only bookshelf leaned up against the railing.

The only things it held were the books on twins, two ancient copies of *National Geographic* my mother had found in a garbage can on Princess Street, and the extra rolls of toilet paper. The pages of the books were crisp and turned with minute sighs, *dolce*. I was always careful to wash the elderberry juice from my fingers first. I flipped through the identical smiles, *legato*. Two-thirds of the way through most of the books were the pictures of almost-complete twins incompletely separated: joined at the hip, or the top of the head, or back to back. But one book had pictures of an entirely different kind: a woman with a third leg emerging from the full skirts of her dress; a young girl with four arms; a bearded man with another face, upside-down, on his forehead; a naked little boy, about my age, with a whole extra miniature body, with arms and legs but no head, protruding from his abdomen.

I asked Nicholas about the pictures.

"Par-a-sit—parasitic twins," he said, reading the chapter heading hesitantly, with his stocky finger sliding underneath the letters. Nathaniel hung over his shoulder and squinted.

"What's paras-tic-tic?" I asked him, without taking my eyes from the book. There was no answer but a sound like *psssssssssss*, and when I did manage to slide my eyes from the page and look up they both had their flies unzipped and were pretending to pee on me before running off to the bathroom, singing like gibbons.

I BELIEVE MY EARLY CHILDHOOD was more chaotic than most, though perhaps this is what everyone thinks about their own upbringing. I've hardly ever heard anyone say they had a normal, happy, uneventful childhood. But seven children in any family is a lot, and the complete absence of girls—somehow my mother didn't seem to count as female—meant there was no balance or temperance to my brothers' energy. I can see now that they were not initially *bad* children, just exuberant, willful, and uncontrolled. The six of them shared something, some unshakable knowledge of their own specialness, which made them expect, and eventually command, attention. They commanded it, and, at first, I hid from it. When the authorities began to warn my mother, I hadn't yet started school, and when the police began to come for them, I was nine. I sat stern-faced in the dark in my dining-room-turned-bedroom, behind the two Canadian flags I'd finally hung across my doorway, and I listened to my mother weeping: A *ballade* for her boys.

Until I was eleven, I grew up entirely on social assistance and pin money from the twin research. Back then social assistance was called "the Welfare." I believe it's still called that by the people who receive it, but political correctness has changed the official jargon. We lived in one of many row houses owned by a slum landlord, who also happened to be the real estate agent with the area's highest house sales every year. When I was in my early twenties, there was an investigation; it turned out that he was selling most of the houses to himself. But at the time I was a child, so all I knew was that our landlord was a big shot in the city. And I knew that he would never fix the leaking sink trap or the rotten step or the sagging wallboard or the window that wouldn't fully close—the house was perpetually drafty and hazardous and smelled like mould and must.

Naturally, when I was very small, there was no money for music lessons, even if someone had noticed that I longed for them. Instead, I *listened.*

FROM THE BEGINNING I HEARD MUSIC everywhere, from the safety of a myriad of silent hiding places. The thudding feet, thrown balls, and door slamming of my brothers gave way to an even more boisterous symphony of the street, to which I listened from behind the elderberry, green and shady enough in summer to hide a small child. The ground was always cool, and damp stained the thin seat of my already-thrice-worn shorts. I leaned up against the crumbling brickwork and listened to hissing buses, impatient drivers, and frantic dogs as a backdrop to the robins' gentle melody line. It was like a song about a lost world.

When I went to school, I hid under the half-flight of steps at the bottom of the stairwell and listened to the fearful buzzer that called children in from the playground—all wound up like metal springs from sugar and bullying, their voices a battlefield—and I felt the vibrations of a hundred feet rise above my head like a percussive detonation. It was a song about the end of the world, where only dust was left in the ensuing silence.

And I, of course, was always late for class.

When I began to sing in public, in my last year of elementary school, it was hard to shake the feeling that it was better to remain unseen. But I was determined not to be like my mother, even though, when I sang, I began with the tunes I had effortlessly learned from her.

ON SUNDAYS, SINCE I DON'T GO TO CHURCH anymore to talk to God, I go to the nursing home to see my mother. It is really the only day I have enough time off. It's hard to know if she ever gets other visitors, because my mother doesn't say anything directly anymore, but usually by the time I get there on Sunday afternoons, the flowers in her room are all dead—and they're the same flowers that I brought the previous week. I know I could ask the staff, but I don't really want to know if my brothers ever come. After young adulthood, they scattered in three directions, leaving me my hometown, and my mother's care, and the fading fame of "The Madrigal Twins" all to myself.

When I went to see her yesterday, this is what she told me:

"The landlord has not prepared the sink. (Pointing at the night table.) Do you have a biscuit? I never can, it's on the sly. Fix him! Fix him! I can't do it! (Hands tighten on the arms of her wheelchair.) Look! (Pointing to the foot of the bed, where a plaid blanket is neatly folded.) The children are all asleep. Oh, tell him they will drown! (Getting agitated; I put my hand on her thin arm. It burns my palm like dry ice.) I saw a cat yesterday. Not cat, no, no. Like marmalade on toast. Jenny thinks that is funny. Funny funny funny funny funny. No, *fanny*. Drowning children!"

"There aren't any drowning children, Mother," I said, before she could get too worked up. I picked up on what I thought was a safer thread: "Why was the cat funny?"

"Cat in the Trap. The Cat in the Trap. The Cat in the Trap."

"*Hat*," I said, finally.

"No," she said. "*Fanny*."

"Oh," I said.

"Jennifer won't eat toast." Jenny was my brother Salvador's girlfriend for about six months, over twenty years ago.

"Jenny's gone," I told her.

"*Jennifer*," she said.

That's how our conversations go. Well, conversations—if

there is a place where our words intersect, where we might appear to be talking together about the same subject, it is purest accident.

I'M THE KIND OF GUY WHO APPEARS to be a bargain garment until the seams are more closely examined. Women like me all right, until they get to know me. Once they do, they decide I'm strange, and a strange man might do anything. They suspect me of being unpredictable, even though I am pretty much the most boringly predictable guy in the entire world. After a few dates, they clamour for a refund.

Every morning I have the same thing for breakfast—a poached egg on toast, a banana, and a very small glass of orange juice. I save the coffee for later—the stuff goes right through me—and I walk along the river to the sorting station, grunt at all the other posties, and sort my mail. By the time I walk downtown, the mail is in my relay box, and I start my route. I can finish within ten minutes either side of four hours, twenty minutes, no matter what the weather. Then I walk home again, through the park by the river, and have a late lunch, rather than eat on my route: canned soup and a sandwich, or some leftover stuff if I ordered in the night before. On the nights I have choir, I usually take a short nap in the middle of the afternoon; other days I fix the leaky tap or rake the leaves or pay the bills. I drink coffee like crazy from when I get home until it's time for me to walk back over to the music shop. My first lesson is usually around three-thirty or four, when school gets out. There is a soundproof practice room with glass windows so that customers can watch the classes in progress without the embarrassment of hearing the mistakes. I think this is meant to be both inspiring for prospective students, and a clear message of safety so that everyone, on both sides of the glass, knows there can be no funny business going on behind the closed door. I teach fifty-minute lessons. There's a toilet at the back of the shop, through the storage room. I always have to go after the first and second lesson, and sometimes the third as well. As I make my way there, Ed always says: "Clean up while you're back there, eh Frederick?"

He means it as a joke, but I do have to clean up a little in order to get through to the washroom door. For days after a new shipment of electric guitars or African drums, I can hardly push the storage room door open, there are so many boxes piled haphazardly along the narrow passage.

On Mondays and Wednesdays I don't teach after six o'clock. On Mondays, I quick-step it along to the United Church, *accelerando*, so I can be there before the choir. On Wednesdays, I run home to meet up with the other three of the Four Consonants. On Tuesdays, Thursdays, and Fridays, I take home some new music from the shop, and Ed is as likely as not to turn up in my living room, especially if he is thirsty.

My weekends are equally routine. On Saturdays, I teach most of the day, and drink coffee unchecked, for energy. After six long days of work I don't have to think too much about Saturday nights, about how I'm not going out on the town with a date nor going home with her. If Ed doesn't come over, and there's no performance at the Grand or the Wellington Street that I want to see, I go to bed early with a library book, and fall asleep with it cracked open on my chest, the pages bent over crisply like unused bed sheets. And on Sundays I go to see my mother, feed her marmalade on toast in the visitors' kitchen, and listen hard for my name in her confused and disjointed speech. Picked out of the bargain bin, it feels like a full enough life.

After the first date, I try to explain all this, but it never gets me anywhere.

I LEAVE OUT THE MOST IMPORTANT THING, though, and that thing is not so much a *thing* as it is a way of being. I can explain to anyone—though I rarely do—what I do on Sundays and Mondays, and how many times I order takeout in a week, and what kinds of books I take out of the library. The numbers and quantities of objects or actions are measurable and definable and lend themselves easily enough to language, whether oral or numerical.

What I can't explain is *music*.

The meaning we attach to the word "music" is entirely a social construct. In other times and places, the constructs were different. Some cultures had no global word that incorporated all music, but had a separate word for the sounds that each instrument produced. So one word might mean the-noise-made-by-a-drum, and another might mean the-noise-made-by-a-flute. Still other peoples used a single word to include vocalizing, banging on drums, and moving bodies. Their musical activity was always participatory, since playing, dancing, and singing could not be imagined as separate pursuits. I find I can't explain *music*, because the words we are accustomed to use simply will not let me. Whenever I try, it seems it is not even another culture of this world that I come from, but a distant planet, where "music"' means the-sound-of-breathing.

IN PLATO'S *SYMPOSIUM*, Aristophanes describes human beings in their original form. The mythology goes a long way toward explaining what seems an almost universal longing for a reunion. In that regard, it does a better job than the Christian bible.

It seems that In the Beginning, we were all twins. Each person was a rounded whole and had two faces on one head, four arms, and four legs, in three varieties: a double female, a double male, or one of each—an androgyne. They never had to walk backwards, but walked forward in both directions. Running was accomplished by turning cartwheels on the lawn. Everyone was perfectly happy; everybody already had their other half. I suppose there was a lot to celebrate.

After a while, people got delusions of grandeur, as people do. They started making attempts to climb up to heaven, so they could attack the gods and take their places. The gods got worried and called a meeting, during which they decided to cut everybody in half. This would not only weaken human power, but instantly double the number of individuals tending the fires of godly worship. So Zeus cut everybody in half, and Apollo went around turning their heads 180 degrees, and gathering the cut edges of skin and tying a knot in the middle of their bellies, so they would all be reminded of the reason for their fate by looking at their scars.

And so we humans are compelled forever to search for our other halves, in unsuccessful attempts to once again become whole. Denied our original form, doomed to twinlessness, we make do. We keep searching, but often settle for second best. As Aristophanes concludes, the desire and the pursuit of the whole is called love.

As I read, I could feel the white lines on the outside of my palms tighten. It is no news to me that I am only half a man.

I take a lot of books out of the library—way more than I could ever read—because I'm in love with the librarian.

I'll admit that after I read the *Symposium*, I stood naked in front of the full-length mirror on the back of my bedroom door, navel gazing with a vengeance.

OF COURSE THERE WERE TIMES when we were tumbled all together, and I was just one of the Madrigal boys—when my mother took us all to the grocery store or, once that I remember, to the park. But in many ways I was an only child. I was five years younger than the youngest of them and so was left behind from the moment I was born. They were already leaping into karate moves and trying out the latest swear words while I was still in diapers. But beyond that, my brothers lived in a world of their own. It was impossible that I should be included; I understand that now. They ran through the world like a double-breasted suit, like a right and left foot, like flame and heat, like breathing and air. They had a lexicon of two, a language of six.

An only child, a sole child—as my mother said, when I was still small enough to think words could only have one meaning. I don't know now if she meant sole or *soul*. Looking back, I see that I had her to myself in a way my brothers never did. I remember laying my head in her lap in the kitchen one night, her stroking my ear, absently, as if I were a sleeping cat. She was there and not there with me. I wanted something more from her, but I was too young to know what. Even the touch of her hand was elusive, a breath of wind when you know there are no windows left open to cause a draft. She nagged or swore or yelled at my brothers as if she were only a shadow of a self that lived in another realm. She could not be called forth, by me or anyone, and seemed to spend those years in a state of longing, hardly ever fully in her body in the present tense. How could I ever know my mother, under such circumstances? Maybe later she came to regret that herself; perhaps she felt if she had given me more of herself, I would not have left her as I did. Maybe it was her greatest regret. I will never know.

If anyone had asked me then, I would have said my mother's greatest regret was that she didn't get to take her twin-bound family to Twins Days in Twinsburg, Ohio. At the end of every school year from the time I was six years old, when the annual event was inaugurated, she would borrow our neighbour's outdated North American road atlas. Mrs. Bern had once driven across the border in a rented car, imagining she would go all the way to Graceland, but she had returned without explanation the following afternoon with a forty-ounce bottle of Captain Morgan, duty-free. Even then, I took some comfort in knowing that the Madrigals were not the only people with unfulfilled dreams.

My mother would flip through the washed-out, un-travelled maps and show me the pink state drooping underneath Lake Erie. Twinsburg wasn't in the atlas, but I'm not sure that mattered. It didn't matter that we didn't own a car, that she held no driver's licence, that she couldn't afford one bus ticket to Toronto, let alone seven to Ohio, or that by the time I was six, my brothers wouldn't have been caught dead on a family excursion with me and my mother. It didn't matter that by the time Twinsburg started inviting twins to town, my brothers were petty thieves and heartbreakers.

She told everyone we were going, except my brothers.

"It'll be a surprise for the boys," she'd say.

She told Mrs. Bern next door when she borrowed the atlas. She told her sister Clara in a blue airmail letter to Australia. She told Angel Hammersmith when she went around the corner to use the telephone to call Greyhound Bus Lines. She told the Chinese couple who ran the corner store. She told the postie, who she was always friendly with, opening the door every day with a smile when she saw him coming, even though she hardly ever got any letters, only bills she couldn't pay.

She worked herself up into a state of trembling anticipation. Her voice would lower to a conspiratorial whisper. She became unbearably bored with the routine of her life, as someone does when they think they are about to escape. She tapped her fingers on the kitchen table and the counter top and the side of the fridge. As the time approached, she stopped cooking meals, instead buying what she called "picnic food" that could be served out cold on paper napkins, and eaten without creating any dirty dishes.

"We'll go to the wiener roast, and the boys will all walk in the Double Take parade," she told everyone. "We'll win a prize for the most twins in one family."

Inevitably, there was a moment when she had to admit to herself that such a scheme was impossible. She was not ever able to imagine what my brothers might contribute to the talent show, nor how she could clothe them in six identical sets of t-shirts and Bermuda shorts. She had no money, and her boys could not be found.

"We'll go next year," she'd say, when the first weekend in August had passed her by. "Next year for sure."

MY MOTHER WENT OUT AT NIGHT sometimes. I try to remember how often—once a week? Once a month?—but the memories are blurred like out-of-focus photographs, one superimposed over the other. There's a picture of my mother on the top, clear and sharp, and underneath a pile of similar images, the lines indistinct and the colours faded. She would dress carefully in her dimly-lit room and leave me in my brothers' care. I don't think I ever had a babysitter. She never said where she was going, and as soon as the door was shut behind her, my brothers would be making their own plans to go out. Really, I was probably safer all alone in that dilapidated, about-to-collapse house than I was with the six of them.

One night I remember she wore a billowy black-and-silver outfit and big silver earrings shaped like shooting stars, and headed blithely out into the jungle of the night. A rare thing: she leaned down and kissed me on the top of my head before she closed the front door gently behind her. Her merriment gave out a false light, however, and she left a heaviness in her wake. Even at eight or nine I could sense this, and I was uneasy enough that I stood in the hallway looking at the inside of the door even after I heard my brothers start down the stairs. They jostled each other like cattle going through a chute.

"Aren't you supposed to be in bed?" asked Samuel.

"Why aren't you in bed?" asked Nicholas.

"Get in your room and go to bed!" demanded Alistair.

And Nathaniel picked me up by my pyjamas, one hand on my shoulder and the other on my thigh, and carried me sideways through the dining room archway and dropped me, not ungently, onto my bed. He'd decided a few days previously to try growing a beard, and after he dropped me, he rubbed the rough stubble against my cheek in what I believed was a form of animal-like affection, much as a lion might rub up against you when it purred—right before it ate you for dinner.

And then he put my pillow over my head and pretended to smother me. I'm sure now it lasted no longer than mere seconds, but it was long enough for me to panic, and at the time I was certain he was going to kill me.

I felt like I was still coughing up feathers ten minutes later as they made their final descent down the stairs and out the door, six pairs of army boots shaking the house like a Molotov cocktail, ready for an atomic night on the town.

THERE SEEMS TO BE A MYTHIC TRADITION about having seven sons. I wonder if my mother was aware of that, and, if so, whether it added to her pride or her grief about her boys. Since most of the stories of sevens are rather alarming, I would guess grief. I don't, myself, consider it a glad heritage.

The Jewish martyr Hannah, and Christian martyrs Felicitas of Rome and Symphorosa of Tivoli, all had seven sons who were tortured and killed for refusing to worship "pagan" gods—or, in the case of Hannah and her clan, for refusing to eat pork and worship idols. It's likely that all these ancient stories have the same origin, but it shows that people liked this story so much that they kept passing it around and appropriating it for their own through a little sleight-of-hand like changing names and dates and hometowns. Hannah-Felicitas-Symphorosa watched her sons being put to death one by one, by various means impossible to imagine. They were first castrated or flogged, then beheaded, thrown off precipices, or cut in two. It is interesting to me that in many of the stories, the mother gets to be a saint, but usually never any of the boys.

According to the Old Testament, the seven sons of Japheth—who himself was one of Noah's sons—were the origin of most of the people of Europe. The Hindu Medhatithi also had seven sons who conquered kingdoms and spread their DNA across the land. Job's first family shared in his famous god-sent afflictions, and his seven sons died when a house collapsed on their heads.

The Guaraní people of South America told stories about seven god-brothers, six of whom were literally monsters. In Greek mythology, one of the seven sons of the sun god Helios, the reckless Phaëton, set the earth on fire with his joy-riding; the others squabbled and pillaged and conquered, and ultimately a few of them got together and committed fratricide. More contemporary fiction is not devoid of this *leitmotif*, either: Tolkien's seven sons of Fëanor died by suicide, murder, and violent accident, and the one remaining brother went over the edge of despair and wandered around alone for the rest of his life.

My brothers and I may not have conquered new lands, nor pillaged the towns and villages of our enemies, nor have we, so far at least, killed each other. We have more modern issues and concerns to contend with: we have been individually and variously laid low by Driving Under the Influence, personal debt, and relentless guilt; we are collectively undermined by commitment phobia and a complex system of non-communication. It would seem we are still worshiping the wrong gods. Our mother, the martyr, has the twenty-first century version of seven sons—and not one acknowledged grandchild to show for it.

THE FIRST TIME I REMEMBER having some small inkling of what was going on, I came home from school to the sharp smell of men's cologne stuck in the dead air of the house, mixed with a faint, sick smell of something else I couldn't then identify. There was a curious presence in the air, as if someone had just brushed past me in the hall. I even turned to look—back and forth, back and forth—though I could see both the front and back doors standing shut from where I stood in the kitchen doorway.

"Who was here?" I asked. We rarely had visitors, and most of them, like social workers from the Children's Aid or from the Welfare, were harbingers of trouble.

"No one," she replied. She was sitting on one of the battered kitchen chairs, rocking back and forth slightly—whether the chairs legs were uneven or the floor wasn't level, or both, I don't know. Her eyes were half closed and focused unwaveringly on her lucky penny on the corner shelf. She looked dishevelled, as if it were morning and she had just woken up.

"What did he want?" I persisted.

"Nothing," she said.

"What happened?" Even at that age—seven? eight?—I could tell when I wasn't getting the truth. You might say I had an instinct for it.

There was a long pause while she, too, seemed to be contemplating the meaning of luck. The kitchen tap was dripping rusty water, *allegro*, making it seem like time was both standing still and speeding up.

"I paid the rent," she said, finally.

She went and picked up the penny, turning it over and over in her hands.

MY MOTHER HAD A SECRET: she sang like an angel. She sang through the deepest part of the night in the kitchen, over the sound of the washing machine that went on for hours: load after load of boys' thin-kneed trousers, in four sizes. For years I sat hidden in the dark doorway of my room and watched her sing her soul out; I couldn't take my eyes off her. She stood with her back to me, one hand on the back of the kitchen chair and the other hand dancing and swaying in the air like a diva's, full of emotion. Even though I couldn't see her face to read the expressions there, I could hear the notes deep in my heart. During the day, my mother was preoccupied and distant. It was at night, unknowingly, that she taught me how to feel. Often, I fell asleep there, my head leaning against the wall, and the pillow from my bed wedged against my side so I would not fall over into the hallway and be seen.

Music is not mathematics, despite the attempts of an array of modern composers to make it so. Music is about feeling, not formula. The best music makes us feel, not intellectualize. I'm not even sure it matters what we feel—love, despair, wholeness, murderous rage—only that we are called to acknowledge that mystery within ourselves. My mother's music was my first feeling—a dozen years of myself exposed, a thin slice of time and purpose, a *cantabile* of meaning. Not only did she birth me, she fashioned my soul with her songs.

As far as I knew during all the years of my childhood, I was the only one who ever saw her sing—whether or not others ever heard her through those thin walls I have no idea. She had a broad repertoire. Old Judy Garland songs: "After You've Gone" and "I'm Always Chasing Rainbows." African-American spirituals like "Swing Low, Sweet Chariot" and "Oh Freedom." Snatches of opera she'd heard who knows where: Rossini's *Il Barbiere di Siviglia* and Puccini's *La Bohème*. "*La destinée, la rose au bois*" and "*L'eau vive*"—the old standbys of her maternal grandfather, sung in a language that had been lost from the family in one generation. When she sang in French, the airborne hand moved to her thigh, where it tapped a lively rhythm, sending her tattered housecoat swaying. She may have been on the Welfare, scraping the pennies together at the end of every month, but she was rich in music. I don't think she could have survived the seven of us without it.

MY MOTHER SINGS NOW FOR ANYONE who will listen. In fact, it is one of a very few ways to get her to stop her incessant, nonsensical chatter; the others involve sedation, radio static, or sleep. You only have to start her off with one line of a song, and she'll deliver the remainder, word- and note-perfect. She stands when she sings, as she always did, struggling up from her wheelchair and placing her veined arm on the fake-veneered supper tray. Sometimes she even still waves one arm in the air for expression, though there is no indication she understands the meaning of any of the words.

Last Sunday, I started her off with:

In Dublin's fair city

And she sang, sweetly:

Where the girls are so pretty
I first set my eyes on sweet Molly Malone
As she wheeled her wheel-barrow
Through streets broad and narrow
Crying, "Cockles and mussels, alive, alive-o!"

"Marmalade," said my mother, interrupting herself.

"Do you want me to bring you some?" I asked.

"Poison," she insisted.

"No, no," I said. "You love marmalade. I'll bring you some. You'll remember."

But she just went back to her singing:

Alive, alive-o
Alive, alive-o
Crying, "Cockles and mussels, alive, alive-o.

It's amazing what the brain forgets and remembers. And what we can't forget, no matter how much we want to.

AT THE MUSIC SHOP, Ed makes tea perpetually. He offers me some every time. I don't know how his bladder copes with it: tea all day and beer all evening.

"I don't drink tea, Ed," I say every time. Sometimes I add, "You know that," but I try not to. I know he doesn't mean any harm by it. I've cultivated patience with people repeating themselves. It seems my whole life is about repetition: the mail route, the scale of C minor, the dripping tap of my mother's mind, Ed's tea, and "All the way through now, one more time" at choir practice.

Ed was the man I first brought my busking money to, all those years ago, for music lessons. He's owned The Whole Note for forty-two years. He taught me how to play piano. But first he found me a voice teacher from the School of Music at the university and drummed up four other pupils from the children of professors so it would be worthwhile for her to come to the shop one evening a week. Not much later, when I made the switch from St. George's to St. Mary's, he drove me to the station and put me on the train to Toronto, and at the other end his widowed sister picked me up and drove me to a tall house in the Beaches where I stayed, free of charge, until I was eighteen years old. Ed tried his best to make sure

I was different from the Madrigal twins in more ways than just being a singleton.

ED OFTEN WANDERS OVER AT NIGHT, not on any regular schedule or any particular day, just when things get too intense at home and he needs a break. It's not that he and Sylvia have a bad marriage, but I guess after fifty or so years with just the two of them, things begin to repeat themselves. So I open the door and he's standing there, and we just nod at each other, and then I say "Rickard's Red?" while he's coming in and taking his coat off, and I go back to the kitchen to get him his beer while he takes a handkerchief out of his pocket and blows his nose. I keep a supply of Red in the fridge for him, and I keep the thermostat on six. If I tried to keep lettuce in there, it would freeze.

Ed chugs back most of the first bottle right away, and then he gets himself settled at the upright. There's a bit of a ritual he has to go through: running his long fingers across my music books—though he always plays by ear—and touching the bent corners of my sheet music; pulling out the bench and wiping his hand across it; stroking the ivories without pressing down on them at all. It's like he's warming his hands up to the very idea of music.

And then he starts, *wham*, his hands are jumping and sliding on the keys, and his butt is dancing on the piano bench. As a contemporary said of Scarlatti, "when he played it was as if ten hundred devils had been at the instrument." Well, that's also Ed, early in the twenty-first century. The notes are hot and wild and fill the whole house with a crazy consonance. Ed's *fanny*—I laughed to myself when I remembered my last visit with my mother—is lifting and his hands are lifting, and there's just no way to stay down. I get up and stand behind him and I sing and wave my hands in the air like an idiot. We do all the old Motown favourites, and then we start on early rock 'n roll from the fifties, and then swing tunes from the forties. As long as there's beer flowing Ed will stay half the night, and some nights we get all the way back to union music and early Gospel tunes before I get tired and remember I have a mail route. It used to be hard for me to get rid of him, but now when I feel like I'd better get to bed I just tell him that there's no more Red.

Last night we were just getting going, still working on Motown, when the sound of someone banging on my door finally broke through. Once I heard it I knew I'd been hearing it for a while.

"Hold on," I said to Ed, and he stopped playing while I went and flicked on the porch light and answered the door. Maya was standing on the porch. She still had that orange suit on, almost fluorescent against the darkness. She has five of them, apparently, one for every day of the work week.

"Hey," she said, "I need a man."

"No you don't," I said. At that point, she looked past me into the living room and saw Ed sitting there at the piano, and then she took a minute to survey the whole scene: most of the double room is filled with straight-backed wooden chairs and an array of musical instruments. You especially can't miss the harp, a 47-string Lyon & Healy with a glistening walnut finish. I traded my car in for it.

"You mean this is *live* music?" she asked. She looked astounded, like she couldn't believe it, like maybe she never heard people singing in their living room before.

I couldn't think of how to answer that, so I just reverted to being polite. "This is my friend Ed; this is my new neighbour Maya."

We all just stared at each other for a minute, and then finally Maya said, "Okay, I need two men."

Ed might be an old guy, but he doesn't get hung up on civility. "No you don't," he said. He laid his hands back on the keyboard longingly. I think he just wanted this weird interruption to be over.

"Look, I already tried Mrs. Halif, but she isn't home. I don't know anyone else yet."

"Mrs. Halif is not one or two men," I said.

"All right, all right, I don't need a man, I need a person. I just thought that would appeal to you more, you know, invoking your manhood."

"Appeal? What is it that you actually want?"

"There's a squirrel stuck in my chimney," she said. "I can see its foot sticking out of the clean-out cover."

"Why didn't you say so?" I said. "Come on Ed, *Sciuridae* in danger."

Ed sighed resignedly, lifted his hands, and played a decisive E minor chord before getting up. "Will we get rabies?" he asked.

Maya led us over to her side of the semi. I admit I was curious to see the place; since she had moved in a couple of months ago there'd been a fair amount of hammering and banging. On a few occasions, I'd even heard her swearing through the walls. It didn't look like she'd done much to the place, though, at least on the main floor. These are small houses with a lot of archways between rooms so you can see the living room, dining room, and kitchen with one glance, practically. She had regular worn-out furniture, and the place wasn't exactly tidy. There were a bunch of open toolboxes cluttering up the hallway, and she'd haphazardly piled a dozen or so lengths of copper pipe along the wall.

The layout was the mirror image of mine—a reverse twin—so I didn't need to ask where the basement steps were. We raided the kitchen for a woven bag and a pair of work gloves, size small, and some scrap pieces of cardboard from her recycling bin for prods.

On the way down I began to catch a familiar skunky scent, reminiscent of my brothers' "science projects" in the damp basement of my childhood. "Smells like—" I began, but Ed had reached the bottom of the stairs, and stopped dead in front of me.

"Christ!" he gasped. The low room was filled with rows of five-foot-high marijuana plants, lined up under grow lights. "Damn good thing Mrs. Halif wasn't home," he said. It seemed to take him a while to get his legs moving again. Sometimes he is an old guy.

Sure enough, when we managed to beat our way through the jungle to the footing of the chimney, we spotted a skinny little grey foot sticking out of the air vent in the cast iron clean-out cover.

"Tickle, tickle," said Ed. The foot wiggled. "Alive-alive-o. Rabies for sure."

Maya put the gloves on, since they wouldn't fit either of us; then she went and stood right back in the middle of the room. Plant leaves draped over her shoulders. Ed shook his head as though that what was to be expected, but I already knew that a dread of rodents was perhaps the only way in which Maya conformed to any out-dated stereotypes of the female sex.

Ed held the woven bag open underneath the edge of the cover. I lifted the door slowly off its hooks, and a whole bunch of black dust fell out onto the floor, pulled by Free-for-All's scrabbling paws. Ed pulled the bag up around the grey body, and I pushed the scratchy little foot back in through the hole so the squirrel dropped down into the bag. Ed snapped up the top, and handed it across the room to Maya.

"Yeah, okay," he said. "You needed two men." Free-for-All stuck a tiny claw through the mesh.

"You guys want a Sleeman's?" Maya asked, keeping the bag at arm's length. I lifted my eyebrows in surprise.

"We gotta get back to the *live* show," said Ed.

"He only drinks Red," I explained. We went back up the stairs and out of her place, Ed walking the half dozen steps around on the path and me hopping over the railing that separated Maya's part of the front porch from mine.

"We just left her standing there, holding the bag," Ed said, solemnly, as he sat back down at the piano.

We just about pissed ourselves laughing. After a while I went and got him another beer and we started in on Gladys Knight and the Pips, where we'd left off.

WHEN I GOT UP IN THE MORNING, I put the empties out on the porch for Luke. He does this part of town on Tuesdays. I get up pretty early—well, I have to—but sometimes he goes by before I get them outside. I don't like to put beer bottles out at night. I tried it once and a bunch of kids smashed them all over the road. It took Norman all morning to clean up the mess; Norman was the old guy who used to live in the other half of the house before Maya bought it. He started before I left for work, and he was still at it when I got back for lunch. He'd cut open his little finger picking up glass, and I ended up taking him to the hospital to get stitches. I even had to cancel the first few students at the store at the last minute, because the wait time was so long in emergency, and I really hate doing that. So, all in all, I learned in just one trial that the beer bottles go out in the morning, and only if Luke hasn't been by yet. I can tell if I'm too late by looking across the road at Tamil's; I know it's okay if there's still a pile of glass ghee and yoghurt bottles outside his place.

I put the bottles out; there was a whole baker's dozen from the previous night. Maya was just coming out her door, too. She had on her coveralls—both of us in our uniforms ready for work—and was struggling with all the gear in her left hand because she had a giant thermos of coffee in her right. The aroma was so strong it made me weak in the knees. I've only seen Maya a few times in the mornings, and it's not pretty. I thought it would be safer to pretend I hadn't seen her, but she was making a racket with all those lengths of copper pipe she lined her hall with.

"Good morning," I said. I really wish I could leave off with the compulsory politeness thing.

"Morning," she grunted. Then she could have been on her

way to blocked drains, dripping taps, and twisting old pipes in new ways. But no.

"I see you got Free-for-All outside okay," I continued. He was in the gutter, fishing around in the debris for a stale peanut.

"*Who?*" she asked.

"The squirrel," I answered, and pointed. She looked at me briefly then, the merest glance. I could see her realizing that I had a name for the squirrel and that I recognized it as the one from her chimney. I could see her thinking that was strange.

"Finking right," she said. Saying "finking" is one of her quirks. Fink, fank, funk. She swears that she doesn't swear. If you want to talk about strange, I thought to myself.

Maya staggered over to her truck and threw the clattering armload into the broken back window of the cab.

THE LONG STREETS OF MY CITY all seem to be going somewhere else. Ontario Street, Montreal Street, Bath Road, the Old Perth Road. They run like sunrays on a page: east, west, and north, and to the south we are bound by an inland sea and the oesophagus of a great river. As a child, those elsewhere-named streets lured me out of town to the promise of something else—it didn't have to mean something *better*. Something else walking the streets besides ex-cons and mental patients and military cadets and drunken, snobbish students. Something else at home besides my six brothers charging through life like a herd of wild stallions. Something else besides a mother six times removed from her seventh child, a mother who hid her great talent in a mould-scented kitchen. Something else in my gawky heart besides being too skinny, and too weird, and too perpetually alone.

A couple of times, I took the city buses to their outer limits. I'd reach the fringes of town, where the increasingly-dilapidated houses tumbled into warehouses, barns, forests, and open fields. I'd get out of the bus and stand on the gravel shoulder and look down the curving highways; the future as invisible as the horizon. Sometimes I'd stand under the underpass of the 401, even in those days four lanes of frantic cars going somewhere else. I sang under the concrete: "Turn, Turn, Turn" by the Byrds and Leonard Cohen's "Suzanne" and "You are the Sunshine of my Life" by Stevie Wonder. It was like singing in the shower, I imagined: the roaring in the air somehow purifying the notes that emerged, *sostenuto*, from my throat. I couldn't go anywhere, but my voice travelled along those roads like a hobo, sleeping in outbuildings, building campfires in fields, begging at kind strangers' back doors. My voice was always on the move.

I could never have sung in the shower at home. My brothers would have killed me for it.

WHEN IT WAS BEDTIME, I got sent to my room. I did not get tucked into bed every night and kissed on the forehead. I did not get read bedtime stories, but I knew the words of a thousand songs before I knew what any of them meant. I knew the words when they were mere syllables of sound, a *Fa-Sol-La* that, as I grew, became "My Bonny" or "O Brother" or "Frail Wildwood Flower," and taught me more than Aesop or the Brothers Grimm ever could. "O Mio Babbino Caro" was both my adventure story and my lullaby.

I kept myself hidden for years while I watched my mother sing. It was like a spell I was afraid to break or I should say *she* was like a spell, and the music she made wove midnight stories in our small kitchen that wafted down the hall towards me like musical tumbleweeds across a barren plain. It was the only joy that touched that house, with its drab and listless air, the cupboard door that wouldn't close, the grime in every crack and seam, those scattered chairs whose screws unwound of their own accord no matter how often or how ineffectually she tried to tighten them with her lucky penny, or a broken thumb nail, or a dull knife. Her music made an otherworldly space around her that shone like the eyes of a cat at night, unblinking, full of a familiar strangeness. She was lit; she was alive. Singing made her tangible and real.

I thought if I moved the spell would break, my mother would break, the music itself would break. I thought the song would drop like glass and shatter into fragments, the *Do-Re-Mi* lost between the floorboards. I knew all the words from before I had memories of learning them, and for a long while I moved my lips as my mother sang. Then I would breathe music in and out, lightly. Then I began to sing with her softly, under my breath, my knees pulled up against my chest, my chest aching as if it would explode with the effort of containment. Finally, after years of this, something broke in *me*.

THE SUMMER I WAS ELEVEN, I started singing in the streets. I was driven there by a double desperation: to make some money for music lessons, and to make music differently than my mother did. The deserted kitchen would not be enough for me; I needed an audience. I was ready to be heard.

The first time, my heart hammered in my throat so fiercely, I don't know how I managed to make any notes at all, let alone true ones. But in those days the music poured out of me like new light at sunrise pours out of the sun, and a glow seemed to be on every face that looked towards the east.

MY MOTHER GREW USED TO NOISES in the house at all hours of the night. My brothers travelled to and from the bars on Princess Street without any regard for her sleep or the neighbours'. The front door opening and closing in the hall beside her makeshift bedroom became part of her dreaming, and she never stirred until much later, gripped by her own peculiar insomnia. I expect during those years she was so tired, and perhaps so disillusioned, that she would have slept through anything, even had she found herself in the orchestra pit of a first-rate opera house on opening night—a thing I don't believe she ever once experienced.

It was nothing for me to dress in the dark. I pulled my thrift store cadet cap down over one side of my head in the way I had practised endlessly in front of the tarnished mantle mirror. I thought it made me look older. I took the stub of a precious 4B pencil—who knows where it had come from—and darkened my upper lip. I had drilled holes in the bottom of my thick-soled boots with a rusty auger I'd found in the empty lot across the street, and filled the holes with bolts and nuts used as spacers. In this way I grew three quarters of an inch during my midnight escapades, and, when required, the metal studs striking the pavement were an accompaniment, *vivace,* to my songs. I walked out of the house solidly, sure-footed and courageous, so as not to give myself away by creeping. I didn't think about the marks my boot-bolts made on the hall floor; they were indistinguishable from the countless dings and dents and scratches that already inhabited that ill-used wood. The front lock was never bolted, and in fact the door handle hung ineffectively in its socket and had no latch. To keep my mother dreaming, I even learned to slam the door behind me by pulling fiercely on the mail slot as I launched myself into the hollowness of the night. Once outside, I slipped along streets like a skinny wraith, gliding from bush to porch to parked car—hulking shapes of darker darkness that hid me along my eerie way.

As I approached the downtown streets, I stopped flirting with darkness and stepped boldly down the centre of the sidewalk. It wasn't far; a seven-minute shadowy journey. I took my cap off and put it on the sidewalk in front of me, open side up. I stood under a street lamp, in front of the alley next to the Limelight Pub, where I could duck back into darkness at a moment's notice. I opened my mouth, and the trembling notes emerged like candles when they are first lit, flickering and uncertain.

When I was a bachelor, I liv'd all alone
I worked at the weaver's trade

It was early spring, and wisps of cloud moved across the moon and stars like a movie trailer for God. It was a big night, in the way that such nights sometimes are—the clouds and the moon and the stars way out there, and on this insignificant street corner in a third-rate city, an insignificant boy belting out the songs of his childhood. An insignificant, wavering noise, in all that endless space.

And the only, only thing that I ever did wrong
Was to woo a fair young maid.

Small gangs of university students staggered past me blindly, but in one group a pretty young woman looked back, and her eyes looked right into mine, clear and bright like a bird's. In an instant, I was looking into the face of my first true love: fine features framed with curling, sand-coloured hair. I was a point of sound, a pinprick of life, a wisp of meaning. My song faltered as her face turned away. But the flame inside me sparked and grew. I was really on the street, singing my soul out. I forgot my mother; I forgot myself. I took a deep breath and sent my voice after the woman who was walking away with my light on her face. She turned back to listen, pulling on the arm of the man she was with.

I wooed her in the wintertime
And in the summer, too
And the only, only thing that I did that was wrong
Was to keep her from the foggy, foggy dew.

"Give me your change, William," she said, and he grumbled sleepily, so she fished in his jacket pocket, and then he smiled. He handed her some coins from his pants pocket, and she stepped forward so she was brilliantly lit by the streetlight above, dropped a small handful of change into my upturned beret, and winked encouragement. I inhaled so deeply that my lungs completely filled with air; I inhaled the whole universe. I was suddenly bigger, older, better than I had ever been before.

I think that was the finest moment of my childhood.

It was also pretty much the most unqualified success I've ever had with a woman.

UNQUALIFIED SUCCESS. The idea is so foreign I'm not even sure what it would look like. Something longer than fleeting, I suppose. Some evidence of stability, a pair of serviceable women's shoes in my closet, an extra jacket on a hook, a drawer in my dresser reserved for the artifacts of a burgeoning relationship: underclothes, a toothbrush, whatever it is that one needs for occasional unplanned sleepovers. I've had those, the sleepovers, but no woman has ever been inclined to leave a spare toiletries bag in the bathroom cabinet or her old slippers by the front door or her favourite wine in the wine rack.

I've been on first dates and second dates and even, sometimes, third and fourth dates. Somewhere in there, we come home to my tiny semi-detached house and sleep together. Most of the women I go out with seem initially captivated by the idea of me, but it always turns out that it isn't really me they want, it's music. We walk reverently through my instrument-littered living room. I don't turn the lights on, but even so, there are always earnest attempts to extract promises to play, and to sing. In my kitchen, we peer with futility into my nearly empty fridge for a midnight snack, and climb the stairs hungrily. It all *seems* fine.

I reassure myself that at least I am not a virgin.

I GO INTO THE LIBRARY two or three times a week, but never at the same time, or on the same day. I squeeze in a visit whenever I have books ready for pick up, or books overdue. Sometimes, when they are really overdue, I put the books in the mail bag, carry them along on my route, and drop them off before I head home. Technically, we're not allowed to carry anything in our mail bags but the mail. I get around feeling guilty by imagining I'm *posting* my books back to their rightful home; in fact, I use and re-use an ancient collection of dilapidated manila envelopes to disguise the returns. Instead of paying for stamps, I pay penance with the straps cutting harder into my shoulders because of the extra weight. When I catch myself at this bizarre behaviour I always think, "This is so *Catholic* of you, Frederick," and I snort derisively at myself, but I keep doing it all the same.

I have to walk right by the checkout desk to get to the hold shelf, so I can tell immediately if she is there. As I am walking along the street, before I go through the library doors, I practise. The look on my face, what I will say. The wind invariably whips up from the lake and tries to snatch out my soul, the way people used to think sneezing did. Breathe, I tell myself, since as soon as I think about it my chest starts to get tight and my throat closes up. It's like I'm eleven again, standing on the corner of Princess and King for the first time.

I get in there, through the library doors, and I look across to the desk, and if she is there my heart stops beating for a minute, and I know that all my efforts to appear nonchalant are going to be hopeless. I tell myself, breathe, breathe, *lento*, but whatever I have practised only half comes out. Like, if I was going to pretend to ask about the large print books for my mother, I think about how I could tell her all about stroke and idiosyncratic memory and engage her in intelligent conversation for several minutes, even if there is someone waiting behind me in line. Instead I say, "Where are your large print books?" And I sound stuffy and officious and boring. She points me in the right direction, with half her face turned up towards me, and her dark hair falling over her cheek. And that is the end of it. So I stand in the rows and rows of Harlequins with hugely-lettered titles, and half my mind kicks the other half, over and over. Sometimes I catch myself knocking my head lightly on the edge of the metal shelving, and when I come to, I realize that now she will think I am taking these books out for myself. Even if she isn't already taken, what self-respecting librarian would ever go out with a guy who reads the abridged versions of romance fiction in 18-point?

AFTER MY FIRST SUCCESS, there was almost always a bit of a crowd when I sang in the streets at night. Even when drunk, the students slowed and stopped for a few minutes under my street lamp, their glassy eyes glazing over even more with some kind of misty memory of home. The night folded close around me then. I could look up in the sky at the pin-poked stars, and around at the faces of my transitory audience, and I could feel the earth turning beneath me. I sang in a kind of bubble, self-contained and protected, while the passersby were part of the larger world, strung on a great web of invisible filaments. Without Filander, I was separate from everything. But I found it comforting to reach out with a tune and touch this face or that one in the crowd, and turn it towards me, as if some kind of musical telekinesis was at work.

They liked mournful Irish lullabies and lively French Canadian folk songs and the tunes from all the musicals that were big hits at the time: "Touch Me, Feel Me" from *Tommy*, and "Could We Start Again, Please?" from *Jesus Christ Superstar*. My entire repertoire was made up of songs I'd heard my mother croon in our deadbeat kitchen, Cole Porter's "Don't Fence Me In" and "Ol' Man River" from the play *Showboat*. There was an intermittent chink and clink of coins dropping against each other in my cap, the donors leaning forward unsteadily, trying with all their might to focus. Even then, the coins sometimes rolled into the gutter.

I sang with my hands in my pockets, and every fifteen minutes or so, at the end of a song, I'd pick up my hat and retreat into the dark doorway behind me and push the coins down into my socks so they slid underneath the arch of my foot, and I'd layer the rare bills carefully along the inside waistband of my underwear. When my brothers came by, as they always did, on their way between bars and pubs and the back doors of restaurant kitchens, they'd cuff my shoulder, tousle my neatly-combed hair, and pick the meagre change from the cap like magpies, before I could stop them. Four of them still needed fake IDs, but already they were accomplished thieves and drinkers.

I COULDN'T KEEP MONEY AT HOME. If my brothers found it they bought beer. If my mother found it, she bought skim milk powder. Either way, I learned quickly. I'd come home to find all my hiding places empty: the toes of my extra pair of boots; the hole behind the panelling that was revealed by lifting the curling corner; the hollow length of my metal bedpost, capped by a broken black knob—you had to turn the whole bed right over to get the coins out. I'd find the bed up-ended regularly, my thin sheets tangled and boot-marked, my blanket trailing into the hallway like the tail of a coiled snake. I'd find the knob days later, hidden by discarded school books or dirty laundry.

So I started to keep my money in the storeroom at the shop. I didn't tell Ed. Even in those years there were places he never looked, and it only required feigning a trip to the toilet to either hide or redeem funds. I slept at night with my coin-filled socks on, and by day put those metallic feet into shoes always worn one size too big. I walked from Saturday to Monday with people's spare change digging into my arches, and hobbled to The Whole Note glad of the serendipitous scheduling that put my voice lessons so close to the weekend.

There were no sound-proofed rooms in those days. We stood in a back corner of the shop, and anyone who liked could stand pretending to look at banjos or metronomes or sheet music and hear us sing: A free concert punctuated by corrections. That first Monday night, in between "Watch the bump in your phrasing, Frederick" and "Lift the breath! *Lift* the breath!" I slipped away from the handful of other children in my voice class—all of them always girls—and made my way to the counter to ask Ed for directions.

That first time, Ed came to the door of the storeroom and pointed. Then, as now, the path to the washroom was lined with haphazardly-piled boxes. I was shorter then, of course, so it seemed even more of an impenetrable cardboard jungle.

"Clean up a little while you're back there, okay?" Ed said, and then he went back to the music book he had open on the glass surface of the display case, following the notes with his left hand, his right hand tapping silently in the air.

I didn't know if he meant it. I didn't even know if he meant me, or the room full of boxes. To cover all possibilities, I washed my hands diligently after I flushed the toilet, and I wiped the inside of the stained sink with the damp paper towel. After that I went quietly back through the storeroom and found a small box that held a set of harp strings and placed the packaged contents into a slightly bigger box, flaps open, that held guitar capos. I can remember I had a moment of wondering if Ed would ever find them there, but I looked around and didn't really know how he found anything, so it seemed not to matter.

I pulled off my boot and my sock and put those first savings into the stolen box, and I crawled behind the tallest tower of cardboard and hid the makeshift bank behind a flaking cast-iron radiator. By then I was so nervous that I went back out into the shop with my sock and boot still in my hand, but Ed did nothing more than raise his left eyebrow a quarter of an inch before returning to the *Miles Davis Songbook*.

"I'm looking for your *middle* voice here, Sandy," said our teacher.

I PICKED UP THE *Globe and Mail* tonight on my way home from The Whole Note. I don't often buy the paper—I usually read the headlines online these days, at the shop—but I did tonight because it had been a pretty busy day, every student coming early and every lesson running late. It's strange, because on the front page there was a little story about conjoined twins that had been born in the Dominican Republic, but I didn't even look at the paper before I bought it.

Surgeon to remove girl's second head.

I still read these things; I don't know why. I always know how they're going to end.

Most people read articles like this out of morbid curiosity. They want to know about freaks. I guess people always have.

They'd been flown to Los Angeles—they are always flown somewhere, the U.S. or the U.K. or somewhere big and important with a need to show off. I expect competing teams of doctors who specialize in separations wait with bated breath for such babies to be born. I don't know how these things are decided, or who decides. Maybe it's simply a matter of who gets to the poor parents first, and the doctors have scouts or spies out all around the world. I imagine they may even open bottles of champagne if they find themselves holding the successful bid.

I say "they" were flown, although most people would say "she." There's a twoness to twins, even those born conjoined or parasitic, despite everyone's best efforts to make it look straightforward, as if one baby's life is being saved. It's almost never true. The extra part is a whole person. A whole person in a leg, an arm, a head, a little finger. Cutting off the extras leaves a shadowy twoness without the two.

I cut the article out and taped in into the scrapbook I keep on the kitchen shelf with the twin books from my childhood. My brothers abandoned them at my mother's, where they sat for years, collecting dust. I found them there After, when I was called home and left on my own to clean everything out.

They are stacked beside the stove like recipe books on how to make humans of all different shapes and varieties, for every taste.

I PUT UP A NEW CURTAIN ROD in the living room. The old metal pole sagged in the middle so much that it was getting hard to open the curtains in the morning; they just kept sliding closed back towards the centre.

I had the wrong bit on the screwdriver, and I opened the end of the tool and poured the bit selection into the palm of my open hand.

It's easy to understand, now, how my brothers so consistently overlooked me: a singleton, a keening baby, a timid toddler, a strangely taciturn small child. And then for a brief moment in middle childhood I imagine I was simply a Voice floating in the streets of their carousing, disembodied and unconnected to their lives. I doubt they gave one thought to where I'd learned such songs—not from their blaring AM radios, to be sure. Soon enough I was swept away from home into the current of my life, and they hurtled into the *tempesta di mare* of theirs.

To them I was at best a brief source of minor puzzlement and spare change. I don't know if they ever really stopped to notice me, or to listen to me sing when they found me on those midnight streets. They held firmly to their own lives and to each other, a six-pack of assimilation. Now that I have some perspective on my own self-absorbed adolescence, I can hardly blame them.

I fiddled with the screwdriver, the chair underneath me rocking slightly on its one short leg.

We had, all seven of us, settled happily into virtual non-communication as adults as well. When I had to tell them something about our mother—that she had fallen and broken her wrist or that her doctors were trying a new, experimental medication—I never called, but sent an e-mail to the garage from the computer at Ed's shop, asking the Ns to forward the information to the others. One of them, Nicholas or Nathaniel, would e-mail back a confirmation, with sometimes a line or two about the weather, or how many cars they had backed up waiting outside the bays. That was pretty much it. We never used each other's phone numbers.

I felt a draft and heard the floor creak and I turned around to see Maya standing in the doorway watching me, dripping from the rain. I dropped the screwdriver and just about fell off the chair.

"Door was open" she explained, shrugging a half apology. She was looking at the curtain rod that I'd just fit into the second bracket.

"Crisp, that's crooked." Weaving carefully around the covered harp, she crossed the hardwood with her boots still on, picked up the fallen tool, and waved me off the chair.

I just stood there in the middle of my own living room and watched her take the bracket off the wall again, level the pole by eye, and re-drill holes for the wall plugs. It didn't seem like she was rushing, but she worked quickly and carefully—*preciso*.

When she finished, she took the pole down and handed me one end to thread the curtain tabs over it. She was all business; we didn't have a conversation or anything. She used hand signals to get me to do what she wanted—hold the pole, pass her the drill, find the screw—like a choir director calling forth music. It was music, *senza misura*. Before I could really think too much the curtains were back up on the new, perfectly-horizontal pole and she was gone. I was left staring at the seat of the dining room chair, where there were gritty little puddles left by her wet construction boots.

"WE'LL GO TO THE BEACH TODAY," my mother announced. She had been out late the night before, and was now manically exuberant. It was mid-morning—breakfast time for my brothers on weekends and during vacation—and it was summer in Eastern Ontario. The air was still and already almost unbearably humid. My brothers were eating overflowing bowls of cereal sprinkled with powdered milk and sugar stolen from the Eat-Rite Diner. The kitchen was littered with puffed wheat.

They all looked at her like she was crazy. The word "beach" had never once been spoken in our family; I myself only had the haziest notion of water, sand, and sky, and I'm not sure where even that much had come from, since I wasn't yet in school.

"You've all got trunks," she said. "Nick and Nat can wear their cut-offs." There was a rare excitement in her voice, like an echo of Twinsburg. "And Fred," she added, "you can wear—"

"Are you *kidding*?" asked Salvador.

"*Beach?*" Alistair shook his head emphatically.

"There's no beach for *this* dude," said Abraham.

"Anyway, we got things to do," said Nathaniel.

"You could take Fred, though," suggested Samuel.

"Maybe he'll even drown," added Nicholas hopefully.

The year before I started kindergarten, after a rash of drownings in the town—including that of Courtney Glass, author of the undefended Madrigal dissertation—there was a community water safety campaign. Every elementary school child was to be given swimming lessons, and every high school teenager was to learn boating safety. In practical terms, this meant that four of my six brothers had been given free bathing suits the previous spring—garish tartan trunks with a drawstring at the waist—and had been taken to the community pool during school time, where they probably learned more about water torture than lifesaving. Instead of swimming suits, the oldest two, the Ns, had each been given a plastic whistle on a lanyard in case they ever found themselves in a boat about to capsize. They had immediately, and carelessly, lost them.

"Suit yourself," my mother said. "But there's a *canteen.*" And she reached down the front of her dress, took a ten-dollar bill from her cleavage—the only place *her* money was safe from my brothers—and waved it confidently in the air over the table.

They took notice, and added up the hot dogs and fries in their heads. My mother thought she had them.

"Get your suits on," she said. "Or your shorts. Or—" she looked at me thoughtfully. "You'll have to swim in your underpants, Fred."

"Underpants, Fred!" mimicked Salvador.

My brothers hooted and howled with laughter. I was used to that, but, even so, my face burned in humiliation. I was old enough to know that some things were private and not to be seen; underwear would be bad enough, but underwear with holes would be mortifying.

"Go on," scolded my mother. "Go on now and get ready. And bring the towels!" She replaced the bill for safekeeping, and my brothers' chairs screeched and their feet shook the stairs. My mother and I were alone in the kitchen.

"Get your shoes on," she said, even though she knew I couldn't tie my laces myself.

In a rare mood and with remarkable energy she rustled us all up. My brothers tumbled down the stairs empty-handed, looking no different than when they'd gone up. She asked to see evidence of their bathing trunks and cut-offs under their jeans.

When instead she caught sight of the elastic of their underwear she sent them back up to put them on "for real." She sent them back up again for all the towels my family owned, three thin turquoise-grey bath sheets that smelled permanently of sweat, which she rolled up and put in a paper Dominion bag to carry.

"Fred should have a pail," she declared.

The house was ransacked for something pail-like. In the end, she fished an empty margarine container out of the garbage and, without washing it, put it in the bag with the towels and rolled down the top to make the bag easier to carry. We were ready to go.

We walked across Princess Street and turned down Clarence. It must have been a Sunday, because the shops were all closed. We walked down to the water, then turned right and followed the curve of Lake Ontario. My brothers either ran way ahead or lagged far behind. My mother called after them constantly, and tightened her grip on my wrist. Heat rash prickled my neck, the backs of my knees, and the skin of my arm under her hand.

I think I whimpered for much the journey—the farthest I believe I had ever travelled on my own two feet up to that point. I could walk that route now in little more than twenty minutes, but at not-quite-five it seemed interminable. After every block I walked *rallentando*, slower and slower, and dragged my toes so much I began to make holes in the tips of my shoes. One long lace had come undone and dragged behind me. By the time we reached MacDonald Park, even my mother's high spirits had wilted.

We walked through the park to the lakeshore, past a massive whitewashed red-roofed tower that my brothers ran around like demented soldiers firing canons during the War of 1812. There was no sand. Instead, a narrow strip of rocky shore curved back to the right and forward to the left, like a giant S. The park was sparingly scattered with families sitting on picnic blankets on the grass. No one was swimming, or even sitting on the rocks.

Undeterred, my mother spread the towels on the rubble, where they lay like lumpy graves. She passed me the margarine container, and I knelt and filled it entirely with two of the smallest stones I could find.

"Where's the canteen?" Salvador demanded after a final frenzied loop around the tower, looking around dismissively at the rocks, the lake, even the handful of sailboats languishing in the windless bay.

"Over there," said my mother. I looked where she pointed and could see a small hut in the distance through the trees, and a short line of people that looked like specks of dirt. "But swim first," she added. She gathered her pink sundress around her knees and sat resolutely on the rocks facing the water. Her shoulders were already pink from the sun.

"Eat first," said Salvador. The rest of my brothers ran up behind him, exploding land mines and firing sub-machine guns. It did not bother them in the least to confuse the timelines of warfare and weaponry.

"Swim," repeated my mother.

"*Eat*," repeated Salvador.

My mother looked at the six of them, standing above her like a battalion of twins on the grass. She was outnumbered and surrendered quickly.

"You'll take Fred," she insisted. It was always her one condition. "And behave yourselves!" She handed over the ten-dollar bill.

Another war cry. Salvador took the money and clenched it in his fist. Nicholas swept me up into his arms so abruptly that the pseudo-pail in my hands spilled its meagre load of greased rocks onto an empty towel with a *clack*. My brothers ran unevenly toward the far side of the park, half carrying, half dragging me. Salvador held the money ahead of him like a torch to guide the way in battle. Over Nicholas's shoulder, I could see my mother lie down awkwardly on the towel and shrink into a pink brush stroke on a strip of turquoise paper.

My brothers ran through the park and right past the people in the line-up for hot dogs. There was a small thicket of trees behind the canteen, and they made their way there. I never knew if they planned such things when out of earshot, or if they operated so instinctively that consultation was unnecessary. Without speaking the four of my brothers wearing swim suits undid the flys of their jeans and pulled the drawstrings from their tartan trunks.

"Here's a good one," said Abraham, and he kicked hard at the base of a maple tree about as big around as my body.

They sat me down facing the tree, with one leg on each side of the trunk.

"Hug the tree, bat-boy," said Samuel. I put my arms around the tree, and leaned my cheek gently against the bark. I knew I only had a moment to get as comfortable as possible.

They tied my arms and legs together with the four drawstrings. They were not boy scouts, so the knots were untidy and plentiful. In short order I was a boy with a tree growing up through me, in a small glade in a busy park, and my brothers were gone.

If anyone had looked closely, they might have seen enough of me to make them curious. But no one did, until, much later, my sunburnt mother wandered through the whole of the park calling the names of her boys, Nick-Nat-Sam-Sal-Abe-Al-Fred! and came across the margarine container, like a solitary crumb, pointing in my direction. I didn't cry out, even then.

"Where did they go?" she asked the tree wearily.

"I'm here," I answered quietly. The pattern of the bark was imprinted into my face for hours afterwards.

I READ IN *NATIONAL GEOGRAPHIC* that one in every four hundred sets of fraternal twins will have different fathers. I knew this was possible with dogs—that some of the puppies could be fathered by a bull mastiff while their litter mates could be fathered by a poodle—but I thought it was just an urban legend about humans. But with *National Geographic*, you know you have to believe what you read. So then I was thinking about different fathers and that maybe I wasn't my father's child after all. Maybe my brothers were only half mine. Maybe I didn't have to own any more of them than that.

I flipped through the rest of that issue very carefully, and thereafter was always on the lookout as I stood in the grocery store checkout line. I read through countless headlines: "Boy Bites Shark" and "Flying Saucer Crushes Cow" and "Hot Tub Time Machine Takes Elvis Impersonator to Ancient Egypt to Meet Cleopatra." I wanted to read something somewhere that would make it possible for my brothers to have been the genetic product of some woman aside from my mother. I would have read that anywhere, even in the *National Enquirer*, and believed it.

SOMETIMES I GO TO SEE MY MOTHER and find her asleep in her room. The lights are on and her bedside radio is tuned to static. I brought her the radio a few years ago—the second radio mistake I've given my mother—thinking that music would calm her, and knowing she wouldn't be able to handle inserting a cassette tape or, later, a CD, into a machine and pushing Play. I thought that a radio wouldn't have to be operated. I thought the staff could turn it on in the morning and off at night, and that the cost to them of a few seconds of their time bracketing the day would pay dividends in terms of the long hours in the parenthesis. I thought she would sing along with the oldies, and somehow be more content.

I was wrong, as I am about most things. The knobs that control volume and tuning are a perpetual fascination to her when the machine is on. Passersby in the hallway might hear a few syllables from an eager broadcaster, or a few chords whispering like an aborted lullaby; they might catch a glimpse of my mother up on one elbow in bed, bent over the device like a scientist conducting an experiment of earth-saving magnitude.

Her fingers turn the dial quickly or slowly, but she always ends her study on the space between two stations, at top volume. And then she rolls from her side to her back and goes to sleep.

When I go in and sit, the way I did this morning, I turn the volume down slowly, so she will not wake up. I examine the ragged lines of her face, noting which of them are beginning to appear in my own mirror these last few years. I feel her skin, which is often clammy when she sleeps, as if the heat inside her body runs to static like the radio, and alternates hot and cold. Sometimes I even reach out my hand and stroke her forehead or her wrist, tentatively, because touch between us is a foreign country. It is a land we visited rarely during my childhood; some things, it seems, need to be practised for a lifetime for them to come easily. I look at other visitors here greeting their aging parents, saying goodbye at the end of their visits, reaching out readily for an embrace that seems second nature. I practise while my mother is unconscious and can't judge my clumsy efforts to comfort her.

MY MOTHER GETS A LITTLE BETTER and then much worse and then a little better again, in the way that people with damaged brains often do. The brain is a strange instrument. When some of the synapses get broken or frayed, these minute electrical strings can sometimes play one note over and over, like a harp being tuned. Other times those broken connections cause the spoken words to leap and tumble and turn and crash like the noise made by a small unmusical child hammering away at the piano.

I take her for walks in her wheelchair. It is often easier to deal with tragedy from behind, without having to look at it face-on. So I push the chair, and my mother sits passively and talks vivacious nonsense into the empty air in front of her as we tour the streets around the nursing home. It is probably more accurate to say that we creep along, *adagio*, going nowhere. The woollen blanket around her knees slips every half-block or so, through some unknown force, since, while we walk, I never see her move so much as a gloved finger. Her body is merely an unresisting house for her ruined mind.

The obvious tragedy is that my mother suffered, too early in her life, a blood clot in her temporal lobe that left her with a peculiar kind of dementia: Wernicke's aphasia. She was young when it happened, and has grown old only in the intervening years—as though her body finally caught up with her mind. Even now, she is still one of the youngest residents of her nursing home. The others stand resolutely on the threshold of death and beckon her forward into old age.

It is easy for anyone to see that such an event, and its aftermath, is indeed tragic. But we all have a human tendency to personalize tragedy. I have no idea who she is, or I should say, was. Maybe most of all I want to know who she was—beyond being my mother, beyond being the overwhelmed single parent of three sets of identical twins and one disappointing singleton, a mother who would do anything to keep a roof over her children's heads, however much it might have leaked. I want to see beyond the details of her harried life to the origin of her exquisite voice. I want to know why she only ever sang alone. I see her always in that childhood kitchen, where there was never enough light. I can see so clearly the paint peeling from the walls, the cracked linoleum, the tilted wooden chairs, but I remember her only dimly. She is slightly out of focus, and, what is more, almost always has her back to me. Perhaps it is a family trait to turn away from tragedy. I can still smell damp plaster and overwashed clothes and overcooked meat—we boys thrived on root vegetables and cheap cuts of beef—but I cannot remember her younger face at all. I can hear the creak of the kitchen floor and the tennis ball against the front of the house and Mrs. Bern's raised voice through the thin walls between our houses.

And I can hear my mother singing. Her voice rose and fell like the beating of birds' wings, their tempo at times languid, at other times *volante*. I realize now that Mrs. Bern would have heard her—getting up after a bad dream for a glass of water at three a.m.—*must* have heard her, through the shared kitchen wall. I wonder what she thought of those sounds, that "live" music, whether she ever said anything about it to my mother, whether it was acknowledged between them that my mother sang alone in the kitchen when even her twins were soundly asleep in their beds, and that her voice was something remarkable and unearthly.

With clipped wings, my mother sits in her wheelchair while I push her across the road to the coded entrance doors of her final home. The last leaves skitter in front of her, and she points along the road at some unseen vision. "There is the peanut feed it chiplets, no it's a, no, I have never seen one that, I've seen it, black and white. I *won't* do that! The sign is mis-crossed, miss-matched, cross-crissed. No way to, go downstairs. Please. Don't tie me up. Not manmade! Not marmalade!"

I did what I always do when she starts to get agitated.

The water is wide, I cannot get o'er, I sang.
And neither have I wings to fly

And she continued:

Give me a boat that will carry two
And both shall row, my love and I.

I punched in the security code posted in large numerals beside the keypad—designed to keep the residents in rather than the public out—and we went in through the yawning doors, singing. The reception staff all looked up, even though they are used to our musical entrances. They are my mother's most appreciative audience.

A ship there is and she sails the sea

She's loaded deep as deep can be
But not so deep as the love I'm in
I know not if I sink or swim.

We went up in the elevator to the kitchen on the third floor, the song ending as the door opened. I made her some toast, and I found the jar of marmalade with her name on it at the back of the fridge, but she wouldn't eat it. She just kept saying "No."

"No, no, no, no, no, no, no."

"What is it you want, then?" I asked her, eating it myself. "Strawberry jam? Peanut butter?" There were always little packets of things in a basket on the counter.

"Wagner," she said, "sand wishes." There was only the slightest of pauses before she was off on a monologue, *stretto*, never finishing one thoughtless fragment before she veered off with another.

WHEN I WAS TEN, our neighbour Mrs. Bern died. For some reason, my mother took me with her to the funeral. It was the first time I had seen anybody dead. It is still pretty much the *only* time I have seen anybody dead, unless you count Mr. Willard J. Sexton whose unmoving feet I saw through the sidelight of his front door when I was delivering his mail. I never saw any of the rest of Willard, just went in to the first shop on Princess Street and called the police and an ambulance, and I heard the sirens cry through the neighbourhood and stop in the correct northeasterly direction, and a few weeks later I saw the family bickering on the lawn about his belongings, and after another while a "for sale" sign appeared in front of his house.

We never had a dog or a cat or a hamster, so we never had any little life lessons about death. We were not animal people; or perhaps it was just that my brothers were so wild that we did not need any more of the jungle inside than we already had.

So, Mrs. Bern was it.

The coffin was open at her funeral.

It is safe to say I did not understand what had happened to her, and I did not understand what death was. I knew Mrs. Bern was not asleep—or I should say, I knew this pale and waxy face would never smile or scowl again, would never call me from her doorway to go and ask my mother for a half cup of sugar, would never whisper that the cookie should remain a secret, since she had not enough to supply all my brothers. I knew this recumbent body would never stand on our corner waiting for the knife sharpening man on his rounds, would never sweep the front step after the rain, would never again wag its finger at my mother with concern about "the boys." I knew that face and that body would not talk or move again, but I think I did not exactly know that it was *Mrs. Bern.*

I saw her lifeless body in the coffin, drawn past by my mother's hand on my thin wrist, jostled by a few ragged mourners in front and behind us. I saw the overdone makeup on her face, could have reached out my free hand and touched the moisture on her upper lip, as if she had broken into a sweat climbing up the ladder to heaven. I looked keenly at her finest dress, smelled the overpowering smell of formaldehyde masked half-heartedly by sparse white chrysanthemums. I took in all that, but still, when we got home I remember sneaking outside to knock at Mrs. Bern's front door, as if she would answer. All I could think about, standing there in the fog, waiting fruitlessly, was the novel realization that she was perhaps the only person besides me, having been awakened in the pre-dawn by music from heaven, who had known or cared about my mother singing.

THE FOUR CONSONANTS EARLY MUSIC ENSEMBLE meets at my house. The practice room at the shop is full most nights with guitar and flute lessons. Besides, the four of us probably couldn't fit our bodies in that sound-proof room, let alone our instruments. We hold it at my place because everyone else has a family. We started out by rotating, but it soon became obvious that children don't stop playing tag around the piano and dogs don't stop throwing up on the carpet and spouses don't stop burning the spaghetti sauce and in-laws don't stop telephoning from Japan just because four people have decided to make music together in the living room.

We've been playing together for over fifteen years, pretty much ever since I finished university. We've played our way through Varrick's prostate cancer treatment, Geoff's affair and subsequent divorce, and the birth of two of Jiro's three children. This ornamentation no doubt enriches the music—though sometimes it's overdone and can get tiresome; too many details to listen to at once, the notes overembellished, cutting into the silence.

I'm usually the one who ends up finding most of our pieces, probably for the same reason: that everyone else has a family. All I am is music. I think for them it can be like changing one more diaper or loading the dirty dishes into the dishwasher after one more meal. More of the same, so they just do it without thinking. And I guess it's true, for them. They don't always live music; sometimes they just live their lives. Music fits in around the edges, fills in the gaps. They can see where music begins and ends. It is containable, comprehensible, controllable. At times it moves them deeply, but they always come back from it. There is always a final bar played or sung, and then a rest. A return to real living: birthday parties, deadlines at work, a glass of wine with dinner, shovelling the walk, making love to their wives.

I think the others see our time together as a kind of escape. They unwind with music. Geoff, Varrick, Jiro—they're all getting a bit older; performance doesn't seem such a big deal any more. Increasingly, they have things to work out with themselves. They no longer need us to have an audience.

It's been a huge relief for me, this shift. I used to feel like I was holding them back when I said I didn't want to play in public. There was some tension in the early years. We spent all this time "practising." It was hard for them not to think they were working themselves up to something, some reward, some Day of Judgement: Would they be good enough? Would they get through the Pearly Gates? Would they be loved?

The word "performance" comes from the Latin *per*, which means "thoroughly," and the Old French *fournir*, which means "to complete." It's strange that it refers to men's sexual achievements as well as to the presentation of a musical or theatrical work in front of an audience. Somehow, in both enterprises, we have to measure up.

I SAVED MY BUSKING MONEY—nickels and dimes and quarters, everything that was left over after paying for voice lessons—squirrelling it away among Ed's new violin cases and broken snare drums. I emerged from my weekly bank-deposit excursion full of dust and paint chips, with a lighter step and a growing feeling of having successfully pulled something off, while all the while Ed determinedly pretended not to notice.

I'd been saving for over three months when I reclaimed my

hidden cash, took it in bulging pockets a few blocks down the road to Steve Packer's father's electronics shop, and bought an AM/FM radio. I gave my mother that radio for her birthday the year I was eleven; I suppose she must have been forty or so, but at the time I had no sense of her age.

I don't remember where the radio idea had come from, or what I thought the giving of it would do for her, or for me. I know I brought the box home reverently, as if it were gospel, capable of saving all of us with the mere tuning of a dial.

I brought it right in and gave it to her, without any wrapping, before my brothers could get hold of it.

"Here," I said, and I held it out to her with my two scarred hands.

She didn't reach for it immediately; she had her own hands in the washing machine, fishing for boys' t-shirts in the cold grey water. "What is it?" she asked me, suspiciously.

"A birthday present," I said. She dried her hands then, on a ragged tea towel, and took the thing from me to examine the pictures and writing on the box. "It's a radio? *Where did you get this?*" And now she was accusing, and I saw all at once that she thought I had stolen it.

"I *bought* it," I said. And then to prove it I gave her the receipt.

She took it from me and studied it carefully. After a few minutes, she took it and the radio and went down the hall. She changed out of her slippers and into her shoes, pushed her arms into the sleeves of her coat and did up the buttons, and then she went out with the receipt in her pocket and the unopened box under her arm.

I said nothing to her when she returned after an hour or so. She was not empty-handed. The box was gone, replaced by bulging bags of groceries. She struggled in through the front door and up the hallway; I did not offer to help her. I said nothing when I heard her rattle the pots and pans in the kitchen, nor when I smelled cooking: onions, meat, tomatoes. I said nothing even later when my brothers came in from God-knows-where to eat supper, filling the kitchen with noise and laughter and swearing, oblivious to what they were eating.

I said nothing after they'd gone out again, when I stood on the sloping floor with the refrigerator door open, finding nothing left there for me to eat.

She never asked me where I'd gotten the money to buy the radio. I never told her, not even to clear my name.

I THINK A LOT ABOUT WHAT MUSIC ACTUALLY IS. Some people think it's simply another language, a universal language that everyone in the world can understand, whether they speak English or Arabic or Cantonese. I don't think this is quite right.

On the one hand, there is some music that doesn't cross easily over generations or cultures. When people trained in a Western musical tradition hear music based on a non-Western musical scale, it's often hard for them to identify with the rhythm. When blues and boogie and country and gospel and jazz were thrown together into the great American melting pot, gradually evolving into rock and roll, our grandparents shook their heads and wondered what all that noise was about. There was nothing universal about it.

On the other hand, as far as anyone can tell, people started singing and playing instruments just about as soon as they took to grunting and pointing and developing spoken language. Lullabies all over the world are sung high and slow, instinctually, like mothers everywhere are pre-programmed to it, whether they live in mud huts or skyscrapers. They bend their heads over their child as they hold him or her to the breast, and they sing. It seems that the first use of music in our lives is to tie us together emotionally.

I think about all this when I sing myself to sleep. Music is the Mystery. There's no way to explain what it does for us, or what humans would be like without it—what kinds of cultures and belief systems we would have built in the absence of beat and melody—or even whether we would still be human without it. Whether we would survive our grief. There has never been a people found who do not make music; it is like trying to find tribes who do not dream when they fall asleep at night.

IN THE EARLY FALL after that first long year of midnight busking, I was picked up by the police. It took me by surprise; I had gotten pretty adept at ducking into darkness. The police, our neighbours from Bay Street, my old grade three teacher who was a lush, anyone who might recognize me—I hid from them all. I got to know my brothers' haunts and the carousing routes they took between them, and got much better at avoiding them, too. Sometimes I had to stop singing in middle of a line, grab my chinking hat, and retreat. It became one clean motion: the music hung on a note while I stooped and grabbed and ran. I don't know what my audience made of my regular disappearances; I expect they were mostly too drunk to care. No doubt I missed out on quite a bit of spare change, though, leaving before the end of a tune.

On the night it happened I didn't see it coming. There was a wind off the lake and a misty kind of rain, and it must have fogged my eyes. I was singing "Shine On, Harvest Moon," and I delivered the last line like I was on a show tour, bending onto one knee, opening my arms from my heart to include all of them in a theatrical embrace, swinging my head up to the right with a triumphant smile.

So shine on, shine on harvest moon, for me and my gal!

"Hello there," a voice said. There was a policeman standing just behind my right shoulder. He was a tower of a man, and looked down at me from what seemed a great height. He must have been left-handed, because his gun holster was hung on his left hip. Kneeling down, my eyes were exactly at trigger height. I froze there, staring at gleaming gunmetal. I was glued to the sidewalk. My knee was getting soaked. The jangled music from the bars up and down the street hung heavily in the mist. My audience evaporated into doorways and around corners, until it seemed I was kneeling alone in the empty street in front of an immense man with a gun.

"Fine voice," he said. "Why don't you stand up so I can have a better look at you?"

I stood up slowly, eyeing my up-turned cap. The cop picked it up with one hand—a colossus bending for quarters—felt its weight, folded it over. The coins clinked a protest, then were silent.

"Past your bedtime, isn't it?" he said, raising his eyebrows. All the blood in my body pumped directly from my heart to my face. Up until then, I think I had really believed in the effectiveness of my penciled moustache.

"Your mother know where you are?" he asked.

I shook my blood-boiled head.

"Crawl out your window using knotted sheets, did you?" He tapped the bulging cap against the side of his leg, below his gun. He did that for a long time, looking at me, narrowing his eyes, sighing. Around us on the sidewalk people passed by in an imitation of being sober.

"What's your name, then?" he finally asked. "Don't bother with invention."

The whole time I'd been standing there, I'd been trying to think of an alias I could give him: Will Begone or Justin Time. Would it be better to make something up, or use the name of one of my classmates? Randall Cheeny, who waited in the stairwell for me? Dougie Fairweather, who threw rocks at my back as I was running home? As soon as he said that I could see it wouldn't be any use, either way.

"Frederick Madrigal," I gasped.

"*Madrigal*?" he repeated, as I knew he would.

"Yes," I admitted. All the blood now went to my feet. I thought about running away—I was good at it—except I'd just given a cop my real name, one of the best-known names, for the worst reasons, in this small city.

"Ah."

"Yes," I said again.

"What am I going to do with you?" he demanded. There wasn't much compassion to be heard in his voice.

"Send me home," I suggested. "I'll go right home. To bed. I promise." After I said "promise" I stopped; It sounded too much like wheedling, like begging.

"Climb back up the sheets, eh?"

I nodded vigorously. I didn't tell him I'd walk straight in through the unlockable front door and slam it behind me with no fear of waking my mother.

"I'll give you a ride," he said decisively, and then after he saw my panic he added: "Don't worry, I won't come in to meet your family—not tonight, anyway—and I won't drop you directly in front of your house. We don't need to give your mother the impression that you're following in your brothers' footsteps. But I'll be waiting to make sure you go right in."

He led me down the block and around the corner to his patrol car. There were a lot of coins under my arches; I tried my best not to limp. My boot-bolts rang on the road. He opened the passenger door for me to get in.

"Try to keep yourself out of the back seat, okay kid?" he asked, but it wasn't really a question.

It took only a minute to get to my house, enough time for me to be overwhelmed by the dials and knobs on the dash, and the static on the police radio. I didn't have to tell him where home was. He stopped just short of the corner, and I went to get out. He put his huge hand on my shoulder and stopped me.

"Monday after school," he said, "you come on down to the station and see me there. We gotta talk about this some more. You don't show up, I'll come looking for you, you understand? You go to Central? You get out at three-fifteen? Right, three-thirty, I'll be expecting you. You know where the station is? Ask for me at the front desk, Constable Miller." He let go of my shoulder, and he handed me my folded-up cap, fat with money.

"You got a fine voice," he said. I got out of the car and shut the door. I could tell he would be watching me in his side mirror as I crossed the street and ran back to the middle of the short block. I hesitated only a minute before I pushed open the dark front door and slammed it shut behind me with my hand through the letter slot, *fortissimo*.

I HAD ALMOST TWO WHOLE DAYS after what I thought of as my near-arrest to stew about Constable Miller and what was in store for me that Monday after school. All day Sunday I grew more and more anxious. I roamed the hallways of our house like a restless dog. If I'd had a tail, I'm sure it would have been tucked between my legs. I tried to distract myself with food, my homework, my brothers' *Penthouse* magazines, but nothing worked. I started out to walk up along Montreal Road to sing under the underpass, but stopped when I got to the arena, and threw rocks for a while at the impenetrable metal siding. Sunday night I had nightmares that always ended with Constable Miller handcuffing me and tossing me into the back seat of his cruiser. On Monday at school I weathered my teachers' displeasure at my lack of completed homework and my distracted state. By the time three-fifteen came and the bell rang, I had to run out behind the school and throw up in a basement window-well before setting out for the police station.

I didn't have to ask for him. Miller was waiting for me in the lobby.

"Well, Frederick Madrigal," he said, "Let's go for another drive."

He drove to the corner of King and Johnson and parked in front of St. George's Anglican cathedral. I didn't know at the time that it was Anglican, or that it was a cathedral. I had never been in a church in my life.

He told me to get out of the car, and I did. We walked right up the front steps and in through the huge double doors, taller than any doors I had ever seen, tall enough for giants twice the size of the giant Miller. Inside, it was dim, but, high up, light filtered through coloured glass. I followed him right down the side aisle to the front. When we got there, I saw that there was a man sitting on what I now know was the organ bench, a few steps up from the floor, and he seemed to be waiting for us. He nodded sideways to Constable Miller, but he kept his eyes on me.

"Sing," he said. Just like that.

I was too surprised to speak, let alone sing. I did nothing but stare. He had on a black robe that covered even his shoes, and I was taken by the impression that he was legless, and would come gliding towards me if he stood up.

"Sing!" he commanded.

"What?" I stammered. "What—should I—sing?"

"It doesn't matter," he said, impatiently. "It's not the song that matters."

I could hear Constable Miller sitting down behind me. I opened my mouth. I wasn't worried about singing; my summer of busking had made me pretty comfortable with performance. I just didn't know what to sing. I tried to think of something religious. I sang the first song that came into my head that had anything to do with church. I'd heard my mother sing it in secret so many times, it was like a lullaby:

I'm in a nice bit of trouble, I confess
Somebody with me has had a game
I should by now be a proud and happy bride
But I've still got to keep my single name.

My voice filled every alcove and flew to the lamps hanging near the vaulted ceiling. There was a most beautiful resonance that was not a dead echo, but a living wish. The sound of my voice in that place was pure and light, like a bird's melody. It was way better than the underpass.

There was I, waiting at the church
Waiting at the church, waiting at the church
When I found he'd left me in the lurch
Lor, how it did upset me!

I saw the man on the organ bench draw his hand down across his face, pulling the skin on his cheekbones down so his eyes looked baggy. He left his hand pressed over his mouth, like he was trying to stop himself from crying out. Many years later, he would tell me how hard it had been for him not to laugh.

All at once, he sent me round a note
Here's the very note, this is what he wrote
"Can't get away to marry you today
My wife won't let me!"

I continued right through to the end, and it wasn't until the long silence afterwards that I wondered if I'd chosen the wrong song. I knew I had sung it well. Finally, the man cleared his throat. He didn't talk to me, but to Constable Miller behind me.

"Well, there may be a few kinks to be worked out," he said. Miller appeared to consider this seriously.

"I expect you are up to the challenge," he replied.

"For that voice?" the man said, rhetorically. "Anything."

I forgot about the woman on the street who'd given me my first coins. This was the beginning of my love affair with God.

THERE ARE THREE KINDS OF PEOPLE WHO SING. The first and the best—the ones I wait for with my fluttering heart caught behind my sternum—are the kind whose immeasurable emotion spills out freely with the words and music. Their faces, their whole bodies, their entire lives, the expanding capacity of their love, pour out among the rafters. If they are outside, they effortlessly carry their audience up to the very stars, until, if we looked down, we would see mere shadows of our earthly bodies far below. But we don't look down while we are listening, for there is nothing important there. Such voices lift the audience up to heaven with them, if there is a heaven—and if there is an audience, for these are the kids that sing in the back of the school bus or the streetcar on their way to their final exams. When they grow up, they sing in stalled traffic on their way to a make-it-or-break-it corporate meeting, or at the laundromat in time with the *chewh, chewh, chewh*. These are the people that start singing to their babies when they are still only one-celled amoebas; the ones who sing to the deer transfixed in the hayfields; the ones who sing all alone at night in their sub-standard kitchens, too exhausted to sleep. If you are lucky enough to be there when they sing, you can't take your eyes off them. Well, I can't, even after years of choir directing, and an early lifetime of spying on kitchens. There's only a small handful of these people in an average-sized choir—maybe four out of twenty.

The second kind are performers; their bodies move and they give great facial expression but they know they're on stage—they only sing when someone's listening, and preferably watching too—and they're conscious of making all the right moves. Oh, they sing well. But you can tell it's not real joy. It's not true despair. They're not feeling, but imagining feeling. It's performance art. There are only a handful of them, too. Another fifth.

The last kind are those whose voices make the perfect notes but they don't *add* anything to the music. It passes right through them, like a ghostly melody through a wall. They just stand there, singing. Looking somehow disconnected from the music, from their own amazing, technically perfect voices. Given that they are often the majority, you can't have a choir without them, but I wonder about singing without any feeling other than enjoyment, and I lament whatever they have done with their souls.

It's one of the reasons I don't believe in God anymore, even though I want to. But I still love the church because I love the sound of the young choristers' feet going down the wooden stairs to the basement to get a drink when choir practice is over. The whole place creaks, like a living thing.

THE LIMESTONE CITY YOUTH CHOIR has won awards at the Toronto International Choral Festival for two years in a row. That's not bad considering that four years ago there was no independent youth choir here. There are the choirs at the high schools and at St. George's—and in fact some of our members are in these other choirs as well—but I like to think we are the only choir in the province without any higher agenda except to sing.

As soon as we got through September, we started rehearsing for our concert at the end of January. We settled on January so no one would expect any Christmas carols out of us. After being involved in the recording of five Christmas CDs at St.

Mary's—one for every year I was there, including the disastrous last—I have vowed never to sing another piece of Christmas music again. Besides, there are all kinds of kids in the choir, from all kinds of ethnic backgrounds and all kinds of religions. For me, Christmas has had its day in the sun.

"Scramble," I called, and they all got ready. Their muscles were pulled tight like the strings of my new harp. I only give them sixty seconds so they know they have to move fast. "According to age!" There are twenty-two of them. There are a couple of twelve-year-olds but the majority are nearer seventeen or eighteen. True to my mathematical predictions, four of them have musical souls, and five of them are trying.

The choristers all pretty much know by now the order of everyone's birthdays, but I still hear the occasional check.

"No, Becky, I'm in April. You have to move up."

"Yeah, April! But March is before April, like, *duh*!"

I handed out the piece of music I'd brought. It was a William Holborne madrigal that I had edited so they could read the notes—I had decided to give myself a bit of a break and not teach them early music notation. I give half the pile to the kid at one end, and half to the kid at the other, and they pass them down the line without looking, until everyone has a sheet. When I say, "Okay," they go ahead and look; they are supposed to be looking at the key signature and the time signature and the words, while I'm looking at my watch, and then they have about thirty seconds left to hear the music in their heads before I expect them to start sight-singing, one line each, all the way down the row. The ones nearer the end of the line have an advantage, since they can usually get a good hold on the timbre and the rhythm before the music reaches them, which is why I have to keep changing the way they line up.

Other than the music I bring in for sight-reading practice, they choose their own tunes. They can each bring in a new piece every few months or so, and we have a session where we all listen to what's been collected—on CD or from sheet music or sometimes the kid will just sing it out from memory after listening to Great Aunt Gertrude, or somebody. They each have to say why they think it's important for us to learn the piece they've brought, what we are going to learn, what the significance of the piece is for them in terms of history, emotion, musical innovation, or whatever. There are some guidelines, though. In any given semester we try not to duplicate composers or styles or eras. The result is a far broader repertoire than I would have imagined they'd choose; they really push themselves and stretch their musical tastes. It's become a bit of a competition in an easygoing way. Once in a while someone will even bring in something that I—or Jiro—have never heard before.

Jiro is our accompanist. He has a small piano lamp over his sheet music, and has trained one of his children to turn his pages for him—a perfectly proportioned, musical child who learned to read notes before she learned to read letters, and can remember when to turn the page without reading of any kind—but is still too young to come and sing in the choir.

We were working on a tune with Becky. She'd brought in a piece that her Polish grandmother used to sing along with on an old LP, and there was a soprano solo part that was a little tricky. It's another unwritten rule that you get to sing the solo or lead part of the piece you bring in, if your voice is in the right range. We went over the first few bars about ten times, until I thought she had it. I gave her a little break while we went through the whole piece, and then started up from the beginning again. She missed again, a quarter beat late, but it didn't even register with me until she stopped singing completely, a few bars in.

"I'm not any good at skipping, either, when the ropes are already turning," Becky said.

I thought she might cry, so I left it until the next week. They're *supposed* to be having fun.

MY FIRST CHOIR, the Boys and Men's Choir at St. George's, practised on Friday nights. I went for two months before I was allowed to sing at a service or concert. The man from the organ bench, who turned out to be Arthur Grey, the choirmaster, first made me learn every song in the boys' repertoire. The music was like nothing I had ever sung before; I learned plain chant and the rudiments of musical notation. To me, we all sounded like the winged creatures who played on the clouds on the covers of our music folders. For the first time in my life, I was singing with other people for whom music was clearly a serious, other-worldly, and, most importantly, public business.

For the first few weeks, since I only came to practise, there was only the singing. I didn't think there could be anything else; that was Heaven enough. But just before Thanksgiving, Arthur Grey kept me behind after the other boys had gone and told me he expected me to attend the early Sunday service even though I was not yet ready to sing at it.

"There is Someone I want you to meet," he said.

So on Sundays at nine-fifteen I pulled on my cleanest, least-worn jeans, combed my hair, and ran out of the house through the falling leaves, zigzagging through the dappled streets. As directed, I sat in the front pew—by this time I knew it was a pew—and listened to the Very Reverend John Harris preach. He was a tall, thin man with a kind face, and his sermons captured me and everyone else in what he called "the hallway of God." "Whichever door you open," he declared, "do it in the service of the Lord." As he spoke, I saw the colours of the window glass dance on the dark floor, and heard the whisper of wings. I began to learn what angels were. I began to imagine a God watching me, and everyone, from the blazing sky.

I was invited to sing with the choir at the Christmas service. We'd practised carols every Saturday from the middle of November. We sang "Adeste Fidelis," Schubert's "Ave Maria," and the "Magnificat." During practice, Mr. Grey always made me sing "Silent Night" on my own, facing the other boys—I thought it was because I couldn't get the phrasing quite right. When I sang it, solo, in front of a packed congregation at the midnight service on Christmas Eve, I was briefly sorry that I hadn't invited my mother—who believed, no doubt, that I was at home, asleep in bed.

I think that was the only time I thought of inviting her; soon, self-centred boyhood, and the joy of finally finding a place to belong, took her almost entirely from my mind. It has been hard to forgive myself for this, even though I was just a child. It's been harder to forgive those adults around me who took me unthinkingly from my mother's life. I know some of them thought they were saving me from something terrible; others, that they were providing me with the opportunity to develop an exceptional talent. They believed I should be grateful, and I was, and I am. That small dark-haired boy was saved, and his musical talent grew—and was put on display. But somewhere, we suffered, my mother and I both. She, because she lost me before I knew enough to sing with her. I, because I was taken alone into a life that was not my own. And in the end the consequences were terrible.

Occasionally, that first year, I would catch a glimpse of Constable Miller in the congregation. Once I saw him pointing me out to the young woman at his side—his girlfriend or his wife. I knew he was laying some kind of claim to me, to my being there in the choir. I didn't mind, really. He was only one of what would turn out to be a number of men who felt they'd saved my life. I never thought of them as father figures, since I'd never really felt my father's absence. If anything, I thought of them as Filander stand-ins, even though they were much older and didn't look like me at all.

NOT LONG AFTER MY CHOIR SOLO that Christmas, there was a meeting of my community benefactors. My mother was either not invited or she chose not to attend; to this day I am not sure which is the case. It was held in the Rectory of St. George's. I was asked to arrive promptly at a certain time and wait outside. Like Pip, I knew they existed, these benefactors, but I'd had no idea who they were until I was called in to stand before them. I expected to see the Reverend and the choirmaster, but Ed was there as well, and Constable Miller, and my grade six teacher, Mr. Bergeson, and the principal from Central. There was also a social worker who had been to the house a few times to talk to my mother about my brothers, but who had never seemed particularly interested in me. I didn't even know her name.

There was also a severe-looking man in a thick black gown who was introduced to me as the choirmaster, Father Gregory, from St. Mary's Cathedral.

"A *Catholic* cathedral," said the Very Reverend Harris, but I didn't understand the remark's significance. I understood very little of what happened during my childhood, or at least, what seemed to be happening then has an entirely different meaning now; I guess that's just the way of it. It seems such a distant place from this perspective, and I'm hardly old yet. We think we can explain ourselves to others by telling them the details of our young lives, our first families; really, I think we are trying hard to look back and understand ourselves in the days before we understood anything.

I remember my hands were very cold—I'd run through the winter streets without any mittens. After less than half a year in the choir, I knew not to stand with my hands in my pockets in front of my elders. I remember little of what was said among the adults at this meeting. I held my aching hands behind my back, worrying about whether that was okay or not, and squeezed my fingers together, five, and then five, alternately, throughout the ten minutes that so profoundly altered the course of my life. I remember wishing for Filander, those other fingers.

I was asked to sing "Silent Night," even though it was January. It was explained to Father Gregory that this was the only solo I knew. I opened my mouth to object to this, since even then my repertoire of songs was enormous, but Arthur Grey shushed me quickly, using the hand movements he used with the choir to signal the dying of a note.

I sang for them, standing on the deep blue carpet in front of the Rectory table. Father Gregory closed his eyes. I thought he'd gone to sleep, but when the last note had risen on the air he opened his eyes upwards as if to follow the lingering C to heaven.

"Ah," he said. "I see." He looked around at the other faces, nodding some mysterious agreement, as if he now understood something that he hadn't previously. "And this has been achieved with virtually no training?"

"I found him on the street," said Constable Miller.

"He's had a few months of voice lessons," said Ed.

Father Gregory raised his eyebrows. "Where did you learn to sing?" he asked me. Other than the actual singing, this small exchange was the only time I was called upon to contribute to the meeting.

"From my mother."

"Ah" he said, "there is music in the family, then! Where does your mother sing?"

"In the kitchen," I admitted reluctantly. He was, no doubt, expecting me to name a choir or a choral society. My embarrassment was because I believed that real music required an audience, and I was afraid that they would find her kitchen singing counterfeit solely because of its solitary location. I did not yet know that music always has an audience, even if there is only one person, the singer herself, to hear it. I did not yet understand how music changes the way the air moves around the world, the butterfly effect of quarter notes and half notes and the controlled intake of breath.

I don't remember what the response to this admission was—whether he smiled or responded in any way, or simply soldiered on with the business of my future.

There was a flurry of talk that I didn't understand. It didn't last very long. It seemed that most of the group was in accord before I had even arrived. Something had been pondered and debated and decided about me, but I did not know for months what that something was. Just before I was told I could go, Arthur Grey said: "I will teach him the treble solo from Allegri's 'Miserere' for his audition," and Father Gregory nodded his approval. I don't expect any of the others had the faintest idea what this piece sounded like. I didn't then, either.

"Well, he can't keep singing 'Silent Night,' said the principal. They all laughed and began to put on their scarves and coats, and I was told I could go home.

In this considered way, the Anglicans handed me over to the Catholics. When I finally realized what had happened, it did not occur to me to wonder if God would mind. I certainly did not.

ED TELLS ME NOW that he had serious reservations about the benefactors' plan, and that he voiced them at the meeting. I don't know if this is true. I don't remember any dissent, but I know that doesn't mean much after twenty-five years. He goes through phases where he gets pretty hung up on this.

"You don't hold it against me, do you Frederick?" he asks, over and over. Given the way things turned out, he needs periodic reassurance that he is not to blame. I give it to him; I don't mind not knowing what the truth is. These days I am not sure there is any such thing.

"I loved St. Mary's, Ed," I tell him. And that is true, while not being strictly Truth.

I HAD A VISIT FROM THE BIBLE. It came to my door accompanied by two earnest young men in suits, not yet done with pimples. "Good day, Sir," one of them said. In my first glance I registered the black book under the elbow of one and a pile of pamphlets in the hands of the other, and started backing away instantly.

"No thanks," I said. I was shaking my head, closing the door.

I do not think they teach them this in soul-saving school, but one of them—the taller one, with worse acne—leaned forward and put his boot in the diminishing crack. The bottom of the door hit his foot with a thunk, and shuddered to a stop.

A hand reached into the crack, waving a coloured pamphlet very close to my face.

"Sir?" said the boy. His voice was apologetic and too young to be doing this, and it was like an echo of a voice that had been unheard for twenty years. I felt sorry for him. I opened the door again.

"If you could just take a copy?" he almost begged. "We have to personally deliver a certain number before—" He stopped himself, and there was an awkward pause, and the two young men looked at each other doubtfully.

"Before what?" I asked.

"Before we stop for lunch," his companion finished.

"How many?" I asked. "I didn't know you guys had a quota to meet. How many do you have to deliver before lunch?"

"Well ... about twenty." The taller one removed his foot from the door, but still held the tract in his outstretched hand. There wasn't much difference between them except for height, a dozen pimples, and the knots in their ties. Their eyes held the same amount of adolescent hunger.

I looked at my watch. "Can you just give me twenty?" I held out my hand.

The two boys looked at each other uncomfortably.

"All right, forget I said that. How many have you delivered so far?"

"Well ... I think it's ... three, Sir."

"*Three*? That's seventeen more."

"Yes, Sir. Unless we get a chance to talk to somebody. That counts more. Like, *really* talk to them. Like, get invited to sit on the porch and have a good heart to heart or something...." Tall One's hand was finally lowering; we all looked at the tiny porch, where one lonely kitchen chair would fill all the available space.

"So do you like pizza?" I asked.

THE ENTIRE HISTORY OF THE *EXODUS* is a strange one. All that hardening of the Pharaoh's heart! All that bloody murder of innocents! All that business about yeast! I didn't remember half of it, though I don't think it was only a memory issue. I suspect the versions I'd been taught in religion class and had heard preached from pulpits had been somewhat sanitized, with all the questionable bits left out. I think that happens a lot. Also, it seems that when God contradicts himself, as he does in spades, it is left to biblical scholars to decide what he really meant—and left to the rest of the flock to just accept the official verdict.

The pizza was two-thirds gone when we finally got to the part about the Ten Commandments and Moses going up and down the mountain like a yo-yo. All that arguing with God! First there are the commandments themselves, a kind of moral summary, followed by many passages that read like the Criminal Code for Israelites, and then a how-to guide on the construction and outfitting of a temple.

Here's one of the parts I totally forgot about: when God called Moses up to the mountain, mostly he told him to bring his brother along, too.

Here's another part I totally forgot about: when Moses came down from the mountain with the word of God written in stone, he found his people bored of waiting for his return, busy worshipping a golden calf, dancing, and singing. Turns out he'd left his brother in charge. Moses was so angry about the calf that he threw the stone tablets on the ground, and they broke. And some time later he had to go up and get God to write it all down again. He was so angry about the singing that he orchestrated the killing of three thousand of his own people in punishment. And then he set up—

"Wait, wait, wait," I said. "He *what?*"

"They were *totally* out of control," said Tall One. "Singing for no reason." He was examining the crust he held in his hand, to see if there was any more meat on it. He decided not, discarded it, and helped himself to another piece, lowering the sagging end into his mouth like manna from heaven.

"He killed them because they'd been *singing?*" I asked.

MUSIC AND RELIGION HAVE LONG BEEN BEDFELLOWS. Some music historians have even suggested that we would not have music as we know it today in the West if we hadn't had the Christian church with its monkish monopoly on musical notation. They suggest that all the early "folk music"—the music of the people—has been lost. What remains in the record is the history of music sung to the greater glory of God.

If I had heard this as a child it would have meant little. I stood in the choir stalls and looked up at the scenes of Jesus's life in coloured glass, and I heard the choir creating harmonic sounds more beautiful than any I could ever have imagined. The notes that countless voices had sung there before us still hung in the air like a sweet fragrance, and we layered our voices over this heavenly scent in choral unity. I could hear music even in the silence. I thought I was hearing the presence of God.

My early lack of religious education seemed part of the Grand Scheme. It made my pre-adolescent conversion more meaningful, as if God had really gone out of his way to find me. I began to believe that everything in my life led to the moment that He came looking. It wasn't merely a Call, it was a Home Visit.

When I was twelve I saw God on my bedroom wall.

It was dark. A faint grey light filtered in from the front hallway, through the translucent white of the Canadian flags: the streetlight through the glass in the front door. My bed was pushed up against the wall opposite the doorway, lengthwise, underneath the fake mantle that hung above the fake fire grate.

There was a real chimney behind there, for the clattering oil furnace in the basement. If I held my ear tightly up against the wall, I could sometimes hear a resonance from the SS's voices in the room upstairs; I could never actually make out what they were saying, but could tell enough from the flow of words and blasts of expletives to determine how far I should stay out of their way. I wasn't doing that then, though; my brothers were all out, my mother was asleep, and the house was dead quiet, but expectant—a *fermata* on the rest. I was lying on my back, staring up at the ceiling.

I had been trying to communicate with God for months. I wrote letters on stationery that I found in the vestry at St. George's. It never occurred to me at the time to wonder if this was stealing since I believed that the paper had been placed there for this manifest purpose, to write notes to God. Honestly, I have no memory now of what I wrote, but I do know I made a serious effort at penmanship, folded the paper carefully, slid the half-sheet under a cracked tile in the fire grate—as if God were Santa Claus or a masculine Mary Poppins—and went to sleep trembling. I woke in the morning still trembling, reached out and retrieved and unfolded the paper, now curiously damp, hoping for who knows what?—an answer written in gold calligraphy, Express Post from heaven.

There was never any answer. The bottom half of the page remained blank as sheet music after the *coda*.

That night I lay there in the dark with a longing so fierce it was like a fever. My skin tingled with it. To say now with any certainty what it was that I longed for seems impossible. Despite the loneliness of my childhood, I was not a sad child. But that night was full of sorrow, a *malinconia*, and I didn't know its source. I held my hands out in front of my face and stretched my fingers wide. I could feel those missing digits, that absent twin. I began to sing a little *duettino*, so softly, *estinto*, from my self to myself, moving my head slightly from side to side for the different parts. It was a song I had been singing for so long that I think I must have made it up in the cradle, or perhaps in the womb—a two-part Aboriginal chant of syllables that could go on and on without a final resolution.

As I sang, the room began to grow a little brighter. The wall beside me began to glow with an unearthly light, not grey like the street lamps, but silvery white and iridescent like mother-of-pearl. With every note, the light deepened and began to form a shape, a presence, a being that shone out from the wall beside my bed. The being became a Being and sat upon an immense white throne. Light spilled into the room. Like the god-lion Aslan singing the leaves onto the trees and the moles out of the earth, I sang the white hairs onto God's great head and the fingernails onto God's hands, until I could see every magnificent part of him in the finest detail.

He was overwhelming.

When God appeared and I had my one chance to petition him personally, I did not ask for world peace. More surprising to me now is that I didn't ask him for another resurrection.

"Get me out of here, God," I prayed. And then I wet the bed.

IT'S ALWAYS HARD FOR ME IN OCTOBER—there's a Sunday that arrives, early in the month, too cold or windy or rainy, and no matter how tightly I tuck the wool blanket around my mother's legs or how low I hold the umbrella over her, the weather is just too bad to take her out walking. I know the staff think I push it too far as it is. When I bring her back, some days in late September, with cheeks red and rough from wind, I know they think I shouldn't have taken her out, that maybe she'll get pneumonia as a result. "How will you feel then?" they seem to say with their accusing looks as we come in through the coded doors. Maybe that's another reason I start her singing before we get back. It pacifies them, and also makes it harder for them to "have a word," as the head nurse would say.

"Can I have a word, Mr. Madrigal? Your mother doesn't seem to be responding to the new medication. Can I have a word? You mother hasn't moved her bowels in five days, and we need your permission to—" Well, you know what it's like. Things you don't want to know about, delivered in a way that makes them seem like the most important subjects in the universe. They take it all far too seriously. Or maybe it is just that they don't realize that all the important things in my mother's life have already happened. Whatever we do now, it's too late.

The leaves were heaped in wet piles in the gutters, and rivulets of the morning's rain still ran down towards the sewers, a little water music for an overcast day. The trees were mostly bare, dark-bolled and agitated. We were passing under a beech when the wind tore at the last few leaves and laid one in my mother's lap.

"Bleeds," said my mother. "Bleeds on the wind. Butter it like bread. I can't see the sky. Can you lift it? Lift, lift, lift, lift. No, that's not what I mean. The reeling, Chicken Little. Did you say you wanted to go? Bleeds like jam. She took it in her hands, but it slipped. I did the best I could. It slipped down, and then the jar broke—not jar, jam—not jam, blood."

We were a few blocks from the nursing home, on our way back. I know all those streets well because we've walked them a hundred times. A thousand times, maybe. She was rattling on, and I wasn't really listening, just walking with my eyes on the sidewalk between my feet and the back of her chair. There's only so much gobbledegook a person can stand. I tune out a lot of the time, tune into something else, some other tune, something more tuneful. I feel badly about it, but I can't help it. In the beginning, I listened to every word, trying to piece together some sense out of her oblique references and repetitions. I wanted to have some meaning to hold on to. Now I usually let the words all run together and they make a kind of wandering melody line to the regular rhythm of my footsteps. I still have a fondness for shoes that make noise when I walk.

I looked up suddenly when the way narrowed in front of me, and there, of all things, was Maya's orange truck parked haphazardly with two wheels on the sidewalk. On the other side of the walk was a high cedar hedge. To get by, I would have had to push my mother's shoulder into the branches on one side, "A new twist for old pipes" on the other.

"Blood makes the best marmalade, the best, oh, marmalade, sneeze and sneeze, no, squeal, no, squeeze. I put it in the jar and in the sand wishes."

I started to reverse, to go back to the cut in the curb so I could get the wheelchair over to the other side of the street. I hadn't noticed Maya at the back of the truck until I heard pipes clattering, and then her head poked around the cap. She saw my mother first. That's where people look when you're pushing a wheelchair. They look at my mother in her chair, examine her face, empty of understanding. Only after they've checked her out do they glance at me—is there blankness there, too, or suffering?—and smile in sympathy and encouragement.

Maya looked at my mother, a good hard stare, and then up at me, and then recognition hit, slowly. It was almost like she couldn't place me in this context. She didn't seem to realize her truck was blocking the sidewalk. Wheelchairs can't turn sideways, I always want to yell at people. But of course I don't.

"Poison in the water, all the children drowning. Get him to fix the noise. It is better if you make it by cutting up the peel with a knife. Tell me the recipe and I'll tell Clara, she brought me a baby."

"Mother of Pearl!" said Maya, and dropped a length of copper pipe about two feet long. It clattered and rang on the sidewalk before rolling under the truck, though she made no move to retrieve it. I didn't think it was possible for a person to look more surprised than she had on the night of the stuck squirrel episode, when she'd interrupted the *live* music, but she did then. She had a pipe cutter in her hand, and she held it out in front of her. My mother held up her arms as if warding off evil.

"A knife! I wish he would fix it, but the children are in bed! Get them into bed, there's a dear dead, dead, dead, no! Help me do it! Poison, *please*!"

"Shike!" said Maya, still looking hard at my brain-damaged mother.

My mother startles easily, and once startled becomes very agitated. I don't know why I didn't just back up. Back right up, without making more of a spectacle of myself, and turn that chair around. But with Maya staring at me open-mouthed, the way forward blocked, I did the only thing I could think of at the time.

I sang very quietly, right into my mother's ear.

I wish I was a little swallow

And my mother took over:

I wish that I had wings to fly
I'd fly away to some dark hollow
And there I'd pass my troubles by.

Maya just stood there at the end of her truck, one foot on the sidewalk and the other on the road. My mother's music gave me courage. I sent Maya a little nod, backed up the chair and turned us around awkwardly. It's always much harder to do something right when someone is watching you. I didn't cross over at the corner; I couldn't pass her after that, even on the other side of the road. We went right around the block and up the next street.

My mother continued to sing. I heard something from Maya behind us; I don't know if she was calling me back or congratulating my retreat. For a minute, I even thought she might have been singing along with us. I had a momentary sense of hearing two voices, though the street was suddenly busy with traffic. Likely it was just a weird echo effect from the limestone houses, that's all.

But I am not a little swallow,
I have no wings neither can I fly.
So I'll sit down here to weep in sorrow,
And try to pass my troubles by.

"WAS THAT YOUR MOTHER?" asked Maya. She was carrying the inevitable armload of copper pipes in from her truck. I was fiddling with the key in my front door, trying not to drop the armload of library books I was carrying.

"Do you have to carry those pipes in every night?" I said.

"So you don't want to talk about your mother?" I have to admit, she was pretty good at manoeuvring one-handed. She just shifted her weight a bit and dug her house key out of the pocket of her orange coveralls with her free hand. The bundle of pipes was balanced on her hip. Another good thing about hips, I thought to myself. My fingers were going to break, trying to hold those damn books against my sheer side.

"You think someone's going to steal lengths of pipe out of your truck while you're asleep?" I didn't *really* think I was going to be able to change the subject, not with Maya.

"I don't know why you don't want to talk about her. It's kind of a guy thing, isn't it, to not want to talk about things? But I'm here for it, you know. I'm happy to listen."

"I guess maybe the lock on the back doesn't work, is that it?"

"Are you ashamed of her?"

"This is not therapy on the front step. I'm just minding my own business trying to get my door open." The key was jammed; the books were slipping.

"Are you ashamed of yourself for being ashamed of her?"

"Feel free to ask any personal questions you like," I said, "and I'll feel free not to answer."

"I could fix that lock for you," offered Maya.

But at that point, luckily, the door finally opened and I practically fell into my front hall. The books landed at the bottom of the steps, heaped like the preparation for a book burning. I kicked the door shut behind me with a great feeling of satisfaction. I was practising being rude, and I liked it.

MY MOTHER HAD GRADE SIX. Where on earth would she have learned the words to Verdi's *Falstaff*, in Italian? Another mystery. I should have asked her Before.

I have a thousand little snippets of memory. They appear like scenes on a broken screen, with thirty seconds or so of the movie playing before once again the characters are frozen in place, heads turned and arms halfway to being raised, mouths opening as if to speak some crucial line in the elusive plot. A thousand narrative snippets, but the thread of understanding that holds them together has been long lost. They might as well be from a thousand different childhoods, for all the sense I can make of them.

My mother and I in the kitchen, the house quiet—my brothers are clearly out somewhere. I am swinging my feet at the table; they don't quite touch the ground. She is eating from my plate, reaching out a decisive hand, picking up the limp broccoli with her fingers, pushing the food into her mouth like one who is starving. She has an air of defiance, as if someone has told her this is forbidden.

My mother in her bed. The curtain across the doorway of her bedroom—the house's former living room—allows a small view of her. She is wearing only a slip and a bra, and one arm is slung over her head, gripping the horizontal rail of the bedframe. In the other hand is a dress, twisted like rope across the softness of her worn belly. Even in her sleep she is hanging on to her dismal possessions as if they might save her from drowning. I stand in the hallway and watch her, but she rests without moving for a long time.

My mother on the front step of the house, sharing with Mrs. Bern a rare cigarette, the two women passing the dwindling butt back and forth between them, their left arms tucked along their bellies underneath their breasts, the folds of their dresses puckered, the wind a little too cold to be comfortable.

My mother in the kitchen with her raw arms in the wringer washer that she got for five dollars, fishing in the opaque grey water for the final stretched-out sock. Me watching her reflection on the chrome edge of the kitchen table, my electric hair like a cat's whiskers, picking up the slightest movements of air, her ragged breathing. There are hardly ever any words. There is never any conversation. I think a lot about what I might have asked her, and told her.

I think, too, about how she missed my years of church solos and community concerts. She missed them all because I didn't think to tell her what she had given me until it was too late.

Those years were the hardest ones for my mother. I can see that now. You might think that three sets of twin boys, at two-year intervals, would be most exhausting in the early years of infancy and toddlerhood. Too many colicky babies screaming through the night, too many two-year-olds sticking table knives into electric sockets, too many four-year-olds under the sink drinking Mr. Clean.

But babies are at least appealing because of their size, and my brothers were beautiful. Dark hair, big dark eyes, and dark complexions combined with fine, symmetrical features; sturdy bodies with perfectly proportioned limbs—they were like infant gods. Add that they were twins, and, in many ways, a sextet. They had no need for mirrors to have their beauty confirmed. It was never a subjective thing. While they were still boys, they got a whole world's worth of attention. They were observed and studied and tested and wired. They were stopped in the street and exclaimed over. They were questioned incessantly. They were admired profoundly. They were envied. They needed to do nothing for all this fame except exist. There were no rules they needed to obey.

There's a natural kind of lull that happens after the age of about eight or nine. In our culture we celebrate early childhood, despise teenagehood, and almost completely ignore the step between the two. In that middle stage, my brothers began to feel deprived of the constant attention they had been led to believe was their birthright. There were still no rules.

It was all sadly predictable. School progress began to falter, and the game of hooky came to be a favourite. Decorative picket fences in the more upscale parts of town began to be pushed over, prize roses—*floribunda* and *grandiflora*—to prematurely lose their delicate heads, and metal garbage cans to be deposited overnight in the middle of busy intersections.

Beer began to be consumed behind the arena. Cigarettes were shoplifted from the corner store. Small change was stolen from my mother's purse, and later from my thrift store cadet cap. The cars of friends' parents were "borrowed" to ride out along the lake with crowbars stashed under the seats for the windows of boarded-up cottages. Beer gave way to pot, which in turn gave way to drugs that were sniffed or swallowed or injected. Boarded-up cottages gave way to suburban houses whose owners were at the cottage. Electronics were hawked at the back doors of pawn shops. Drugs were dealt at the side doors of bars.

And I, her singleton child, was taken away to another life.

In the years that I was away from home, my mother coped as best she could with the departure of the Ns from Terminal 3 at Pearson International Airport, where they boarded a plane for Australia and landed briefly, unannounced and unwelcome, on the doorstep of our Aunt Clara and our transplanted cousins; it seemed this emigration to the desert was inspired by the atmosphere getting too hot for them to stay in Canada. My mother coped with the three-year Medium Security sentencing of Salvador for the punching of his girlfriend Jenny, and the subsequent attempted suicide—or perhaps it was merely an accidental overdose—of Samuel in a motel room in Barrie. She coped with the disappearance of AA into the cesspit of gambling and cheating at cards. Or at least, attempting to cheat. They were beaten to within an inch of their twin lives in the washroom of the Akwesasne Mohawk Casino by three heavily-tattooed guys from Syracuse, New York.

I knew little of this at the time. St. Mary's Choir School was a distant cocoon. It might as well have been a distant planet. But I think my singing might have been some comfort to her.

The double irony is that the Ns came back when things had cooled down some, and opened a garage on Everett at Sherbourne—they both had legit mechanics' licences from Down Under to hang on the wall. Salvador was sprung for good behaviour after only serving nineteen months, and, after Jenny died in a car accident caused by a drunken pimp, he joined a group called Men Against Violence Against Women and eventually became its chief spokesman. Samuel voluntarily entered a residential treatment program, converted to Buddhism, and got a Youth Worker diploma from George Brown College. AA recovered—though Abraham still has a limp and an eight-inch scar across his left shoulder blade—and apprenticed themselves to a heritage bricklayer in Perth, the "prettiest town in Ontario." These things all happened After. My mother doesn't know any of it.

I WALKED HOME ALONG THE LAKEFRONT and around the corner of the bay. The ferry was just pulling out into the steely water, and the wind whipped up paper scraps and brown leaves along the curb. I needed a warmer coat, but I hadn't yet located it; once I was home, I couldn't seem to remember to look for it. That's one of the things about living alone—you fill up every closet by yourself. When you want something, you have to look through them all to find it.

Maya had apologized before I left for my next visit to my mother, though I don't really know why. Or, at least, she'd delivered the closest thing to an apology that I imagine she ever gave. She'd come out onto our shared front porch at about noon, while I was sweeping the leaves off my front step. She looked like she'd just gotten up, but at least she wasn't wearing orange, since it was Sunday.

"So," she said.

It's a small porch attached to small, conjoined houses, so we were pretty close together, with just a small railing in between. She didn't have a jacket on over her pyjamas, and I could see her shivering. I stopped sweeping and leaned on my broom.

"Uh," she said. She was waving her hand in the air, like she was trying to help the words out. "About the other morning...."

I was just leaning on the broom watching her hand. She was

doing exactly what I do when I'm trying to get choristers to articulate more clearly: a kind of decisive swing of the wrist, fingers open.

"Well, don't mind me, okay?" Finally, she successfully conducted her own sentence. "I'm just a little rough around the edges."

There's this idea about Twin Worlds. Philosophers have discussed it, quantum physicists have created formulas for it, writers of science fiction have used it as a foundation for plot lines. The concept is that there are really many earths, many Fredericks, not just this one: here, now, me. In fact, there are an infinity of Fredericks. Every time something happens, when something else could have happened, a whole world branches off in which that thing *does* happen. If you can imagine it, this means that every time a person acts, every single human being, over six billion of us, many new worlds are created, since it is also possible not to act, or to choose to act differently. There is always more than one possibility. In some of those other worlds I may have my twin, Filander, or a successful concert career, or a mother who didn't have a stroke. It's comforting, sometimes, to think that this is not our only reality. Another me in another world knows what to say to woo the circulation supervisor when I walk into the library. Another me never hears from any of my brothers ever again, and silences the refrain of my unwelcome past. Another me straightens my back, looks my wacko neighbour in the eye, and says, "Fink off, Maya."

In this world, this is what I said: "Don't mention it."

And then Maya, satisfied, went back into her house to get herself more coffee.

THE PHONE RANG AND I PICKED IT UP, though I never answer the phone on practise nights.

In my living room, Varrick, Geoff, and Jiro were poised over their respective instruments, tuning up quietly, with as much reverence as they would before a performance. My inexplicable answering of the phone wasn't rational. It was a split-second impulse. Afterwards, I thought a long time about what had made me reach out and grab the receiver, but I couldn't come up with any explanation.

At the other end of the line, a man's voice was saying "Hello? Hello? Hello?" It seemed like that went on forever.

"Hello," I said finally, *sforzando*. Jiro's violin squawked an eight *v.a.* A-sharp, and we all winced.

"Fred?" said one of my brothers. I didn't know which one. I hadn't heard any of their voices in many years.

"Frederick," I said, more from habit than anything.

"It's Sal." I didn't know if he'd heard me or not. I didn't know if it mattered. In my left hand, *sinistra*, I held my lute out from my body, as if it was in danger of desecration.

"Hey buddy," he continued. "How's it going? Long time, eh?" Geoff stood up, leaned over, and took the lute from my hand. They were all trying not to look at me in an obvious kind of way. Varrick and Jiro suddenly felt the need to search for phantom sheet music on the shelf over the piano, and Geoff fell to tuning my lute with devout concentration. Singers and musicians are often really keyed to the intonation and emotion in another's voice. It's a blessing during a piece and a hazard during an overheard conversation.

"Yes," I said. "Long time." I pulled the phone towards the dining room as far as it would go, and turned to face the wall. I knew the guys would still be able to hear every word, but it gave all of us the illusion of privacy. I don't know why I don't go buy a cordless phone.

"I guess you've been doing okay." I'm not sure if it was a question. It seemed more like a statement, but I wondered how he would know. Or why he would care.

"Pretty well, yes." It didn't occur to me at the time to ask him how he was in return, the way you are supposed to.

"I guess Mom is doing okay, too."

"Oh, as well as can be expected," I said slowly, still holding back warily. I knew he was the lead singer in this strange *opera seria*. I just had to wait for the lines, and then follow with the harmony. We did that for five minutes or so, point and counterpoint, all about how he calls and gets monthly reports from the nursing home, and how business was going and what the AA or the Ns were up to—though none of it really registered. I just went "huh, um, yeah, oh," and he finally wound down to a remark about the rainy fall we were having. Then there was a small silence, and he cleared his throat decisively.

"So, look, I know this is a bit nuts, me calling out of the blue. I won't beat around the bush any more. I called to ask you something. A favour, I guess. A big favour."

"A favour," I repeated. *Duh,* as my young choristers would say. Behind me someone knocked over a music stand and cursed. Everybody was getting nervous. Disquiet had infected the air.

"I want you to sing at my wedding," he said. "Well, both of us do. Johanna and I both do."

What struck me most in that moment was not that my brother Salvador had called after an eight-year silence to ask me for something. It was not that he dared to speak to me, let alone ask me a favour. It was not that he was getting married, or that he was getting married at—quick calculation—forty-two years old. It was not even that he had asked me to *sing*, for God's sake, of all the less confounding things he might have asked. What I couldn't fathom, in that moment, was that when he said "both of us" he referred, not to himself and Samuel, his twin. "Both" meant himself and this woman Johanna, of whose existence, until that moment, I was completely unaware.

"Uh, Salvador," I said finally, with exaggerated timing, "I don't sing in public."

"Hey, this is not public, Fred. This is *family*—with just a few friends, you know." He spoke like he had completely missed my point. He did not see this fact as particularly significant, and certainly, in his mind, it had nothing to do with him.

"Johanna thinks—*we* think—the whole family should be there, and you singing, well, it's a kind of a reconciliation thing, isn't it?"

I got the details of the wedding down, somehow. I don't know why I did. A failure of my momentary bravado. Reconciliation, my ass. I simply didn't have the courage to say *No, Fink Fank and Funk Right Off*, and hang up. Or maybe it was merely that suddenly I had a pencil in my hand, and a pencil calls for one to write. Given the way the conversation was going—a conversation they were all pretending not to listen to—Geoff had thought that a piece of paper and a writing implement would come in handy, and these things had appeared in front of me in the form of a staffed exercise book and his notation pencil. I wrote the date and the place in the margins of the instrumental piece we were in the middle of composing together, at the end of a bar of rising eighth notes scrawled in his almost illegible hand.

My brother Salvador was marrying Johanna in a church, of all places.

THE BATHROOM WAS UPSTAIRS at the very back of the house. It

was a long way to go, every single day, through enemy territory.

My mother was out. I was getting ready for bed, and my brothers were all still home. I held my wet toothbrush in my left hand, and my whole arm shook.

"He's a dickhead," said Salvador from the hall. His voice came clear and deep through the thin door.

"Yeah," said Samuel, "a gownie dick-head."

"Too big for his own boots," Salvador continued. "Always carting around all those fucking *books*, as if he could fucking *read*. Like he's fucking *better* than we are."

"And all that fucking pansy *singing*," said Samuel.

"That *faggot* singing," amended Salvador. "Like some fucking *super*star."

"What are we going to do to him, the piss-pot song-boy?" asked Samuel. It was part of their routine, this patter, whenever my mother was out. Never exactly the same, but always designed to terrify me before they ever laid a hand on me.

I thought my knees were going to buckle, and I struggled to hold myself up. The edge of the sink dug in to my rib cage. I spat into the sink, quietly. Saliva hung from my lower lip.

"Make him eat shit?" suggested Salvador.

The bathroom door didn't lock. I kept my eyes on the handle, waiting for the inevitable.

"*Whose*?" asked Samuel. It seemed like it was an important question, and there was a brief silence. Maybe they were thinking about the answer. But then I heard multiple feet going downstairs and Nicholas shouting up from the bottom:

"Are you guys fucking *coming*, or what?"

"We just have to take care of dickhead first," explained Salvador.

"Just *leave* the little shit for once," called Nathaniel. "We're gonna be late."

"We'll be quick!" said Salvador, and he turned the handle and pushed open the bathroom door. He and Samuel tumbled into the room like bulls bursting out of a rodeo pen. They went for my ankles, one on each side. The legs of my pyjama pants were pushed up to my knees so they could get a good grip. I didn't fight them. It was easier to submit; I didn't get hurt as much. Their four hands were on my ankles, and then two hands moved to my wrists, their grip strong and solid.

The bottom of my pyjama shirt was against my chin and over my face, so I couldn't see. I was lifted and turned, and I could feel the hair on my head fall, pulled by gravity, and my arms were straight out from my sides, held there by my bullying brothers. They were having a good time; great round laughs escaped their flashing teeth.

Upside-down, I was lowered into the toilet bowl. Slowly, slowly, slowly. There was an extra pull of weight on my head; each hair felt heavier. I could see white porcelain beyond the folds of flannel. I could smell—

"Come *on*!" cried Nathaniel's voice, far away and hollow. "Brent is *here*!" And the front door opened and there was an exodus and the door was slammed shut.

And I was on the bathroom floor, my pyjamas bunched and twisted in odd directions.

I didn't move until I heard four more feet thunder down the stairs and out the door. A car pulled away, squealing faintly. I let all the sounds echo and fade. The toilet ran, and I lay there for a while and listened to the burble.

When I finally got up, a little water ran down my neck and underneath my collar. The top of my head was wet—the ends of my hair—but there were no towels. I pulled my shirt right way round.

I spat into the toilet. In our house, the seat was always up. I spat again, and saw a line of blood in the bowl. I'd bitten my tongue.

ST. MARY OF THE ASSUMPTION CHOIR SCHOOL heard my audition of the Allegri treble solo in April of that year. In addition to my regular choir practice, I sang twice a week with Arthur

Grey, occasionally assisted by Father Gregory, learning a fair number of the treble and soprano parts that are common for both Anglican and Catholic choirboys to know, all in the space of two and a half months. The "Miserere" was the focus, but they did not want me to get bored.

The scout heard me sing in the chancel of St. Mary's. He offered me a scholarship on the spot. Or rather, he offered my scholarship to Arthur Grey, and I thought that meant they were going to pay my choirmaster so I would sing.

Father Gregory sent someone right away to go and fetch my mother in his car, and in the meantime, one of the Ladies Brigade brought us coffee. She handed the tray around to me as well as to the men, so I took a steaming cup and drank the bitter liquid black, as they did. It was my first cup of coffee, an invitation into the world of men. Those roasted beans are the jazz music of the taste buds. I was instantly hooked.

My mother, apparently, was doing her hair when the car came for her. For some reason, when she saw the brother's black robes at her door she thought I was in trouble with the law, or perhaps dead, and came weeping, with a paisley kerchief tied around her head. They gave her lukewarm coffee to calm her down, and then told her about the scholarship. She sat on a metal stacking chair directly across from me and looked at me like I was a stranger. They explained again about the scholarship. She drank more coffee, now cold. The dye in her hair seeped through the bandana. I sat on my hands on my metal chair and swung my feet back and forth, and she watched my knees as if she were transfixed.

"Where is this St. Mary's Choir School?" she finally asked.

"Why, *Toronto*," said the scout, as if it would be impossible not to know such a thing.

My mother put her hands up to her mouth and gasped her loss.

It was only then that I understood that my prayers had been answered: I was going Somewhere Else. All I felt was a surge of pure joy.

IN THE LIBRARY, it always feels like there's an audience at the check-out desk; all the other library clerks pausing to listen, book jackets open, scanning pens arrested in mid-air. One day last week when I went in, she was standing right there, behind the desk directly in front of me, doing something at the computer. I was breathing okay. She smiled when she saw me, *dolcissimo*. Our interaction went like this:

"Oh, hello," she said. I never know if she is just happy to see everybody in the library, happy to see all those people reading, even if it was only an internet screen. I handed over my books.

"Hello," I said. She ran the books one by one through the scanner. There were only three of them. Then we were just standing there.

"It finally stopped raining," she said, maybe because I wasn't moving.

"Yeah, that's good. Finally. Wow, that was a lot of rain."

"I suppose we shouldn't complain—it'll be winter soon enough." Was she trying to help me out, or did she talk about the weather to all library patrons? The trouble is, it's impossible to tell. I had this almost overwhelming urge to fall at her feet.

"Well, I'd rather have the snow really; the envelopes don't get so wet." I usually went in at the end of my mail route, so she was used to seeing me in my uniform. It was probably one of two things she knew about me. One, that I was a postie. Two, that I was an inarticulate idiot.

"Your books are overdue," she said. "Seventy-five cents." She smiled at me again.

You have a lot of opportunity to look at someone's hands when those hands are checking your books in or out. They are small olive-white hands, with perfectly proportioned fingers. They look soft, strong, warm, gentle. Friendly. The nails are short, unpainted, pink ovals. She wears a thumb ring on each hand, but her fingers are all bare. That's a good sign, I guess, but not as clear a one as it used to be.

My fingertips touched her palm when I handed over the quarters.

Then, a couple of days later, I got an automated phone message: Bolton's *History of Jazz* was finally in at the library for me; I'd started at number 36 on the wait list. When I went right over to pick it up I passed by the music section and piled a whole bunch more books onto that one without really looking at them, just so it would take longer. Once I'm actually inside the building it doesn't seem quite so bad. *This* time I can do it, I think to myself.

"Sure took a long time to get this book," I said to her. After the first sentence comes out of my mouth, I always know it isn't going to be any different.

So when I went on a Friday a few weeks later with my returns—everything I took out with the Bolton that I wasn't really ever going to read—I got as far as the third step before my knees locked. Luckily, Luke was pan-handling outside. He was watching me, wondering what the hell was going on, I'm sure. There was this skeptical expression on his face, like I might need therapy. He didn't say anything though; he likes people to mind their own business, so he does the same.

"Take my books in for me and I'll buy you some lunch," I said to him. He's always up for some lunch. He didn't ask any questions then either, just picked up his cap and his recycled pens and pencils, and came down the steps to take the books out of my arms. He was only gone a minute. He sure didn't waste any time trying to chat anybody up in there. I could probably learn some things from Luke.

We went to the Sea Biscuit, where the service is pretty much instantaneous, since Luke gets to feeling awkward quickly if there's nothing to do with the cutlery besides twirl it around. I bought him clam chowder with an extra order of pumpernickel bread, which is his favourite. He says the bread stays in there well, making him feel full for a long time afterwards. His eyes were a bit runny, and his hands shook just a little holding the spoon: a harder day than usual, so I was glad I'd caught him.

I had the fish and chips, which is my favourite. I didn't worry too much about the leftover pizza at home in the fridge that I'd been planning to eat for lunch. I just wouldn't have to order in supper.

"Good morning for business?" I asked him as we chewed. Luke has a different occupation for every day of the week; on Fridays he usually sells used writing implements outside of the library. I don't know where he gets them, but I guess it's possible that lots of people leave pens and pencils around, especially in the library. Probably in some cases the same ones they bought from him on the way in.

"Not bad, not bad," he said in between slurps.

We pretty much eat in silence. It's hard to make small talk with someone you don't know anything about, without asking questions. I haven't asked him any really personal questions since we first went to lunch together almost three years ago. I was curious about his life, I have to admit. How did this smart guy end up on the street? Where did he come from? He'd just appeared downtown one day without any history. I'd asked him a few things, I don't even remember what, and he'd answered "yes" or "no" to everything, without elaborating. Then I'd asked him if he had any family.

"Maybe," he'd said, in a puzzled kind of way, after giving it considerable thought. He said it like it was possible that he didn't know. I tried to imagine how that could be, and it just stopped me dead from asking anything else. I thought there was quite a bit of wisdom in that answer, and I've never forgotten it. So now we eat lunch together a couple of times a month, and we make a few remarks about the weather or how well or badly business is going, and the rest of the sounds are slurping and chewing noises, knives clicking on plates and glasses thunking on tables, the intermittent rise and fall of voices from nearby tables and the cook shouting at the waiter in the kitchen: an *aleatoric* symphony.

Luke finished his soup and wiped the inside of his bowl with the last of his dark bread. "I'd better get back to work," he said.

He left me there finishing my French fries. He doesn't like to see me pay the bill.

IT WAS THE MONTH BEFORE I LEFT for St. Mary's. My blazer and my robes had already arrived in a brown paper parcel, had been tried on for size, and were taken off somewhere to be altered so they would fit my skinny frame. God did indeed move in mysterious ways.

During those nights, I watched and listened, sitting sleepless, for my mother's music. I leaned up against the wall inside my flag-curtained doorway, the heat of summer making my shoulder stick to the chipped plaster with dull sweat. I watched and waited. My last nights in that condemned house were filled with familiar sounds: the tocking of the electric clock that lost three minutes in every hour, so I learned early that time was relative and unpredictable; the endless rushing of water through pipes not-well-buried in the walls, since my brothers never bothered to jiggle the handle of the toilet after they had flushed, and no landlord was ever going to come to fix the broken valve despite his promises, or the exacting of advance payments; the hum and click of the old refrigerator, the constant creak-breathing of humid wood floors; the tiny scrabbling of mice; the thundering of my brothers' feet on the stairs, gods descending and ascending to heaven, their near-private second storey of the house; the slamming of the front door at all hours, the punctuation at the end of house-bound musical sentences.

I waited for my mother to resume her kitchen singing. Since my audition, there had been a strange and particular silence during the late hours when my brothers were out carousing and my mother and I were alone in the house. She sat mutely at the kitchen table, staring at the wall in front of her, for hours on end. I could just see her almost motionless profile; every once in a while, she would lift her tired hand to brush a few stray hairs from her forehead, or to examine the skin around her fingernails. At the time, I felt those weeks of waiting only as a curiosity, gradually supplanted by a growing excitement about my new life at that unimaginable place: St. Mary of the Assumption Choir School, Toronto.

I waited in vain, but I was not overly troubled. Once she heard that I could sing and saw the result of that singing in the chancel of St. Mary's—her dyed hair, under her kerchief, seeping like blood on the brain—my mother's music suddenly stopped. I never heard her sing again with all her faculties intact. I knew this silence had something to do with me, but I easily imagined it was fierce pride that had stilled those angelic notes, and not, after all, a feeling of betrayal, or jealousy, resentment, fear, or even relief—all things that I can now conceive during my worst moments in adulthood. My mother's music was gone from my childhood, but at the time I didn't mourn the loss any more than I mourned the loss of childhood itself.

I DON'T REMEMBER SAYING GOODBYE to my mother. I remember Ed came to the house and parked his station wagon on the curb outside the front door. I was waiting for him. If there had been a leave-taking, it had already taken place. My brothers were not home. They were never home in those days, except to raid the fridge or use the shower or turn my bed upside-down, though it had been a long time since they were rewarded by spare change—the substance of their lives was lived elsewhere. My mother was somewhere upstairs; I had the distinct impression that she was in hiding. Arthur Grey and the social worker sat in the kitchen like an abandoned meal. I looked over my shoulder down the long hallway after Ed pulled up, and saw them fidgeting there in silence. My hand was already on the door knob.

I swung open the door and stepped out into the late summer mid-afternoon heat, dragging my suitcase and the parcel of new school clothes over the doorstep. Ed got out of the car and came around to put my bags in the back, and the choirmaster came down the hallway.

"Did you say goodbye to your mother?" Ed asked me.

"Yes," I answered, not looking at him. Had I? Was I lying?

Arthur Grey came out, and Ed and Arthur shook hands and nodded solemnly at each other, as if they knew they were engaged in a most serious business.

"The boy's mother here?" Ed asked him.

"Upstairs."

"Should I—?"

"No," said Arthur Grey. "Better not."

"Should I see your mother?" Ed asked *me*, then. I could see he wasn't sure about the choirmaster's answer. He put one foot on the bottom step. The heat wafted around us. I was sweating, and rubbed my palms on my pants.

I looked up at the man who had introduced me to God. He shook his head, one shake, so small that I do not think Ed saw it.

I shook my head at Ed, holding my breath.

The moment passed. The two men shook hands again, and Ed went over and opened the passenger door of his car, and I stepped away from the house of my childhood for the last time.

All the windows were rolled down in the car. We pulled away from the curb, and over the engine noise and the 8-track of Buddy Holly on Ed's old car stereo, I heard the scream of a dying animal. I am almost certain that Ed did not hear it. But Arthur Grey—standing on the sidewalk outside my mother's house, beneath the open window where she stood looking at us pull away, her two hands covering her mouth, her small frame collapsed against the window jamb, as if she would fall over without its support—Arthur Grey must have heard my mother's cry, though he made no sign that he had done so. He stood, motionless and expressionless, his nostrils flaring slightly, gazing after us until we turned right at the end of the short block; I turned to look back at him, but he was quickly out of sight.

Neither the choirmaster nor God did anything at all about my mother's grief, which only served to prove its insignificance.

I turned to face the front, and I believe Ed started humming with the music.

GOD FOLLOWED ME TO TORONTO. In fact, for many years after the bedroom wall incident, God followed me everywhere. I saw every occurrence as being divinely ordained. God was at Bluffer's Park and in the shops on Queen Street. He was in the front room of that tall house in the Beaches, and in the boy-filled corridors of my school. The hand of God orchestrated the music of my life and the lives of all those around me.

Even though some music historians think that all the early folk music has been lost, great composers have always drawn on the music of the common people for inspiration. There are fragments of folk tunes and ancient chants in the works of Josquin des Prés, J.S. Bach, Martin Luther, Johannes Brahms, Béla Bartók, and pretty much everyone in between. The music made for the glory of God came first from humans singing about thoroughly human things: the harvest, or prowess in battle, or lustful love.

Back then I thought it was the other way around—that all Original Thought originated with God. Newly Catholic, I bought the bit about Original Sin being the fault of mortals too eager for temptation. I didn't see myself as a sinner, but as one chosen. I was encouraged to think this. My benefactors saw themselves as Samaritans, and I was the battered—but saved and converted!—Jew on the road to Jericho. My brothers were, of course, the robbers; my mother didn't figure in the story anywhere. I did not wonder at all about why God had forgotten her. I had forgotten her myself.

I CUT OUT THE PICTURE of the two-headed kitten. I wonder how many people around the world cut it out, like I did, and pasted it into a scrapbook? It's not that I think what I do is so unusual. It's more a matter of my sense of the oneness of me. I sometimes wonder whether if I had gotten to keep what I still think of as Filander's extra fingers, whether I would have felt more of a twoness, or less.

Sometimes it does seem like there are pairs of everything. But other times it seems there are infinite one things trying to become two.

The kitten theme came with me to the sorting station that morning. Dave, who sorts next to me, told me he'd gone to the humane society after work the previous day and picked out two six-week-old kittens for his kids.

"So small they both fit in the palm of the wife's hand," Dave said. "Both kittens, one hand." He is the fastest sorter I've ever seen, and, even as he was talking, his hands kept efficiently filing pieces of mail into their designated slots.

"You know they got over fifty cats and kittens there now? They don't have room to keep 'em all. They're killing 'em, eight or ten a week." I could tell that he was really proud of himself for saving two living creatures from certain death. I thought of the two-headed kitten, sure to die.

Dave finished his sorting, sliding the elastic bands onto the bundles without even looking. Some guys just dump those elastics back into their bags when they're on their routes, but Dave wears his like jewellery, blue bracelets as precious to him as gold. When he finally got this job, he'd told me, he was drinking methadone every day to try to keep away from the pills—he was that depressed. I always want to ask him if he ever ran into Luke on the streets, but that seemed ridiculous, like Canadian tourists in Bucharest being asked if they know the Romanian's friend's first cousin Reuben Pretty in South Dildo, Newfoundland. So I just looked at Dave, and at his bangles, and I thought, we have that in common, at least: being saved by the mail.

He always finishes sorting before I do, even though he has a heavier route, north of the university, and so has quite a bit more mail to sort. On his way out, he glanced back over his shoulder at me. "Maybe you should go get yourself one," he suggested. "Be a bit of company for ya."

I raised my hand goodbye, but I didn't say anything. It didn't really even register that he was still talking about kittens. I was looking at a piece of lettermail, a long white envelope addressed to Ed from his sister Annie. Annie, my foster mother. I turned it over a few times, looking at the familiar two-toned stamp. It felt like a message in a bottle.

Later on, after I'd gotten my mailbags from the collection box and walked all the way up one side of Princess Street, I walked into Ed's shop and that so-intimate bell rang over the door like a spiritual homecoming, as if I were being called to worship in some mysterious Eastern religion.

Ed was tuning a guitar for a young woman with red hair—I mean *red* hair, the colour of cranberries.

"From India," I said to him, and I waved Annie's letter in the air.

"Excuse me," said Ed, and he handed the woman the instrument, made some vague, ineffectual hand signals at her, and finally said, "You try it."

He came over and took the letter, weighed its thickness in anticipation, and slit it open with a grapefruit knife, still sticky from breakfast.

There were four folded pages. I didn't wait for Ed to look at them. I went back out through the tinkling door, an excommunication in miniature.

In the background, fading away behind me, the berry-headed woman was plucking the A-string over and over again as she turned the key, and the string slid up past A and down underneath A, the elusive note tormenting the air with its absence.

ANNIE HAD GONE TO WORK at Child Haven International in Hyderabad, India, the year after I left St. Mary's. I believe that when she got there she took up with a different kind of God than the one she was used to.

The four sheets of Annie's letter to Ed lay on the shop counter for days, gradually getting smudged with peanut butter fingerprints and gathering toast crumbs inside its creases. She always sends photographs of happy children eating bowls of rice and playing with crudely made wooden toys in a flagstone-paved courtyard. Ed leaves them spread out where I can't help but see them, because he knows I won't read the letter, despite his invitation. Part of his life's work seems to be engineering a quiet reconciliation between me and Annie, but I can't help him much with that one since he doesn't really know why we're not talking.

AT ST. MARY'S I WAS NO LONGER one of the Madrigal boys. I was no longer the singleton in a land of twins. There was no longer two of everything. I worked hard to forget that I'd been born into my particular family and fiercely resisted any attempts by anyone to encourage me to remember them. I made friends at school and found power in music. There was only One Best Voice, and it was mine.

Ed brought me to the train station, and his sister picked me up at the other end: Toronto, the endless city. In direct contrast to my hometown, where all the streets led elsewhere to more important places, the streets of Toronto go nowhere except to more of Toronto. It is as if the city proclaims itself the most important place with every street, avenue, road, and crescent. I arrived at Union Station, a small boy even at twelve, with an unwieldy suitcase and an awkward parcel of private school clothes. Struggling off the train, I lost hold of the parcel and watched speechless as it tumbled down the steps past the attendant and broke open on the platform, bursting navy pants and maroon ties like ripe milkweed. The platform was crowded with people getting carelessly off the train, stepping over my too-white shirts. Already this city was different from the one I had come from.

I followed with the suitcase, bumping it down the steps, until the attendant took it in a mighty hand and set it on the platform easily as if it weighed nothing at all. There was a woman waiting there.

"Frederick?" she asked. She was younger than Ed, but had a more serious manner. She had on a flat black skirt that covered her knees and matched the colour of her hair exactly. She was thin and insubstantial in some ways, but she took charge, bending down and gathering the spilled clothing into competent arms, producing an extra plastic bag from her large handbag to gather up the stray never-worn navy blue socks. It was clear she was prepared for anything. Childless herself, she could still take twelve-year-old boys in her stride. She was nothing like my mother at all.

"My mother doesn't even know how to tie a knot properly!" I said to her in humiliation. I am ashamed still, thinking of this moment, but for different reasons. But Ed's sister always spoke of my mother with an understanding that I did not possess.

"Your mother was doubtless thinking about bigger things than knots," she said simply, and, despite not knowing what she meant, her words still stung me a little. She straightened with the parcel under control and, having re-tied the knot over the torn brown paper, took the suitcase, shook her head briskly at the waiting porter to indicate that she had no need of his services, and set off down the platform so quickly that I had to trot to keep up.

She looked back only once to make sure I was with her. "I'm Annie," she called out. "Call me Annie."

Empty-handed, I just managed to keep her in view in the

high-ceilinged station, dodging between travellers and bumping my knees on suitcases vaster than my own. She wove expertly through the crowd and led me out into the sweltering heat, late afternoon and no wind off the lake. I didn't even know the lake was still there, only a few short blocks away. I was landlocked by skyscrapers, more belittling in real life than anything one could imagine from photographs or television.

The school was not very far from the station, and she drove by it slowly, pointing out the junior boys' entrance, now abandoned for summer; it seemed that she had done her homework. The two-storey red brick facade was disconcerting in its solidity amidst the steel and concrete. We seemed to drive a long way, that first day, but later, with a mere week's experience, I knew that for this city the distance was remarkably short and traffic-free.

She pulled up in front of a tall house in the Beaches: a whole flight of steps ran up to the front door through a rock retaining wall, the garden a smeared palette of colour with late summer flowers. There was summer furniture on the big front porch, a whole arrangement of wicker chairs and side tables and large wooden planters spilling blooms onto the deck. She unlocked the front door, and we stepped into cool air, mutely lit, a relief from the glare and the heat.

"Here we are!" Annie announced, as if that was all that needed to be said, and the bags hit the hall floor, *strepitoso*. She had carried in all my worldly possessions with such assurance that I hadn't even offered assistance.

I didn't know anything about front gardens. I didn't know anything about air conditioning. I didn't know anything about French doors. But through the panes of glass, in the large front living room that really *was* a living room—a real sofa and chairs, no beds at all—stood the largest and finest, and the first live grand piano outside the music shop that I had ever seen. Even then, because of Ed, I did know something about pianos.

ON MY FIRST DAY AT ST. MARY'S, Annie knotted my school tie, explaining what she was doing as she went. I was standing in front of the hall mirror, and she was standing behind me, easily a head taller, and held one end of the red tie—a red I would quickly learn was called *maroon*—in each hand. I watched my reflection in amazement. She had taken me to get my hair cut the day before, and I still found the tops of my ears pale and unrecognizable.

"This side should be longer than this side by about this much. The long end wraps around the short end. Fold this over here and poke it through..."

She knotted it tightly around my neck, and rested her hands on my shoulders for a minute. She had slender hands, but their weight was not insignificant. Our eyes met in the mirror, but it was impossible for me to guess at the expression on her face.

And then she untied the knot, and told me to do it again myself.

THE LETTER FROM ANNIE was still lying on the counter a week later, half hidden by sheet music and Ed's scratchy notes to himself. I saw a corner of it when I answered the phone.

It was a call from a father wanting music lessons for his kid. Ed had disappeared into the storeroom, whether to unpack some of the new shipment of boxes, piled precariously and bulging into narrow aisles, or to sit sideways on the lid of the cracked toilet seat with his back against the wall to do a few sudoku to exercise his brain, I didn't know.

"We're thinking voice would be best," said the man. "Then we don't have to worry about the instrument getting damaged."

This sounded pretty suspicious to me right off, but I did what I always did with potential students, and asked him to bring his son in sometime between the hours of such-and-such, and so on. He said the kids were already home from school and that they were free that afternoon and would be right in. I hung up the phone without thinking too much more about it. People say lots of things on the phone, and even face to face, that turn out not to be true at all. But, I didn't even have time to turn more than a few virtual pages of the online Naxos catalogue before I heard the bell tinkle, and I looked up and saw the whole family coming in through the door. Or I should say the bell *jangled*, and the door burst open, and a tousle-headed child of about nine or ten burst into the shop like a baby kangaroo. I instantly understood the father's remark about the instruments, and I knew who this kid was right off, even before the more sedate entrance of the rest of his family, and the formal introductions.

There were four of them: father and mother and two boys. It was hard to tell which boy was older; they were about the same height but looked so different from one another. Maybe even twins, but in no way identical. It was also hard because tousle-head didn't stay still long enough for me to get a good look at him. He charged from the row of hanging guitars to the world drums to the open keyboards, and everywhere he went he plucked strings and slapped skins and crashed keys, so the shop ran wild along with him.

I wondered—not for the first time—where the hell Ed was when I needed him, but I was also grateful for his absence, since he deals less and less well with things going out of control in the shop.

A shelf of music books slid sideways as tousle-head ran by, and cascaded, in slow motion, onto the floor.

His parents introduced themselves like reasonable human beings, but made no effort to rein him in. They were both tall and thin and had deep eye sockets, and their bodies vibrated lightly, like they never got quite enough sleep. The brother stood just behind their mother's elbow, reading a sepia-toned graphic novel with great concentration. You could tell they were all bookish, the whole family, aside from the kangaroo—they had the controlled movements of body, the fractional pause before speech, and the intensity of spirit common to many people generally immersed in worlds inside their own heads.

"My grandmother was very musical, and we thought Daniel shows some promise in that direction," said the father.

"We thought it would channel some of the *energy*," the mother added.

The guitar pick display crashed to the floor, and a rainbow of plastic triangles scattered in all directions.

Sometimes children aren't seen by their parents. They're not seen because the family culture is so strong that it can't value—or even recognize—anything *other*. Bookish families don't understand the child among them who doesn't care to read; sporty families relentlessly drag their non-athletic offspring to inexplicable ball games; agnostic families think the born-again child is a kind of alien from another planet; child philosophers are routinely disregarded by their couch-surfing antecedents; musical parents don't relate to children who don't have the capacity to play the triangle in the school band, but would prefer to conduct science experiments that fill the house with smells of sulphur. There's usually no deliberate or even conscious intention to leave aside, neglect, or discourage the displaced child's interests. And we can hardly blame parents for believing overmuch in both heredity and upbringing. At some level, we all continue to believe we can create what we wish out of our lives.

"He doesn't need voice lessons," I said to the parents standing in front of me. Behind me a banjo string was plucked too hard, and broke with a sharp twang. "He needs *hockey*."

ED EMERGED FROM THE BACK a few moments after the door had jangled shut behind them. "I heard a commotion," he said. His hair was standing on end, and his eyelids were heavy, and I wondered if he'd been asleep back there. I thought that, even for Ed, this was strange, and I suddenly saw that he was old and getting frail. I realized, for the first time, that he was much older than my mother, and my mother had been in a nursing home for twenty years.

"The commotion," I said, "is in my head." I was thinking of the child who felt unseen because his mother was exhausted from dealing with the six changelings who happened to be born first.

MOST BABIES, ESPECIALLY THE YOUNGER CHILDREN of large families, get used to falling asleep amid the general rumble and roar of infant life: siblings clamouring, pots boiling over, mothers losing their fragile tempers. Babies normalize their noise environment and dream through such harsh music as if it were merely the sound of dust motes drifting past their cradles.

My mother once told me that for the first two years of my life, any loud noise would set me screaming. If that were true, I must have screamed more or less all the time. Seven hundred and thirty days of screaming. No wonder my mother was done in by the time I came to consciousness.

When I was born, my brothers, at ages five, seven, and nine, were beyond silencing, even for the ten short minutes it might take for my mother to rock me to sleep and put me in my crib. If they were in the house, their feet thundered on the stairs, their voices rang in the halls, their misdemeanours crashed and shattered on the kitchen floor. The house was a tempest, and I was tossed, howling, on its waves.

This is my first clear memory:

I am sitting on the floor in my childhood kitchen, my legs stuck straight out in front of me. My bothers are all at the table; I suppose they were there to eat a meal, though I have no idea which one, or what they are eating. I can see the backs of the Ns and the chrome legs of the chairs. Underneath the table is a snake pit of tangled limbs and chair legs, everything in motion. There is a great commotion, over top of which I cry and shriek, though few tears run down my cheeks. And there are my mother's legs; her slippers are red with yellow flowers, the fabric interrupted on the insides by the premature emergence of bunions. The hem of her dress brushes my ear as she bends down. In front of me, she places an upside-down cookie sheet that fits perfectly, lengthwise, over the span of my legs. My bare toes curl under the cool metal. Into my left hand she places a wooden spoon, then takes my small fist into hers—engulfs it with hers—and brings the spoon down upon the tray, *bam-bam-bam,* three times. Her touch has not been gentle, but desperate. It seems she has not spoken to me at all, though if she had, in reality, I may not have heard her; there has been no let-up in the ruckus at the table. Her hand lets go of mine; her legs and dress recede. I can remember the sharp intake of my breath, that shudder that comes to children at the end of a long bout of crying. And then I banged the spoon on the tray until there was no more noise outside of me:

Bam-bam-bam-bam-bam-bam-bam-bam-bam-bam-bam-bam-bam!

My mother taught me how to make music to regain control, the way she did. This is only my interpretation, of course. She would never have said anything like this. We never talked to each other about music at all.

IT WAS SUCH A STRANGE THING TO TRAVEL, in the space of only four hours, and a distance of a mere 250 kilometres, the great and unaccountable differences between my mother's house and Annie's. Nothing was familiar. I went from chaos into order, from dirt into cleanliness, from squalor into privilege, from cacophony into music measured by silence. I went from choking on everyday despair into inhaling trust, and expectation, and hopefulness. My young lungs filled with that peculiar oxygen, so tentatively at first, as if from the very beginning I half expected it not to last.

I went from being a youngest son in an overcrowded family to being an only child, and, though I still missed Filander, I gradually grew used to Annie's focused attention.

As foster mothers go, Annie was efficient, generous, even devoted—but not affectionate. There was never a moment when she absentmindedly kissed the top of my head, or tucked me in at night and pulled the sheets up underneath my chin. Perhaps she thought I was too old. Perhaps I *was* too old, and only long for her physical affection now, when as an adult I can see something missing from my entire childhood, some essence of belonging to someone else—someone *human*. I was never at home in another person. Why I should have expected to be at home in Annie I do not know. While I did not understand then that she loved me, I did recognize that she wished the best for me. And she demanded the best from me, in a singular, intense way, and within a narrow range of possibilities.

Annie believed in God-given gifts, and believed equally that it was a Sin—capital S, despite not being Catholic—not to use those gifts for the edification of the world. She had a mid-century, middle-class sense of good child-rearing practice: wholesome meals, cleanliness, and moral fortitude.

I put on my school uniform, and my previous life wore thin and faded away like my hand-me-down jeans. Annie threw those jeans out and bought new ones for me to wear when I wasn't at school. She bought me new socks and underwear at six-month intervals. At Christmas, there would be new shirts and sweaters under the tree and new sheet music rolled in my stocking. She drove me to school when the weather was inclement, saying the damp would ruin my voice. She looked over my report card with her mouth curled like a *fermata*, on guard for any evidence of slacking off. She attended every concert I sang in, including the last one, and many of the church services, although she was not a church-goer. She believed that God came to where you were, especially if you were singing. Making and sharing beautiful music was apparently at the very top of his list of what was good.

I FELT IT WAS MY DESTINY to be at St. Mary of the Assumption

Choir School. I began the year self-confident, sanguine in the direction my life was taking—or rather, for the first time, I felt like my life had a direction, and that it was inevitable that things were looking up. The year before, I had taken to singing in the streets in desperation, and I had gone to St. George's in gratitude; both events had seemed like happenstance. St. Mary's Choir School was different. God had chosen me. It felt like everything I touched would turn to gold.

Despite my new and growing sense of the rightness of things, I was still, by nature, reserved. At home, Annie and I danced around each other congenially, while our mutual confusion about our new roles and responsibilities slowly worked itself out. In my first few weeks of school, I watched the other boys warily. I waited to see if I would be teased and taunted, or ignored. I made no assumptions about finding like-minded peers or developing friendships. Up until then, my only friend had been Filander; I did not look for that to change. At that point, I wouldn't have said it even mattered to me. I thought music, and God, and the ephemeral Filander, were all that could possibly matter in the world.

THE JUNIOR BOYS WEREN'T ALLOWED off the school grounds at lunch time. We ate our bagged lunches seated at long tables inside the basement cafeteria, and then, rain or shine, were evicted into the curiously fresh Toronto air in the quadrangle behind the school. There was no alcove underneath the stairwell for me to hide in. In the playground during that first month I stood up against the reassuringly solid brick wall of the school and watched as boys hurled balls and shouted rules and flung themselves across the pavement like the erratic atoms we learned about in chemistry class. It seemed to me, a boy unused to the unwritten rules of playground games, just as random and chaotic.

"Play it, play it, *play* it!"

"What do you *mean*, you dickhead?"

"You're *out*, Kevin. Out!"

"Look out beloooow!"

"Send it here, *here*!" cried a sandy-haired boy, running by so close to me that I could feel the air move as he passed. A soccer ball was kicked in his direction, and he stopped it expertly; everything was still and quiet for a frozen second as he stood with one foot on top of the ball, before he turned to travel past me again, keeping it close between his two feet, outmanoeuvring the small group of boys who now surrounded him.

It was a warm September, and the sun shone directly down on us. I could feel the heat of the bricks against my shoulder.

Absently, I twisted the toe of one foot into a crack in the paving, digging at a small line of gravel. It was hard to know where to settle my gaze, so I often looked down, trying always to give the impression that I was contentedly self-occupied—the second-best strategy in the absence of hiding. I started to gather the small pieces of rock into a pile, and noticed with alarm that my once perfectly polished shoe was scuffed and dusty. I was under the impression that our uniforms were sacred. I didn't yet understand that it was the job of junior boys—even those at a Catholic choir school—to push the limits of decorum: the length of our hair, the tightness of the knots in our ties, the relative shine of our shoes, these were all tested regularly. There was an almost constant dance between boys and teachers to see how far things could slide. But that day, I anxiously rubbed the toe of my shoe on the back of my left calf.

"Move *over*, Eric!"

"Pass it! No! No!"

It was as if I were hearing a colony of seagulls floating and wheeling and crying, so far from the sea, in the city air currents.

"Hoy! New boy!"

I looked up, and the boy who'd passed me earlier was calling from an opening in the jumble of moving bodies, with his arm outstretched and his finger pointing, and I saw the ball coming sideways, flying toward me along the ground like a tracking device that might explode when it reached me.

It was instinctive, I suppose, though I never knew I could have such instincts. I drew my leg back in a panic, and my scuffed toe connected with the black and white leather. I heard a hollow *thuk*, and felt a jolt run up my leg like an electric shock, and saw the ball sail, like a winged miracle, towards the boy who'd called me. It landed perfectly a short distance in front of him, and once again he lifted his practised foot and held the soccer ball motionless for a split second.

"Good one!" he shouted at me, and he twisted his way through the boys who were closing in. He dribbled the ball with his feet all the way to the fence, and kicked it, finally, through the net made from carefully folded blazers. I could just see the top of his head, bobbing up and down in the crowd, and hear him whooping with joy.

I looked down at my foot like I had never seen it before. Beside me, a ghostly Filander stretched his leg in awe. I saw a shoe made entirely of gold, and I laughed out loud.

IT SEEMED ENOUGH THAT I HAD DONE IT ONCE. After that, I could pass off my disinclination for playground games as disinterest rather than incompetence. The kick became legend, and for a long time—long enough—they continued to believe that I had a rare talent in soccer, as well as in music, and that I simply chose to concentrate my efforts on the latter.

At lunchtime, whenever it was dry, I sat with my back against the brick wall of the school, my knees bent in front of me, and relaxed a little. When the ball threatened to come in my direction, I sometimes caught it and rolled it a short distance to Kevin or Eric or Brian as they ran past, and other times pretended I was focused on my sheet music and simply didn't see it. And sometimes I was, though out of the corner of my eye I watched the other boys run into autumn, trading shirt-sleeves for blazers and fall jackets. Knapsacks were brought out to serve as goalposts, and the seagull-like cries wove themselves into a song that caught on the wind and rose above us; I imagined the sounds, far out over Lake Ontario, finally evaporating into the clouds.

IN EARLY OCTOBER, I stood in the bright kitchen and watched as Annie spread peanut butter on one slice of bread and grape jelly on another, fit the top and bottom together carefully, cut the sandwich into triangles, and then took a piece of plastic wrap from the carton in the drawer.

"I could do that," I said, finally.

"What? Make your lunch? Do you want to?"

"Yes. I could get my own lunch. I always did at home." I didn't tell her that, in the previous year, I bought my lunch with my busking money, running into the corner store on my way to school and grabbing a bag of Cheezies or a Hershey Bar, and a pink lemonade.

"Go ahead then." She handed me the sheet of plastic wrap and moved out of my way. I thought she would go back to her *Globe and Mail* on the dining room table, but she stood beside the fridge, her arms loosely folded across her chest—Annie didn't ever lean on counters or put her shoulder up against walls.

"Do you like the school?" she asked. "Are you settled in now?"

"It's fine," I said, and there was a pause. I was still getting used to this new life, and we were polite and rather formal with each other, every day for months behaving as if we were meeting for the first time. My answer seemed wholly inadequate, given how I felt about St. Mary's, but I wasn't used to being asked about things. It took me a long time to understand that this was called *conversation*. Annie worked hard at it from September until January of that first year, when at last I finally started to catch on, steadfastly asking casual-sounding questions on a variety of subjects that she hoped might elicit more than a perfunctory—and somewhat suspicious—response from me.

"Are you learning any new music?"

"Yes," I said, "I am." But I didn't elaborate. I didn't know she would want to know the names of the songs.

I held the plastic wrap awkwardly and made a hash out of wrapping up my sandwich. To her credit, Annie let me muddle along without interference, although I was over-conscious of her presence and bit at my upper lip. Even when she passed me a paper lunch bag from the cupboard, she kept her eyes tactfully on the French blue hydrangea bush just outside the patio doors, and once in a while hummed the opening bars of the overture from *The Marriage of Figaro* to accompany the vibrating refrigerator.

"Are the other boys nice?"

I thought about my classmates, many of them still nameless to me, in their indistinguishable uniforms, running boisterously through the oak-panelled hallways.

"Nice?" I repeated.

"That's probably not the right word," she said, and she laughed. "I'll have to learn what the right words are for things, won't I? The words young people use these days?"

And so I was able to smile, and nod, and successfully avoided having to answer her previous question. When it was clear that she wasn't going to go back to her newspaper until I had finished, I realized I would have to be direct.

"Can I have *two* sandwiches?" I was looking at the side of her face, ready to slide my eyes away when she looked at me, but she didn't turn her head, just tipped her chin down and spoke as if the pebble linoleum had asked the question.

"Of course," she said. "Help yourself. You should have told me you wanted a bigger lunch." I wondered then why it had taken me two weeks to get up the nerve to ask.

Peanut butter and grape jelly and two more slices of bread. Annie was very precise in the kitchen: there was a separate knife for each jar. I'd watched her carefully while she was making the first one. Like her, I spread the butter to the very edge of the crust. When it was done I got out the plastic wrap carton, ripped off another piece—much too large—and made another mash-up job of the wrapping. Annie picked up the paper bag, and started to put the second sandwich in on top of the first.

"Can you—I mean, can I have that—can you put it in a different bag?" Her hands stopped moving. "I'll eat it at morning recess," I explained. She looked at me then, or at least her eyes flickered sideways, and then she simply went and got another bag from the pantry cupboard.

When she reached to choose an apple from the fruit bowl, she almost-looked at me again. "Do you want two apples?"

she asked. "You could eat one for afternoon recess." She didn't wait for my response, but put one apple into each paper bag. And then two orange juice boxes, four Fig Newtons, and two twists of sliced celery were divvied up.

"You can do it yourself from now on," she said. We both stood in the kitchen looking hard at the two fat bags of food, and not at each other. Outside, the hydrangea's colour had deepened into navy blue, and then to black. After a minute, she reached over and turned the kitchen light on.

ANNIE NEVER SAID A WORD against my mother, and, before the fall break of that first year, explained to me matter-of-factly, and without blame, why I would not go home at holidays and why my mother refused to visit.

"She thinks it would be too hard for you," she told me, "going back and forth. We try to tell her otherwise, Ed and Sylvia and I, but....." It seemed all we could do was wait. What none of us understood was how that initial reluctance of hers would grow quickly into an absence too big to gulf. Within a short time, we were strangers; there was nothing of that old life that called me.

Meanwhile, as she so fruitlessly waited, Annie took me to the ROM and the Gardiner, as well as to Fort York and the Science Centre and the zoo. Once we got used to each other, we went regularly to the music collection in the Metropolitan Toronto Reference Library and came home with our arms full of music scores and librettos. She fed me large platefuls of food; there was simply no opportunity to be hungry. She taught me how to hold my fork and knife properly and to sit at the table for an hour over several courses of always-delicious supper, and how to play Brahms, Schubert, and Schumann afterwards, to aid, she said, in our digestion.

And so, a few years later, when I stopped singing and, on top of that, gave up the possibility of Juilliard, it was for her a betrayal of everything she thought sacred. She'd been grooming me for God and greatness, just as my hometown benefactors had been. She could not forgive me. And even worse, she could not forgive her God for allowing me to choose as I did.

IN THE BEGINNING WAS WAR. And on the Second Day came rhythm. All those spears and clubs being beaten on the dusty ground, the drums calling from tribe to tribe, the frenzied stamping of feet. Afterwards, the making of flutes from the shin bones of the enemy, warriors blowing their souls right through the hollow places after sucking out the marrow.

My time at St. Mary of the Assumption Choir School seems so long ago, now. It's easy enough to imagine what it was like. Testosterone and music—what unaccountable power grew in those of us who took our singing seriously! We ran through the hallways like delinquents and sang in church like angels. It was an odd mix, to be sure.

I sang for God. Not for the glory of God, not for His exultation. I believed my music went right into God's ear. I thought I had a direct line to Our Father in Heaven.

I EMBRACED THE GOD OF THE CATHOLICS as fully as I had embraced the Anglican one a year or so earlier. There was no doubt in my mind that they were really one and the same Being. Or sometimes, after some reflection on the conundrum of the Holy Ghost, I conceded that there might have been two—a god and his ghostly twin, like Filander—sharing out human souls like penny candy. I didn't mind, either way. I knew so little of religion then that it did not occur to me that there were in fact many other gods to contend with.

In the school's eyes, of course, I was not remotely Catholic. I had not been baptized in the Catholic church—or anywhere—nor had I taken my First Holy Communion. I did not know the Catechism or the saints' days or the Ten Commandments. As a result, I was an alien of sorts—at any given time there were only a handful of non-Catholics in the entire school—

but even this did not subject me to "outsider" status. While I attended compulsory religion class with my classmates, I did not go to confession or take communion with the other boys. I did attend mass every Sunday because of choir, and quickly learned to say Our Fathers and Hail Marys and the Apostles' Creed and the Act of Contrition, though I was sorry for very little at the time.

During my first year there was some talk of a Rite of Christian Initiation, but Annie was not enthusiastic, and they didn't push it.

"I don't know that we should make you *that* unrecognizable to your mother," she said.

Since I was not Catholic, I did not understand how these things could be that important. I thought I already had the whole of whatever God was in my hands.

Still, I was curious about the Eucharist, and whether or not an active imagination might be called for.

"Is it really wine?" I asked Eric when he came back to the choir stall, the blood of Christ still moistening his lips.

"It's blood," he said.

"No really, does it *taste* like blood?"

"It tastes like wine," he said, grinning. And he hiccupped and laughed at himself under cover of the organ playing the closing bars of "Ave Verum Corpus."

"What does that wafer thing taste like?" I asked Kevin after the mass.

"I don't know," he shrugged.

"What do you mean, you don't know? Is it like meat?"

"It's like nothing," he said. "It just tastes like nothing." He shrugged again; he wasn't the least bit interested.

THE WHOLE ST. MARY'S JUNIOR CHOIR sang at mass in the cathedral every Saturday evening and early Sunday morning during the school year. In addition, there were a number of us—perhaps a dozen or so—who were regularly selected to sing at funerals. Most people have probably assumed professional mourners had gone out with Dickens, but that would hardly be accurate. While we weren't paid for our services, St. Mary's was; I suppose it was part of what allowed the school to offer scholarships to boys like me. Certainly, there were a lot of scholarship boys in the ranks of the funeral choir, in a blatant "give and get" kind of process that I wish could have been handled with a little more circumspection, given the implications.

The coffins were always closed by the time they got to the church, so Mrs. Bern, thankfully, remained the only dead person seen during my boyhood. But there is something palpable about coffins when you know they are not empty. Especially in church, they emit an aura of contagion, as if something of the dust of death could escape that well-polished box, no matter how tight the seals. Occasionally, I would search the faces of the mourners in the front pews, examining them for the evidence that God would need to assign them to either a northward or southward direction.

The priest finished the Lord's Prayer, began to walk around the coffin sprinkling holy water, and then went around again with the thurible. At the end of the Prayer of Absolution, I got up by myself to sing the "In Paradisum," while pallbearers flanked the coffin and got ready to carry it out of the church. I knew what the Latin words meant in English; we were all required to know what we were singing about, no matter what the language. The body, and the dust of death, always made an exit with the promise of angels, martyrs, and eternal rest. I thought about that in practical terms as well. What I remember most is my belief that I would get to go to heaven without my brothers; my mother I left languishing in limbo with careless omission.

"PICK POCK," MY MOTHER SAID. "Pick pock rock red pock pick."

"Strawberry picking?" I suggested.
"Pick Pock," she said.
"Pickpocket?" I tried again.
"*Marmalade*," she said.
"Robertson's Thick Cut?" I asked.
"*Poison*," she said, with finality.

I SAID GOODBYE TO MY MOTHER and got up to go, but I turned back when I got to her door and watched my mother's lips moving from across the room. She was seated in the blue wingback chair, her head framed by machine-stitched tiny golden lilies which, from the distance of the doorway, looked like starbursts around her limp curls. There was no one nearby. She was talking to ghosts, her eyes focused on a point halfway to the window, greyed with rain.

What is the value and the purpose of life? It's not the first time I asked myself this question. Sometimes it seems that there is nothing *except* this question, and all our earthly activities are a way to avoid looking at it squarely. There were lots of times when the phone rang at home, I admit it, when I had a flicker of hope that the nursing home staff were calling to say, Sorry, Mr. Madrigal, *Frederick*, your mother's gone ... *passed away*. A flicker of hope, and a flicker of guilt, and a flicker of the question that can't be answered, and then the whole thing gets shut down by the part of my brain that can't deal with these things. I answer the phone as if there are no big questions, and after the call go back to making music or taking a shower or eating leftovers for lunch.

Sometimes it happens—the hope, guilt, question, *click*—when I walk into her room and find her deeply asleep, her breath so shallow and imperceptible that she could be—could *almost* be—dead; the air of the nursing home, *diminuendo*, trying to rend another human soul from shadowy existence. There is nothing like the sleep of the old to make us understand the fragility of life. And they sleep everywhere: seated at dining tables or in wingback chairs as often as in beds, blue eyelids and no dreaming.

Watching my mother across the room, seeing her lips move, hearing the faint whisper of words that never make any sense, I thought of the almost twenty years of Sundays that I'd witnessed, and taken part in, her unearthly, fragmented conversations. Twenty years of trying to hide from the meaning of a life without those elements of humanity that we consider ubiquitous: connection, communication, comprehension. To say something of meaning to another; to hear back a scrap of truth, a shred of lie, any words at all that, once strung together, form a sentence: subject, object, verb, and that carry a thought, wrapped like a gift, between two people. Cheap or expensive, it *is* the thought that counts. *I went to the store; Mrs. Bern did my hair; I always liked vanilla ice cream best.* Straightforward meanings, neat and clean. I would have been happy enough with these. More complex sentences would have been pure luxury: *My husband left me when my youngest child was born; I kept his lucky penny on the shelf.*

Perhaps only one side of the equation was required to be fully functioning, in this case, me. I was clearly still connected to my mother, even if only by guilt—how else might I explain my weekly nursing home habit? And I still communicate with her: "Are you cold? Here is your sweater; My dear, Mrs. Bern has been dead for many years; There is turkey soup on the menu for lunch." Does it matter that she doesn't understand me? If people have relationships with cats, or gerbils, or iguanas, then surely this is worth at least as much? But I think the difference is this: If I talk to a gerbil, I can *make up* the gerbil's answer. If I talk to my mother, I cannot pretend to know what she is thinking. With this argument, it is comprehension that bogs me down, mires me in confusion, both about the meaning of what has been said between us, and whether understanding is something human beings absolutely cannot do without.

That expression, *passed away*. Such a strange way to say

dead. Passed away to *where*? I always think. Wherever it is, most of my mother's brain has already gone on ahead.

THE ONLY PART OF MY MOTHER'S BRAIN that hasn't totally gone on ahead is the part that makes music. Singing is the only thing that connects her still to the vast and quaggy mudpuddle of human emotional experience, and the thread is as thin as a silkworm's unwound cocoon. Sometimes when she sings, I can see her struggle perplexedly with *feeling*, as if there is something suddenly present that is both hauntingly familiar and unaccountably strange. When I'm feeling brave I watch her face, and I can see a momentary depth appear in her eyes, as if she can sense fullness or loss or hope, and understand what these emotions are—though not, I think, how they are intimately related to her own life.

Feeling arrives for her in the midst of a song, drawn up and out by the way notes lie next to each other, the rhythm of their expression, the melody line. It has no context other than itself. Mournful songs make her feel sorrow, but she cannot connect the sorrow to the sloping kitchen, the Welfare worker, or her lost sons. Happy songs do not make her think of fantasy journeys to Twinsburg, her far away sister Clara, or that dusty lucky penny on the shelf. Fierce and defiant songs do not make her think of how she paid the rent to our landlord with her body, month after month, the only way she could see to keep a roof over all of our heads.

Some people would say that emotion resides in the heart, not the brain, and harbours there like a ship at anchor until called out to sea by either storm or uncanny calm. Perhaps that is why my mother can still sing, why she can still feel. In her twenty years of being institutionalized, she has never had so much as a heart murmur.

When I am brave, I look in her face when she sings; but then I always turn away, with feelings of my own.

I THINK ABOUT MYSELF AS A CHILD before I was sent to St. Mary's, stiff-legged, wedged into shadowlands. The hallway seems long, longer than I know it really is, and the bare bulb in the kitchen is like a halo around my mother's head and shoulders, its harsh glare diffused by the distance and the darkness clinging to the corners of the room. The acoustics in that decaying house are inexplicably excellent, her voice perfectly clear and sweet, and the rest of the world enrobed in a silence so profound that I can hear her measured breathing and even the ends of each breath, when a note hangs in the air, *al fine*, before the next one sounds. How many times did I wake to her melodies, and creep out of bed to listen? It could be a hundred times, or a thousand. It could be every night of my childhood, for what I cannot remember are any nights except a small handful where there was anything else except being woken in the dark hours by my mother's singing to herself—or to ghosts perhaps, but never to me.

I think of those nights; I examine them closely; I pick at them like I picked at my scabs as a boy behind the elderberry bush, lifting the edges of memory to see if I can make my blood flow, red and bright and clearly visible. I think of the things I can recall: my mother singing, the elderberry bush, Mrs. Bern's secret cookies, my mother's striped dress, the bully who used to chase me home from school—whose name I only sometimes remember. Flickers of memory that, gathered all together like grains of sand in a glass, might fill a week or two of consciousness. Where is the rest of my boyhood? Where are all the other things my mother said to me: the scolding for "borrowing" her lucky penny (I *did* do that, I confess); the admonitions to finish my soup, the grease cooling around the edges of the bowl while I tapped a rhythm on the metal edge of the table with my spoon. Where are those moments—aren't they inevitable?—when she would have been too tired, or too lonely, to censor her pent up feelings in front of her youngest child. When she might have said how much she missed Clara, who'd gone by ship to Australia, or how hard she found it not to get to Twinsburg with her boys, or how she hoped I wouldn't think badly of her when I was grown, because she'd only done what she could do.

I sometimes have a feeling that all the memories I long for are in my head, trapped somehow in the topography of the pinkish-grey folds of my brain, sulcus and gyrus, my head a different kind of renovated house, the detritus swept into the cracks and covered up by more recent events. I poke and prod carefully, in selective corners, looking for any sign of her I may have lost: small stories about *her* childhood, an abbreviated explanation for her incomparable voice and her seemingly endless repertoire, an inconsequential, fragmentary mention of her hopes and dreams—all spoken in my hearing during some vulnerable moment that I have merely misplaced. If I look hard enough, think hard enough, surely I will unlock an entire catalogue of long-forgotten snippets, indexed by month and year, retrieving them as easy as pushing the brass pin down with my thumb and sliding open the drawer, laying them out on the table, rearranging them into categories, and adding them all up. Taking some little thing she might have said in an offhand way while wiping the cracked countertops with a rag made of small boys' underwear handed down four times, adding it to something she said on the third day she lay in bed with the flu, no food in her for seventy-two hours, and adding that pair to what she said half under her breath, with terrible foreboding, as the police came to the door for the first time.

Why can't I remember the things I *want* to remember? Sometimes I think about taking psychedelics or getting hypnotized, somehow giving my memory a boost. But it seems to me that the best a hypnotist would do is increase my susceptibility to hopeful suggestion. I've spent enough time in my mother's nursing home to see how false memories can be created out of nothing but unfulfilled wishes and unlived dreams. And I would rather have no memories at all.

The worst a hypnotist would do—helping to uncover all the things I've tried so hard to forget—would be unbearable.

LUKE WAS OUTSIDE THE LIBRARY. "Want me to take your books in?" he asked, with a calculating look.

"No thanks," I said, and I ran up the steps without stopping. I guess I was pretty short with him. I didn't want to commit myself to lunch. Who knew what kind of space I was going to be in when I came out again?

Luckily, Luke doesn't take offence easily. I guess that's the good thing about living on the street; you just have to learn to ignore rudeness. I know most people don't even look at him when he talks to them, let alone answer him back.

I ran up the library steps, my books in the mailbag banging against my thighs. I'd taken a lot of books out in the previous weeks, but I hadn't read any of them. I'd gone home at the end of my route and collected them all up, not even bothering to change. I had a new adult student coming to the shop at two-thirty, so I didn't have much time, which was just as well. No time to hesitate.

I pushed through the doors, *inciso*. I almost bumped into an old woman with a cane who was coming out, but I didn't stop to apologize. I didn't feel badly about it until I was walking out again. Right then I just needed to get to the circulation desk, get the thing over with, once and for all.

I got to the desk so fast, I didn't even notice that she wasn't there until I got there. There was this other woman, no one I'd ever seen before, with lipstick showing on her teeth when she smiled. All I could focus on was that spot of lipstick, like it was under a microscope, and everything else was a blur. All the sounds in the library came at me like a swarm of bees, dangerous and insistent. The music of pages turning, patrons sniffing and coughing, a hollowness of echoes in the stacks. I thought the whole building would hear me if I spoke. There was nothing to do but reach into my bag and hand over the books, though I was cursing myself up and down. Had I got the day wrong somehow? Was she just on break?

"That'll be three fifty," the vampire said, blood on her teeth.

"I'll pay next time," I whispered. I didn't have it in me to lurk about pretending to look at new acquisitions to see if she might appear from the staff room. I went right back out and gave Luke all my change—five dollars and ten cents—for lunch. He'll probably buy a pack of cigarettes instead, but *he* gets to choose, right?

AFTER AN OCTOBER WEEKEND where the clouds shuttled across the sky like they were late for God's convention, it began to rain. After two days of rain I even heard thunder—though I looked for lightning to no avail. At the dentist's office on a Monday afternoon, waiting for the dental hygienist to be ready to clean my teeth, I'd had the chance to read any number of old magazines that looked like they were discards from the library. I read about a guy named Tony Cicoria, who got struck by lightning outside a phone booth right after calling his mother. Up until then, he was an orthopedic surgeon who favoured rock and roll. Afterwards, he turned into a classical pianist and composer—though I think he kept his day job—and turned out a piece called the "Lightning Sonata" to some level of acclaim. It's funny how different parts of stories stand out for different people. The writer made a lot out of the lightning bolt; I made more out of the fact that he was calling his mother.

I DID WRITE TO MY MOTHER while I was at St. Mary's, but they were dutiful letters, hard won from me by Annie, who threatened to withdraw her services if a letter wasn't posted every month at the very least. Since it was Annie who taught me to play very well indeed on her grand piano, and Annie who kept the piano tuned well enough for the most discerning ear, I was perceptive enough to comply. I have to point out now that it was also Annie who housed me, fed me, did my laundry, and drove me to school when it rained, though these things seemed to have largely escaped my notice at the time.

Consequently, once every month I sat at the dining room table with a thick piece of cardboard under my foolscap paper so I would not ruin the cherrywood finish, and I wrote two or three desultory and largely invented paragraphs about my friends at school, or our class trip to the museum, or the size and appearance of my new basketball shoes, but for some reason I never once wrote to her about music or singing.

My mother did not write back regularly, but sporadically I would receive a crumpled envelope with a new stamp, the original address scratched out, and my name and Annie's address written over the top in child-like handwriting. Inside were her few lines of mundane news in grammatically incorrect English, which I was careless about, with a torn and crumpled five-dollar bill inserted in the folds, which merely embarrassed me. She never wrote about any of my brothers. I didn't find this perplexing. I assumed she didn't want to relay the perpetually bad news; at the time, it supported my efforts to pretend that they didn't exist—that none of them existed, even my mother herself. I wanted to believe I had been hatched by Music alone and let loose in the world to sing. She also never wrote to me about music, neither mine nor her own. It was as if we had made a secret pact to avoid the one subject that mattered most to both of us.

YESTERDAY AFTERNOON, my mother told me this story: "Once, you knew the day it happened, but the fork slipped out and came to, but there was no other way but marmalade. You can put the fork where the children are, in cats. I went to see him. It was dark and hard, and orange. Dead on the table, my hand."

"Really? Dead?" I asked.

"Where we went before along the table in the land of milk," she answered.

She's talked a lot about food over the years, and cutlery, and cats, her children, and people from her distant past—who she sometimes remembers the names of, and at other times refers to by some quality of their being that is obvious enough for me to figure out who she's talking about.

Sometimes I still write her stories down. I have notebooks filled with her gibberish, with words highlighted, circled, or underlined, arrows slicing across passages if one thing seems to relate to another. For instance, if I were writing today's sentences, I would circle "marmalade" and draw an arrow to "orange," and insert a question mark to hover over the word, as these things may—or may not—be related. I've gotten good at picking out the bits that seem connected, even as she's talking, even as I'm tuning out most of what she's saying. The nouns jump to foreground, and the rest of her sentences—all the filler—recedes. What I might register from the above, then, is "Fork, marmalade, fork, children, cats, orange." And then "dead." "Dead" always gets my attention.

When I was a boy, people always assumed I wanted to know something about my absent father. They were mystified when I showed no interest in him—neither his past deeds nor his current whereabouts. When I said I did not care, they assumed there was some suppressed rage deep inside me about being abandoned by him while I was the smallest of infants, that I couldn't manage to communicate. But what I couldn't communicate was that I felt no need to create a relationship out of thin air, with someone I had never known, just because we shared some questionable genetic material and a relationship with the same woman. I had spent much of my adult life strenuously avoiding most of the people I was related to and had known very well when we were all children together under my mother's leaking roof. I had no illusions that biology guaranteed likeness, or connection, or understanding, or even respect.

This position perplexed me somewhat when it came to my mother. Twenty years of Sundays—the long distance between young manhood and almost-middle-age—was no small investment of time in a relationship of biology, if biology was of no account. While most college kids were going home to Sunday dinner to get fed their one home-cooked meal of the week, ham and scalloped potatoes or roast chicken and dumplings, I was going to the nursing home and feeding my mother with a plastic-coated spoon, minced beef and mashed carrots. Then, as now, all these years later.

MAYA WAS RE-CAULKING HER FRONT WINDOW by the dull glow of her porch light when I got home. Even in the dim light I could see her hands were red, and she was making that funny shape with her mouth that people do when they are cold but, despite the pain, are determined to hold on long enough to get the job done. I was still adjusting to the early darkness. If I'd been any less tired, I would have gone back downtown for a coffee rather than have to pass her going in my front door. As it stood, I could see there was no way I was going to be able to get inside without a conversation.

"Do you go to see your mother every Sunday?" she asked, as I was digging around in my coat pocket for my house key.

"Yes, I do." It seemed like a harmless enough question. With Maya I find I have to weigh the balance between civility and discourtesy to determine which is more likely to end the conversation sooner—always the goal at the forefront of my mind.

"That's very good of you," she said. The scales tipped.

"I don't know if it's good or not," I said, shortly. "It's just what I do." I get fed up with people's accolades. People seem to think I—and countless others in similar positions—do what we do for simple reasons like *good* or *right*. The reality is so complex, it's impossible to talk about. It would take me my whole life to explain it.

I couldn't find my key. I put my bags down and unzipped my coat so I could check my inside pockets. Maya unzipped her jacket, pulled out a new tube of body-warmed caulking, and fitted it into her caulking gun.

"Well," she said, "I think it's good of you. Nobody's making you do it. Nobody's holding a gun to your head, saying, 'Go and see your mother.'"

"Actually, it's a condition of my inheritance," I said. I finally gave up and found the key I kept tucked under a corner of my Welcome mat.

"Is it?" She looked over at me. Her index finger, topped by a blob of white caulking, pointed to the heavens.

"No," I said. "There is no inheritance." Of course, that was a lie, if we were talking about more than money. I put the key in the lock and turned it.

"Does she know who you are?" she asked. She wiped her finger on a rag made out of an old sock.

"Isn't it a little cold for that?" I asked in return. She had cupped her hands around her mouth and was exhaling hot air.

"Just getting a jump on winter," she explained.

I pushed the door open and stepped across the threshold.

"That's kind of an obvious place to hide a key," she called after me. "Any idiot could find it there." I closed the door behind me. "Just saying." Her voice came after me through the mail slot. I stood in the warmth for a minute, my back against the closed door.

I DIDN'T BOTHER TO TAKE MY COAT or shoes off, but walked straight through the house and out the back door. My rake was leaning up against the house, and I stood for a moment looking through the dusk at the fallen leaves, slick with decay. Maya's whole tree was there, a million pieces of shed tree-skin, shrivelling against the fence. All that death in one place. And that was just my yard. How many billions and billions of leaves fall from Canadian trees every October? Leaves in my yard, I thought. My yard, my street, my city, my province, my country, my continent, Earth, the solar system, the galaxy, the universe. I used to write that on the insides of my St. Mary's textbooks when I was a kid. We all did it; back then it felt like a testament of faith, a secure spot in the vastness of creation.

Sometimes I miss God. He would have been good company raking leaves by the yellow light over the back door. If God were around, you could talk about astronomy, or electricity, or even belonging or not belonging. You could talk about anything at all that was on your mind, because he knew it all already. No secrets from the Big Guy in the Sky. You could watch the dark clouds sweep across the dark sky, obliterating the faint stars, and not feel that terrible fear in the pit of your stomach. The fear you feel when you know you are all alone, no matter what, and the scars on the sides of your hands are burning.

The light over the door flickered and went out, and for a minute I was standing on the lawn, leaning on a rusty rake under a giant maple tree, and the unseen hand of God swept the cobwebs from the sky.

And then Maya's porch light came on, her back door screeched open, and her head appeared sideways, like a trick at a magic show, followed by her orange jumpsuit, right side up.

"Hey," she said, as if we hadn't just had a conversation out front.

"Hey," I said, my lungs frozen, as if I could undo things by not breathing. As if I could undo Maya noticing that I was out raking in the dark. I leaned harder on the rake, and the tines bent underneath it. All the stars were suddenly gone, obliterated by clouds, and the wind picked up and tossed crumbling leaves over my head like confetti.

"Want some help?" she asked. "The rain's coming." She sniffed the air like a farmer, but I imagined all she could smell was copper pipe and ABS solvent. "It's my tree, really," she added. As if her ownership of the tree was the reason I'd say yes or no.

I only have one rake, I thought, in awe at my own flash of brilliance, and then said, "I only have one rake," with relief. She disappeared inside, and the door screamed closed. I breathed out, looked up, and the wind blew leaf crumbs into my face.

Twenty seconds later she kicked her door open again, came out onto the porch with her hands full of what I first took to be lengths of pipe, and pushed the door closed behind her with the flat of her foot.

"*Lots* of bloody rakes," she said. She leaned her collection against her side of the fence, chose one with some deliberation, then vaulted over the pickets with one hand.

She raked like a whirligig. Leaves tumbled in miniature cyclones around her small frame; burnt orange ashes on an orange backdrop, everything back-lit in an eerie light on a wind-blown autumn evening.

She wasn't even out of breath. I held the brown paper bags while she piled the leaves in. I wondered if I could possibly feel any more useless than I did around her. When we had seven bags stuffed with leaves, leaning full of life up against the pickets as if they were seven convicts waiting for the firing squad, we both stood leaning on our rakes like something painted by Jean-Francois Millet. Totally pastoral. Except for Maya's porch light and orange jumpsuit.

"I was going to light up the barbeque," she said.

"It's *dark*," I said, surprised.

"It's not snowing," she said, which explained nothing. There was a long pause, and she just stood there looking at me as if she'd asked me a question.

"Won't be too many days left," she added. "You eaten?"

"Oh," I said, finally figuring out the answer. "Sorry. Ed's coming over tonight. I have to go get ready." I waved my rake in the direction of my burnt-out porch light. "But thanks for asking," I added, for some reason. "And thanks for helping with the leaves." Sometimes I wonder if I ever tell the truth to anyone.

"Ed?" she said. "Is that his name?"

"*Live* music," I said. "Yeah."

"Can I come?" she asked.

"It's not a *concert.*" I said.

"I don't expect a finking *performance*," she said. "I can sing too."

"No," I said. "I'm sorry. I don't sing—I really don't sing in public."

"Public?" she repeated, narrowing her eyes. Her visible disappointment was the first sign of vulnerability I had seen in her face.

ED AND SYLVIA CAME TO TORONTO to see Annie—and, I suppose, *me*, during the years I was there—every two or three months. Annie liked to make a fuss about the meal, cooking all day on Saturday in anticipation of their arrival. There was always a roast or a ham or a turkey, and more vegetables on the table at one time than I had eaten in months in my former life. At Annie's house I ate things I hadn't known existed, and I couldn't imagine how or where they grew, nor how she transformed them into dishes that none of us could stop eating until our stomachs grew too close to the table and we pushed our chairs back to try to find some relief. I am sorry I didn't have the foresight to ask her to teach me to cook, but at that time I was too busy consuming music to imagine that I would ever want such mundane and pragmatic skills as cooking *food.*

"Annie," Sylvia would say every time, "You've outdone yourself." And Annie would be pleased. You could see it in the way her cheeks rose up to meet her eyes, and a dimple emerged on the right side of her face. Those evenings were when she was happiest, I think.

"It's lovely to have all the family here," she said once. I never thought about the fact that her husband had died young or that they, like Ed and Sylvia, had had no children. To me Annie seemed utterly self-sufficient, and I was inclined to worry that an adolescent boy in her house was something she was suffering through for the sake of her only brother. I didn't see that when she said the word "family" her eyes gathered up everyone seated around that gleaming cherrywood table.

But those evenings were my favourite at Annie's house, too. After Ed had had another beer—in those days he drank Canadian—and Annie had poured the smallest glasses of Harvey's Bristol Cream for herself and Sylvia, and a tumbler of soda water for me, the adults would toss their napkins onto their scraped-clean plates and push their chairs away from the table in anticipation. It was the moment we all waited for, even though the food was always good.

Ed went and sat at the piano. He rotated his shoulders and snaked his spine. He inhaled deeply. He closed his eyes and tilted his chin up and down a few times, and with one final deep breath raised his hands above the keys.

And *wham*—he was off, his hands jumping into the music as if their fire could save the world, as if everything burned as the music came out of him, as if the phoenix was merely biding its time in the ash.

Annie and Sylvia sat in the wingback chairs and sipped their sherry and tapped their toes and swung their legs and even, when the sherry bottle had been tipped a few more times, added their fine alto voices to the song.

Once, after another couple of beers, Ed looked up at me in between tunes, when it hadn't yet come to him what he would play next. It seemed like something pierced him, and he put his fingertips on his Adam's apple for a minute, as if there was something stuck there. There was an odd silence.

"I wish your mother would come," he said to me finally. "I wish she could see you now."

And then his hands were on the keys again, and he was belting out Johnny Cash as if music was the Last Supper and he was singing to prisoners on death row.

Sylvia and Annie were looking at me carefully to gage my reaction. I smoothed out my forehead and joined Ed singing.

WE WERE AT THE SHOP, and it was another slow day. Ed was doing an inventory of the sheet music, but we hadn't ordered anything since he last tallied everything up, so I knew he was just trying to pretend that there'd been enough turnover in the past few months to actually make a difference. I was doing my usual, checking out NPR music, reading ChoralNet, surfing YouTube, going from one song to another as if I was being led down a path by breadcrumbs. I kept the volume at a kind of middle range, and I kept my eye on the door, waiting for Anita, my next student, who was late again. Depending on my mood, I'll either dig up old favourites that I haven't heard in years, or I'll try to find something I've never heard before.

Ed has a pretty low tolerance for bad recordings, so if the first couple of notes indicate that someone was holding a cell phone over their head at a concert, I quickly move on. The result is that we hear a bar or two of an awful lot of tunes, and only occasionally a whole piece of music. On that day, he'd heard a half dozen short clips in other languages, and finally a decent recording of a pink-shirted choir singing in Hungarian on the top of a building.

"Eh? What's that?" he grunted at me. When I didn't answer, he got up from his pile of faded show tunes and came over to stand behind me at the computer.

"There's the translation," I said to him, pointing to the bottom of the screen: *Why don't they wash* MY *son's stuff in washing powder ads?* it read.

Who knew, but all over the world, impromptu community choirs were popping up—made up of regular folks, some of whom had never sung in public before—creating songs about whatever it was that bugged them about early twenty-first-century life.

I wax every month but no one ever notices.

These Complaints Choirs perform on street corners and outside subway stations, as well as in concert halls.

Why does CapsLock get stuck at the worst possible moment?

We listened to the rest of Budapest's complaints, and moved on to St. Petersburg, Tokyo, Jerusalem, and Copenhagen—these last dressed in black and red, singing in a public parking garage, the ones in the back row standing on upturned milk crates.

Since the world is going down from global warming, hate, and mistrust, we would like to complain that the weather doesn't get better right away.

When that one ended, we both stood there for a while, speechless as the credits rolled up, and then just staring at the black screen with yet another handful of Complaints Choir videos listed. Behind me, Ed had his eyebrows ruckled up and was tipping his head from side to side like a bird. I just waited, almost holding my breath.

"*People who smoke don't realize how much they sti—ink,*" sang Ed, finally, and then he nodded at me like he was passing along the baton.

"*I can't get shirts to fit because my arms are too long,*" I sang back.

"*People come in here with sticky fingers and they touch everything.*"

"Right," I agreed. "It doesn't matter what they're eating, animal, vegetable, or mineral, it's always sticky. How about: *Why don't people print neatly when they address envelopes?*

Don't they know someone has to read them, even if it's only a machi—ine?"

"*It doesn't matter if they print neatly or no–ot; I can't read it anyway.*"

"*My neighbour's tree had about a billion leaves on it and they all fell in my gar—den.*"

Ed snorted. He was on a roll. "*My wife wants me to retire but I don't know what I'd do with myse—elf. I'm too old to keep up with how fast things are chan—ging,*" he sang. "*And I'm too old for se—ex.*"

"*I'm too young to not to be having se—ex, but I haven't slept with anyone in almost three—ee—ee years.*"

And then the bell on the door sounded, and we looked around to see Anita already standing inside the shop, her umbrella dripping rain on the tile, her mouth a round O of surprise.

IT ISN'T THAT I NEVER THINK about my father; I do. Not very often, but once in a while, when I'm kind of brought to it by force. Not on Father's Day or predictable times like that. More like this: somebody will make some casual remark or ask some innocent question, and I'm suddenly brought up against it: I know nothing at all about him. It's the only thing I think about, that there's nothing to think about him at all.

I was at a party—one of Ed and Sylvia's parties, actually, so there was a lot of home-made music happening. A different room, a different jam session, practically. I just wander around at these things, room to room, mostly just listening, but I do sing along quietly sometimes too, if there are enough voices going and I can keep my distance. I enjoy the small-scale notes: nobody's performing, there's no separation between the audience and the music, everyone pretty much just joins in and plays or sings or both. Music *is* and *does*, the way it used to. The way it should.

Sylvia's one of those perfect hosts: greets everyone at the door, makes a million little one-bite *hors d'oeuvres*, all from scratch. Always damn good food. She greets me at the door, and when she's kissing me, left cheek, right cheek, she whispers the names of all the available women in my ear.

"Jacklynn, the redhead, tall, Vogue glasses, plays the piano *very well*; Maura, frizzy dark hair, bit of a lost look but nothing to be concerned about; Kathleen, now *she's* pretty interesting, artistic director at the Grand, quirky, but not really a flake at all, despite the look of that skirt."

I guess I am supposed to spend my evening checking these women out, courtesy of Sylvia's undercover dating service. And sometimes I do, but generally from the other side of the room. I'd do much better if Sylvia left me to my ignorance; I'm pretty good at pretending that all the beautiful women are married when I don't know otherwise. I don't seem to make such an ass of myself if I believe my co-conversationalist to be already taken.

I went from the living room to the kitchen, got myself a beer, and started wandering. There's a huge sunroom in the back of the house, with a woodstove in it for the three seasons we don't get enough hot sun in this country. It was a cold night—a November rain in October—so lots of people were in there. All the cold-blooded ones, anyway.

Ed had rolled in the upright Steinway; they always do for parties, and then call the piano tuner to come in after it's been moved. I went and leaned in the doorway. There was a redhead on the bench playing Schoenberg—Jacklynn, no great mystery. Sylvia was right, she did play *very well*, though I didn't think the selection was really party material. Not an Ed and Sylvia party, at any rate.

As soon as I had that thought, she must have realized it herself, and did a neat slide into James Taylor's "Shower the People You Love with Love." It worked, because by the second bar she had half the room accompanying her fine alto voice, me included, and a guitar and a banjo appeared for a quick tuning.

And then there were two quiet words that materialized in the breath between lines.

"Nice voice."

There was a beautiful woman at my elbow. The skirt was one of those wacky brightly-coloured affairs, in sections like the petals of a flower, light like feathers. Quirky Kathleen, artistic director of the Grand. She was talking, it seemed, to me.

"She does, doesn't she," I agreed.

"I meant *yours*."

I had heard a thousand appreciative comments about my voice when I was a schoolboy, but it had been a long time since then. Kathleen's remark came accompanied by intense looks from her reportedly single women's eyes, clearly an opening to an episode of flirting. I cleared my throat. Sylvia had probably whispered in Kathleen's ear about *me*, I realized. We were both standing in the doorway, and everyone going in and out of the room pushed us up against each other. I think Sylvia made four or five trips in and out with plates of food during the course of that one song. I had my beer bottle up above my head.

"You don't have a drink," I said, finally noticing. "Can I get you something?"

"Red wine," she said. "On the rocks."

I raised my eyebrows.

"I know, I know," she apologized. "It's weird. I get it from my father; you can blame him. He taught me how to like my red wine cold. He also taught me to keep the salt and pepper in the fridge. And to eat the peel of oranges." Her hair was full of static, and a dark tendril floated in the space between us and attached itself to my shoulder.

"The *zest*?"

"Yeah, the zest," she agreed, and made a face.

I went and got a wine glass and some ice cubes and poured the Moroccan wine. When I got back to the doorway and handed it to her, she said it.

"Don't you have weird things you learned from *your* father? You know, you read the newspaper backwards, or you flush the toilet before you finish peeing, or you open your mail with the latch of your belt buckle? Because, you know, that's the way *he* did it?"

So there it was again, staring me in the face. I could easily imagine that my father did not regularly read the newspaper any which way or remember to flush the toilet at any time or get any mail besides eviction notices. But I didn't actually know for sure. And I didn't actually care. But I sure didn't want to get into that with Kathleen.

"Can't you learn to enjoy your red wine at room temperature despite your quirky father?" I asked, jokingly, evading her question. But as soon as I said "quirky" I blushed, as if she could somehow hear Sylvia's roster.

"It's much more comforting to be able to blame someone for my idiosyncrasies—and my faults," she explained, smiling up at me. I couldn't really tell if *she* was joking.

I felt the need to change the subject.

"So do you eat the zest with the orange, or afterwards?"

"With," she said. "Just like I'm eating an apple."

"Don't they put some kind of wax on those things?"

"I wash it first. In hot water."

"I'd never have children," I said. But I was thinking of my father, not hers.

KATHLEEN CALLED ME THE WEEK AFTER the party. "Hey," she said.

"Hey," I said. I had no idea who was calling. Mostly when women call me they want music lessons, not dates.

"It's Kathleen," she said. "We met at Sylvia and Ed's—"

"Oh, *right*, Kathleen." But I guess I still sounded vague, because she said: "I told you you had a nice voice and you told me I drank too much."

"Oh, no … I didn't say that … I didn't say that…?" My hand was suddenly sticking to the receiver.

"Okay, you didn't say that. But you did raise your eyebrows at me."

"I did?"

"When I got that fifth glass of wine."

"I think my forehead was just itchy," I said. "Just some kind of dry skin, forehead thing." I was scratching my head with the palm of my left hand as I said it, pressing hard, noticing how the skin wrinkled up on the down stroke. I was beginning to get it that she was teasing me, and if she was teasing me she was maybe going to ask me for a date. I fell back on small talk, since I didn't know whether or not that would be a good thing. "Good party, wasn't it?"

"From what I remember," she said, "it was great. You do have a lovely voice."

"*Do* you drink too much?" I asked. It would be good to know what I was getting into, just in case we were going to get to the date part. Be in the moment, I was telling myself. I'm just not very good at staying calm when facing the future, especially when it comes to relationships. I always want to know what I'm getting into before anything happens; I want to know the worst of the worst. And then usually, in short order, I go down on one knee and then the other, tie my running shoes, and run.

"Sometimes," she admitted. There was a small silence, as if she were considering her next move. She made it: "That's pretty personal."

"Oh, yeah, I'm sorry, I shouldn't have asked that. I should have said—"

"So now I get to ask you something personal: Do you like fish?"

"*Fish?*" I said. "Like fish in an aquarium or fish to eat or "Save the Whales" or what?"

"I was thinking planked salmon," she said. "On an open fire. Beside the lake. On Saturday night."

"*Uh…*" I said, "Saturday night coming? This is the *Thanksgiving* weekend…?" I hadn't expected that level of date, like going right to the coda to start playing the notes. The "be in the moment" theme was shot to hell already.

"You can bring the wine," she said. "I prefer red."

"Yeah, with ice. I noticed that," I said. I think she was pleased I remembered *something* about our interaction.

"Come in the afternoon; we can walk on the beach," she said, and she gave me directions to her cottage, which, as near as I could figure, was a good two hours' drive away. I don't know what it is about people giving me directions, but as soon as I have to start with the rights and lefts and stop signs and gas stations at the fork, I completely lose sight of saying no.

I HAD PICKED UP THE PHONE about ten times before the weekend to tell Kathleen that I didn't own a car and that, anyway, I really had to go and visit my mother for the nursing home's Thanksgiving luncheon—even though it wasn't always clear whether or not she even knew who I was. I wouldn't have said that last part, of course. In the end, after a lot of procrastination and random plunking of harp strings, I called Enterprise and booked a subcompact for twenty-four hours, noon Saturday to noon Sunday, telling myself I could take my mother out for a drive on Sunday morning before I brought it back. Make it worth it, I thought.

"Only reason I have any cars left is because someone just cancelled," said the rep. He wasn't anyone I knew, even though I deliver mail to the showroom. "You're a lucky guy. This is one of our busiest weekends of the year, you know."

I had one hour and twenty-seven minutes to mull over the question of luck as I was driving along the shoreline of Lake Ontario. Was it luck to find another whole continent when all you were looking for was saffron and pepper? You can easily see how those early explorers thought they had found the ocean, in perpetual high tide mode. Little waves lapped the shore in an imitation of salt water, and the sun lifted their edges into thin golden horseshoes. At least it's a fine day for a drive, I thought to myself. I was pretending that the drive was what it was all about, not thinking about arriving at my destination, and especially not thinking about *planked salmon*. Across the vast expanse of water, nothing was visible except sky. There's something unnerving about that far horizon and the way it continually beckons. Most of us can't live like that. We need trees or hills or skyscrapers to keep us from the longing. We need to be boxed in. Limits save us.

I got as far as the ferry at the end of Bath Road, and I waited for a while in a small line-up of cars, looking out across the narrow strait to the cliff on the far shore. There was a giant chocolate lab in the station wagon in front of me that was steadily obscuring the vehicle's rear window with drool.

I ejected the CD from the player. I'd been listening to the Deller Consort sing the madrigals of Clément Janequin. I wanted to see if I could hear the dog panting, but of course I couldn't. The windows were closed, and the wind whipped any sounds right out across the Bay of Quinte and tumbled them among the rocks on the far shore. I put the music back on, and watched as the dog's sides heaved in and out in 2/4 time. I could see the ferry across the bay, starting its return journey.

And then I re-started the engine, backed up as far as I could without ramming the car behind me, and did a five-point U-turn on the narrow dead-end road. Driving back along Bath Road, with the lake on my right this time, Alfred Deller and I sang a *duettino* at the top of our lungs.

I POPPED THE CD OUT AGAIN to listen to DNTO on the CBC, and I caught the news. I was only half listening, but I turned it up for the weather report. There were thundershowers expected for Sunday. I looked out across the water at the two-toned blue, the blazing sun, and the stark trunks of trees, with their almost-bare branches etched haphazardly into the sky.

I stopped at a rare pay phone near an Esso station, fished in my pockets for change, and made two calls. The first call was to the nursing home, to ask them to get my mother ready to go out. The second was to Kathleen. Car trouble, I told her home voicemail; I had neglected to bring her cell phone number. I often thank God for voicemail. I didn't apologize too much about my inability to arrive. I suggested to her safe, airless, cyber-message that she give me a call when she got back into town, but I don't know if I meant it.

Somebody had pulled the plug on the anxiety that had been building as I drove west. East seemed a safer direction for a Saturday afternoon. The wind scattered leaves across the highway in eddies of red and rust; I watched a murder of crows fly up into a giant hardwood and perch like ripe black apples ready to fall. I counted them as I went by: seven for a secret never to be told. Relief filled the car, and I could breathe deeply again.

When I got to the nursing home, I parked in the circular drive where it said "No Parking, Fire Lane." As soon as I got out of the second-floor elevator, I was accosted by Marilyn, whose curious brand of dementia causes her to think the common room outside of the locked ward is the living room of her former house.

"I'm sorry," she said, shaking her head regretfully. "I'm not up for guests right now." She was blocking the hallway with her canes stretched out like arm extensions and cocked like duelling pistols. Her wispy hair was dyed blonde, but it hadn't taken very well, and she was thin and reedy, but at the same time wiry and muscled, like a stray dog. You could easily imagine her with a shotgun in her hands, standing on a derelict porch, guarding her property, baring her teeth.

"Hi Marilyn," I said. "It's Frederick." I was eyeing the locked ward door behind her, maybe twenty feet away, on the other side of the common room entrance. The television was blaring, but the room was empty, sofas sitting vacant. Despite the noise, it looked like a place that should have white sheets on the furniture. The whole place smelled of death and desertion.

"I don't care if it's *God*," she said. "I'm watching my show now. You'll have to come back later." I am sure I heard a little growl from the back of her throat.

"What show are you watching, Marilyn?"

"*Star Trek*," she said. *Space Cowboy* this week, I thought. Last week she'd told me her favourite show was *Friends*. *Gossip Girl*, I'd thought then.

"Oh, I love that show," I said. "It's my *favourite*. Can I watch it with you?" How we lie so easily to the old, I thought. I was still eyeing the ward door.

"I don't know," she said petulantly. "I wasn't expecting visitors. I haven't done my hair." She lifted her thin hand up to her forehead, and pushed the hair from her face. This small action called back a shadow debutante.

"You look just fine," I told her. "Really fine." A memory flashed across her eyes, herself at twenty in front of an oval mirror, perhaps, and she softened. Her eyelids were translucent blue, and sagged over her eyes as if they were over-weary of looking out.

"Are you *sure*?" she asked.

"I'm sure. *Better* than fine. *Beautiful*, in fact. You're beautiful." And then there was a look in her eyes that *was* beautiful, as if we—any of us—have the power to call up beauty by mere words.

I ended up sitting there with her for a full twenty minutes, holding too-tightly to the elongated triangle of wilting gerbera daisies I had bought for Kathleen, watching the Enterprise float through deep space, because I didn't have the heart to slip away any sooner. I patted Marilyn's arm and left the flowers on the seat beside her, but she didn't look at me at all when I got up.

I punched in the code, four-three-two-one, and opened the door up. It always amazes me that even four-three-two-one is too complicated for the demented mind. As I stepped into the locked ward, the light changed, and I had a vision of Kathleen arriving at her cottage with an armful of groceries—kalamata olives, prosciutto, roasted bell peppers, and other antipasto, I imagined—and not seeing her phone flashing my message until she got home on Sunday. Guilt is such a familiar emotion that I don't always notice when another slice gets added to the sandwich. But this time I did. I thought, no, not bread, but rusks from Belgium. Lay the guilt on the rusks with the provolone, Frederick, I thought to myself. Lay it all on, and eat it all up. Trouble is, it's indigestible. There's no way to get rid of it. It stays in our bodies like toxic waste.

WHEN I GOT NEAR MY MOTHER'S ROOM, I could hear her voice, that rousing tune:

Of all the money that e'er I had
I spent it in good company
And all the harm I've ever done
Alas it was to none but me.

Louise must've started her off. She was standing just inside my mother's door, leaning on an unused IV pole, shaking her head in some faintly awestruck way.

"Love to hear your mother sing," she said, wistfully. "My father used to sing this one when he came home after losing his shirt at poker." The curls of her hair fell over her shoulders like an advertisement for youth. She'd only been working there a few weeks but she knew enough to keep trying the first lines of songs until she found one my mother knew, and to stay still at the edge of the room if she wanted my mother to keep singing.

And all I've done for want of wit
To memory now I can't recall
So fill to me the parting glass
Good night and joy be to you all.

And then I remembered my own rented good ship Enterprise, parked outside in the fire lane for the past half hour. I went in to get my mother.

"Louise," I called back over my shoulder, "can you help me get my mother ready for a drive? I called ahead but I guess no one—"

"Money?" asked my mother.

"You don't have any," I told her, and pulled open a drawer to look for a sweater.

I REALLY *DON'T* KNOW IF I MEANT IT about her calling me again. I thought about it, walking home from the car rental place on Princess. The place is on my mail route, so I kept going into shops by accident—my automatic pilot—as I walked along, even though it was already getting dark. I'd found a ticket on the car when my mother and I got out to it. A little passive-aggressive message from the nursing home staff.

Did I mean it? Why had I driven almost all the way to Kathleen's cottage and then turned around? Or maybe the question was better put like this: why didn't I turn around on Princess Street, or at the Townline Road intersection, or at the diner in Sandhurst? Maybe the question should be why didn't I drive straight to the nursing home to pick up my mother? *Why* did I waste all that gas?

I stopped in to see Ed.

"Hey *bro*," he said, when the bell had stopped tinkling. He tries hard to be a holdover from the sixties.

"Hey *pops*," I said. I don't let him forget his age.

There was no one in the shop except a young couple looking at a banjo; she was cradling it in her arms like a baby she didn't know how to hold—no mothering instinct there—and he was saying, "Go on, Stacy, try it," and looking at her like she was the Madonna herself.

I looked at Ed and cocked my eyebrow.

"We've been doing this for seventeen and a half minutes already," he said valiantly, under his breath. "Go on, try it, try it, *try* it!" His eyes bulged a little as he spoke.

"You want to come over later, drink some Red?" I asked him, laughing.

And then he remembered.

"Whoa," he said, looking at my new Scottish cable sweater, pure virgin wool, hand-knitted. "You're kinda *dressed* for success. Didn't you have somewhere to go today? Aren't you supposed to be there, uh, *now*?" He looked at his watch. "Twenty-two minutes," he amended. The young couple were still at it.

"I don't know, Jason," she was saying. "It's so, *like*, in*timi*-dating." She had her hand on the strings and was patting them as if they were attached to a small dog that had just been sick on the carpet.

"You could close early," I said to Ed, ignoring his question. We did that a lot with each other; knew the unsaid line was, *Don't go there*. You can't get away with that with women. Give them a gentle "back off" message and they just get more determined to find things out.

"That's a *great* idea," he agreed.

"You have to just let yourself get a *feel* for it," said Jason.

“SIR?” I SAID. I HAD GONE TO THE SCIENCE TEACHER. He wasn’t a young man, but I thought his subject would make him more open to possibility. I might have gone first to the English teacher, but that was a woman. “Sir?”

“Hm?” He looked up from his desk, where he had been marking our lab reports. The skin under his eyes sagged, and he had a habit of rubbing his rough chin. Outside his classroom windows, the dirty snow announced the spring of my first year. There was an empty Tim Hortons cup beside his left hand, with the rim rolled up. *Please play again*, it suggested. “Ah, Madrigal,” he said. “You still here?”

“Yes,” I said.

Briefly, he went back to his marking, but, when I continued to stand beside his desk and stare at him, he put his narrow finger on a page to keep his place, and gave me his full attention.

“Need something?” he asked. “Problem with your ride home?”

“No, sir. I take the subway.”

“Then what?” He rubbed at his five o’clock shadow.

“It’s the toilet,” I finally said.

“The *toilet*?” he repeated. “If there’s a problem with the *toilet* no doubt the janitor will see to it this evening.” He was not angry, but dismissive.

“It’s the walls,” I explained. “There are things written—”

But I didn't want to tell him what. "I tried to wash it off, but it's in ink. Black marker."

St. Mary's is a small school, so there was only one student washroom, on the second floor. Four urinals, two stalls, two sinks, sunflower yellow walls, an automatic hand dryer that didn't work, and a wall mirror with a chipped corner.

When I'd gone in after lunch, I'd seen it.

"This is a boys' school, Madrigal. There are bound to be rude things written on the walls."

"Can you get it painted over, Sir?"

"Just ignore it, Madrigal. Ignore it. After a while you won't even see it." He put a red checkmark on the page.

THE PAPER RAN A PHOTOGRAPH OF AN X-RAY of the twin girls' fused skulls with the story of the failed surgery. Not one or two now, but none. There were two heads stacked on top of each other: brain building blocks. On the bottom skull, I could clearly see the eye sockets, jaw, neck bones, clavicle. There was the assumption of a whole body below, not captured by the x-ray lens. On the very top of the top skull, looking upward, a tiny face with condensed features. But, the article said, lips that sucked, eyes that blinked, a brain with firing synapses.

I thought about how our assumptions limit us: this child has a body; this child does not. So, this part is an appendage to that part. This part is the real part; this part is a parasite. This part deserves life, and this, *other*, is careless about death.

I stared at the paper a long time, scissors in hand. *Craniopagus parasiticus*. The label was almost like a spoof, too strange or silly to be true. Finally, I cut out the article, then cut carefully around the photograph, and, in some kind of fugue, cut around the outline of the girls' skulls, two heads together, two faces, one assumed body. Then, with a decisive single movement of the scissors, snipped along the thick fault line where the two heads joined. The pieces floated down and lay separately on the table, one face down so the used car ad from the other side of the page was visible.

I turned it over quickly and arranged the heads so that they faced each other. Then I imagined them singing.

"NO, NO, NO," I SAID. "*Really.*"

"Look," said Salvador, "I'll get Johanna on the phone. *She'll* ask you." There was a bump, and a knock, and some urgent whispering at the other end of the line.

"Hello, Frederick," said a woman's voice, lyrical and unmistakably upper-crust English. "It's a little odd meeting you for the first time by telephone, but, well, I'm pleased to meet you, I'm sure." There was nothing about this voice that I could connect with my brutish brother—past, present, or future.

"Yes," I agreed, "it *is* strange." And then I realized my gaffe and added, "Nice to meet you, too, Johanna." The *really* strange thing was that it was true; just listening to her speak one cheerful sentence had infused my surroundings with weightlessness. The phone receiver threatened to float away out of range.

"Salvador wanted me to impress upon you how much we want you to sing at our wedding."

"Look, I'm not really sure I can get there for the wedding. I have commitments on the weekends: my students, my mother—"

"I've heard so much about you; it would be such an honour." She continued as if I hadn't spoken.

"I don't know how much Salvador has told you," I said, "but—" I didn't quite know how to continue.

Johanna was gracious. She also utterly ignored my aborted explanation. Our meeting, she said, was seriously overdue. She assured me that it wasn't a mere formality that they had asked me; she placed the highest value on family ties, and she had heard so much about my "lovely voice" from not just Salvador, her intended, but from every one of my brothers.

I realized then I didn't actually know anything of substance about Salvador's present or future, and I knew only one angle of our seven-sided past.

I did manage to keep declining the request to sing, despite the siren's luring. It was so far from what I considered possible that I couldn't even think about it. I *didn't* think about it. I was not able to be quite so categorical on the question of my attendance at the wedding, so when I got off the phone that element was still, for me anyway, up in the exosphere. Johanna, I am sure, felt she was able to report some success to Salvador. I could imagine the two of them, at the other end of the cut line, planning their next assault on what they might see as my weakening resolve.

LUKE FOUND HIMSELF an ancient rusted-out wheelbarrow. The front wheel squeaked and squealed when it was pushed along, and the metal tray rattled. I heard him coming all the way down the street. I winced, worried on his behalf about the complaints of the neighbourhood, people unhappy to be woken an hour before their alarms were set to go off, and middle-class-uncomfortable with the thought of someone so unclean going through their garbage—and perhaps even more uncomfortable to think that he could make a little money out of what they had so carelessly discarded.

I was out in the front, just about ready to pull the door shut behind me and leave for work, when the squeaking made me look up to see Luke wheeling around the corner. I'd forgotten it was Tuesday. I went back through the house quickly and out the back door to grab the empties stashed on the back step. There were two cases of Rickard's Red. Once my hand was on the front door knob again, I had another thought, put the clinking cases down on my small front porch, and went back in to get a spray can of WD-40 from the basement.

I tucked it under my arm and went out to meet him in the middle of the road, beer cases dangling from each hand and the can of lubricant in my armpit. It was a crisp morning with the faintest daydream of frost, and our breathing left cloud traces in the air like small banks of fog. Luke was dressed in the three jackets he wore through most seasons, and he had a wildly-striped stocking cap pulled right down over his eyebrows. He had no gloves, and when he laid down the handles of the wheelbarrow—oh, sweet silence!—he beat his hands against his thighs to try to warm them up. I didn't need to ask him if he'd slept outside overnight; this small action gave me the answer.

"Good find!" I said, admiringly. Luke smiled a half smile, on the right side of his face.

"Guy put it out for the garbage," he said, shaking his head. "Perfectly good."

I admired it some more, its once-yellowness, its worn rubber-treaded wheel, the shredding comfort grip on the left handle. A number of Luke's colleagues worked their routes in confiscated shopping carts, but Luke had consistently refused to use one himself, saying it was worse than stealing groceries. I am not sure how someone with those kinds of scruples ends up on the street—or perhaps he ended up on the street precisely because of his moral standards. It appears that Luke doesn't believe in getting something for nothing, unless it's from me.

"Well, thanks for picking these up," I said, as I always do. "Saves me a trip to the depot."

I added my cases to the wheelbarrow, lowering them carefully onto the piles of loose bottles and cans. I hesitated with the WD-40, not knowing if I should just spray the wheel axle myself, or let him do it. In the end I decided to hand the can over, and I motioned at the metal hulk.

"I thought you could use some grease on that wheel," I told him, a little self-consciously.

He looked at me very seriously, nodded a few times, and stopped slapping his thighs. He reached for the can, tucked it underneath his arm, picked up the wheelbarrow handles, and continued on his way down the street, the wheel listing and complaining, leaving a trail of metal rust flakes on the whitened pavement. I stood looking after him for a minute with my hand still held out, then I collected myself and went back to my porch for my shoulder bags. I walked the other way to work, so Luke and I didn't pass each other again, but I could hear his new old wheelbarrow stop and start up again, *decrescendo*, a number of times before I got out of earshot.

DELIVERING THE MAIL IS AN OCCUPATION some two and a half thousand years old. I wish I could say that it was always an honourable one, but it seems that some of the earliest postal systems may also have been refined mechanisms for gathering secret intelligence regarding the activities of more remote populations. It's that old thing again, about how military inventions go on to become so widely used that everybody forgets what we were fighting about in the first place.

At any rate, it seems to be an honourable occupation these days, and much sought-after, even though a lot of what we get to deliver are bills, solicitations for money, packages ordered on eBay, and ad mail—our "bread and butter." Nowadays, would-be posties can pay their dues on casual rosters for years, waiting for an open route, kind of like teachers who substitute, hoping to get their own classroom one day. Strangely, once they arrive at this destination, most of my colleagues are single-minded in their attempts to get through the thing as fast as possible. It is not time, but speed itself that is of the essence. Those starting out first pare quarter hours, then, as their experience grows, whittle minutes and seconds off their clocked time, sometimes going to what seem to be bizarre extremes for the sake of thirty seconds. Giselle arrives at the sorting station an hour early every morning and has left again by eight o'clock, while the rest of us are still sorting and waiting the required time for the arrival of our nine o'clock packages—she sneaks back for hers at the end of her run, and delivers them from her own car on her way home. Dave has perfected the "moving drop," which involves unlocking his relay box, putting what he finds there into his own letter bag, and re-locking the box, with both his feet still moving along the pavement. Although our contract requires us to take a certain number of breaks, and we're given plenty of time to remove the shoulder bags, eat lunch sitting down somewhere, and find a washroom, I don't think I know anybody who doesn't have their tuna sandwich tucked inside their overcoat, to emerge briefly between numbers 37, 39, 41, 43, and 45. In residential areas, cutting across lawns is standard, and holding over a piece of mail going to the end of your route for one more day, when there's nothing to deliver to the middle, is not unheard of. It's like they're playing a music piece with a constantly accelerating tempo, because once they've finished their route for the day, they get to go home and have their real lives begin.

This whole real life thing might be the difference between me and them. I am not sure if that is because I alone consider my mail route a legitimate part of my real life, or whether there is simply nothing in my fake life that feels any more real than this. Whatever the reason, I prefer the mail route metronome to be set *Allegro non troppo*, so I have enough time to notice things. I see things that most other people miss. This morning, for instance, there was an open telephone book—the Yellow Pages—in a tree in front of the Crawfords' house; someone had been looking up "Golf Courses – Public" in the middle of the Raglan Road. Yesterday there was a red wallet containing five hundred and twenty dollars in well-worn twenties—somebody's drug money, no doubt—in the wet gutter in front of the rooming house on Montreal Street. That necessitated a stop at Constable Miller's police station—though he's long since retired—after work.

I know the last names of pretty much everyone who owns a house or runs a business on the streets I deliver to. I can often guess someone's age and sex and birthday and religion and approximate household income without meeting them, just by seeing what kind of mail they get. Bills from *National Geographic*, vegetable seeds from William Dam, notices from collection agencies, promotions from Pennington's, the Child

Tax Credit, Easter cards. It's mostly only old people who are still sending handwritten cards and letters.

You get to learn a lot more about people, too, just by watching the changes that occur on their doorsteps, or inside their shops. I see when people put up Christmas lights, and when—or *if*—they take them down. I see when someone's got a lover sleeping over, or when they've bought a new car. I see who plants crocus bulbs in the fall, and who cuts down perfectly good maple trees in the summer to give their yards more light. I see who replaces double-hung windows and storms with low-e, argon-filled glass, and whose plastic down-spout breaks off and is never replaced. In the shops, I see when all the sales start and end, and how many t-shirts, tambourines, and swivel chairs are purchased in between. I see who sits in the booths during their coffee breaks, in the darkest corners of the restaurants, waiting with their hands around a cracked mug for an erstwhile lover to appear.

THE NEXT TIME I SPENT OVER AN HOUR in the library before I could get my nerve up. I examined the hold shelves and tried to predict other people's personalities based on their requests, which was a waste, since the whole time I was there no one came in to collect their books. I stood at a computer terminal for half an hour and played solitaire, a game I hate. I gathered one forgotten mechanical pencil and two gel pens to give to Luke on my way out. I read the front page headlines from the *Whig Standard* and the *Globe and Mail*, but I would not have been able to repeat even one of them five minutes after hanging the newspapers back on the racks. I played mind games with myself with my watch, saying that I would do it when the second hand reached the twelve, again and again, like a kid who shouts "one, two, three—go!" to himself countless times before jumping from the high diving board.

Finally, the minute hand got too close to the hour when I was supposed to teach a lesson at the shop, and I had to either jump or come back some other day and go through the whole blistering procedure again. I started towards the circulation desk, and then I was somehow heading back the other way, back into the safety of the book forest. I swear it was completely involuntary. I leaned against a metal bookcase, and a shoulder-width of large print books slid to the back of the shelf. I just needed to get myself past the point of no return—the place on the floor when she would notice me walking towards her, with a look on my face showing my intention to speak. The point where turning around would be more humiliating than continuing on.

When I was about six feet away she looked up and smiled. Even then I wondered if it was a patron-greeting smile, or something warmer. I still have no premonition for true disaster, looking for it, as I do, all the time—and so am mostly wrong.

I forgot to smile back, but I did open my mouth to speak as I crossed the last few feet towards her. I knew if she looked away, even for a moment, I would lose the string that was pulling me in and I'd veer off in another direction. She was wearing a white cardigan, buttoned to the top, with a kind of indoor scarf flowing in folds around her neck. Her sleeves were pushed halfway up her forearms, and, when I arrived at the desk, I could see that her skin was freckled and her arms wiry.

So my mouth was open and she was looking at me expectantly. I put my fists on the counter, and leaned in.

"I suppose you're with someone?" I asked her, though that was not what I'd been planning to say at all. A library kind of silence followed. The echoes of distant footfalls died away, and I wished with all my heart I had not jumped. I leaned so hard on the counter that my knuckles hurt, and the pain held me together for the sixty seconds I had to wait for her response.

"You're asking me this because—?" Her voice was confused, but not wary, which for some reason I took as a good sign.

"Yes," I said.

"You were maybe thinking about asking me for a date?" She was really being very helpful.

"Yes."

"Why are your eyes closed?" she asked then.

I opened my eyes.

"Really, you want to go on a *date*?" *Now* she looked doubtful. I was beginning to get a very bad feeling—an even worse feeling than I'd had at the edge of the diving board.

It felt like there wasn't any water in the pool.

I nodded.

And then, as is the way of these things, there was suddenly someone behind me, with a preposterous handlebar moustache and an armload of books to check out, waiting for us to finish.

She rubbed her hands together thoughtfully behind the counter. She opened her mouth several times and closed it again. The man behind me cleared his throat, to make sure we knew he was there.

"Well I'm honoured, Mr. Madrigal," she said finally. "Thank you for asking me. I really am *honoured*. But I *am* married. I've been married for fifteen years." I think my eyes were closed again.

"*Happily*," she added.

I opened my eyes, but I couldn't look up at her. I could see I had nothing in my hands but three well-used writing utensils.

“SO YOU THINK YOU MIGHT BE GAY?” Maya asked.

“*Me*? No. Not a chance.”

“That’s been said before,” said Maya. She was leaning hard on the “privacy fence” between our properties. I wanted to tell her to lighten up; it looked like she was going to push the whole thing over. I couldn’t stand the thought of a shared back yard.

“Yeah,” I said, “but in my case it’s true.” I didn’t tell her how many times I’d been asked that question in my life, mostly by women who were on their way out the door; they almost always asked it compassionately, as if they were doing me a favour. As if they were helping me get in touch with something deeply buried. I thought it was just easier for them to walk out the door if they thought they were helping to set me free. *That*’s not the thing that’s buried, I always wanted to say.

“So why don’t you have a girlfriend or a wife or something?”

“How come everything has to be so personal with you? Don’t you understand about boundaries, personal space, you know, good old-fashioned tact?”

“No,” she said, and she looked up at me with a mild belligerence, still waiting for an answer, still leaning on the fence rail. I had come out to drag the sodden and overfull bags of leaves out to the curb for the last leaf collection of the year. I was easing the bags, one at a time, across the slippery grass, trying not to rip the paper—at least not while Maya was watching.

“Or maybe,” she said, “you’re shy? Or just a little repressed?”

"What about minding your own business?"

"What's that?" she said. "Citrus Plumbing?"

It is a proven fact that when one has been asked two objectionable questions, the inclination to answer one of them, in order to avoid the other, is almost overpowering.

"Maybe I suffered the tragic loss of my lovely young wife to invasive ovarian cancer, and I've never recovered," I said, exasperated. The bags were heavy with wet leaves. I was trying not to grunt out loud.

"So did that happen?" She raised her eyebrows, as if to suggest I could have made up a better story.

"No," I admitted. "But it might have. Then how would you feel, asking me personal questions like that?"

"I would feel so honking good that you finally opened up to someone. I'd rejoice. I'd have a party," she said. "I'd invite all your friends and family," she added, as an afterthought.

The damn bag I was moving caught on a maple tree root, and no matter which way I pulled, it wouldn't budge.

I didn't have anything to answer to, but Maya kept looking at me as if I did.

"You just go ahead and assume that would be a good thing," I said, finally, "but can you quit leaning on the fence?"

"Do you *have* any friends or family?" she asked. And then she jumped over the fence to help me with the bag.

"WHERE'S ALL THE BARS, THEN?" wondered Brian. There was a small gang of us in the street, and the Milky Way was twinkling a trail of silver dust in the clear night.

Nothing in Stratford seemed to be more than three stories high. Even to me, after more than two years in Toronto, it seemed quaint and rather boring. It was a handsome place, but a boy's desert. All the shops were closed, and we wandered through the town feeling superior, and very sorry for the resident teenagers.

"What the hell do people do here at night?" asked Kevin in

disgust. His voice broke on the word "hell," which ruined the effect, but nobody laughed—or at least, not so he would hear them. He was the first of us to enter that much-anticipated and fearful door to manhood; the previous week he had come to school with an admirable collection of razor nicks and told us all about shaving with his father's Gillette Trac II.

It was the latest I'd been out at night—without an adult—since my pre-adolescent busking in the streets. Three years is a long time in a boy's life; having lost my familiarity with the dark, I was a little nervous about the deserted streets, the dark corners, the narrow alleys that ran between buildings, the dark water lurking in the river, and the dark face of the big sky.

"This was your dumbass idea, Bricks," James said to Eric. "So you better come up with something to do."

"Just waiting for you to ask!" declared Eric, and he took a flask out of his inside pocket with a flourish and showed it around like a magician holding a rabbit by the ears.

"Whoa!"

"Now you're talking!"

Immediately there was a huddle of boys around the Old Monk, and it was passed from hand to hand. James got it first, tipped his head back, and doused himself generously with rum.

"Ohhhh shit!" he gasped, wiping his mouth with the back of his sleeve.

"Allll right!"

"Yesssss!"

"Here Frederick, over to you!"

"Naw," I said, nervously. I had stood a little outside the circle, hoping to escape notice. My hands were in my pockets, and I didn't take them out to reach for the bottle. I held my breath and waited.

"Lame," declared Kevin.

"Ah, leave him alone," said Eric. "More for us!"

After a while they began to sing, their voices rude and jarring, cutting into the quiet like an alarm clock that rings just after the insomniac has fallen asleep. They linked arms and stomped pirate-like down the middle of the pavement, those on the ends of the line kicking tires and slapping the hoods of parked cars for percussive effect.

For I am a Pirate King!
And it is, it is a glorious thing
To be a Pirate King!

I expected windows to fly open and sirens to wail. But the whole town was like a postcard, and it seemed it could not be made into something real, no matter how much we tried to disturb its surface sheen.

For I am a Pirate King!
And it is, it is a glorious thing
To be a Pirate King!

"Hoy! Frederick!" Kevin called back at me over his shoulder and held the flask up over his head in a second-chance invitation.

I ran to catch up and burrowed into the middle of the line. We turned at the corner and made our way down toward the river, whose black surface seemed irresistible to over-tired and slightly drunk boys looking eagerly for mischief.

"Give me that," I told him. There was one swig left, and it was mine.

For I am a Pirate King!
And it is, it is a glorious thing
To be a Pirate King!

"JAMES! JAMES! YOU SPACE CADET! Take the other side!"

"Here!"

"Ouch! You *fuck*, that was my foot!"

They were tackling a mail box. It was like a swarming; the

box's curved top was invisible in the dark crush of rum-infused boys. I half expected to see, at any moment, a triumphant boy hold up a pair of Nike sneakers.

"Lie it down! Lie it down!"

"It's on my fucking *foot*, you asshole!"

"Have you got it? *Here*! Like this!"

It lay flat on the ground like a dead thing covered in dark blood. Like a swarming gone wrong. They stepped back for a moment to admire the sight, puffed themselves up, cuffed each other on the back and shoulders in congratulatory excitement.

Eric took off his fall jacket, tossed it in the grass, and rolled up his sleeves like a fighter. The other boys took off their jackets, too, even though it was midnight-cold in October.

"Pirates, ho!" he called, and once again moved in towards the body of the beast.

We were on a strip of green beside the river. The five of them lifted the box, dropped one corner, stumbled forward a few steps, dropped another corner so one metal leg made a long rent in the grass.

"Up here a bit, it's deeper."

"No, no, no! *Wait!*"

"It needs to be deeper, you dickweed. Not there!"

"That is *my fucking foot*!" yelled James.

"One, two..." said Eric's voice.

"THREE!" they all yelled together, and they pitched the box as far as they could—it travelled about two feet—into the Avon river. The letter flap clanked closed as it fell, in a kind of death screech, and the splash it made was enough to soak Kevin and Brian, who were nearest the water. They jumped backwards, laughing. The box sank quickly, releasing giant grunting bubbles to the water's surface, which made them howl with laughter. The river was only deep enough in that spot to just cover the box, and it lay on the riverbed completely visible below the rippling surface.

From the sidewalk, its hulking form was hidden by the inky

silhouettes of my classmates. I thought of my mother sending me ratty five dollar bills in a mailbox like this.

"*Awesome!*" said Eric, in satisfaction. My hand was on his bent back, as if I'd helped by extension.

I looked anxiously up and down the deserted street.

"*Wicked!*" agreed Kevin.

THE STARS ARRANGED AND RE-ARRANGED themselves into new constellations on my bedroom ceiling. I was still alone, of course. The room was pitch-black like a night with no stars, moon, or planets, yet I could still see pinpricks of distant suns. I could feel the light years of emptiness between myself and *others*, the *married* librarian, my co-workers, my neighbours, all their cats and dogs and gerbils and occasional laying hens in clandestine backyard coops, the skunks under porches, the coyotes nipping at the heels of subdivisions, my whole city and all its streets that ran to other places—the entire unbearably crowded planet—and the unknown and distant planet where someone, some*thing*, a creature beyond my imagining, looked out into space and wondered what to make of existence.

I longed for the certainty of my lost boyhood, ached for Filander, yearned for God. Such nights, if held in God's hands, might only be a practise run for dreams. But there was no sleep, and no going back, and no Filander—not even the fantasy of him was left to me—and no God, and I watched the second hand travel unhurried round the tiny clock face as if there were no hunger for morning. I alternately watched the flow of seconds for ten minutes or so at a stretch, then closed my eyes for as long as I could bear the darkness—a different kind of darkness, somehow both more grey and less flat—only to open them to find that in this way I had passed nine minutes, or only seven, or perhaps just three. Nine or seven or three minutes closer to morning, but also to my death, an end that, in God's absence, held no more security than life did. I thought about how death is something we can't know, the end of a hundred thousand moments we can't understand. It is not The Mystery but merely one mystery of an uncountable number, like the stars.

I reached for the clock and turned it face downwards on my night table, but the faintest glow was still visible around its edges, so I placed it in the bed beside me and smothered it with my extra pillow, killing time. A cloud of pinpricks formed, like the specks behind my eyes when I rise too quickly, then scattered and became a line of tiny lights; a straight, small arrow of light where life is just what happens to us in between the banging on the cookie sheets with a wooden spoon and—*what*? The final letter dropped into the slot, the final episode of *Star Trek*, the final piece of toast with marmalade, the final sounding of a note, even if sung by those who sing like angels? What is the point of raking leaves that are sure to fall again another year, visiting a mother who does not know who I am? What is the point of telling the stories of our lives to others, or telling ourselves about the truth—or falsehood—of our stories?

What is the point of *music*?

Was my life's songline a composition in binary form, the second half similar to the first, but played in a different key? More singing with my mother, only with her remembering fewer and fewer words? More turning around on Bath Road, only perhaps with more decisiveness? More letters slipped into mail slots, but at a quicker pace? More drinking beer with Ed as he gradually hollowed out into someone who defined himself first and foremost by his failure to reproduce? More walking the line between singing and not-singing, the notes echoing faintly before dying into silence?

Outside, without warning, a crow cawed, an unforgiving sound, still full of the black taste of night. Another answered, closer, and then they took up their call-and-response, and one by one the stars, inside and outside my window, disappeared from view. There was a brief lull, when it seemed the dark would be eternal. And then again the caw of crows, double and triple calls, answered in increasing numbers, a round of harsh and tuneless notes, like untameable sounds descending along the road to hell.

Almost imperceptible, the light bubbled up to meet the sky. But then it was suddenly luminous, as if lit by a glowing ring around the earth. The crows continued their atonal talk, holding on to the night's edge with their sharp-clawed toes. My eyes were wide open, and now I could see the outline of the window frame, and now the hump of the extra pillow beside me and the curve of the footboard on my bed.

It was my birthday. It was a particular birthday, and I was a particular age—not an age that others would recognize as significant, not yet the labourious turning of a decade. But the dotted line between the first half and the second half of life, the exact day between the time of my birth and the end point of the average life expectancy for men in Canada, and in addition, as if that wasn't enough, only ten years short of the age my mother was when life for her was effectively over.

IN THE BIRTHDAYS OF MY EARLY CHILDHOOD there was only one cake, instead of the two that appeared for all my brothers. It reinforced the notion that twoness was normal and that I was somehow deficient, unsubstantiated by confectionary.

On birthdays—my own or anyone's—I missed Filander most. On non-birthdays his shadow played beside me, sang beside me, went shyly to school beside me, however reluctant he was to put his hand up in class to answer the teacher's questions. When I hid in the elderberry bush from my brothers, *soltanto*, I was defended by his spirit.

I both knew and didn't know that he was fantasy. All children engage in magical thinking, and I was no exception. My five senses declared that he did not exist, but I knew something beyond sensing—like the mystery that occurs when people sing together, and the music becomes more than instruments and voices. Filander was like that music, mysteriously radiating energy into the universe, an essence that swelled and expanded to fill every crevice of creation. I knew him by morphic field, echolocation, pheromones, and infrared light. He could not be argued with.

On my birthdays, faced with only one cake, all I felt was confusion. On each new birthday, I hoped my mother would have noticed him sometime in the preceding year, trailing after me to my makeshift bedroom, sitting in a vacant chair in the peeling kitchen, attached like a conjoined twin to the side of my palm when I reached out my hand for an extra piece of toast or a glass of watery milk. Now he was attached on one side, now on the other, never anchored quite as securely as I wanted, left or right, but still there hazily along the fault lines, those bright scars, the testament of my faith that I was not, could not be, alone. But every year a singleton cake made its entrance down the long hallway, having been hidden on the floor of my mother's tilting wardrobe to prevent it from being eaten prematurely by my foraging brothers. Once it appeared and was placed on the chrome table in front of me—the one day of the year I would sit in a chair while one of my brothers stood impatiently behind me—I couldn't help but have a small moment of doubt about Filander's existence. I was almost relieved when my brothers demolished the evidence, *scorrevole*, before I could blow out the single set of candles—and, most years, even before my mother could light them.

We try all our lives to make the world into something we can understand. It is the best argument against the existence of God that I can think of. My mother bought our birthday cakes from Dominion, and who knows what favours she had to grant in order to afford them.

I ESCAPED IT IN MY FIRST YEAR in Toronto, because November arrived almost before we knew it, and there was no expectation that by that time I would have made friends good enough to invite over. That first year, for my thirteenth birthday, Annie and I walked up to the Danforth—with a striped golf umbrella, just in case—where we ate *moussaka* and I drank well-watered Assyrtiko. But by my second year at St. Mary's, and my fourteenth birthday, Annie was insistent that we have a party to celebrate, as if I had to prove, somehow, that I was a regular boy and not a misfit.

I was in a quandary that I didn't know how to solve: who to invite that Annie would approve of? Kevin, Eric, Josh? Instinctively, I knew the three of them together would be a mistake, but to choose any one of them was impossible.

"But I don't need a party!" I said to Annie, for the seventh time. "Really. Last year was fine; let's just do that again."

"What about that boy you sang the duet with? He seems nice," she said. "Cool. He seems cool," she corrected herself. I made a face.

"I'd just as soon go and eat Greek food," I told her. "Just you and me." I didn't want to tell her his name.

"Invite him to come along with us," she instructed. That was really the end of our discussion, except for some amount of reminding on her part, and some amount of avoidance on my part, so that the days slipped by in calculated inaction and I never did ask anyone. On the day, after school let out, Annie and I walked up to Greektown with our fall jackets clasped tightly around our necks against the swirling wind, and I had a single sip of ouzo in a shot glass after our meal.

BUT IN THE END, I got a party anyway.

The basement lunchroom was the only part of St. Mary's Choir School that was not beautiful. The oak-panelling in the rooms and hallways above stopped abruptly on the landing halfway down the stairs, where grey-painted cinder-blocks took over, and the high windows of the classrooms above gave way to flickering fluorescent lights. The room was small, and necessitated two shifts of boys, all seats taken in both sittings. The younger boys got the earlier shift; I suppose the administration thought our immature stomachs more delicate and so were disinclined to make us wait. Despite the crowds, I never had to stand and eat, as I had had to do at home. There, we would all—my mother and myself and all my brothers—have been able to sit down together, since the long rectangular tables in the lunchroom each had eight chairs, arranged in two lines along its longer sides.

There were seven boys already at the table when I arrived, a little breathless, from math class. Not one of them looked at me as I sat down and opened up my lunch bag; in fact, they were rather curiously *not*-looking at me. But I was hungry and concentrating on unwrapping my tuna sandwich.

"One, two, *three*—" said Eric, and suddenly there were seven presents in front of me; every boy had pulled out a box from where he'd hidden it under the table or under his arm or in his blazer pocket, and tossed each box, underhanded, backhanded, under a knee or facing backwards, onto the table, making a seven-note thudding tune and a jumbled pile of bright gifts.

"Happy birthday, dumb-nuts," said Kevin. One of the boxes fell to the floor at my feet.

"Open that one first," said Brian, and he bent down to retrieve the small square box, waved it under my nose, and then hit me in the ear with it. Everyone laughed.

I was meant to open them all.

They were small things, tokens—I can see that now, but at the time I might as well have been given the Crown Jewels—or all the sheet music in Long & McQuade. The one from Brian, opened first, was a Rubik's Cube, and was subsequently passed around the table in admiration. There was a harmonica, which, despite the fact that I never really wanted to learn to play, became the first instrument I ever owned myself. There was a giant Hershey bar that James had gotten from his aunt who lived beside the legendary chocolate factory in Smiths Falls.

They weren't merely presents; I was opening a tower of inclusion. I was being invited in to a place I'd never thought to go. Once in, I found I desperately wanted to be there.

I MAY HAVE GIVEN THE IMPRESSION that I haven't seen any of my brothers since my homecoming twenty years ago, but this is not entirely accurate. I had not seen all six of my brothers *together* since leaving the house of my childhood when I was twelve years old. My contact with them in any other form or number has been infrequent and sporadic. Singly, they occasionally email, or, doubly, sometimes even show up on my doorstep or in the locked ward of the nursing home, with an irregular rhythm that is measured in light years and celestial orbits. I have not seen any one brother alone in over thirty years. Stereotypical twins, they always come in sets of two, like ear plugs or altar candles. It is as if they need to be mutually bolstered to accomplish the act of arriving in their hometown, visiting our mother, and announcing their presence—to me, at least.

They can announce themselves to our mother all they like; she has no idea who any of them are. Oh, she knows she had sons in numbers; she still sometimes talks about the six of them in her indecipherable ramblings. But she couldn't equate these overgrown men with the thin brown creatures she longed to show off in Twinsburg, Ohio. The odd time a duo visited while I was there, she looked from one identical face to the other, and seemed not to find it untoward that the same person was seated on both sides of her bed simultaneously.

But I hadn't seen them, even one set of them, in a long time when I came home from work that unseasonable late fall afternoon, still exhausted from the godless night of no sleep, to find my welcome-mat askew, my front and back doors wide open, and all my brothers crowded into my backyard—I'd say it was postage stamp-sized but I avoid workplace analogies—standing at ease on the newly-raked grass, a twelve-pack of Keith's and a two-four of Rickard's Red piled in the centre of their half circle, like it was a double-decker fire keeping them warm. My supply of fuel for Ed's late-night visits, almost burnt down to embers.

If I'd seen it coming, I'd have closed the front door with myself streetside, and run back to the shop to dust the neglected shoulders of guitars and the hips of drums, back to the nursing home to sing with my mother, back to *anywhere* but my burgled house and this twin-invaded backyard.

But I didn't see it coming, and they hadn't heard me coming, so I stood on my small back porch, momentarily unobserved, completely unnerved, looking down at the tops of all of my brother's heads, some of that mass of dark hair now flecked with grey. The tiny yard was a sea of cramped and crowded movement, like an over-sized orchestra warming up in the pit. There was head turning and emphatic gesturing and back slapping and outbursts of laughter, deep and resonant, oboes and the lower notes of cello. The Ns were clinking bottles as if they had just declared a toast. Samuel was attempting to feed Cheesies to Fly-by-Night, holding out his orange offering on the palm on his hand. Alistair was blowing his nose in a blue plaid handkerchief. Abraham was leaning sideways talking to Maya—speaking of orange, God help me!—across the fence.

The ghost of Filander moved past their middle-aged bodies like an ache. I thought about the dust on the guitars, and my legs started to move backwards, but AA saw me, and Abraham lifted his hand and held his palm out in my direction, and they all stopped talking and looked up.

Alistair honked, wiped his nose back and forth, and slipped the cloth into his jeans pocket. They all leaned forward and stretched out their hands, inviting me to come down from the conductor's rostrum.

"Hey buddy ... hey brother ... Frederick ... happy birthday! *Surprise*! Happy Birthday! Happy Birthday! Long time no see!" they all said. "Maya showed us where you kept your key."

"Happy birthday!" echoed Maya, raising her bottle; she tossed it over the fence to Nicholas and, almost one-handed, vaulted over the pickets.

MY BROTHERS AND MAYA STOOD IN MY YARD drinking beer with their jackets on until the sun moved behind Maya's maple tree, and we were all enveloped in shade and rapidly cooling autumn air. Instead of leaving, as I hoped and expected, they simply moved inside and took up residence in the erstwhile living room, each one taking a place behind or beside an instrument and randomly plucking or plinking notes at odd times in their boisterous conversation, an accident of music. The whole time, my heart felt like it was caged in iron, and I could only inhale with short shallow breaths. Every time I exhaled, I felt my heart shrink and condense, until I had something metallic and foreign inside my chest, beating a retreat. My mouth was parched as if there were a whole desert inside me—sand storms, cactus plants, and mirages. Every time I was called upon to talk, I found my jaw stuck together and was compelled to lick my lips and swallow numerous times before I could get any words out.

We had a lot to catch up on. Or I should say, I had a lot to catch up on, since my life—in its outer form at least—hadn't changed a bit since I had last talked to them or seen them.

My contribution to the conversation went pretty much like this:

"You still directing that choir, then?" asked Salvador.

"Oh, yes," I managed to reply.

"How's old Ed?" asked Abraham, in a momentary lull some half hour later.

"Oh, fine, he's fine, doing well enough."

"Still with the post office?" asked Nathaniel, at a time when several brothers had gone outside in the dark to smoke near the frost-ravaged flower beds. "Mail still goes the old-fashioned way, does it?"

"Yes, yes it does," I stammered and nodded, but my reply was lost in the ensuing discussion—heated debate, rather, and growing more heated as the smoking brothers returned—of the merits of this or that email program, or this or that server, or this or that brand of computer.

I can't accurately convey what those hours were like for me in my invaded house. Sometimes there was one voice talking, *toccata*, but more often there were three or four or five brothers speaking at once, *tutti*, in a kind of vocal competition that was jovial, intense, erratic, and physical. Nobody sat still for long, and congenial shoulder punching and exuberant back slapping were *de rigueur*. Maya's alto voice—always a surprise to my ears in the midst of the tenor and baritone sextet—sounded confident and clear, and flowed through the conversation as if she were used to such rowdy gatherings and had six older brothers herself.

The details were understandably hard to follow. Catching the occasional word or phrase, piecing together fragments of meaning, I did manage to learn that Abraham was on Day 36 of his most recent attempt to quit smoking; Alistair had just come back from a fishing trip in the Dominican, having caught himself a girlfriend from Nova Scotia while there; Salvador's bride-to-be was very much looking forward to meeting me; Samuel was thinking of becoming a monk; and the Ns had been recycling motor oil for three years longer than the national average.

The Ns had come for a car show, and had convinced AA to come along for the ride. The SS had been sent on a mission from Johanna, to act as emissaries of persuasion in her Madrigal family reconciliation plan. They had been to see my mother, *en masse*, earlier that afternoon, and had found her anxious and confused and fearful of being arrested. They had tried again, two by two, and had found her more congenial, but still rather focused on Pyrex.

In addition, I learned that Maya had been a blacksmith before she'd been a plumber and had changed careers because she found the work too hard on her back; that, contrary to appearances that evening, she was an only child; and that her hair was not naturally auburn, but blonde.

At some point my brothers began to talk about my childhood and their adolescence, as was perhaps universally inevitable during the marking of a family birthday.

"You were such a little egg-head," Alistair said to me. "Wasn't he a little shit?" he asked the room.

"He was always so fucking *serious*," said Samuel to Maya, as if letting her in on a bit of secret gossip.

"Remember that time we brought him a watermelon for his birthday, and told him it was a dinosaur egg?" said Nathaniel. "He fucking *believed* us! He took it to bed with him for a week, remember?" They all laughed.

"When we finally cut it open he thought it was full of dinosaur blood and he wouldn't eat it!" said Nicholas.

"Oh yeah, what about when he stuck his arm in the wringer washer?" said Abraham. "We told him it would get flattened and just pop right back, like Bugs Bunny! There we all are with our sleeves rolled up, like we were waiting to take our turns, and the idiot sticks his arm right in!"

"Or the time he decided he was going to sing everything, instead of talking. God, that went on for ever! Like we'd go to the table for supper and he'd sing "Please be seated" like we were at some fucking opera!"

They all laughed some more. I didn't remember any of it. Like my mother, I didn't remember a thing.

"You never stopped singing," said Samuel. "Waving your

hands around. It was like *The Sound of Music* all the time, except nowhere near so upbeat. No, no, it was more like a cross between a musical and a morgue!"

"Damned good voice, though," said Salvador, and the shock of his pronouncement was like an explosion inside my head—and that seemed to be, at last, the final word on the subject of my boyhood.

After that, Nicholas went out to his car and brought in a case of Australian wine, and Maya went next door to get some of her basement grow-op harvest, and someone decided he was starving and picked up the phone to order pizza, and someone else decided *he* was starving and got up to order Chinese, and the doorbell rang more times than twice, and mountains of food in cardboard boxes and paper bags appeared in installments, and Samuel went outside to *his* car and brought in a birthday cake with white icing and blue letters that read "Happy Birthday Frederick." All these things have run together in my mind, but I know that there was a considerable time lapse between them, and that, when the cake appeared, I had already been breathing second-hand *cannabis indica* smoke for some time, the room hazy with it, the instruments stoned and silent, having clearly decided they wouldn't get a word in edgewise.

I don't remember anything much after the cake, because once I saw it, it seems I fainted dead away.

Luckily, my uninvited company merely thought I had had too much to drink, and my six brothers, like careless pallbearers, dragged me sympathetically up the stairs to bed.

"SO YOU THINK YOU MIGHT BE ADOPTED?" asked Maya, during our Monday morning exodus in uniform. "You're so different from your brothers."

"I *wish*," I said, before I could stop myself.

GOING BACK TO WORK AFTER my brothers' visit was a relief. Delivering the mail is simple and straightforward. I just walk through my route putting goodwill into people's doorways. Other than the ad mail—which on good days I can argue is at least not harmful—and all the bills, and the occasional notice from a collection agency, most of what I deliver is friendship, connection, and love. It might be a stretch to put the bulk of my job aside to consider the few postcards, greeting cards, and handwritten letters that get sent these days as the true meaning of my weekday mornings, but I suppose everyone justifies their work somehow, even stock traders, helium balloon sellers, and soldiers.

But pretty much all the hate is now sent by email, text message, and twitter. "Dear John" letters are dispatched with a click. Bullies hound their victims online. Terrorists use the internet to plot destruction. I find it comforting that most of what I push into mail slots won't cause that kind of suffering.

ONCE IN A WHILE, NOT VERY OFTEN, Eric's father picked him up in his Cutlass Supreme. It was more like a boat than a car, and had a T-top that added to the nautical effect. Very rarely, if I happened to be on the school steps when the car pulled up, he offered me a ride. His father drove with the panels off in almost all weather except outright precipitation, so most days it was a cold ride and I sat in the back seat with my hands between my knees. There was never any conversation in the car that included me, and if Eric and his father ever spoke to each other I couldn't hear what was said over the blistering noise of downtown Toronto streets. Not one to go out of his way for any child, including his own, Eric's father drove me to their house in the Beaches, and I walked home to Annie's from there.

What this meant was that, a handful of times a year, I ended up standing, chilled to the bone, outside the automatic garage door attached to Eric's house. He never invited me in; I got the impression that he wasn't allowed to. But he was never quite ready to let me go, either.

We stood in his driveway with our hands in our pockets. Eric would talk, and I would try to figure out what to contribute to make it look like I both cared about what he was saying and knew what he was talking about.

"See the game last night?" he'd ask me.

"Yeah," I'd say. "Killer."

And then he'd mention a player by name, and their particular brilliant and astounding goal, or pass, or miss, and most of the time I wouldn't know whether we were talking about football or basketball or hockey.

"Wicked," I'd say, in agreement, or, if his tone was one of disgust, "lame, yeah, really lame."

Sometimes he talked to me about movies he'd seen or his favourite TV show, which was *Magnum, P.I.*—a detective series I had never watched. Even then I didn't like the idea of uncovering secrets.

At some point the cold would become alarming, and I would stomp my senseless feet and try to tuck my elbows eve n tighter into my rib cage.

"Better get going," I'd say. "Thanks for the ride."

"No problem, man. I'll walk with you." And he would toss his bag underneath a juniper bush, and I would shoulder mine, and we'd set out to walk the eleven blocks between our houses.

In the middle of Grade 10, Eric started smoking, and as soon as we'd rounded the first corner he'd look over his shoulder with a calculated bravado and light himself a Marlboro. He always used matches rather than a lighter, huddling next to a power pole or a parked car or a stone retaining wall to outwit the wind.

One day there was a delay in this routine—he'd been talking about a girl named Emily whom he had met at his cousin's party—and he stopped next to a mailbox and dug around in his pockets. "Va-va-*voom*, man!" he said, lit his cigarette and sucked at the smoke in relief. It would have been his first nicotine for the day.

Instead of tossing the spent match onto someone's lawn, as he usually did, he pulled opened the flap of the box and threw the still-burning match inside. "Fucking crazy!" he said, laughing. He looked up and down the street, across the intersection, and at the nearest houses. There was no one to be seen except for a distant middle-aged woman walking away from us with a poodle. He lit another match and threw it in after the first, and then another. His cigarette was stuck in the corner of his mouth, and waggled up and down when he laughed.

"Got any paper?" he asked me.

"Don't *do* that!" I said, too loudly. I felt nothing except panic. But I surprised him, and he hesitated just a little, and the wind blew out the flame.

"You *wuss*," he said, but there was no malice in it. He put the matchbox back in his jacket pocket and, without any further reaction, resumed walking towards Annie's and talking about Emily. "You should see her *tits*," he told me.

No detail of Emily's body penetrated my confusion. I had surprised myself with my own power.

SOMETIMES A PERFORMER OR CHOIR or band will come to sing for the residents on the locked floor of my mother's nursing home. Once in a while, on a Sunday afternoon, I show up for my regular visit and find the place in an astonishing state of preparation.

The singers bring with them an apparent need to alleviate the suffering of others, and provide an hour or so of, at worst, a diversion from listlessness and confusion, and, at best, the musical stitching of a thin thread of memory onto the selvage edge of lost lives. Perhaps the time the residents spend listening will count, minute for minute, as a direct detour from Death, who waits at the hall door for all of them, uninvited.

I visit with my mother in her room for a while first, as it takes the staff a symphonic amount of time to propel, tilt, cajole, and wheel everybody into the dining room. They make a party out of it; an admirable attitude, since doing anything at all out of the ordinary in that place is twenty times the work. The cook, inevitably in the middle of supper preparations, generously puts out lukewarm tea and coffee, and leftover muffins—which go down as quickly as they do when they are fresh, inefficiently chewed by loose dentures and swallowed haphazardly, or crumbled onto the parquet flooring and poked perplexedly by canes.

The musical tastes of the demented elderly are in general fairly narrow: they want to hear the songs they sang as twenty-five-year-olds, songs from the pop charts and folk tunes from their summer kitchens or sing-alongs from around the campfire. The ones they love best have simple sentiments as well as melodies, and a lot of repetition. They want to recognize the tune, to remember the words. They want the tune and the words to bring back time—not youth, exactly, but the feelings of youth: the struggle and solidarity of the war; the innocence and pain as well as the lust of love; the joy of being alive and immortal. They want to know again what it feels like to see unlimited tomorrows stretched out into the distance like a long coastline that invites adventure, and fades gently into the mist. They want to turn away from the rocky promontory at the end of the road.

They recline in the familiar, put their feet up on the notes, and hang their hearts on the lyrics.

Goodnight Irene, Irene goodnight

I am an expert of detection among the old. With some residents, the only way I can tell the songs they want to hear from the songs they don't involves tiny and irregular movements of index fingers tapping on the arms of wheelchairs, or the slight lifting and lowering of tongues inside open mouths, or perhaps simply an excess of drool. If Franklin is present, there may be a frenetic keening, akin to a hound accompanying a piano, but he is the exception rather than the rule.

From glen to glen, and down the mountain side

My mother sings along. I always position her near the front of the room, where there is a small ramped platform permanently set up near the kitchen door, ever hopeful for any kind of free entertainment. She stands the whole time, so I have to watch her out of the corner of my eye, in case she begins to waver. She can last longer than you would think; the music opens her airways, fills her lungs, toughens her muscles, and strengthens her bones. I don't know what she makes of these occasions, supposing she ever tries to make anything of *anything*. Her voice is clear and sweet and carries to all the corners of the room, and her memory is flawless for the words of any song anyone can think to begin.

I spied a poor cowboy all wrapped in white linen

In this, as in many things, my mother is different. Some of the others do join in, remembering the chorus near the end of the song, finally catching up and rasping out the last three or four words of each line. The staff often sing along too, as well as the occasional visiting family member holding the thin-skinned hands of loved ones, but their voices generally have a heartiness they do not feel.

While they are singing, all the eyes in the room change. The demented eyes lose their vacancy or confusion, and a rare light shines bluely out of them; the undemented eyes fill with unbearable sorrow. I don't know which is worse to see. It is always exhausting.

If you want anymore, you can sing it yourself, Uh-huh, Uh-huh, Uh-huh.

At the end, the residents don't start to applaud until the staff do, standing in doorways and leaning against walls, cueing them. The bringing together of hands turns out to be just another social convention that drops away with lost synapses. They clap their palms together lightly, surprised to feel living warmth at the tips of their own fingers.

"TWO PEAS IN A POT," said my mother.

"Is that right?" I said. Does she mean me and her? I wondered. Is she anticipating the dinner menu? Is she remembering all those twins?

"He *made* me do it," she said. Did she mean our old landlord?

"Yes, I know that now," I reassured her, just in case.

"I did not want to wear the soap," my mother said. "Old Maid, old Maid."

We were sitting in the dining room, waiting for the supper trays to make it to the tables. She had picked up the knife from her place setting—they were all purposefully blunt, those knives—and was turning it over and around in one hand, running her thumb intently up and down along the smooth handle, with her head turned determinedly away, as if she was playing a game of being blind, trying to figure out the mystery object that she held in her hands by feel alone.

"What do you have in your hand?" I asked her.

She didn't look at me; she didn't look at her hand. She didn't stop rubbing the knife handle. She didn't stop muttering. There was no sign at all that she had even heard me. I looked across at Jack, and he looked at his wife, Isobel, who was smiling warmly and vacantly around the room. Jack and I had shared a lot of looks across the table in the past month of Sundays, since Isobel had first arrived.

"How are you today, Isobel?" I asked. Unlike calling my mother, using Isobel's name would at least guarantee that she would look at me.

"Do you know me?" she asked, surprised, the way she always

does when first spoken to, as if she herself is always the stranger.

"I *do* know you," I said. "We've eaten supper together a few times, haven't we? You and Jack and me and my mother." I looked around the table as if helping her out, introducing her to all those people once again.

"Oh," she said, and visibly relaxed. "Well, yes, I am a good, I ... I see the ... yes, we are having ... did you know that when ... Jack is my ... Oh, yes."

"Jack tells me you were dancing last night, Isobel. Did you enjoy the music?"

"Oh *yes*," she said, and for a split second I can be fooled into thinking she has understood the question and made the right answer. "They fly off ... when I can ... it all was so ... so hard to *say* why it is so ... do you see when I ... always wanted to know ... Jack did that."

Isobel's brand of dementia has caused her to lose pretty much all the nouns out of her speech. Jack is the only noun she can still always hold on to. My mother, on the other hand, is full of nouns that no longer mean the thing intended.

"Cut myself with the ring," my mother said. "Cut it off rather than use it. He tied me to the bed. No, bad."

The kitchen staff were slowly making their way to our table, and trays were rattling all around us. Finally, plates were lowered in front of us, and Jack reached across to his wife's meal and began to cut the pre-cut roasted chicken breast into even tinier pieces. He lifted his eyes to mine for an eighth-note.

"We had forty good years together," he said, and then turned his head away.

"Light. Light. *Leitmotif*," said my mother, and she dropped her empty teacup on the floor.

THERE WERE THREE MESSAGES on my voicemail when I got home:

Hi Frederick. This is Jiro. Can you come over sometime

this week and help me get the seats out of the van? Any evening is good. Just let me know.

Beep. Erase.

Hi Frederick, Salvador here. Johanna and I were just talking about the music selection, and uh, well I guess we need to talk about that, huh? We're kind of undecided between John David and Elton John. So, uh, maybe you could call me back. Or call and talk to Johanna. That'd be best. She's really the one who's organizing this thing. Talk to you soon!

Beep. Erase.

Hello? Frederick? It's Alex, Alex Hughes. I was hoping to talk to you about.... Look, I just want—shit, I'll call back.

Beep. My finger hovered for a few seconds over the delete button, but I didn't push it. I pushed Replay instead, and listened to Alex's message, over and over, maybe ten times. I sat on the bottom step with the machine balanced on my knees, and the rain from my boots all over the hardwood floor. His voice brought everything back. Talk about shadows.

I MET ALEX HUGHES at my first St. Mary's choir practice. I hadn't particularly noticed him in any of my classes, but at choir he stood next to me, holding the right side of our shared choir book, and tossed his blond forelock out of his eyes with a flick of his head at the appearance of every rest and fermata. Each time he did this the page jumped slightly and I lost my place in the progression of notes for a split second. It didn't really matter—we were singing a piece that I knew off by heart from St. George's—but I remember feeling quite frightened on his behalf when the choirmaster rapped his baton on the edge of his music stand to interrupt our singing and told Alex he had until the next morning to get his hair cut.

"You should know better by now," he admonished, severely enough for the first day.

I lowered my head in an effort to avoid notice, but Alex smirked into the corner of my eye and elbowed me mildly in the ribs as soon as the choirmaster's back was turned.

"*Arse-pick*," hissed Alex. I bit my lip to keep from laughing.

"FREDERICK AND ALEX," SAID THE CHOIRMASTER, "you two stay back."

It was like a gun had sounded for the beginning of a race to the exit. All the other boys picked up their book bags and ran off through the hallways, throwing their blazers over their shoulders, eating the Crunchie bars and Granny Smith apples that their mothers had packed into their school bags. I listened as the echoes of the boys' receding footsteps faded into the late afternoon. I turned my gaze to the windows and watched the trees tremble, watched as the line of cars at the entrance gradually dwindled, watched as the street lights came on by ones and twos along the street outside.

Our classmates had run off into late afternoon freedom and left us with fading echoes. I don't think it occurred to either of us to mind; we wanted to sing more than anything, and we each had our own way of silently passing the inevitable waiting time in between practise pieces. While the choirmaster, hunched over the lectern, arranged and re-arranged the score to suit our voices, Alex closed his eyes and slept, or half-slept, his breath deep and easy as if the practice room was the only place at school he could truly relax.

I listened contentedly in those moments the way a wild animal might listen for the wind in the grass or the rain on the leaves, silently singing along with the natural musicality of our habitat: Alex's even breathing beside me; the choirmaster's breath, the quick inhalation of a great idea and the long exhalation of disappointment; the electric clock on the wall over his head, its ticking as loud as a metronome; the reluctant creaking of the radiators; the branches of the naked trees against the long windows, like sentinels in the gathering dusk.

When I look back from this distance it feels quite companionable. The other boys may have been set free to join the ball hockey tournaments at the end of their streets, or to play with their new Nintendo sets, or even to practice scales on their families' pianos. I felt freer than that, cooped up in that classroom.

When we were finally asked to sing, we sang like the sun coming out from behind a turbulent cloud, the bruised sky gathering light until its white strength hurt the eyes. When the choirmaster was particularly happy with us, he squinted and clicked his baton blindly against some nearby surface: the desk, the music stand, the hard palm of his own hand.

Afterwards, Alex and I left the school together. As it turned out, we often took the same subway train, made the same station change—though he stayed on much longer than I did—so it was natural that we stayed together, waited by each other's lockers, came out of the school doors and turned right together, walked past the cathedral together. Natural that we crossed the street together, and that I waited—more or less—while he kneeled and prayed in front of the Statue of the Virgin, his cap in his hands, his coat on the ground under the knees of his trousers, the holes in the heels of his socks almost always visible above his regulation black shoes.

The first time I was with him when he stopped to pray, it was November of my first year. A few leaves had outstayed their welcome and fell from the trees like tiny missile shells, curled and dry and brown. The evening wind was full of the sound of their skittering.

"Which way do you go?" Alex asked me. He held the door with his hip and tried to catch an oak leaf that had hit him lightly on the side of his head.

"Subway," I said, and pointed north. "Dundas."

"Walk to Queen with me instead," he suggested. "I have money for pizza. I found five dollars this morning in the church yard! We can take the streetcar home instead."

I shrugged, and we turned south. He ran up the bank onto the retaining wall and walked along the edge, putting one foot carelessly in front of the other, without particularly looking. When he got to the end he jumped down, throwing his backpack into the air at the top, and catching it neatly seconds after his feet hit the pavement.

We had come to the cathedral. He pushed his bag into my chest and turned to the stone Mary. She was slightly larger than life, her height augmented by a pedestal, her head tilted to one side, her hand reaching out towards us. Alex stood on his toes and put his hand up, but there was still an arm's length between them. All the same, I felt like I was witness to a secret handshake.

And then he unzipped his fall jacket, twisted himself out of it, and laid it at her feet. He knelt down on this makeshift pillow and bowed his head. I looked quickly around to see if any of the other boys were still around, lurking in the shadows out of range of the street lights, but I could see no one, just buildings and trees and tumbling leaves.

I turned back and watched him. I knew he was praying. I didn't understand yet about Mary, or confession, or sin; I hadn't been Catholic long enough. I just waited. I don't know why I did, that first time. Maybe it was because I was holding his school bag, and I didn't think I could just put it down beside him and walk away. Maybe I was thinking about the pizza, my stomach as hollow as the city air. I wasn't impatient, only a little worried about being seen. I moved along the road a ways, walking slowly, putting some distance between me and him. After a few minutes I heard running behind me and I turned to see him digging his arm back into his coat sleeve and reaching out for his bag.

"Thanks," he said. "It's fucking *cold* out, isn't it?"

I didn't answer. We reached Queen Street in silence, turned, and after another block he handed over his bag again and turned into a pizza shop.

"Wait a sec," he said. Through the glass of the dirty windows I could see him point energetically into the display case and then fish around in his pockets for his money. He came out with two fat slices of pizza, each with its own triangle of cardboard for a plate.

I burnt my tongue, I was so eager. We stood on the street corner and ate in great adolescent boy bites, strangers moving around us unheeded, the flow of commuters trying to get home after work. With our appetites temporarily sated, we wiped our hands on the legs of our school trousers.

It was when we started walking again that I asked him. "What were you praying about, anyway?" It was a question born of both innocence and curiosity. My own prayer had so recently been answered: We were in Toronto, and we were singing. What more there could be to wish for, I could not imagine.

He didn't answer, but ran a little way in front of me, turned suddenly and threw his backpack into the air in my direction. It slid through my outstretched arms as if it were a basketball being dunked through a hoop.

WE WERE KEPT LATE TOGETHER OFTEN after that, perhaps once a week. It may even have been the same day each week—every Tuesday perhaps—but I don't remember that now. Week by week we sang together in the practice room after the others had been dismissed, while outside the days shortened, brittle leaves flew off the trees, and dirty snow gathered at the edges of the streets.

Outside, fall ran into winter; inside, our voices grew like curling weeds at the height of summer. When we pushed through the double doors at the end of practice, the frosty air rushed eagerly into our lungs, and Alex always pulled his scarf up around his mouth, as if to protect his voice. He wasn't one of those boys who suffered the cold for the sake of looking tough.

"You taking the streetcar or the subway?" he would ask me.

I would shrug. It didn't matter to me at all.

ST. MARY'S IS ON A STREET almost hidden from noise, an arterial backwater, a miracle of calm. Only occasional sirens punctuate this oasis, and they reach through distantly and waveringly, as if made of the same fabric as a Saharan mirage. But step to the end of the block, and the rush and whirl and roar of Toronto breathes like something too-loudly alive, rasping and coughing in the smoggy air. Cars and trucks, buses and streetcars, bicycles and jaywalkers are drawn in and pumped out of Toronto's heart by veins and arteries whose rhythm is circumscribed by the working day and the theatre-going or drug-dealing night.

We walked out into the street, crossing in front of a lane of stopped cars, and boarded the 501. Alex had his bag in his hand, and stepped lightly through the congestion at the front of the vehicle, seeking more open space. We always went to the very back of the car, finding seats side-by-side or opposite each other, singing a duet or a duel accordingly. If a duet, our voices tangled and swirled around the streetcar in unison, filling that small space with perfectly synchronized sound and vibration. If a duel, we sang in rounds, watching each other carefully to anticipate the frothy notes, delighting in the harmony created by an echo of the melody line. In the beginning, our feet didn't even touch the floor, but swung back and forth like lazy metronomes with pointed toes.

My life flows on in endless song
Above earth's lamentation
I hear the sweet, tho' far-off hymn
That hails a new creation.

After a few bars, old men turned on their hearing aids, college students removed their Walkman earphones, babies stopped crying, and their mothers turned to us in hope and gratitude.

Thro' all the tumult and the strife
I hear the music ringing
It finds an echo in my soul
How can I keep from singing?

Alex had an intuitive sense of the speed of the traffic, the timing of the streetlights, the number of people waiting to board or disembark at each stop. Sometimes he adjusted the tempo of a tune as he went, but more often he discarded the note from one song and picked up a note from another, seamlessly, as if he were an old woman with her knitting—as if he'd been knitting for fifty years and could knit without thinking of speed or tension, as if he could change colours of yarn without looking, never dropping a stitch. And so he would turn from Robert Lowry in an instant, and join the last note to another, stitch to stitch, and my voice would follow with a split-second of hesitation too small for untrained ears to hear.

Fare thee well, for I must leave thee
Do not let the parting grieve thee
And remember that the best of friends must part, must part
Adieu, adieu, kind friends adieu, adieu, adieu
I can no longer stay with you, stay with you
I'll hang my harp on a weeping willow tree
And may the world go well with thee.

It seems strange now that we were so careless with our voices: careless of the other streetcar riders, careless of their haphazard applause. We sat in the back of the streetcar and sang, our school ties loosened, our blazers unbuttoned, and our coats laid across our knees in the rush hour warmth. We were simply singing; it was neither performance nor gift, and we spared no thought to how it was received. We wove our music into the *clang* and *clang-clang* of the muted bell, the whine of the engine accelerating, the *clacket-clacket-clacket* as we bumped through the tracks of other lines at intersections, the mechanical sighing of the brakes, every two blocks, all the way along Queen Street.

FIRST THING THE NEXT MORNING I sprang for Call Display. I never answered the phone again without looking to see who was calling.

The phone rang only sporadically, not any more or less than it usually did. But I was preoccupied with waiting for that phone to ring again. Every time it rang, I left off what I was doing—tuning the harp or making toast, it didn't matter—and went to look at the display. There was some interrupted music that month, notes broken off mid-breath, a B-sharp hanging in the air, *perdendosi*, while I was already moving across the room to the phone. The notes broke and hovered briefly as they had done when, at age eleven, I had ducked into the alley near the Limelight, my cap full of coins, waiting for my brothers to pass me by. The phone would peal; something about the triple *pas de deux* ring of boots warned me that they were coming up the street. The caller ID would appear; I recognized their drunken shouts. One ring, two rings, three rings. As then, I peeked out from the safety of darkness to watch them move on.

Increasingly, I began to sit or stand beside the phone while I sang or played, or to move it to a practice chair beside me as I moved acoustically around from harp to lute to piano, to the spot in the front north corner where my voice sounded best in the small rooms.

Alex's second call came on a night when Ed was there, his bottle of Red dancing on top of the upright. We were singing Gospel tunes and I stopped suddenly after "*O brother, let's go down, down in the river to pray—*" and Ed played two bars into the gap between rings, and then he stopped too when he heard it sound again. He looked at me like I was nuts—the incident of Maya and the squirrel represented the first time we had ever allowed an interruption in all our years of playing music together. I think he was really afraid disruptions were going to become habitual.

I leaned over to look at the phone while it rang for the third time, and he raised his eyebrows and titled his head at it, like he was saying, *So pick it up already, you've gone this far!* But I just stared at the phone and the name on the Call Display, A HUGHES, and Ed just stared at me, and it rang three more times before it stopped. I kept staring, but this time there was no message. I felt like all the blood had run out of me, and I looked down at my feet and thought I had better sit. I landed on the end of the piano bench beside Ed. I put my elbows on my knees and my head in my hands. There was no music left in that room at all.

"You're taking this brother thing far too seriously," said Ed.

There was a kind of dread that grew in me, a premonition that whatever significance that call had had, it was large, ungainly, and unwelcome. I was afraid, I suppose. I could imagine no occurrence that would inspire those calls, except more catastrophe.

"THAT WAS LUCKY," SAID ALEX. He'd been watching me the whole time. He'd seen me close my eyes and pray and kick, and had watched the soccer ball land in front of Kevin, who'd called for it to come to him.

"You're not kidding," I said. I rolled my eyes at him. "I never kicked a ball straight in my life."

"Me neither," he said; he shrugged, as if it wasn't important. "They might leave you alone now."

"Will they?"

"Yeah, well," he said. "They might." He looked impassively across the courtyard. Kevin had kicked the ball through make-shift goalposts and there was a wave of distant cheering. Alex looked down at my foot. "Made of gold, that foot," he said, "making a kick like that." He stuck his own leg out in front of him and pretended to kick the air.

"Mine's made of shit," he said, and we both laughed out loud.

THERE IS AN ARCHANGEL in the Limestone City Youth Choir by the name of Blake, though he looks like he should be named Gabriel or Raphael, or Michael at the very least. Fine features, cherub's curly hair, translucent skin like the veneer on a Renaissance painting. So he looks a lot like an angel, but mostly he looks almost exactly like Alex. Blake reminds me so much of Alex that it is sometimes hard to remember to call him Blake. He sometimes even tosses his hair, *lusingando*, just as Alex did on my first day at St. Mary's.

Unlike mine, Blake's musical talent was fostered almost as soon as he could talk. His family had the resources to make music something he could take for granted right from the beginning. His infantile banging on kitchenware was rewarded with preschool music lessons. His mother and father pick him up after rehearsal, and you could tell, somehow, that the whole family was cultured.

I'm so conscious of Blake's perfect voice that sometimes it's a strain to hear the other voices singing with him. I catch myself exerting all my energy not to pay attention to him, not to think about how much he looks like Alex. I work hard to have him be just like the others, just one great voice in a choir of great voices, just one more seraphic face that has no reference point with my past. He has no idea how I struggle, having him in the choir. He seems not to notice that I stutter a little when I speak to him, guiding his perfect voice gently even further upwards. He simply comes to choir and sings because he loves singing. That's the thing about that small handful of choristers with souls—they never hold it against those who haven't got a clue how to act in the presence of the divine.

But a strange thing happens when I listen to Blake sing. I want everyone to hear him, the whole world. He opens his mouth and such sweet, evanescent sounds come out that it creates a pain in my chest, a trapped bubble of piercing emotion. Trapped, so I can hardly breathe.

ALEX HAD OVERHEARD ME talking to Kevin. We were outside the cathedral, and Alex was leaning up against the statue of Mary, affectionately, as if he were a faithful dog waiting for an afternoon walk. The clouds swept across our patch of sky and tossed wind chaff in our flushed faces. A pigeon swirled in the air above our heads and landed ungracefully at our feet, cooing for crumbs.

"The Eucharist tastes like *God*," Alex said.

"Well," I persisted, "what does God taste like?"

He moved his mouth slowly as if he were chewing and tilted his head, as if to better remember, and he looked up at Mary, haloed by sky.

"Stone," he said. "Wind." He looked along the street to where we could see Annie's car rounding the corner. He hesitated. "Love," he said finally.

The station wagon pulled up to the curb, and I pulled open the passenger door and climbed in, leaving him with his stone Mistress, waiting for his ride. Both of us, despite our faith in the divine, shared a longing for something merely human, something we had so rarely experienced.

TO BEGIN WITH, I KNEW LITTLE about Alex's home life. I don't think he was secretive; I just didn't ask. Initially he was brought to concerts and funerals by a dishevelled couple who were preoccupied with leaving quickly, a couple I assumed were his parents, until the following semester, when he was brought by a tall man with a two-day beard who straightened his tie and brushed the shoulders of his blazer and admonished him to tuck in his shirt. After that year, he came on his own, and if there was ever anyone in the audience who'd come specifically to hear him, he never mentioned them, or appeared to look for their faces before the house lights went down. There were rumours about a group home, but in my first years at St. Mary's I had no idea what that meant, and assumed he lived among some extended family consisting of many generations of Hughes' under the same roof. Frankly, I had enough trouble explaining my own living situation to wonder too much about anybody else's.

I did manage to notice that while I was always hungry after school, Alex ate as if he were starving. It was as if, once released from singing, and having fulfilled his self-imposed obligation to pray to Mary for forgiveness, he finally realized a bodily hunger that had been secondary for much of the day. It was as if he ate music for breakfast and lunch, and only realized at suppertime that that wasn't quite enough.

MY MOTHER DOES NOT EVER TRY to escape from the locked ward, like some of the other residents do. For a while there, this one old guy, Vincent, managed to get out every couple of weeks, one way or another. He can seem very rational and charming, and if a nice family came in to visit Great Aunt Maud or someone, he would lurk about by the coded door at the end of visiting hours, pretending to tie his elastic-laced shoes. Then he would just follow them out, explaining to them quite lucidly that he comes in every evening to visit his poor demented wife, and asking for their honest opinion of the facility.

"The food isn't as good as at the other place," he would say, mournfully. "My wife would like to have more donuts."

The staff finally resorted to taping a life-size colour photograph of him on the outside of the ward door. Underneath are the words: "This is Vincent. He is A RESIDENT. Please do not let him out."

I had rooted for Vincent; it was like a geriatric version of *One Flew Over the Cuckoo's Nest*. The main difference was that there was a lot more drool. After that once-successful route was lost to him, he did on one occasion try to climb out his second-floor window. Luckily, he is a large man, and he got stuck before he even got one knee through the small opening, and a personal care worker found him and laughed herself silly, which I initially thought was rather unprofessional. If Vincent had ever seen The Chief rip the washstand off the floor and pitch it through the window, the plaques had eaten away his memory of it. Or perhaps he just wasn't ever that strong.

There was no sign of Vincent in the corridor. Nor was my mother's wheelchair parked along the hallway with the others, and there was no one at the nurses' desk. When I went into her room, someone had pulled the curtains closed and flipped the lights off and she was sitting alone in the near-dark. She looked up only briefly, and then she made a caught-animal noise and began to beat her hands together in her lap, like there was something lying there that she was trying to kill. I was still thinking of the movie, so I didn't get what was going on. I went right over and held onto her wrists, gently at first, and I started a line for her.

Oh Danny boy, the pipes, the pipes are calling

I was trying to pull her up but it was like her legs were somehow locked around the footrests and the whole chair kept coming with her. I added another line:

From glen to glen, and down the mountain side

Glen!" cried my mother. "The bells of St. Clements! Lemons and limes! Oranges! *Marmalade*!"

I had my arms around her waist now, and was getting frustrated with why nothing was happening the way it usually did, and she began to fight me. Her right palm pushed against my sternum while her left knuckles caught me under the chin, so I bit my lip. I licked a trickle of blood from my tooth. Her arms were surprisingly strong.

"Come on, sing!" I said, interrupting my own singing for a moment and continuing to pull at her. I didn't know what was up with her, but I'm not sure now why I was so sure at the time that I was doing the right thing.

The summer's gone, and all the roses falling
It's you, it's you must go and I must bide.

"Marmalade!" my mother yelled. "Marmalade!"

"What *is* this thing with marmalade?" I said, exasperated. I love marmalade as much as my mother does, but there's only so long a guy can talk about the stuff without losing it.

"Poison, poison, poison, poison!" she screamed. I had a sense of movement behind me. I was sure by then the staff were hovering in the doorway, wondering what the hell was going on, wondering if they should intervene. It was probably hard for them to tell who was abusing who. It was hard for me to tell, too.

"Stop it!" I said, still struggling to pull her upright. "Stand up! Stand up and sing, goddamn it!"

And then she reached out and slapped me across the face. I let go of her waist and backed off, putting my own hand on the sting. There was a silence so profound I could hear the slap echoing in my ears. It was terrible music.

"Get in the car," said my mother, then. "Fix the trap, tap, cap. Get in the car. Green eggs and ham." She had her hands on the arms of the wheelchair and she was struggling to push herself up, but she couldn't seem to manage it. I just stood there, three feet away, and watched her.

"She's strapped into her chair," said the nurse, Helen, from the door.

"She never hit me before," I said.

"You need to undo the buckle."

"Never. Not even when I was a child."

"It's a child-proof buckle," she explained.

"What the hell is she doing strapped into her chair?" It finally registered.

"Green eggs and damn, green eggs and damn," said my mother, weeping. Crocodile tears, I told myself. I was still angry, and trying to calm down, but then it was just easier to shift the anger along to something else.

"She fell yesterday," said Helen. "She didn't hurt herself, but we thought—"

"Why didn't someone call me?"

"Jennifer said she would make toast," complained my mother. She was still trying to get up.

"You just need to undo the buckle. I *did* call you. I called five times. I left two messages. We thought you must be away."

It was my own fault. I hadn't answered the phone for three days. It hadn't rung for three days, because I'd turned off the ringer. I hadn't picked up my messages for twenty-four hours; the red-light blinking had gone unheeded. I'd been trying to escape.

"Tap, tap, tap, tap, TAP!" said my mother. I took a step, leaned forward, and tentatively pushed aside the bottom of her cardigan so that I could pull the strap out of the buckle. Now that I saw it I couldn't imagine how I had not seen it before. It seemed like all that flailing about was so damned obvious.

"I would have hit me, too, if I'd done that to myself," I said to her. She looked up right into my eyes and held my gaze for perhaps three whole seconds. Her cheeks were damp, as if the tears had seeped into the lines of her face, and run, willy nilly, unguided by gravity. Something caught me inside, so I staggered sideways, sat down on the edge of her bed, and put my head in my hands.

But only for a second.

"Tap, tap, tap, TAP!" As soon as the buckle was undone and I'd moved away again, she pushed her arms down and got herself to her feet. I looked up and half reached out in case she might fall, but I didn't want to touch her, didn't want her to know I was devoid of the faith that she could stand. She opened her mouth, and this is what came out:

But when ye come, and all the flowers are dying

"Oh!" said Helen. "She remembered the song."

If I am dead, as dead I well may be

"She remembered what song you were singing." Helen was starting to repeat herself. Sometimes I think dementia is infectious. The staff at nursing homes are especially prone to it.

Ye'll come and find the place where I am lying

"Don't you or anyone ever tie her into that chair again," I said. "Write that on her chart, her file, her door notes, wherever you write those things." I still didn't look up. I could hear her hesitating, and then another resident's alarm started, and she moved away from the doorway and down the hall.

And kneel and say an ave there for me.

I waited until she got to the end of the line. "Do you want me to make you some toast and marmalade?" I asked my mother. It was the only way I knew how to apologize.

FROM THE CHANCEL, we could see the priest's back, and the end of the draped coffin, and the mourners in the pews. To most of the boys, it always seemed a terrible thing to die at Christmas time. What would you do with the presents? they asked each other. Alex and I were more inclined to believe that a special call had been made from Heaven, and who was anyone to argue?

The smell of incense was heavy in the air, and Alex was, as usual, off in his own world beside me. I elbowed him from the safety of my cassock, pushing his arm forward and finding the sensitive spot between his third and fourth rib. I counted three seconds and jabbed him again, counted three more and leaned into his side as far as I could with the point of my bent arm. Elbowing had taken on the status of ritual.

"Mmmmuhh," he said, quietly. But he sat up a little and reached for the music book. His *Agnus Dei* solo was up next.

We were both in what we came to call "the death choir."

He got up, straightened his gown, dipped his head a couple of times, finding the deep part of the music, and opened his mouth.

Agnus Dei, qui tollis peccata mundi, miserere nobis

One of the younger boys joined him about halfway through, and for the conclusion the full dozen of us entreated God to take away the sins of the world. We all sat down again when the last notes faded. I kept my elbow ready. We'd done this often enough that it was possible for most of us to let our minds wander until we heard the signal—two or three opening bars from the organ, or the quiet clatter of the thurible and smell of incense—that would bring us back to the matter at hand: singing someone into their grave. I am not sure what the others thought about; maybe food or comic books or, for some of the older boys I'm sure, how far they could get their girlfriends to lift their skirts. Alex always almost-slept, but I have no idea what he almost-dreamed. And I—I didn't go far into my mind—just as far as the coffin standing draped before the altar.

Unlike the other boys, I thought about death quite a lot during those funerals, but always in a fairly pragmatic way, and without any doubt about my own fate after dying. I was concerned, rather, for all those who had somehow avoided the pointing of God's finger—deliberately avoided, I thought at the time, for I believed it a sin to refuse God's call, assuming naively that he bestowed the same opportunities on everyone, and what made the difference was our mettle.

IT WAS AN EARLY WINTER. Snow had come at the beginning of December and settled in like an unwelcome in-law, waiting for

Christmas. For obvious reasons, my books got seriously overdue at the library, and my fines escalated to alarming amounts. I suspect it would have been cheaper to buy the books outright than to pay all the late fees, but I did not want to claim that I had lost them. Being careless with due dates was bad enough. I didn't think a librarian would respect someone who was careless with the printed word. I didn't want to give her any more reasons to think I was an idiot.

But I did anyway. The Monday afternoon I took them back, the weather was consistent with a trip to Hell, if Hell had been bitter cold instead of blazing hot. I didn't see any sign of Luke. In fact, I didn't see any sign of life out on the streets at all. I couldn't even see the great dome of St. George's in the next block; a blue whiteness spread across the sky like God's windows had frosted over. There was a hearse parked in front of the Greek Orthodox church, and a couple of once-dark cars haphazardly parked, but it looked like people were pretty much doing their mourning in the warmth of their own living rooms. A poverty of people, and an abundance of stinging snow, and it wasn't even officially winter yet. I slid up the library steps with the oversized book-filled plastic bag hugged to my chest, my hat pulled down over my eyebrows, my eyes squeezed three-quarters shut, and my head down like a charging bull.

I plowed into her just before I got under the portico. She let out a little "Unh" sound on impact and reached for the railing to steady herself. She had on a red coat with a hood pulled tight around her face, so I didn't immediately realize who she was. All I could see was her nose and her little round open mouth. Then she tilted her head up to look at me, but her eyes were mostly closed against the stinging snow.

"*Oh*," I said. I could feel a sudden heat in my half-frozen face.

"I'm sorry!" she said. "This weather!" And she tucked her chin back into her scarf, and made her way down the steps, watching her footing, her right hand on the metal railing.

"No! My fault!" I called after her, too late, not wanting her to get away without an apology, but she didn't turn back again, so I don't think she heard me. At the sidewalk she went left, down the street towards St. George's, bent into the wind blowing up from the lake.

As if in some kind of delayed reaction, the plastic bag broke and books dived from my arms to toboggan down the empty library steps. I watched them, torpidly, as the sleet obscured their titles and the authors' names. Judging by the jacket art, there was a wicked snowstorm in every story. Within a few minutes, you really couldn't tell a book by its cover.

"SHIT!" ALEX SAID; he'd clearly just thought of something. He pulled the zipper of his parka halfway down and fished around in his inside pocket for his watch. "*Yes!* We have time!" He was exuberant. "Let's go get some *summer*! Come on!" And he started to run through the squeaking snow without waiting for my agreement. I stood and watched his knapsack jumping up and down on his back like a diminishing monkey. When he got to the corner he called over his shoulder once more: "Come *on*!"

It was impossible not to follow him.

He zig-zagged over to Jarvis, with me twenty yards behind him, both of us slipping in slush and grime and the detritus of Toronto winter. An old man with a three-legged cane shook his mittened fist at me as I went by, and Alex got caught up in the leashes of dachshunds with matching plaid coats. At the intersection he waited for the light, and, when I caught up with him, he tossed the snowball he'd been making into my shoulder, where it exploded like a soft grenade. Ice chips ran down my face and neck like a baptism in boyhood, so long overdue.

And then we were running and diving and slipping, sliding, caterwauling, whooping, throwing and catching, ducking behind the streetcar, playing chicken with the couriers who rode their bicycles in shorts even in the winter. We ran among office blocks and past churches and pawn shops. I had no idea where we were going.

We threw ridiculously tiny icicles broken off from the bottom of No Parking signs, firing them like miniature spears at the backs of each other's heads. We turned another corner, and I stopped to catch my breath, bent over double, my hands on my knees.

"Come *on*!" he yelled, and we were off again, my heart hammering out the beat like cymbals in an orchestral *finale*.

We entered a park. The paths were not well cleared, both of us fitting our feet into the half-frozen footsteps of previous walkers, stretching our boy-legs just a little to match the stride of men.

And finally he stopped, panting, in front of a huge and ornate house made of glass—in the fading light lit up from within like the true house of God—and looked at his watch again.

"We've got—half an hour—before—it closes," he said, the words on his out-breaths ragged with running through the frosty air. And then he solemnly walked up the path and held open the door to summer.

We went inside. I was hit with a ferocious warmth, and the sight, and the scent: surely the fragrance of Eden itself, of fresh, damp, living green—so many greens, but also gold, white, sky blue, and magenta. Tiny flowers and tall ones; shrubs with large leaves like hearts or porcupine-like needles; trees that almost touched the high roof of glass and others that climbed like snakes upon the railings—a riot of shape, colour, smell.

But it seemed that we were not there to admire the greenery. Alex wiggled his shoulders so his knapsack fell to the floor behind him. He unzipped and removed his coat, and rolled it haphazardly under his arm. Then he picked up his bag with the coat hand and grabbed my arm with the other.

"Over here," he said. "This way." He'd caught his breath a little, but his voice still had an urgency to it. He pulled me down pathways and through doorways, the melting remains of snowballs brushed lightly from our shoulders by giant ferns and palm fronds. We passed a few other people on our way, but not many: a young family with a red-faced baby bundled in a sling, an old woman with a magnifying glass, examining the stamen of a flower I didn't know the name of. I thought I didn't know the name of anything in there.

Finally we seemed to have arrived.

"Here," he announced. "This is the best spot." And he pushed me in behind an unfamiliar kind of tree with a thin trunk and leaves at the top like the giant fans I had seen in illustrations of the bible, with great big bright green sausages hanging seemingly upside-down beside my ear.

"Dude," I exclaimed, "are those *bananas?*"

Alex shushed me, as if I had sworn in church. He closed his eyes, took a measured breath, and opened his mouth.

Ave Maria
Gratia plena
Dominus tecum
Benedicta tu in mulieribus
Et benedictus fructus
Ventris tui, Jesus

I cannot describe the almost unbearable poignancy and purity of his voice rising among the leaves in that green-drenched hall. I shrugged my own coat off my shoulders, and let it drop between the tree trunks in that tropical world.

We sang together:

Sancta Maria, Sancta Maria
Maria, ora pro nobis
Nobis peccatoribus
Nunc et in hora
Mortis nostrae
Amen Amen

In my heart I can still hear that ethereal music, even now, over twenty years later. We were both there for God, and there was no doubt for me then that he came down to meet us. If there was one moment of perfection in my life, it was lived there, behind the banana leaves in the conservatory of Allan Gardens. Our two voices together were like warp and weft, poem and paper, kiln and clay.

THERE WAS A CURIOUS SILENCE in the locked ward when I arrived. Marilyn was watching television in the living room, but she made no move to waylay me. She didn't even look at me as I went by, but sat totally focused on *Corner Gas*, her eyes sinking into her skull and her cheeks gaunt.

There was a vibration in the air at the nursing station, the staff busy in controlled and furtive movements, though the crowd of wheelchair spectators were unusually subdued and they all looked haggard and hollowed out. Helen and Louise were on shift, one of them bent over an open filing cabinet drawer, the other flipping urgently through red file folders, her eyes flickering back and forth while she was reading. There was another woman I didn't recognize there too, a new staff member perhaps, standing a little to one side and wringing her hands.

Someone died, I thought to myself, and I looked quickly for my mother along the rows of wheelchairs, though she never sits out in the hallway with the others. I turned left and went down the hall to her room, and I have to admit that I don't know whether or not I was hoping to see her once I got there. I know I had inhaled deeply at the desk, walked down the hall at an accelerated pace, *stringendo*, with my chest constricting like I had stage fright, and didn't breathe again until I got to her room.

She was sitting in her chair, her hands crossed at the wrists and lying lightly on her lap, fluttering a little as if there was a gentle breeze blowing across her tiny room. The movement was small, but telling enough. She wasn't dead.

But something *was* wrong. The shape of her face had changed somehow, and she sat uncharacteristically silent, neither singing nor talking. I thought maybe she'd had another stroke, and I went and put my hand gently under her chin to lift her head so I could look at her eyes.

Touching my mother is always a shock, though I try to do it as often as I can stand. The skin of the infirm is as thin and as fragile as last year's leaves. Her face was neither warm nor cold; she seemed not to have any animate temperature at all; she felt the way a book does, or a piece of wood, or a leather shoe. Her eyes travelled across my face, but only because it was the thing right in front of her, and not because it engendered any memory.

I ran my thumb across her jawbone, and understanding hit me. And then I took a moment to recognize and register what I was feeling as relief. I looked around the room. I went and opened the drawers in her dresser, one by one, and rifled through her meagre possessions, a few cardigans and blouses and brassieres. I looked under the bed. And then I went back out to the nursing station, where the trio had changed positions slightly, but were still single-mindedly occupied with the same pursuits. I went right to Helen.

"Has someone died?" I asked. I wanted to know, first, if there was a bigger emergency they needed to deal with.

"Not yet," said Helen, and she looked over at the new woman meaningfully.

I tried to read the new one's tag, but the hand wringing was still going on, right in front of her name. It was a cryptic enough answer, but I got the sense that if anyone was going to be dead imminently, it was Hand-wringer.

"Then *where* are my mother's *teeth*?" I asked.

As soon as I got to the question mark Hand-wringer ran

towards the ward exit. She tried the door handle forcefully before she seemed to remember about the code, and it took her several tries to punch in four-three-two-one and get it right. Some of the wheelchair occupants turned their heads mutely to watch her departure, and some of them just kept right on staring at the floor.

When she was safely on the side of the living room with Marilyn and *Corner Gas,* and the door had closed behind her, Helen, Louise, and I looked at each other with our eyebrows up, and then the two of them transferred their focus to each other, muscles jerking and twitching, as if some form of sinewy communication was going on between them.

"Should I show him?" asked Louise, finally, and Helen nodded reluctantly.

I followed Louise down the hall in the opposite direction from my mother's room. We turned in at the staff kitchen. Instead of the usual box of Girl Guide cookies, piles of used coffee mugs, old newspapers, and paper napkins, the counter was lined from one end to the other with residents' false teeth. Sets of teeth were scattered on the little round table, uppers and lowers in random order. On top of the microwave, a pink and white tower of teeth balanced precariously. Beside the sink sat a box of Polident powder and a toothbrush.

Louise gave me a minute to take all this in.

"She thought she'd give them all a really good cleaning," she said. It seemed a generous thing to do to stop there. "I don't suppose you know which ones are your mother's?"

I started to react slowly. At first it was like a kind of gasping for air, a kind of disbelief escaping from the depths of my belly. Then Louise's throat made a noise like she was trying to hold something back, and that was it, we were sunk. When Helen came down the hall to see what the racket was, she found us holding our sides in agony, the tears streaming down our faces. I think because Louise was laughing, Helen just assumed that I was, too.

WHEN I GOT TO THE SHOP the next afternoon to give a voice lesson, Ed was sitting behind the counter, as far away as the dark side of the moon, holding his bristled chin in his wrinkled left hand, his fingers splayed across his face. His right hand rested on the cradled telephone, as if he had long forgotten to remove it. There was a heavy presence with him in the shop, like bass clef notes below the staff, that I felt even as the door chime tinkled shut behind me.

"Sylvia?" I asked him. "Annie?" I knew right away that something was wrong with *someone*.

He looked across the counter at me. His lids were heavy, and his eyes dull with confusion. He wiped his hand across his mouth and inhaled wetly, as if he had forgotten how to swallow. "No," he said. "I'm okay."

"*What happened?*" I asked. I was still a distance from him, across the floor of the shop, the door slowly shutting behind my back, the room hollow.

"Nothing," he said. The word came out of him and he flinched, and his breath caught in his throat. I practically ran across the shop floor to the counter.

"*Who?*"

"I'll be fine in a minute," he said. "It'll pass. It's nothing." I only understood then that he was in physical pain, himself.

"This isn't nothing," I said. "What does it feel like?" He looked translucent and thin, as if some of the life had leaked out of him.

"No," he said. "It's nothing. I'm fine now."

"I think I should call an ambulance."

"Don't you dare," he said.

I stood there for a small minute, just waiting to see if he would take his hand off the phone. My bag of students' sheet music was suddenly heavy, the strap cutting into me, weighted with other people's notes that were no use to me at all, and I let the bag slide off my shoulder and down my body until it rested against the bottom of the counter. I put my hand out and laid it on his forearm, and I was surprised at how bony and frail it seemed, for all his apparent strength and height. As soon as I touched him, he shuddered as if being woken unexpectedly from sleep, and rubbed his face forcefully with his liver-spotted hands. I let go of him and reached for the phone.

"I'll kill you," he said. "Just help me into the back. I'll sit back there for a few minutes. I'll be fine."

"I have a student coming," I said. "Barbara."

"Then hurry up. Get me in there before she gets here. If Barbara knows anything, the whole damn town knows."

So I went to the front door and turned over the OPEN sign to CLOSED, hung out the "Back in 5 minutes" clock face, and turned the bolt in the lock. Then I went and got him up and led him into the storeroom—he leaned on me heavily—and moved several boxes of hissing snare drums one-handed, to clear a way to the beat-up office chair he'd recently gotten out of Steve Packer's garbage. It was like clearing a den of snakes.

"I'll be all right in a minute," said Ed as he sat down. "I'll be fine."

I pushed down on his shoulder with some kind of non-verbal signal that I hoped would keep him sitting there for a while.

"Don't you dare call Sylvia," he finished.

I went back out—closing the storeroom door carefully behind me on my way—and, of course, I called Sylvia.

"I think he's okay now," I told her, "but I don't know what happened. He's threatening to kill me if I call an ambulance."

"All right," she said, "I'll take the heat for taking him to the hospital. I'm on my way. I'll be there in five minutes."

"Bring your key," I told her. "He's in the back."

I went and looked in at him in the storeroom one more time. Some of the colour had returned to his face, but his eyes were closed and he didn't open them when he heard the door. If he heard the door. I listened for his breathing, and it was ragged, but even.

"You called her," he said angrily. "I'm going to kill you."

"Don't you dare move!" I told him fiercely in return, on my way out again. I'd never talked to him like that before.

Then I unlocked and opened the shop door. It was starting to snow, and my next voice student was standing on the sidewalk, a young woman who had dreams that were bigger than her voice. She was looking at her watch. "Sorry, Barbara," I said. "Come on in."

I held the door open and then I shut it behind her and locked it again, leaving the clock and the CLOSED in view to passersby. I didn't want her to see Sylvia coming in, and Ed going out. She followed me in to the soundproof room. I shut that door too, although there was no sound from Ed in the storeroom, and positioned her music stand so she had her back to the glass.

Then, somehow, we had a singing lesson.

SYLVIA STOPPED BY MUCH LATER that night on her way home from the hospital to let me know that Ed had been admitted. They'd taken five vials of his blood and done a CT scan, and were planning a liver biopsy for the following morning.

"Ah," I said.

"Yes," she said. There was a pause. It seemed that neither of us was surprised.

"Do you want to come in?" I asked at last. I was holding my front door open, and snow was drifting in onto the toes of my corduroy slippers.

"No, no, I've got to get going. I'm pretty tired, and I told him I'd be back first thing in the morning." She turned to go. "I'll call you when I know something," she said. "I'll call you at the shop."

"I don't know if it's related," I said quickly, "or if it's something else, but he's been a little *confused*—"

"No," she said, and she put out her hand as if she could stop Truth by willpower alone.

"*Disorganized*—" I continued.

"No. Don't even say it," she said.

She was careful to hold on to the railing as she went down my single porch step.

I watched her back and shoulders turn white as she opened and reached inside the passenger door for the snow brush and circled around her car on the road, it was snowing that hard. She swept the windshield, but as soon as she had it almost clear on one side, it was covered again on the other.

I slipped my feet out of my slippers and into my boots, and kept her company by attempting to sweep the snow, first from the hallway, and then from the porch, the one step, and down the walkway. My porch light was burnt out so I left the door wide open behind me so I would have some light. The broom lifted the grains of snow into an arc over my head, and soon my pyjama shirt was soaked through with the double precipitation, though I couldn't feel the cold.

I knew we were both thinking about my mother.

"HEY," I SAID.

"Hey," Ed replied. He turned his head slightly in my direction, though his eyes appeared dull and focused inward. That didn't change as I entered his line of vision.

He was in a semi-private room, but the other bed was empty and unmade. The guardrails were up on the bed he was in. The head of the bed was angled about halfway up, and he had a sheet tangled between his legs as if he were rope climbing. His hospital gown was twisted and a bare inch of skin was visible all the way down his backside. There was a pulse monitor attached to one of his fingers, and I could see various other wires emerging from the sleeves of his gown. On the machine beside his head, a green line rose and fell reassuringly, making a music entirely of the body.

"How's it going?" I asked him.

"Going, going, gone?" he suggested. He was trying to make a joke, but the hint of sarcasm and taste of fear in his voice meant that it fell flat; he could hear that himself, I could tell.

He turned and looked out the window, but there was nothing to see there but his own reflection.

"It gets dark so bloody early," he complained. His voice was bitter.

I went around the end of the bed and pulled the two sides of the curtain across the window. The hooks made a noise like a death rattle as they slid across the track. "Where's Sylvia?" I asked.

"Taking a break," he said. "Having a coffee. Gone to worry for a while in the cafeteria instead of in this room." He looked at me defiantly, and I could tell they'd had a fight. I could tell he'd sent her away for fussing over him, but it was all I could do not to fuss.

"Of course she's worried," I told him. "We're all worried." I thought about how I couldn't say *I'm* worried; how we shield others from direct knowledge of our deepest selves. I thought about how he couldn't say the two words to me *I'm scared*, when his body and his tone of voice and his shuttered eyes were screaming it. We could both see that his life was only a thin and fraying thread on a full spindle.

"*Worried*," he said, like he was spitting the word out.

"Do you need anything?" I asked him. I didn't have any idea what else to say.

"I need the devil," cried Ed. "Where the hell is the devil when you want to make a bargain?" There was a silence.

"I'm here," I told him, finally.

I STAYED AT THE WHOLE NOTE every day until closing time, to give Ed a bit of a break. I'd offered to look after the place until we were sure he could handle it—I took a week of vacation from work—and then Sylvia had called to see if I might be good for another week or two of afternoons.

"Of course," I'd said to her. "However long you need."

So it was two weeks and counting. I ran through my mail route like the best of them, for the first time wearing a watch and actually looking at it in between pushing envelopes into slots or handing parcels across countertops. For the first time *ever*, at twelve noon precisely, ditching my undelivered ad mail into the recycling dumpster behind the apartment building near the end of my route—though not without losing sleep over it.

I opened the shop at twelve-thirty; there was a sign on the door in Sylvia's handwriting, explaining that, due to circumstances beyond management's control, The Whole Note would be closed every morning until further notice. A handful of regulars keep asking when Ed would be coming back, but I didn't know what to tell them. All the gusto had gone out of him. He came to the house only once in that time—dropped off by Sylvia because she wouldn't let him drive—and spent the evening sitting on the piano bench, *flebile*, running his fingers in the lightest possible manner along the closed lid, his foot never leaving the damping pedal: a doubly silent elegy for I knew not what.

I hadn't even needed to replace the Rickard's that my brothers drank in my backyard. He only wanted orange juice.

"Drink mighta got me into this," he said.

So I hung out in the shop, dusting guitars and waiting for customers. I held my voice lessons with the soundproof doors open, so I could hear if anybody came in. After the first day, I thought about tackling the inventory in the storage room, but after standing in the doorway staring at the disorganized piles of boxes for twenty minutes, I couldn't decide if that would be helpful or controlling. After the second day, I thought about setting up a small business software program to track sales and expenses, but there'd only been one sale of any significance, a reconditioned Fender guitar, and I didn't want Ed to have to face any more bad news. By day three, I had given up all bright ideas and mostly surfed the internet and listened to YouTube when the place was empty. Those days it was most of the time.

ED FINALLY CAME BACK to the shop in mid-December, a fainter and more acerbic version of himself. He got muddled easily, and complained often of the cold, keeping the thermostat at a temperature I knew he couldn't afford. The weather continued to be terrible. Every time the shop door opened to let in a customer, the wind whipped in behind them like Zephyrus on a jealous rampage. People kept their coats and hats on in the store, trying desperately to warm up, and ribbons of slush from their delinquent sleeves dripped across the glistening banjos, while icy fingerprints were left on the saxophones and trumpets. It drove Ed crazy, and he wandered around the shop with a soft rag and an ill humour.

I still went over to the shop every day, even when I didn't have any students, though once Ed was back I didn't stress myself even more by rushing through my mail route—even in those unseasonable blizzards I delivered every single piece of ad mail, in a kind of penance. I'd stop on my way over to get Ed and myself some lunch, and get there between one and two, so I'd have time to watch Ed eat before my first lesson. Sylvia had called to say that he was hardly eating at home, so I was doing my bit to keep his strength up. I brought him his favourite foods—crab cakes or Montreal smoked meat on rye from the diner, with the occasional peanut butter and banana sandwich I made at home—but he ate everything like it was sawdust, and left a lot of crusts.

Despite the fact that no one wanted to go outdoors at all, business picked up a bit in The Whole Note going into Christmas; we finally sold last year's model baby grand, at a discounted price. I convinced Ed not to order another, and one day when he'd gone home early I rearranged the shop so the piano's absence was not so obvious. He'd always had a piano in the store; if nothing else it helped him pass the time when business was slow. It was yet another marker that, after a long period of consistency and tranquillity, things were changing, in fits and starts and revelations of mortality. The world was becoming a place we couldn't rely on. To what end, I did not know.

THERE IS SOME MUSIC THAT MAKES PEOPLE want to dance, the beat irresistible, the pulse infectious—the whole tune a thumping package of energy creation, like nuclear fission among the heavy elements. Other music uplifts and inspires; we hear a series of notes, and somehow we can imagine nothing less than universal tolerance, celebrated diversity, world peace. A few bars and the very fallible and much maligned human spirit is good enough, at last, and forgiveness is granted even to our worst enemies. Other music makes us so grateful that we are here, alive, and have *music,* that we can find ourselves laughing out loud with the joy of it.

And there is some music—and it has existed in every era and is found in every style and genre—whose sole purpose seems to be to facilitate the expression of sorrow, where that sorrow has been caged somewhere inside us, a wild animal we are afraid to release, for fear it turns and devours us entirely.

There was an animal like that caught inside Ed.

When we were in the shop together, I sang to him. I began with every piercing song from my mother's repertoire, and initially he would just listen without comment. The only way I knew he was listening at all was that when I stopped, he would invariably ask for another. After a while, he would ask for a specific song by name, and as more time passed, his requests were pulled from an ever narrower selection, a shorter short list. The first weeks I sang him dozens of different songs, and then a week came when he wanted only four or five, and the next week he wanted only one. I didn't argue. He was like a child wanting the same bedtime story over and over, even though every picture and every word had been memorized long ago.

The water is wide, I cannot get o'er
Neither have I wings to fly

It seems both ironic and obvious that the song that comforted Ed in his shop also comforted my mother in her kitchen.

"Aren't there more verses?" Ed always said, when I stopped. I dredged up a few more, half remembered. There are enough verses to suit both shops and kitchens, childless men and mothers.

Martinmas wind, when wilt thou blow,
And shake the green leaves off the tree?
O gentle Death, when wilt thou come?
For of my life I am weary.

The tune has been sung, with minor variations, and the words, with major variations, for over four hundred years. It can be traced back even farther, in fragments of melody and phrase, to other, much older songs. It comes to us from the depths of time.

"Sing it again," Ed demands.

SLOWLY, I BEGAN TO UNDERSTAND that loss can make us cranky with what we have that remains. We look around, and everything is meaningless. Why did you take this and not that? we yell to the heavens. Other things I could have spared! I do not need the extra bedroom, or the V8 engine! Leave me my eyesight, my sturdy legs, my lifetime of memory, my sense of hopeful possibility! We examine everything as if there is a contest underway. As if we can make a trade, as if it were not too late to compile a long list of all that we could do without. As if the weight of them could be traded against something merely held for ransom. Things we were once attached to, all the threads that weave us into neighbourhoods and businesses and countries, become clearly expendable. The morning paper with everyone else's bad news. The public bus service with the express stop at the end of our street. Sidewalks and breakwaters. Pianos and banjos and clarinets. The Whole Note in its entirety becomes redundant. *Music.* Choirs and angels and churches and synagogues. *God.* We would trade it all away, we realize. We just want back what we have lost.

ON THE NIGHT OF MY FINAL Christmas concert at St. Mary's, Annie pinned the sprig of holly onto my jacket, holding the two pins in her teeth as she gripped my lapel with both hands, and pulled it away from my chest with such force that I lost my balance for a minute. She had been fierce with me all that afternoon and evening, saying no more than necessary; when she did, she was curt and talked at me from a distance.

She pushed the pins in deftly, one at a time, around the holly stem; the light of her eyes was shuttered, and she would not look at me. She moved through the world as if her spirit had been transported elsewhere—to hell perhaps—while her body remained in that house in the Beaches and did everything that was required of it, but bitterly. At the time I thought it was a little like voodoo; years later, once I'd watched Ed realize that he was suddenly, unaccountably, inexplicably, *old*, I realized at last that it was their family way of expressing unspeakable grief.

THERE ARE PEOPLE IN THE WORLD who are working on theories about which most of us know nothing, and understand even less. These days, the evolving concepts of science are as obscure to most of us as is the language of the Wessex Gospels. We go about our daily lives without any real sense that for hundreds of years, chemists, mathematicians, physicists, and astronomers have been determinedly trying to find God, and that many of them feel they are very, very close.

It is in the intersection between quantum mechanics and general relativity where most contemporary scientists believe this deity, the theory of everything, may be found. There need be no exclusion of one for the other, except with the literalists. It is only necessary to break everything God touched down into a quantum particle, and to stretch time, and to call his first work a singularity.

At the quantum level, it seems it is possible for two things to behave as if they are related to each other, even though there is no communication between them, and no other discernable explanation for their connection. It is as if I go through my life singing or not singing, randomly and unpredictably. But as soon as I sing, Filander is found to be singing, and as soon as I stop, Filander is also silent.

This would be equally and instantaneously true whether we were in the same room, or whether one of us was singing, or not singing, on the moon.

Einstein called this "spooky action at a distance" and refused to believe it. I call it obvious.

CHRISTMAS DAY. WHEN YOU'RE ALONE, it's hard not to be self-conscious about it. As soon as I woke up in the morning I had a sense of all the Christmas trees, real and fake, all the presents, all the *expectation* in countless houses and apartments, cottages and trailers, residences and shelters across the continent. The weight of it all kept me in bed for a good while past my usual rising hour. It didn't matter; there wasn't any rush.

Despite everyone's conviction that the day's weather should admit only languid, large-flaked snow, or at second best that crisp and brilliant azure sky dotted with cumulus clouds—the kind of sky that seems at any minute inclined to crack open and reveal Saint Michael and all the angels in their heavenly glory—my experience is that the weather is usually perfectly ordinary, running to grey rain or blinding blizzard as often as any other winter day, and that the streets and sidewalks invariably remain bordered by frozen grime.

This Christmas was no exception. I looked out the bathroom window onto a dull sky hovering unapologetically over my yard and my back neighbour's frosted roof. In thousands of houses across the city, people were going downstairs to open presents. I went downstairs and opened the fridge.

I didn't have anywhere to go until eleven-thirty, so after I poached my egg and ate standing at the counter, I went and sat on the piano bench in the front room, facing out, and polished a small patch of the hardwood floor with my sock feet. I did that for a while, looking around the room at the silent instruments, the lute in its stand, the Japanese flute, the harp I'd traded my car for. I didn't miss it, the car. An empty driveway made me feel less like I had to have somewhere to go.

I thought I might listen to some music while I got ready, so I got up and rifled haphazardly through the CD shelves, looking for I don't know what, but something different, something I hadn't heard in a while. My fingers ticked through the plastic cases, shelf by shelf, but nothing seemed to suit. I got to the bottom shelf, and was about to give up and go get dressed, when I found the four recordings I had from St. Mary's, one for each year I was there. I shuffled through them and picked out the last one, turned it over slowly, and looked at the picture of myself and Alex on the back: St. Mary's singing twins. My dark head and his blond one. Our shoulders touched, but there seemed to be a singular distance between us that the camera could not efface.

I opened the case, and a tightly folded paper sprang out, as if it had been trapped there for years, aching for freedom. It was a thin concert program: a single page folded over. When I opened it, a strip of paper floated out from among the folds and landed printed side up, beside my knee. *Please note that for tonight's performance, the "Silent Night" duet will be sung as a solo by Frederick Madrigal.*

My hand was trembling a little, but I managed to get the disc out of the case and put it into the player. I checked the playlist and skipped to the last track, pushed "play," and held my breath.

In the bleak midwinter frosty wind made moan
Earth stood hard as iron, water like a stone

People think that Christmas is a difficult time to be alone because of the absence of family, loved ones, company of any kind. I am not sure that that is exactly right. There are some days of the year that have threads running through them, threads that stitch a particular day with all the other such occasions we have known. Christmas is a day like that, swollen with what has been, vivid in memory, indelible like the pen marks on the door frame that show how much we've grown. What makes Christmas hard is the recognition of how much, year to year, things can change.

Snow had fallen, snow on snow, snow on snow
In the bleak midwinter, long ago.

I remember being in the recording studio with Alex, before we had any idea how much things would change. Our adolescent voices held the final note and then died away, and the final notes of the piano died away, and the CD player clicked over to the next spot in the roundabout, but it was empty. I turned the machine off.

After a while, I got up to find a suitable shirt to wear to the nursing home luncheon, and got out the ironing board, and wrapped my mother's present—a soft toy cat, black with a pink nose—and signed the card I would bring to Ed and Sylvia's for supper, along with a bottle of fancy Italian soda that almost looked like wine.

The boy who'd sung that carol—in those days always his favourite carol—followed me out into the still-grey streets, but I didn't recognize him. We walked along together to the nursing home, my breath white in the dull air, but we didn't look at each other or speak to each other. Not even once. Not even on Christmas Day.

ANNIE HAD LEFT THE ENVELOPE PROPPED UP in front of the cookie jar on the kitchen counter, wedged in place by the silver-topped crystal salt shaker. I picked it up, felt its heft—three or four folded pages, not just one—and noted the return address: The Juilliard School, New York. My hand shook a little, and I was over-conscious of Alex standing in the doorway watching me. I knew what that letter meant: one more step towards my goal. I imagined myself ripping it open with him looking over my shoulder; then I imagined myself placing the envelope back on the counter, face-down and unopened, nonchalantly collecting a handful of peanut butter cookies and going through to the music room to eat them sitting backwards on the piano bench, the way we always did. Both courses of action seemed impossible.

"It's okay," he said. "I already got mine."

"You did?"

"Yeah. It came yesterday."

"Fat or thin?" I asked him, just to make sure.

"Fat," he confirmed. I knew he couldn't tell from across the room, but he didn't seem to have any doubt about the thickness of my envelope.

So I opened it, even though I knew what it said. I took a paring knife from the drawer and slit the flap neatly, removed the folded sheets reverently. Even though I already knew—had known in fact since I first learned what Juilliard meant to boys like me—I wanted to see it, wanted to hold it in my hands and see the words singing on the page, words written to me, Frederick Madrigal:

> Bachelor of Music Live Audition Repertoire
>
> Faculty may ask applicants to sing several scales to check vocal range.
> All compositions must be performed from memory, and should include the following:
>
> I. An Italian art song or aria from the 18th century or before.
> II. An art song in English (not a translation).
> III. A third selection in any language.

When I'd read all three and a half pages, I took the lid off the cookie jar and offered some to Alex.

"Why didn't you tell me yesterday?" I asked him.

"I was waiting till you got yours," he said. We made our

way to the piano, dribbling crumbs. I swept them under the sofa with my sock feet. I was still holding my audition letter in my left hand. The auditions weren't until March of our senior year, and auditions did not guarantee acceptance. But I knew that neither of us was the least bit worried.

"D'you know what you're going to sing?" I asked him.

"Not yet," he shrugged, nonchalantly. We wiped our hands on our school pants, swivelled on the bench, and began to play Mendelssohn's "Allegro Brillante," our four hands on Annie's perfectly-tuned grand piano.

ERIC WAS SITTING ON HIS KNAPSACK on top of the stone retaining wall across from the senior boys' entrance. We'd come out together at the end of the day. It was a habit of his to sit on his text books and sheet music; I always kept my own bag slung across my shoulder, one hand on the strap, like a soldier carrying a kit bag in which he has stored everything necessary for life.

"You get your letter?" he asked me.

"Yeah," I said. He looked at me and nodded, and one side of his mouth went up, to show he knew it. "Did you?"

"Oh, well ... nah," he said, as if he'd been going to pretend he didn't care, but changed his mind.

"Bad luck," I told him.

"Nah," he was resigned. "I'm just not good enough." And he was right, so I made sure that the line of my mouth stayed firm and straight, so he wouldn't know I knew it. But still I marvelled at his passive acceptance of a life without music, something that, in that moment, I myself was still utterly unable to imagine.

"Anyway," he continued, as if to reassure himself, "my father wants me to be a lawyer." I didn't know what to say.

"Bad luck," I repeated. He shrugged and steadied his expression so I couldn't read it. We all knew how to do that so masterfully. We all knew, too, that it meant something underneath the surface was being smoothed over, covered up, buried. There was a small tremor in his hand, and he rubbed his face to hide it. I could tell he was desperate for a cigarette but didn't dare risk it.

On cue, the Cutlass Supreme turned the near corner and pulled up in front of the school. Eric got up quickly and shouldered his knapsack, but his father didn't see him immediately, and honked. At the sound of the horn, Eric tucked his chin into his parka, as if to hide his face.

He didn't look back at me, just climbed into the passenger seat and closed the door carefully. Nobody offered me a lift. Like a soldier, I tramped down the white road. I didn't need a ride in an icy car.

I DIDN'T WRITE TO MY MOTHER to tell her the news. In keeping with the best child-rearing practice, Annie allowed me increasing latitude to make my own choices, good or bad, and watched me suffer the consequences of bad ones without pity. By the time I was in my senior year, she generally left me alone to write to my mother or not, and, in general, I did write several times each semester, though my letters held no warmth and little substance.

Despite this, after I got my letter from Juilliard, Annie did ask me if I had written. I don't remember now if I lied outright or was merely evasive. It wasn't that I didn't want my mother to know. But I didn't want to crack open any door that might lead to the possibility of me going back for a visit before going to New York. Toronto, and Annie's, had come to feel like home. I had arrived there by extraordinary means, and I didn't want to be reminded of what I had left behind.

JANUARY CAME IN LIKE JANUARY DOES: dissonant, delusive, and cold. Despite the hype, there was no new beginning to things; there were just false starts, repetitions, and a few extra pounds from eating so much at other people's houses.

At first it seemed that everything was basically just going to go on the way it had been going. Any changes were like small bumps in the landscape, hardly even noticeable if you skirted carefully around them. I spent a lot of my free time at the shop with Ed, without any sense of where or how that would end. Day to day, there was no improvement in his outlook or in his ability to run the shop on his own; the fundamentals continued to elude him. He ordered too many harmonicas and misplaced the receipt—along with about fifty others. He blocked the route to the bathroom with precariously-piled instrument boxes. He plugged in the kettle but never made tea. Even when people asked for help, he seemed unable to sell the smallest piece of musical merchandise to the most credit-card-happy customer.

On days when I sent him home early, assuring him a dozen times that I would stay and lock up, Sylvia and I had clandestine telephone conversations about what to do about Ed.

"Okay, he's on his way home," I'd call and tell her. Partly I didn't trust him to get all the way there without an accident. He refused to let me drive him home, and wouldn't hear of Sylvia dropping him off in the mornings. I wanted her to be looking out for him, so we wouldn't lose time if he didn't appear on schedule.

One day early on there'd been a two hour-fifty-five minute gap between his leaving the shop and arriving home—a driving distance of about seven minutes—and Sylvia had alerted the police after only half an hour. The cops had suggested waiting a little longer, but Sylvia had gone out driving through the neighbourhood, in ever-increasing concentric rectangles around their house, peering through the windshield and cursing the defroster. She'd found his car outside the bowling lanes, and went in to find him sitting at the lunch counter in bowling shoes, drinking a root beer float.

"He never bowled in his life!" she told me after. "And *root beer*?" Apparently, Ed hadn't had a single real beer in months.

"He can't seem to enjoy anything," Sylvia said. I knew she

wasn't enjoying much herself, between worrying about Ed and trying to keep him safe. After that, we both made him promise that he would always go right home, and, surprisingly, he did.

"He's been drafting his will," she said. "He's suddenly obsessed with what to do with everything. The house. The shop. The canoe. Everything."

"Oh," I said. "Maybe that's a good thing?" I was thinking about my mother. "Isn't it a good thing to have a will?" I was leaning on the counter, and The Whole Note was empty, so I didn't have to worry about keeping my voice down to protect Ed's privacy.

"He's obsessing about it," she said. "I'm not sure it's the best thing for him right now. He thinks he's going to die any minute. He wouldn't talk about it for years when I wanted him to, and now he won't stop talking about it."

"He hasn't said anything to me about it," I said.

"That's because you're in it."

"In what?"

"In the will. He wants to leave you the shop. He thinks you'll leave it open, run it yourself. He's put a clause in there that it's yours if you'll run it, and if you don't, the place will get sold and the money will get added to a music scholarship fund at the university. Oh Frederick, I'm only telling you this because I've been trying to talk him out of it. It just sounds like a make-work project for you; I know you don't want to run the shop. You'd end up having to handle the sale of the building and all the inventory and everything."

I looked around me at the racks of hanging guitars, the disordered recorders, the curling sheet music; a thin layer of dust lay over everything. Salt stains on the worn carpet. I breathed in that so-familiar musty, musical smell. I didn't know what I would do without the place.

"No, I can't really run the shop," I agreed.

"It's not making any money, you know. It's costing us money to keep it open."

"I know," I said. My elbow was on the accounts ledger.

"But you can't tell him that," she said. "He won't hear anything like that. He just refuses to believe the evidence." Her voice was overtired, and I thought she might cry. But then I heard her sniff deeply, and I imagined her wiping a handkerchief across her watery eyes. "He's here now, Frederick. He's in the driveway. I have to go."

"Okay," I said, "talk to you tomorrow."

That was how it went. Every day, seven minutes of conversation with grief, about grief. It was almost more than I could stand.

I'M A POSTIE; I DON'T MIND WEATHER. It's one of the requirements of the job. Guys who hate it when it rains for three weeks in a row aren't going to last. But, *Jesus*, it had been raining for three weeks in a row, a bitter cold rain that got under your skin and into your bones—and into your vocal chords. Voices were damp, and notes were flat; students and choristers were painful to listen to.

"Holy Raindrops, Batman! Could it get any wetter?" I handed Ed two pieces of mail across the counter. The ink was running on the envelopes. My poncho made rivers on the floor.

Ed took them distractedly. He was more interested in the Joe Louis he was trying to unwrap to eat with his tea. I took the packaged cake from him, ripped open the plastic, and handed it back soggy. Funny thing, the guy can still move those fingers like lightning over the ivories, but he has trouble unwrapping a fake chocolate cake.

"Dammit, these're both for you," he said with his mouth full.

"I know," I said.

Ed grunted and tossed them under the counter. He has an old person's fondness for letter mail.

When I got back just before three, I had to dig them out from under the Yellow Pages and the Fender guitar catalogue. I put them out on the counter and was ready to slit the tops with

Ed's plastic peanut butter knife, but Juanita came in early and got her umbrella stuck in the door so I had to go rescue her from being pierced by a spoke. After her lesson, I had to dig the letters out from under the Community Telephone Tree for Ticket Sales and the hand-written accounts book. I just can't convince Ed to download accounting software; he has to do it by hand.

He was using the plastic knife, so I took a music stand clip off the display on the counter to open the envelopes. The first one was an overdue cheque from one of my students, but the second was a handwritten letter. I read it—it took all of three seconds—and then made some kind of involuntary noise, a quarter-note of surprise, and avoided looking over at Ed.

He came and stood over my shoulder, chewing his peanut butter toast. "Don't mind me," he said.

"Huh," I said. I held it up so he could read it. To do anything else would have given him an even clearer signal that it was important.

Please, it said. *Call me back.*

There was a phone number, but no signature. It really didn't need one. I could still recognize the handwriting. I put the letter down, and Ed looked directly at me with his forehead all tightened up. I could see that from the corner of my eye. I kept my focus on the page, because there wasn't anywhere else that was safe to look.

Ed was still breathing peanut butter into the damp air.

"This a new kind of fan mail?" he speculated.

I grunted. I didn't know what to say. I just felt sick. I had seen the spectre face-on and had recognized it as the Ghost of Christmas Past.

ALEX GOT HIS HAIRCUT AS DIRECTED by the choirmaster, and came to school the following day—my second day at St. Mary's—with his severed blond forelock tied into a tuft at the end of a chopstick, like an oversized paintbrush. He held it between his fingers like a cigarette holder, inhaled loudly at the end of the stick until the saliva rattled in his mouth, and pretended to drop ash into the obsolete inkwells drilled into our wooden desks. Then he dipped his sham brush into the non-existent ink, and tried to paint an imaginary moustache on the face of one of the itinerant boys milling around his desk. It was my first experience of his quirkiness.

"You idiot," said the boy, and struck the thing out of Alex's hand with a backhanded swipe. It arced to the floor and skittled under the cast iron radiator beneath the classroom window. For a moment, Alex was left with his empty hand suspended in the air, before he raised his other arm and began to move in some kind of parody of an Egyptian dancer. The bell rang, and the boys moved off, trailing their laughter behind them. When I looked back from the doorway, his waving snake arms were still in the air above his head, and the grin on his face was only just beginning to fade.

Nobody ever shortened my first or last names at St. Mary's, but Alex Hughes got teased mercilessly for his name. Boys called him Lick Shoes, which just goes to show that, if so inclined, kids can make any name into torture. He got teased for a lot of things, actually; he was the kind of kid who seemed to invite ridicule. He didn't do anything about it, didn't beat anybody up or call anybody names in return. He didn't run away, either, as I had done at Central Elementary when the bullies were after me. He didn't hold his breath in terrified anticipation, as I had with my brothers. Alex laughed it all off, but there was something about that laugh—how it always ended on a higher note than you would expect—that once I got to know him better, could tell was insincere.

ST. MARY'S WAS A DIFFERENT KIND of high school. It wasn't only the absence of girls that made it an anomaly. It was the presence of music more than anything. Like a holdover from another era, it took "twentieth-century boys" and "Western art music" and put them together like you might put bulls in a china shop—if you expected the bulls to act more like nightingales, and expected the china shop to be rather more like upscale Berkeley Square in London's West End. In lots of ways it was a fantasy on everyone's part. While I was there, I wasn't afraid of anything, even death; I thought I was already in the afterlife.

For Alex, boyhood was another kind of afterlife, much worse than anything I felt I'd suffered through before arriving there at the place—or so it first had seemed—of my salvation.

I DIDN'T SLEEP MUCH THE NIGHT AFTER the letter arrived at The Whole Note. After choir, the feeling of deep unease had grown on me, and I'd gone around the house making sure all the latches were closed on the ground floor windows and checking for drafts and stuffing a rag into the mail slot in the front door, as if the past could seep in through the cracks and find me. I didn't know what to do with the letter after I'd opened it. I hadn't wanted to bring it into the house, but that impulse was outweighed by not wanting to leave it anywhere else, for fear it should be found. I thought about going out to the yard and burning it, but I couldn't find any matches. In the end, I sat on the edge of the bathtub and ripped it into tiny pieces over the toilet, flushing about seven times to make sure they made it all the way out to the sewer. When that was done, I wandered around the house for hours, playing a few notes on the harp, opening the door of the fridge to stare at the empty shelves, and checking the phone for a reassuring dial tone.

At bedtime, I just couldn't settle down enough to go to sleep. I was sitting by the waiting sound system, thumbing through my CDs, when the phone rang. I leaned over, my heart thumping *istesso tempo*, and checked the caller ID. Of course I couldn't sleep at all after that.

WE WERE IN THE SCIENCE LAB, dissecting rats. Alex had been paired with Eric, and I with Kevin, and the four of us stood around the two rats laying spread and pinned on the square table, the air heavy with the stink of formaldehyde. Our science teacher was talking to us about *urogenital systems* and *body cavities* and *seminiferous tubules*.

"How can you tell if it's a boy or a girl?" asked Eric, poking at the rat with the end of his pencil.

"Males will have a penis and scrotum—" the teacher began, but the whole class was laughing.

"Look, Lick Shoes," whispered Eric, "it's bigger than yours!" He poked some more, and a tiny pink penis emerged from the white fur.

"—and females will have a urethra and the vaginal orifice—" There were howls and hoots, and some boys at the next table put their fingers in their ears.

Eric and Kevin laughed. Alex was laughing too. His fake laugh. So I laughed too, but I didn't think anything was funny. I laughed, I think, to cover my own embarrassment.

"Okay, boys, settle down," called the teacher. "They're just *body parts*."

THERE WERE FIVE SOUNDPROOF practise rooms at St. Mary's, grouped at one end of the long hallway that ran the length of the second floor. Each room had a resident piano, a scattering of music stands, a small handful of stackable chairs, a chalkboard—though there was rarely any chalk—and a wooden bench under a row of coat hooks by the door. On the outside of the door itself, under a notice that said "No Food or Drink Allowed," was a sign-up sheet for time slots before and after school started, and for lunchtime. The junior boys had a monopoly on lunchtime; we weren't allowed off school grounds, and were less likely to be able to arrive early or stay late.

Most days, Alex booked himself a half-hour slot. The rooms weren't perfectly sound-proof. I could stand in the window alcove at the very end of the hall and listen carefully while the muted notes of five different melodies ran together like disparate colours, creating a blanket of white noise. From one room, piano; from another, perhaps violin or viola; from most, treble and soprano voices.

Alex favoured the room closest to the stairs, though he invariably approached from the hallway, which was lucky. If I ran up the stairs quickly enough at the end of morning classes, I could check for his name on the list, duck into the room, take the paper bag out of my backpack, lay it on the bench, and run back into the stairwell before any of the other boys got there.

Only once, the very first time, did I write his name on the bag, so he would understand it was for him.

Sometimes I crouched on the landing for five or ten minutes, pretending to tie my shoes. When I'd heard five doors slam I came back to stand in the window alcove, and I waited while backpacks and book bags were searched for sheet music. I heard the strings start up, first in one room, then in another. The music was almost always something we were learning in choir or band. A voice from the third room joined in, and then the fourth: piano scales. From the door closest to the stairwell there was no sound. It always made me smile, that ten minutes of silence. I knew Alex had found his lunch.

I WENT THROUGH MY DAYS at St. Mary's in a kind of ecstatic dance in which it seemed that everything I sang turned to gold and gilded the lintels of the school, the beakers in the science lab, and the choirmaster's baton. For the first time in my life, I felt I was *connected* to something, had friends, and loved learning. I drank it all in—the glittering concert halls, the names of the fancy cars that dropped off and picked up my classmates, and the thoughtless disregard we displayed for the street people when, once the cars had pulled away, we ran around the corner to the coffee shops and bought *lattes*—the latest new thing. I came to know a whole different class and culture, and pretended I belonged there. My shadowy friendship with Alex Hughes was a secret thing I never admitted to. Now I see him always standing tragically just outside our circle; then, I paid him little public attention.

His successes, while celebrated, were tinged with an air of inadequacy, as if the entire school felt he could do better and was holding something back from God. In hindsight, I am not sure he could have done better, except to be less tired and to stand up for himself once in a while. His voice was exquisite, and he always gave his singing his utmost. If there was any drop of him that he did not pour out into those ethereal notes, I did not hear it. He was pure Voice. But if my coming to St. Mary's had displaced him from that most illustrious spot, it almost seemed that they were waiting for me, so quickly did they announce my supremacy; indeed, one might have thought that they had chosen me precisely for this purpose.

He was punished for things that seemed trivial or contrived. It was as if they thought they could discipline the affectation out of him. Once he was kept late because his tie lay over his shoulder like curled seaweed after he had run to choir practice, another time it was because he had neglected to put the sheet music in order, and another, because he walked to chapel without his shoes, his red heels showing through the holes in his fraying socks. His shoes had been taken off his feet while he was held down by a group of boys, and the scuffed brogues had been hidden behind the creaking hall radiator by Kevin—we all knew, but Alex never once spoke up in his own defense. He took the teasing of our classmates and the punishments of our teachers with laughter, as if he were careless of the calamity that followed him from room to room. He appeared determined to enjoy the joke along with the rest of us. Knowing he could not escape notice, it seemed he resigned himself to being the centre of ridiculing attentions.

Set down a notch, no longer the One Best Voice, they made Alex Hughes into a kind of shadow twin, a *doppelgänger*, despite his fair hair and pale complexion.

In the end, it seems that I was the dark-hearted one, as my Madrigal heritage would suggest.

"LOOK HERE," SAID ED. He was behind the rack of hanging guitars, and I thought for a minute that he wanted to show me something. I half stood up, one heel still resting on the lowest rung of the wooden stool.

"What's up? Another mouse?" The previous week, he'd discovered tiny chew marks around the sound hole of an ergonomic Iberica. He'd gone immediately to the hardware store up the street and bought a four-pack of lethal looking plastic mouse traps, loaded them liberally with peanut butter, and set one in each corner of The Whole Note, hidden behind upside down music stands. I didn't really want to know whether he'd caught anything.

But today it wasn't about a mouse, though it sounded just as serious. He came quickly out from behind the guitars, sending them all swinging like someone had walked into the shop with the North Wind behind him.

"Do you have enough money?" he demanded.

"I think I can buy us lunch," I said, and reached for my wallet.

"I didn't ask if you have *any* money, I asked if you have *enough* money."

"Enough for lunch?"

"Enough for life!"

"I think I should go get us a couple of muffins, at least. You could make some tea." I thought maybe his blood sugar was getting low.

"I'm not hungry," he said, and he almost stomped his foot with impatience. He was across the counter from me by this time, and he leaned toward me with his elbows on the concert posters we'd been asked to put up, making dents in the head and left knee of the lead singer of a band called Tapeworm. "Do you have enough money to live on? Do you need a car, a new car? Does your house need new windows? Maybe a new kitchen? You know, stuff like that."

"You're asking me if I need a new kitchen?" I asked, incredulous.

"Right. Oh. Right." He stood upright, and his eyes rolled in his head a little. "A new piano?"

"Are we talking about your will, Ed?" I demanded, finally catching on. I could see from the way his eyes flickered that I'd got it. "If you leave me any money, I'll kill you," I told him. "And then I'll just hand it all right over to the scholarship fund, so you might as well save me the tax implications!"

"A new lawn mower?" he asked.

"I don't need anything more than I already have," I assured him. "In fact, I need a lot of things *less*."

"A new toaster?"

"Not one penny, or I'll kill you."

"Ha," said Ed. "But I'll already be dead."

"I'll throw your urn in front of a bus," I said.

ED'S ILLNESS. MY BROTHER'S WEDDING. Alex's phone calls and then his letter. There was an element to all the things that were happening in my life that felt otherworldly. It was like a return to my childhood when, other than during my midnight singing, I never once felt my life was in my own hands. Even when things began to get better, I first felt it was because of my benefactors, and, after my conversion, that it was the will of God. After my mother's stroke, when God left me as suddenly as He'd first appeared, I felt—and still feel—like a piece of driftwood in the cold waves of Lake Ontario. But drifting with the sun shining, and with land always in sight, so it really wasn't as bad as it sounded. I don't want to sound like I'm complaining.

It used to be that when people turned away from God—or God abandoned them, whichever way it happens—they turned towards science. But who can credit science anymore? Physics these days is like science fiction. Parallel worlds, time travel through black holes, eleven dimensions, string theory. This last belongs to quantum physics, the physics of the very small, subatomic particles like quarks and a bunch of other things like neutrinos that nobody has ever heard of. It seems that all these subatomic particles are simply notes on a plucked string, and change as easily as a harpist plucking the string in a different place produces a different note. Physics is the harmony and chemistry is the melody and the universe is a symphony, and it's all supposedly a neat package of cosmic music. But there are still questions about whether anyone is plucking the strings, writing the score, conducting the symphony. The hands of God still cannot be proven. Or worse, disproven.

The new kind of "fan mail" jangled my nerves, even while I was at work. I began to feel anxious while I was still in the sorting depot. I started to put any letters addressed to me in my jacket pocket instead of in the mailbag, defying years of well-entrenched habit, just in case Alex sent another one.

I read my letters in the washroom of the bookstore, but there were only notices of concerts or offerings of new music products. Sandra must have thought I had a digestive problem;

locked in for five or ten minutes at a stretch, and red-faced and sweaty when I handed back the key. Once I tried throwing everything out unopened, but retraced my steps up the block and fished them out of the garbage can again, fouled by spilled Coke and a banana peel. Lots of days I added fifteen or twenty minutes to my route time; people who'd set their watches by me began to shake their heads and look at the time as I passed their elastic-bound bundles over their shop counters.

I've known all along that you don't get away from the past that easily.

"I'LL SING YOU A SONG FOR YOUR BIRTHDAY," Alex announced. "I don't have any other present."

He had come to join us in the cafeteria, pulling a chair from another table to a corner of ours. There were eight of us already there, and the table's surface was spread with chip wrappers, the ragged crusts from salami sandwiches, chocolate milk cartons, and orange peels. Nobody had moved even an inch to make room for him, so he sat on the very edge of his seat and held his empty hands in his lap.

The birthday presents were for me, and I was overwhelmed by this novel manifestation of friendship: a Rubik's Cube, a brick of chocolate, a trading card-sized hologram of a naked woman whose enormous breasts shook from side to side provocatively when the card was tilted back and forth. That—along with the monogrammed bottle opener I'd gotten from Kevin—was already in my pocket, both tucked away immediately after their unwrapping before the lunchroom monitors caught sight of them. I am not sure which of them would have embarrassed me more.

"Which song would you like?" asked Alex. "Not 'Happy Birthday'—that's too predictable. Name something you really like that you haven't heard in a long time. Just say the title. I bet I'll know it."

There were a lot of eyes on me, waiting eagerly for my answer. I couldn't think. There was a buzzing kind of noise in my ears, a tinnitus of indecision.

"I can't think of one," I finally said.

"What about 'The Last Rose of Summer?'"

"Oh shut *up*, Lick Shoes," said Kevin. "He said he can't think of one."

"'The Water is Wide?'" he persisted. "'The Fields of Athenry?'"

"Folk music is just plain lame-ass stupid," declared Eric.

"I don't think *any* music is stupid," said Alex. He wasn't defending himself, but an art form.

"Right then, how about singing 'I am a Loser,'" suggested Reid.

And he started, of course, laughing at himself as he did so, making up the words as he went along:

I am such a loser all the time
I am just a stupid jerk
Oh a loser and a jerrr—rrrk

All the boys were laughing; we were all laughing. But even singing those terrible words his voice was beautiful.

On my way home from school that afternoon, I tucked the hologram into the crack between my subway seat and the wall of the train, leaving only a small corner exposed. I imagined someone finding it, maybe an old man, maybe the cleaners, maybe another boy my age who would be amazed at his good fortune. The bottle opener I was afraid to simply leave somewhere, having at that time a ridiculous sense of the likelihood of being tracked down in a city of several million merely by the initials FM. Instead, I got off and walked between Castle Frank and Broadview and threw it from the overpass into the Don River.

“ASHLEY, IS ANY SOUND COMING OUT of your mouth, or are you just moving your lips?”

“I hab a coud, sir.”

“If you have a cold,” I told them all for the hundredth time, “you need to stay home until you are better. Next week everyone will have a cold,” I said to Ashley.

“I dibn’t want to biss anything,” she said. “I lub choir too much to stay homb.”

It’s hard to give them heck when they say things like that.

“Come on down and sit in the pews, at least. You won’t miss anything, and we’ll all miss getting your germs.”

A conductor channels electricity, heat, light, or sound. All of these things are produced by a good choir, though sometimes miracles are a required ingredient in the recipe. I was tired and in need of a miracle. A good number of them had taken turns having colds and flu and broken legs and mysterious rashes. They’d had aunts visiting from China and had gotten new puppies and had been given way too much homework by unsympathetic teachers. Some of that homework, doubtless, had been peed on by the puppies. The excuses had been legion. All this to say that rehearsals had been missed. And Ashley knew exactly how to mollify me.

I took them through “Danny Boy” one more time.

“Okay, okay,” I said, when they’d barely gotten through the last line. “Let’s take a break.”

Jiro put his foot on the soft pedal and looked over at me. "I'll go down with them," he offered. What he meant was, "You stay here," since we both always go. It takes two of us to monitor both the water fountain and the washrooms. He turned off the piano lamp, swept his child up onto his shoulders, and motioned for Ashley to join them.

"Wash your hands before you touch anything," I told her as she went by, but I knew it was wasted breath.

I sat in the pews on the opposite side to where the germs had been sitting. I could hear the kids' feet going down the wooden stairs, in a curious multiplication of sound that made me suspect I was conducting an army choir, and they were all wearing their combat boots in church. After a minute or two they'd gotten to the bottom and gone along the hallway, and I could hear only the faintest of noises: soprano calls and distant laughter. I looked at my watch and closed my eyes. I had ten minutes.

"Are you all right?" said a voice.

I opened my eyes and saw Alex standing in the centre aisle, his fine hand resting on the end of the pew. As I looked at him, he tossed his blond hair back with a shake of his head, and I saw with relief that it was Blake, not Alex.

Alex is not twelve. Alex hasn't been twelve for twenty-five years.

"Sir?" Blake said. He tilted his head to one side, and did the hair thing again. It was uncanny. But he looked genuinely concerned.

"Thanks, Blake. I'm just tired."

"You're never tired," he asserted.

"Well, I am today," I told him. "But I'm okay. Don't you want a drink?"

"No. The water down there tastes like chemicals."

"There's ginger ale," I suggested.

"I don't like ginger ale," he said, and then he hesitated. "Actually, I'm not allowed ginger ale."

"Ah," I said. "Yes. We should get juice, I suppose. For choir nights."

"You won't tell anybody I said that, will you, Sir?" he was suddenly anxious.

"No, I won't say anything," I reassured him. "I'm good at secrets." He was relieved, and changed the subject.

"Do you like directing our choir?"

"Yes, I do, very much," I said. "Do you like singing in it?" I slid over so he could sit down. It seemed I wasn't going to get rid of him.

"Yes," he said, sitting. He pulled a hymnal out of the slot in front of him and flipped the pages absent-mindedly. "I'm good at it, aren't I? Is that being conceited?"

I laughed.

"No, that's not being conceited, and you *are* good at it. You're very good at it. We'll see what happens after your voice changes, but you could probably have a career in music if you wanted to."

"I don't know yet," he said. "I'm only twelve."

"Right," I said. "No rush. Just keep singing." There was a bit of a lull then, as the book fell open and he ran his finger down the lines of a hymn. His lips were moving slightly; he was singing the music to himself. Then he flicked his hair back and lost his place.

"You remind me of a boy I went to school with," I told him then. "He was very good at music too."

"Did he make a career out of it?"

I didn't answer right away. I saw an eighteen-year-old Alex "Lick Shoes" Hughes pulling on his coat in the cloakroom and running out into the snow, crying. His gloves fell out of his pocket as he went, but he didn't stop to pick them up.

I could hear the first pair of army boots coming up the stairs.

"No," I said, finally. "He didn't."

"LET'S GO BACK," SAID ALEX. "I'm tired. Aren't you tired?"

"I'm not tired," I told him, but I was dead on my feet.

We'd been taken to see *The Pirates of Penzance* and were going the next day to a matinee of *Twelfth Night* before boarding the chartered bus for home. We'd gone back to the motel with our chaperones after the performance, changed out of our school clothes into our "civvies," waited patiently for them to be convinced by our deep breathing, and then had risen from our beds fully dressed and exited by the back door.

It was all Eric's idea. He had produced a flask of rum stolen from his mother's liquor cabinet, and some of the boys were drunk. They were singing loudly.

Oh is there not one maiden breast
Dah dah dah dah dah dah-dah dah-dah.

"Frederick? Where's Frederick?" called James. "*He* should be singing this!" Much had been made out of the fact that the play's protagonist and I shared the same name. And that we had been taken to a play where someone sang about women's breasts.

Oh is there not one maiden breast—

"Maiden breast, fuck me!" said Brian.

"I'm going back," said Alex. "They're just being assholes." We were slightly behind the row of boys strung across the road like lanterns in the wind. "They're going to do something stupid."

"They're just having *fun*," I said. I was trying to believe it.

"Hoy, Frederick!" Kevin was in the middle of the string of boys, and was looking for me over his shoulder. "Where are you?"

"I'm *going*," hissed Alex.

"I've left some for you," Kevin shouted back, and he held the flask of rum up over his head like a trophy.

I was in the centre of an expanding universe. The line of boys was moving forward and Alex was moving backward. Their bodies drifted in slow motion, like planets in orbit.

"Come on, Frederick, *please*," pleaded Alex. "Let's go." His hands were in his pockets, and his shoulders hunched forward defensively. He looked like an old man nervous about falling.

"Hoy, *Frederick!*" shouted Kevin impatiently. There was no doubt in his voice that I was one of them.

Out of my orbit, I ran to join them, singing along.

For I am a Pirate King!
And it is, it is a glorious thing—

Eric broke off the singing and turned to watch Alex pass beneath a streetlight and run off alone into the dark.

"You better not narc us out, Lick Shoes!" he called after him. "If you do you'll be shitting teeth for a week!" The whole line of boys laughed.

"What a loser," someone said.

In front of us the Avon River slid darkly by. Stratford was as far as I'd ever been from home, but there was something about how I was feeling that made it seem that I was as close as I'd been to my Madrigal heritage in a long time.

LAKSHMI, GODDESS OF WEALTH AND PROSPERITY, was recently reincarnated in India, but instead of having only the four requisite arms, she also has four legs—an improved version. Or I should say *had*, because doctors cut off all the spare parts—four of her limbs, much to the distress of the local people who worshipped her.

I read the article over three or four times before I got out my scissors. I thought long and hard about those extra arms and legs. So much more substantial than fingers.

These days stories like this make pretty much every major newspaper around the globe. I wondered how it would be, as an adult, to read such reports about oneself. I imagined this newspaper cutting—with dozens of others, and photographs from every angle, and maybe even medical reports—being put carefully into a scrapbook on the other side of the world. How would it be to know that all the world had once seen you as something else, no matter how ordinary you now seemed. No matter how alone you appeared to be.

Lakshmi's twin was referred to as a "parasite" by the surgeon who led the operation. The procedure to eliminate the evidence lasted twenty-seven hours and involved more than thirty doctors. Goddess or host, Lakshmi survived the operation.

I wondered what they did with the discarded arms and legs: perhaps buried or incinerated them or pickled them in formaldehyde for medical research. What *do* they do with body parts no longer wanted on the voyage? I looked at my hands; thought about my missing fingers. Thought about missing Filander. Thought about being alone.

Six flesh and blood brothers, and I want the one I haven't got. I can't even say Filander died, because he never even existed except in my endless longing. For me, there was not even the comfort of his loss.

When Lakshmi was grown, I wondered how she would feel about losing her divinity.

THERE ARE MORE LISPS AMONG THE YOUNG than you would think. The choir was singing *She's like the Swallow*, and "swallow" was coming out more like "thwallow." There's nothing you can do about that but wait for them to grow out of it.

She slike the river that never runth dry

Likewise, you can only wait for them to grow into their bodies, for all the body parts to come into alignment—and you can only hope they don't ever look closely enough in the mirror to notice how discordant they really are. There are small child heads on trunks that seem practically adult-sized, and large heads on tiny bodies, so thin and frail-looking that I wonder how they can carry their brains around without wobbling like bobbleheads. Some of them have arms so long that they can almost touch their knees without bending over; others have legs like stilts and walk as if they are always too far from the ground. They are like those paper people divided into three sections—heads, bodies, and legs—and somewhere in the universe a hand reaches down and flips the pages around so everything is mismatched, the head of one on the body of another. They are mythical creatures, children. Sometimes I feel as if I am conducting in a cartoon.

She slike the thunshine on the lee thore

We had the parents there. We had been rehearsing for weeks for the occasion, and I had nagged them to be on time, and tidy. And, since it was an official concert, the kids got pretty worked up about it, excited and nervous and more inclined to look as if they had been dragged there against their wills, and were going to throw up or faint while singing. Like dogs, children yawn when they are anxious. The result is that it is generally hard to tell that they are thoroughly enjoying themselves. I just have to trust that the parents know this as well as I do.

'Tis out in the garden thith fair maid did go

There are exceptions. Those few who grin widely, even ludicrously, the entire time, in between the syllables of the words to the song, unable to contain their delight, and oblivious of the concept of performance anxiety: Ashley and Emily and Ryan. Or those whose faces, like miniature opera virtuosos, portray the emotional content of the song so well that even a deaf person would understand what they were singing about. They can make us believe that their teenaged hearts know exactly how it feels to be betrayed by a lover: Blake and Stephanie. These are the few who carry the choir through evenings in front of an audience, as if their beaming and expressive faces have the power to light even the most stage-struck of their peers.

How foolish, foolish you must be
To think I loved no one but thee

When we get to the end of the song, Jiro looks at me from the piano, and we wait through the exuberant applause, fifty people sounding like two hundred, in a four-fold appreciation of their talented offspring. As if they could get their children to smile by clapping, or clapping harder. As if to prove they do not drag them, screaming, to the Limestone City Youth Choir.

The lights are dimmed in the church. We ask the parents to sit in the first few rows and we put tall candles at the ends of the pews; the resultant atmosphere is like an intimate pre-historic gathering in an isolated cave. There's something about darkness in churches that insulates you from the world, and can make you feel smaller even than when standing under the bowl of the night sky and praying to the stars.

The clapping began to die down, and I nodded at Jiro, and he began to play the next selection on the programme, the Kenyan children's song *Kanyoni Kanja*. The lisp is not so noticeable now, because there's only one family in the audience that actually understands the words.

The theme for this year's concert is "Songs of Childhood." I've used this one a couple of times, and it's getting harder and harder to help kids find something other than the Beatles, Michael Jackson, or Mötley Crüe. That's from the ones whose parents played music at home, so they actually heard tunes from somewhere other than the television. Those who didn't suggest the theme songs from *Fraggle Rock* or *Inspector Gadget*.

"No, no, no," I say. "Children's songs. *Folk* songs. Lullabies."

They go back again and ask their parents, and, if they have any nearby, their grandparents. Eventually they get the idea, and "Kumbaya" and "Mocking Bird" and "Lavender's Blue" straggle in like lost boys. We sing them all until we know them, and then they vote on the eight or ten we'll do for the parents.

A month and a half ago, when we were first picking out songs, Becky put her wavering hand up while I was re-arranging their standing order so those having growth spurts would be in the back row, and, without waiting for me to call on her, blurted her question in my direction.

"Sir," she asked. "What about you? What about *your* songs from *your* childhood?"

Some people claim they see their lives flash before their eyes when they are in the gravest danger. Me, I heard my mother's entire repertoire in the split second before I answered her.

"That was so long ago, Becky," I joked. "All those songs are in the old folks home!" And I moved right on to "Oyfn Pripetchik" and "À la claire fontaine."

But all through the concert I kept thinking about my mother, standing alone in our kitchen, singing and swaying, while a small boy sat silently, listening intently, effortlessly memorizing the words, just out of sight down the hall in a dark doorway.

THERE WAS A LETTER FOR ME lying on the mat when I pushed Annie's door open. I recognized the handwriting straight away; it was from my mother. I ripped it open and unfolded the single page, looking only for the five-dollar bill. I did, for once, feel grateful for it, though I was inclined to think of the hand of God in this stroke of luck rather than my mother. I didn't even read what she'd written, and left the letter crumpled on the hall table beside the vacant envelope and my soggy gloves. I went back out again right away, leaving the gloves to stain the wood as they dried.

There was a hardware store on the Danforth; one of the kind, now all-but-disappeared, that sold everything. I wandered up and down the aisles as if I were a criminal furtively looking for the "common household ingredients" with which to make explosives—except I wouldn't have had any idea of what those might be. Within a short while, a clerk came and asked me if she could help me find something, but I told her no. After that, she saw something to rearrange on every shelf I walked past, and kept her eyes steadily at my hands—which began to shake a little under her scrutiny.

I lingered a long time in Home Décor, staring at the innumerable gallons of paint stacked in precarious towers. The shadowing clerk relaxed a little then, knowing that I couldn't slip one of those monstrous cans underneath my jacket.

Finally, in Automotive, I found the touch-up paint for cars, in miniature spray cans. There wasn't a lot of choice of colour, and I deliberated a long while with the clerk so close behind me that I could hear her scratching behind her ears. There was no yellow, no off-white or cream; I finally chose Bright White. I wanted to practise putting it in my pocket to make sure it would fit, but I didn't dare.

After I paid for the paint, I stuffed it into my jacket pocket, and ran as fast as I could back to Annie's, knowing she would be getting home soon, and worrying about my suddenly-remembered gloves drying on the hall table. I ran up the steps two at a time and pushed open the door.

My gloves had already been carefully removed to the top of the radiator. Annie's half-folded umbrella was dripping obediently in the stand. Annie herself was bent over, unzipping her boots.

"Oh, I—"

"Is something wrong?" she asked me. She unbuttoned her tweed coat and took a hanger from the closet, sending the others into a rattling complaint, *risvegliato*.

"I just needed—"

"Yes?" She uncoiled the scarf from around her neck. "What did you need?"

I did think about lying, but I couldn't think fast enough.

"*This*," I said, and I took the paper bag from my pocket and shook the spray paint out into my hand.

"Frederick," she said doubtfully, "I hope you're not going to take up model airplane building?"

THE NEXT DAY, I waited until I had Geography, which was in a classroom on the second floor right next to the washroom. Once the bell rang for class and the hallways were clear, I ducked past the BOYS sign with my Bright White bulging in my pants pocket. I shook the can vigorously, as instructed in tiny print on the tiny can; the tiny ball bearings rattled like dice being rolled by elves. I held my breath for as long as I could and sprayed, watching the paint obliterate the letters L ... I ... C ... K ... S ... H ... O ...

The nozzle jammed, and I wiped it clear with a wad of toilet paper from one of the stalls, careful not to get any paint on my hands. I continued spraying, turning my head away from the noxious fumes to gasp air as I worked. If I kept my eyes wide and my vision out of focus, the letters looked like random lines, a careless doodle, an indecipherable secret code. They were just black lines with no meaning. E ... S ... S ... U ... C ... K ... S ... C ...

The can was empty. I shook it again, wiped the nozzle several times, turned it upside-down, and hit it against the edge of the sink. Nothing more would it spray.

There was a giant Bright White cloud-shape of paint on the yellow wall. At the bottom edge of the cloud, still visible, were the letters OCK. A Bright White drip trickled down through the O.

I put the empty can in the bag and threw it in the garbage. I unrolled half a roll of toilet paper and threw that into the garbage on top of the can in the bag. I washed my hands, scuttled out of the washroom waving my wet hands in the air, and ran up and down the hallway to try to leave the lacquer smell behind me. I had thought the whole operation would only take a minute, but it had been more than ten, and as I ran I tried to think of what excuse I'd make for being so late for class.

"DID YOU SEE IT?" HE ASKED ME, but his mouth was full of pizza so I could pretend I hadn't understood what he said. "Did you see it?" he tried again after he swallowed.

"See what?"

"In the washroom."

"What?"

"What they wrote."

"Oh," I said, "that. *Ock*. I didn't know what it meant. Do you?"

"What?" he said.

"Ock. O-C-K. Someone wrote Ock. What the heck does that mean?"

"Ock?" he repeated, confused.

"Dumbass thing to write," I told him. "Doesn't mean anything. *Ock*-ock-ock-ock!" I stuffed my last bite of pizza into my mouth and flapped my arms like a chicken until he laughed.

"HEY FRED," SAID MY ANSWERING MACHINE, in my brother's voice. "Just checking in. Johanna wants to know if you could recommend some instrumental music—you know, some background noise—for the part where the communion business is happening. Got any ideas?"

Beep. Erase.

There was nothing in my fridge except some mouldy strawberry jam, half a jar of kalamata olives, four slices of black forest ham, and an empty pizza box. I took out the pizza box and unfolded it, then folded it up again—flat this time—and jammed it into my overflowing recycling bin. I ate the ham and a handful of olives as I made my grocery list, and piled the pits on the counter beside the new book I'd ordered online.

I'm not good at grocery shopping. I'm not good at food, period, so I guess for me shopping is just one element of a whole package of nutritional incompetence. I do know what's good for me, but I don't want to have to buy it or prepare it. I don't object to trying new foods, like some people do; I just can't seem to care enough to think about ingredients or recipes or the temperature of the oven. I think it's got something to do with the fact that I had to start preparing meals for myself at eighteen, and never graduated to cooking for two. I'm still an adolescent eater.

I've heard that it's not a good idea to go grocery shopping

hungry, to preclude buying up the entire store. In my case this isn't a problem, since buying too much is preferable to buying nothing. If I weren't hungry, I'd never go. Besides, since I don't have a car I have to carry everything home, which places definite weight restrictions on the appetite.

I took my knapsack and walked up to the Loblaws. It hadn't snowed for a week, and the snowbanks that lined the streets were grey and hard.

I suppose there was a time when I thought quite a bit about cooking for two. Sooner or later, I had imagined—perhaps *assumed*—I would find a woman I liked well enough to be with. Human beings are fundamentally hopeful creatures. We can hold on for a long time, but, as the years pass, it's hard not to notice that there is less and less evidence for hope. I can't say that I've given up, but I don't think about it much anymore. Big things get buried in the mundane. Life goes on. Oneness just is.

My breath rose translucently as I walked. The store was busy, and there was a bit of a traffic jam at the automatic doors, with people coming and going, and a general lack of available carts. A woman in a pink ski jacket came out with a small cart, pulled on her gloves, and lifted out a couple of overfull cloth bags, and I was in the right place to grab the thing. If I just fill the bottom of the cart, I can usually manage to carry the stuff home without too much trouble. I am, after all, used to carrying heavy loads. I could always take a taxi, but there's something depressing about the thought—something too obviously solitary about it—so I hardly ever do.

I wheeled up and down the aisles, knowing what I needed without looking at my list, because it's what I always buy. Bread, orange juice. I try not to look at couples and families in there, but I always look in other people's carts if they're shopping alone. Eggs, cheddar cheese. I look to see what they're buying, to see if I can guess if they live alone. It's usually pretty obvious. Frozen dinners.

I was standing at the deli counter, contemplating supper, when it happened.

"Weeell, *hello*," Kathleen said. She had come up beside me, her hand still resting proprietorially on the front edge of her shopping cart. Her coat was off, and shared cart space with a host of fruits and vegetables, a bag of whole wheat flour, and a twelve-pack of plain yoghurt.

I was instantly in a panic. "Hello," I said, flustered. "What are you doing here?"

"Probably what you really mean is *What the hell are you doing here when* I'm *here?*" she suggested. I wasn't sure whether she was joking or angry.

"Oh, no," I said. "That's not what I meant." But it might have been. And then there was a pause that it seemed up to me to fill, so I said "*Well....*" I didn't know whether one meaningless word would be enough to make something else happen. In a glass case beside me a half dozen chicken carcasses rotated on a spit.

"You could have called me." Okay, so she was angry.

"I *was* going to call you," I said. "Didn't I call you?"

"You left me a voicemail," she said.

"Only one?" I asked. The heat—I hadn't taken my jacket off—and the smell of roasting chicken was making me feel light-headed.

"Only the one."

"Well, I was going to call you," I assured her. "*You* should have called *me*. Things have been busy—Ed, and the shop, and all."

I assumed she'd have heard about Ed's health, and she didn't ask for clarification, so I guess I was right. Or maybe she was too mad to care what the hell I was talking about.

"I fed some of the salmon to the dog," she said.

"I *was* going to call, *really*, and ask you—I was going to see if you wanted to—I was going to invite you to—come to Toronto with me, for my brother's wedding."

How can it be that things come out of our mouths that are not at all what we planned to say. Somewhere in a Twin World, another Frederick bravely admitted that it was only cowardice that made him unpredictable. I thought about him longingly. The chickens mocked me as they turned.

I WOKE UP IN THE MIDDLE OF THE NIGHT with a jolt. I had been dreaming, and realized in my dream that I'd been tricked. I'd never had any intention of going to Salvador's wedding—my plan had been to rustle up a terrible cold or flu at the last minute—and now not only was I going, I was planning to take a woman who had a car and a cottage and who cooked planked salmon on an open fire.

It was raining ice; I could hear it clanking against my bedroom window. I looked at the clock, groaned, then quickly tried to reassure myself—told myself to keep calm, breathe deep, sleep was still possible—but really, by the time I get to that point it's already too late. It would be another godless night, the weight of the universe pushing in on me, my heart a black hole. All black holes have what's called an event horizon; when things get drawn in past this point, they can't be seen by anyone on the outside. That was it: the story of my life.

The furnace came on, and the duct work began to creak as it warmed. I got up, put on my robe and slippers, and went downstairs to the kitchen, turning the thermostat up some more as I went through the living room. The strings of the sleeping harp vibrated as I passed.

I poured some milk into a mug and put it in the microwave. I made it too hot, and burnt my upper lip. Plans are often better in my head than they ever turn out in real life. *How* could I have let this happen?

And then in an unwanted and unwelcome vision, my spirit hung in the air over the Loblaws deli counter, and I was looking down at my own face tinged green from the heat and the florescent lighting and the sheer stupidity of the moment. I knocked my forehead against the top edge of the fridge, *largamente*. A skin formed on the surface of the milk.

Like the third ghost of Christmas, I flew again, still unwilling, and lingered high above the chancel and all the children of the Limestone City Youth Choir, and Becky was asking her earnest question—what about the songs of *my* childhood? I could see myself standing slightly below them, music stand glinting in the muted light. But the scene replayed with a different result. I didn't laugh it off, or make a joke, or move right on to "Danny Boy."

"The songs of my childhood are curious lullabies," I said.

I watched as I told them instead about St. Mary's Choir School, and my favourite Christmas carol, the one I eagerly awaited every year, once the snow began to fall. The one I sang to myself a thousand times walking between the school and the cathedral, my head down, watching the rhythm of my feet.

Earth stood hard as iron, water like a stone
Snow had fallen, snow on snow, snow on snow

I walked with the rest of the choir, boys jostling each other and slipping on patches of ice. Father Gregory watching us to make sure we didn't get too out of hand. A younger boy holding the side entry open while we all filed in, leaning with all his weight upon the great wooden door.

And then I was suddenly younger, and hadn't yet left for St. Mary's, and the cathedral was St. George's, and belonged to the Anglicans. The junior choir boys were filing into the rectory door, and it was a crisp night, a Christmas Eve, and the snow fell on our hair as we took our hats off and looked up at the soft flakes falling like silent stars. I was in front of the congregation, every pew full, stepping forward into the light with a child-like reverence for holiness, and I sang the solo just as I had in my final year at home.

Panis angelicus
fit panis hominum
Dat panis coelicus
figuris terminum
O res mirabilis!

There was such a quiet in the congregation, and my voice rose through the vaulted ceiling and into the dome, walls like poured cream in the candlelight. In the silence afterwards, a baby made half a cry and was hushed, a man coughed, and the spirit-filled space closed in around all of us, warmed with a sense of destiny.

Afterwards, I walked home alone through streets of houses lit with strings of coloured lights and friendly with hope. My own childhood house was dark, and I undid my tie before I crept in to go to bed. But I didn't go to bed; it wasn't Christmas, it was every other night of the year when I waited for my mother to sing. I sat just inside the doorway of my room, holding the curtain that hung there raggedly, watching her rise from her chair and put one hand on the Formica countertop, watching her centre herself, take a breath, and begin to sing what was surely one of her favourites—a song I knew by heart before I was five, she sang it so often.

The water is wide, I cannot get o'er
Neither have I wings to fly
Give me a boat that can carry two
And both shall row, my love and I.

I leaned my back against an oak
Thinking it was a trusty tree
But first it bent and then it broke
So did my love prove false to me.

My mother was singing to the kitchen walls, and I was

hiding. She sang this song as if her heart were breaking with it, a sweet and piercing pain, the notes so full and clear, even in that cramped space. I watched as I pulled aside the red curtain and stepped into the light of the hall, a bare bulb hanging from a broken fixture. How easy it seemed, to walk the ten steps towards her, to open my mouth and sing along. I *did* know the words. She saw me coming, and she didn't stop singing, she sang and I sang, and she reached out her hand to me, almost there...

And then I was standing in my kitchen, alone, singing one of the defining songs of my childhood, my hand on a granite countertop, the milk cold in the cup.

Oh love be handsome and love be kind
Gay as a jewel when first it is new
But love grows old and waxes cold
And fades away like the morning dew.

WE WERE WAITING IN THE HALL in single file—a long line of navy blazers, hardly visible in the half-darkness, punctuated by bright white collars and maroon ties and lit by the whites of eyes, those twin windows of the soul. We weren't allowed to talk, so each boy moved slightly, shifted his feet, leaned to one side as the boy next to him searched his pockets for nothing or bent forward to scratch his knee, so that words could pass back and forth between us without being detected by the choirmaster or the monitors, who would put you down for detention for the first offence, and make you sit out of the performance for the second.

I pretty much never risked it. There wasn't anything important enough to say except for the music itself. I waited in a kind of calm anticipation for the cathedral to fill with people; we could see a small view of the left aisle from where we stood, and flashes of dress or dinner jacket moved across this small screen like fragments of a dream as we are waking. I watched this space with interest, making a game of fitting the fleeting movements to the notes in my head—a pre-concert of my own creation. Even though I was watching, my eyes remained unfocused on the specifics. I registered colour without my brain naming the colour; I registered leg or arm without reference to bodies or anything except rhythm and beat. There was a roaring kind of echo as our audience filled up that great space, footfalls ringing on the stone floor, handbags dropping on pews, people talking freely amongst themselves.

Alex was directly in front of me. We would be singing a duet together, Arne's "The Lass with the Delicate Air," arranged for two voices. Usually, our only interaction came just before we were about to start moving into the cathedral toward the choir stalls, when I would give him a poke in the ribs with my elbow or a kick on his shin with my polished shoe, the signal that it was time for him to return to this world from whichever other place he normally inhabited. But that day he was already in the real world, and fully present. For once, he too was focused on the patch of light ahead, the high doorway where colour and movement and sound flickered. He was craning his head, moving this way or that as the line of boys ahead of him undulated like the body of a snake in a cave.

I watched him for a little while without thinking anything. His movements and those of all the boys in front of us and the monitors transecting the hallway and the growing audience made a symphony. I was content to conduct. But after a few minutes, his activity began to register as out of the ordinary.

He was trying to see into the cathedral, as if he were trying to pick out a face or a recognizable cuff or collar or pant leg. But nobody ever came to concerts for Alex. I couldn't think of who—or what—he was looking for.

I turned my head towards the wall and spoke quietly into Alex's ear, with only a minimal moving of lips. "What's up with you?" I asked him.

"I had a dream that my mother was coming," he answered, his eyes still focused on the distant doorway.

"Hughes! Monday detention!" hissed Braithewaite, the monitor.

The long snake was moving, curling out of its dark den into the incandescent house of God. We entered singing.

"DID SHE COME?" I ASKED, though I already knew the answer. During the concert, I had seen him look, and look—his eyes travelling back and forth, back and forth, across the rows of people seated in the pews—and finally give up looking, and stare hard at his choral book, though he knew every note it contained.

It was a Sunday, the day after the concert. We'd come home from mass together on the streetcar, singing Sydney Bertram Carter's "Lord of the Dance" with all our breath. Annie had made us pancakes and had gone out for a walk before we were halfway through the stack, for fear of missing the fading sunshine.

Neither Alex nor I were overly concerned about the sun, and had gravitated to Annie's music room when we'd finished eating. I was lying on the settee with my legs hanging over the wooden armrest. Alex was lying on his back on the carpet, his bent legs resting on the piano bench.

"No," he said. He lifted his legs straight up in the air and began to pedal an imaginary upside-down bicycle. "Well, anyway," he added, "I didn't see her."

"It was just a dream," I reminded him.

"She might have come," he said, hopefully. "I don't actually know what she looks like."

"You must have a picture," I protested.

"No," he stated. "They don't give you anything until you're eighteen." He put his calves back on the bench.

"Not too much longer to wait, then," I reassured him.

"I guess," Alex said, staring at the plaster medallion on the ceiling. Then he hummed a few bars of a tune I didn't recognize.

"What's that one called?" I didn't have to ask who the composer was; I knew it was him.

"I don't know yet," he answered. "It's about my family."

"Do you even know anything about them?"

"No."

"Nothing?"

"No," he said, "so I have to make everything up."

"You can have all mine," I said flippantly, "and make a song about them."

Alex was never flippant. "You only want to get rid of them because you know them," he answered earnestly. "If you didn't know anything about them, you'd do anything to be introduced."

I thought about not knowing my brothers, but all I could see was relief. "I don't think so," I said.

And then, as is often the way with boys, we'd done enough talking. Alex leapt up and launched into "Simple Gifts," the old Shaker song that Carter stole his "Lord of the Dance" tune from, as a round. Alex started with—

'Tis the gift to be simple, 'tis the gift to be free
'Tis the gift to come down where we ought to be
And when we find ourselves in the place just right
'Twill be in the valley of love and delight.

And after the first line of the second repetition, I came in with—

When true simplicity is gained
To bow and to bend we shan't be ashamed
To turn, turn will be our delight
'Til by turning, turning we come 'round right.

I don't know how many rounds we sang, trying to make

things right. It might have been an hour; it might have been two. We were inside the music, and it was inside every cell of our bodies. Distantly, from far away, I heard the front door, and felt the draft, when Annie came home from her walk. I felt the delicious full feeling from the pancakes wear off, and I saw the light change in the garden as clouds covered the whole sky. We wore our voices right out, but only stopped when Annie briefly poked her head into the music room to interrupt us and beg for a change of tune.

We watched her retreat once again to the kitchen through double sets of French doors. She wore pink knitted slippers, and her feet made no sound on the hardwood.

"I think my mother was probably a prostitute," said Alex hoarsely.

THE HOUSE OF MY CHILDHOOD is up for sale again. I took a walk down my old street on Saturday during a brief reprieve from the myriad forms of frozen precipitation we'd been getting for weeks. The grey-toned blanket of the sky was ripped into a hundred irregular pieces. The sun shone weakly through the narrow spaces between the cloud fragments, brightening the January sky and casting thin shadows under the bare trees. Lots of people sitting inside their houses noticed that the light had changed, pulled back curtains, looked out their frosted windows to search for an explanation. A few even came out into the street to gaze at the sky, or, like me, decided to go for a walk; we had almost forgotten sunshine, and shadows were the stuff of dreams.

The "For Sale" sign trembled a little in the wind.

It seemed a strange time to try to sell a house, in the dead of winter. I thought of the young couple I'd seen earnestly fixing the front step, wearing designer jeans spattered in flecks of lime paint, with the knees frayed and worn. The two of them, straightening their tired backs and wiping their sleeves across their foreheads to keep the sweat from stinging their eyes. Looking at each other and then not looking at each other.

"Getting divorced," I bet myself. But then I thought maybe they had just planned it this way, planned all along to fix it up and sell it, move on to another. Some people do that, I know. As if a house is just a roof and walls and wires and pipes. But our histories are there, underneath the new surfaces. Everything gleams and shines, but memories are still trapped in cracks and crevices and false walls and chimney flues. My lost boyhood, sealed in there like a time capsule for ghosts.

I'd been planning to go down to the river by Belle Park, but I turned the other way instead, back towards downtown. In between the doors at the real estate office, I picked up the most recent copy of *The Real Estate Book*, ducking in and out quickly so I wouldn't be seen by the agent on duty. The office was on my mail route; I can't go anywhere downtown incognito.

"AS YOU CAN SEE, THEY USED THIS as their office, but it could easily be used as a third bedroom." She was stating the obvious, but that is often the nature of real estate agents. I'd picked her from one of the new realty offices on the edge of town, her photograph, with the announcement that she'd recently joined the firm, confirming her youth.

"If you need the space," she said. "If you needed the third bedroom."

I grunted. I wasn't giving her anything. We were up in the front room, overlooking the street. I'd steered her upstairs as soon as we'd entered. I thought starting upstairs would be safer.

The house was full of beautiful furniture, but empty of clutter—*staging*, they call it now—and there was a curious echo when she spoke, an airless kind of vibration, as if the life was already gone out of the house along with the occupants. We'd left our wet boots on a cork mat in the hallway downstairs, and our feet made no noise on the refinished floorboards. Everything was immaculate; even the tops of the baseboards had been scrubbed. The walls of the office were inclined towards the yellow of ochre, and there was a fine wooden double pedestal desk pulled up in front of the window. Colourful framed prints hung on the walls, Aboriginal artists like Moses Beaver, Daphne Odjig, Norval Morrisseau. I went around trying to read the signatures, while *Inexperience* tapped her stockinged foot in the doorway. All numbered originals.

But I was just killing time, and I knew eventually we would have to go back downstairs and look around.

"Improvements to the house include all new windows, those, you know, *energy efficient* kind," said the agent. She said "energy efficient" like it was something she'd memorized out of a handbook. "The house is super insulated. The oil bills are very low. There are copies of the spec sheets for the house down on the kitchen counter. If you want to go downstairs?"

I think I was beginning to make her nervous. I grunted again, trying to smile reassuringly, and motioned for her to go on down. I held tight to the handrail behind her, relaxing my grip only enough to slide my hand down the freshly painted wood. I could hear a thunder of feet charging down stairs, perhaps from the house next door in the row. *A big family,* I thought to myself. At the bottom of the steps, she turned to her right and stopped under the living room archway, looking up at me expectantly. I could hear a door slam and tennis balls being thrown against the bricks, *giocoso*, somewhere outside.

"The living room," she said. She rested her hand lightly on the back of the leather sofa. "See, the windows are all new downstairs too. And they've really opened up the house to the light. It's made quite a difference to the feel. You can see right through to the kitchen." I poked my head into the room, and sure enough, the cheap paneling had been removed from the wall between the living room and dining room, and an interior window had been cut between the dining room and kitchen.

I went down the hall and stood to the left of the original archway, just inside the dining room. There was a dark table, stocky and square, with two chairs along each side. A vase full of pink roses was set on a beaded mat in the middle of the table, and a solitary pink petal had fallen onto the gleaming wood. My chest was tight, but I pivoted on my sock feet until

I was leaning inside the doorway, looking down the hallway into the kitchen. It wasn't very far at all, perhaps six or eight feet. There was no door there now, the door jamb completely replaced so there weren't even any rectangles chiseled out for the hinges.

No cracked asbestos tiles, no chrome table, no sagging plaster, no dripping tap.

The agent followed me down the hall and went to step into my line of sight, but I quickly put out my open hand to signal her to stop. She jumped back nervously, and I was sorry, but I couldn't help it. When she got back to her office and told them about it, they'd teach her about the speed dial buttons on her cell phone, and the code words for "Help!"

I kept my hand up to block the hallway, and I looked. I turned my head and listened.

There was a kitchen island where my mother would have stood leaning up against the counter. I couldn't see her sway, or watch her expressive arms keep time. I couldn't hear her singing.

"Would you like to see the kitchen now, Mr. Jones? I'll just get you that spec sheet?"

"I don't need to see any more," I said.

She was happy enough to go and get her shoes and put them on with her hand on the door knob. I slipped my own boots back on, and we both went quickly out on to the front step. The street was deserted.

The door shut behind us, and she fiddled with the lock box. The wind was blowing her hair sideways, and she brushed it away impatiently.

"Why are they selling?" I asked. Suddenly it seemed the most important thing in the world. "Are they getting divorced?"

She looked up for a moment, a strand of hair caught in the corner of her mouth.

"Oh, I—no, they just—they're just *moving*," she said, flustered. "They're just moving someplace *else*."

THERE WAS A BRIEF SHIFT IN THE WEATHER later in the month, one of those slightly warmer days when the air turns the snow to rain, but the ground holds firmly to winter. Cold rain fell down in sheets slantwise against the vinyl and clapboard and brick on the sides of buildings. It covered the dirty streets and froze into a smooth, treacherous, shining blanket. It was the ultimate worker's compensation claim waiting to happen. I strapped metal coils onto my boots and walked my mail route gingerly, like an old man with thin bones.

From Dave's cell phone I had called Sylvia to tell her to keep Ed at home. On my way down Princess Street I let myself into the shop, cancelled my afternoon music classes, and wrote an apology for the door in case any customers actually made it out—though I wasn't too worried about the possibility. The Whole Note has few enough customers these days even in the best of weather. I stomped and slid and tiptoed through the almost-deserted streets in an erratic tempo, accompanied by the faint music of falling icicles, and grasped at railings, lamp posts, and letter boxes whenever they appeared. Luckily, the rain stopped before I was completely soaked; the water solidified in the creases of my coat and crackled as I dug into my mailbag.

WHEN I GOT HOME FROM THE SHOP on one of those kind of days, Alex Hughes, Second Best Voice, was sitting on my front step.

There had been one other time much earlier in my life when Alex found out where I was living and sat waiting on my step until I arrived. I'd gone home after Introduction to Financial Accounting and found him halfway up the outside staircase that led up to my student apartment, directly above the vents, his clothes and his hair steeped in the sweet stink of dryer sheets.

He'd been drunk. He'd stood up when he saw me and thrown up over the railing. I'd taken advantage of that preoccupied moment and run away. I'd hid in the university library among the periodicals and read about landscape architecture, whose aisle I haphazardly found myself in. When I dared return, late that night and for weeks afterwards, I could smell the lingering stench of vomit lifting on the hot air under my feet.

Although I hadn't seen him since, and we were both more than two decades older, I didn't have any trouble recognizing him. His face still looked young—younger than mine did, I think. His darkening blond hair was long enough in front for him to need to flick his head back when he looked up, and he still had a shadow in his eyes—though it was different, somehow, perhaps now holding more ferocity than deference.

He had a newspaper folded up under him, and he looked pretty cold.

"Frederick," he said, and he got up stiffly, and held out his hand.

I took it, and shook, though I worried even in the moment that he might take that for a sign of some sort, and made it as brief as possible. He wasn't wearing any gloves, and his hands were like cold iron. I didn't look; I was afraid of what might be visible in the space between his cold hand and the cuff of his jacket.

"I called," he said. "Did you get my messages?"

I think someone should write a book about the history and uses of the invocation of left messages: that act of sending information, where there is a time delay between sending the message and its delivery, and often a physical distance between sender and receiver. How this time and space disruption allows for interpretation, suggestion, insistence, and bluff. In fact, in the neat absence of procurable proofs, the doors are thrown wide open to downright lying. It's not really a very secure system of communication. It wasn't the first time I used this to my advantage.

"Messages?" I said. "No." We were standing on the porch, and his newspaper was still lying on the top step, unraveling in the wind. Neither one of us did anything about that.

"Look," I said, "I can't invite you in; I've got to go out tonight. I've only got a minute or two to get ready." I didn't want to tell him I was going to choir. I didn't want to say anything about music at all.

"Sure," he said. "No problem. I'll come another time."

"I'm pretty busy these days," I told him. "Sorry."

"Right," he said. He was nodding slowly, sizing up the situation, figuring out what to say next. He half turned away, and I thought he was just giving up, but he turned back again, and that look in his eyes turned out to be determination. "We could talk. We could finally get past it."

"I don't know what you're talking about," I answered back.

"You—"

"There's *nothing* to get past!" I interjected. There was more than a shadow in my voice; there was a full body of raging anger. It was so foreign to me that I didn't know how to feel it. I didn't know where all this disquiet was coming from. I just wanted my perfectly guarded life back.

He opened his mouth, and closed it again. He just stood there looking at me, it seemed like a long time, pursing his lips and nodding slightly to himself, as if he had half expected my response.

"I'm sorry, Frederick," he said apologetically. "I didn't mean to bother you." There was a peculiar look in his eyes. As if *he* felt sorry for *me*.

"WHAT DO YOU THINK OF THAT NEW PIECE?" Alex asked me. We were sitting beside the path, under a tree in the Allen Gardens conservatory, and Alex was brushing tiny stones from between his knees and tossing them ineffectually at the trapped pigeon that strutted a revolving path around us, just out of reach, waiting for crumbs.

"Which one? The Purcell?"

"Yeah." He sang the first line, the notes flowing like water, his *cambiata* voice, in that moment, untroubled.

Come, come ye sons of art, come, come away

"Woolly," I pronounced, deepening my own voice and tucking in my chin as I said it, the way our choir director did.

"Arse!" Alex said, laughing, and he hit my shoulder with the back of his hand. A trickle of dust fell down my neck.

"Woolly, woolly, woolly!" I repeated with fake seriousness, as I ducked and rolled out of his way. It was a word the choir director used often in those days, in a room full of choir boys, some of whom could no longer be counted on to sing the right notes. My own voice had changed, but Alex's hadn't fully. There's a certain quality to a boy's changing voice; it's not quite treble, but it's not quite anything else yet. Alex's voice was lurking in an alto-tenor range, but some of his notes were true renegades. He didn't seem worried by it. He just laughed when a note broke, as if it were something easily put back together.

"You could knit a sweater with that voice!" I said. He threw his book at me, and the startled pigeon fluttered three feet into the air and landed a little farther away. I caught the book and opened it upside-down, pretending to read, still imitating our teacher.

"Master Hughes, please sing *baaaaa*!" I put my hand to my ear.

"*Baaaaa*, *baaaaaaa*," said Alex, obligingly. "*Baaaaaaaaaaa.*"

"I can't hear you Master Hughes! Can you *baaaaa* louder?"

"*Baaaaaaaaaaaaaaaaaaaaaaa*!" he brayed.

"You sound like a real sheep!"

"I know," agreed Alex.

"Real sheep shit."

"*Baaaaa, baaaaaaa*," said Alex.

"Why do we need to have shits in the choir, anyway?" I said, mimicking the voice Kevin had used when he had said exactly that to Alex earlier in the afternoon.

"Fuck off." Alex's voice changed then. He said it lightly, but there was a waver—and a warning—in his words that wasn't due to his voice breaking. He wasn't playing any more. He reached for the book he had thrown at me, grabbed it out of my hands, snapped it shut, and unzipped his knapsack.

"What?" I asked, "I was just teasing!" But then I was uncomfortable in the silence that followed. Alex had his head down and was collecting his things—his choir notebook, a mechanical pencil, the crumpled pizza wrapper—and ramming them into his bag. He stood up, and bits of gravel rained down around him. He brushed off the seat and knees of his pants.

"I better get going," he said.

The afternoon felt ruined, but I didn't know why. I was angry at myself for it. I suppose that was why I couldn't let it drop. I had to take it out on someone.

"You should try standing up for yourself, for a change."

Alex picked up his bag and put it on over his blazer. The pigeon spotted a crumb and sidled up to him, pecking the ground and cooing.

"Fuck off," he said to the pigeon, angrily. He kicked at it, and it flapped up and away like a dirty newspaper in the wind.

"Why don't you stand up for yourself, sheep shit?" I asked him. I was goading him so he would answer me.

Alex turned his head then, and gave me my answer. "*Fuck off, Frederick*," he said between his teeth. His face was bright red, and his eyes were like wood. And he turned toward the exit without asking me if I was coming.

I sat slumped on the path in shock. Alex reached the banana tree and didn't look back.

"Wait!" I called after him. "Wait!" I got up frantically and looked around at all my homework spread out around me, my music book turned to *Ave Verum*, black and red and green pencils piled like the end of a game of pick-up sticks.

"Wait!" I yelled. I didn't know if he could hear me. He didn't even slow down.

"Why don't you just tell *them* to fuck off?" I screamed at him. He turned a corner and disappeared.

I stood there until the pigeon came back. When I kicked out

at it, dust tickled down inside my untucked shirt and fell onto my open music book like lost notes.

I DIDN'T EVEN WAIT TO SEE if he picked up the newspaper. I closed my front door with Alex on the other side of it. I was late for choir—or I would be if I didn't get a move on.

I went upstairs to splash my face with cold water.

I couldn't help myself; I went into the front room and approached the window from the side, moving my head slowly around the edge of the curtain, so I could look out onto the street without being obvious about it. Alex was still out there, leaning his hip against a car parked on the road opposite my door, head bowed, huddled into his coat, and sucking his cheek in indecision.

As I watched him, he fished in his jeans for his keys and unlocked his car. He got in and drove away without looking back at my house.

ALEX HAD ALREADY BEEN AT ST. MARY'S for three years by the time I arrived. Until that point, he had enjoyed a kind of immunity from the worst of what the rowdies might deliver, since he did have a very rich voice; before mine, the former One Best Voice, which was currency at St. Mary's. Before puberty he had more range than I did, and an alarming breath control—a talent he used as often to win breath-holding wagers as he did to hold a note during choir practice—as well as a remarkable memory for a musical score. We were so often paired in choir, a duo of fine voices—the Two Best Voices—and were selected to perform solos and duets at countless masses, concerts, and funerals. Our teachers, unknowing of its relevance, even referred to us on occasion as "our St. Mary's singing twins." Fair to my dark, erratic to my staid, I was so sure he was nothing at all like me—nor, I was doubly sure, like Filander.

I was newly come from a public school where my notorious brothers had paved the route before me, but it was a road I had refused to travel. When the bullies at Central discovered I was more inclined to hide than fight, they sought me out everywhere. I thought it was clear what side of *that* road I would always be on.

At St. Mary's, there was no longer any reason to hide. My voice went in front of me, both my sword and my shield. I did not know—didn't care to know—why Alex's voice did not protect him the way mine protected me.

When I said the two words to Alex Hughes that changed the course of both of our lives, he did not look shocked, or even surprised. Rather, his chalky face suggested he had known all along what was coming, and only ever wondered when and exactly how. He looked at me only briefly, the colour draining from his over-heated cheeks, his blond hair hanging limply across his forehead. His eyelids narrowed slightly in that ever-frozen moment—or perhaps I merely imagined it—and his eyes fell from light to dark, the way I thought an animal's would as the knife was at its throat. He'd known all along that I would betray him. He looked like Jesus once kissed by Judas.

ED WAS SITTING BEHIND THE COUNTER and he had his feet up on the shelf underneath. He'd pushed aside the accounts ledger and the tea-stained mugs and the plastic recycling that ends up there because he can't be bothered to take anything back to the storeroom and put it in the blue bin. I had to lean over the counter to hand him his letter, and the edge of the glass stuck in my chest. He didn't really look at it as he took it, just held it loosely in his hands and kept staring at the toes of his sneakers. He wiggled his feet back and forth as if he were hearing some silent melody, but I couldn't decipher the tune from watching the rhythm.

"It's from Annie," I said. He seems to need a lot of encouragement these days to interact with the things of this world.

He looked at the envelope then, and grunted.

"Open it," I said, and I stood there waiting for him to put his feet down and find a knife, even though I was dripping melting snow across the display of classical guitar strings. He clattered among the cups and found a knife that actually appeared to be unused, but wiped it across his pant leg anyway. I watched until he had the knife inserted under the flap, then turned to go back out and continue my route. I had the next door shop's pile of mail in my left hand, and my right hand was on the bar of The Whole Note's door, when he said, "*Annie.*" It seemed he was saying a lot more than just one word with her name.

I turned back to look at him. The letter and knife were still in his hands, but he hadn't used the knife and the letter was still unopened.

"Why don't you write to her?" he asked. It was like he'd saved up pennies for twenty years just to buy that one little question.

"Why doesn't *she* write to *me*?" I answered. It was impulse. I didn't really think about what he was saying or why he would ask me that then; I just felt resentful, and didn't want anything else to be my fault. Heat flared inside me, licked the inside of my skin with instant fury. "Why are you on about this now, anyway?" I asked him whitely.

"It seems like you blame her for something," Ed said. He was angry too.

"I'm not blaming Annie for anything," I argued. "I'm grateful to all of you." But I heard the tone of my voice and the force with which I spoke, and I knew I didn't sound grateful at all.

I put my hand back on the bar and pushed. I heard the shop bell tinkle, and, as the door opened, a bus roared by and threw slush across the sidewalk like an unwelcome offering from a careless hand. I went out into the street, and it seemed like the whole world was a roaring bus, overfull with impatient riders, the ill-mannered driver counting the stops until the end of his shift.

I WAS SEVENTEEN YEARS OLD before I knew the true story of Filander. It was Annie who told me about polydactylism. She looked it up in a dusty volume of the Encyclopedia Britannica, searching haphazardly under *poly-*, after I told her about my missing half, my parasitic twin, and showed her the scars on the outside of my hands.

"*Wherever* did you get such an idea?" she said. She had that air about her, as she often did, that suggested, in the nicest way, that my vocal talents made up for my lack of brain function.

"My brothers told me," I explained, and as soon as I said it I had the terrible feeling that she was going to be right about my brain. How could I have believed *any*thing told to me by my brothers, and for so long?

"I have the proof," I insisted, holding up my hands, holding on desperately to the frail shadow of my twin slipping from my grasp. "Look!"

And then she got the Encyclopedia from the shelf under the stairs.

"Poly ... poly ... poly..." she muttered to herself as she flipped the thin pages. "What's it called? *Poly*-something...."

I didn't want it to be called poly-anything.

"It's *Filander*!" I said then. It might have been the first time I had said his name out loud. It was the last.

It was about a week before my final St. Mary's Christmas concert at Massey Hall. I am not sure what inspired me to share my deepest secret with a woman who was guaranteed not to play along with a fantasy, no matter what the emotional fallout might be. In that house, truth always came before feeling. For Annie, Truth was God.

"Nonsense," she said. "It's a gene mutation. It has nothing to do with twins."

She looked up, exasperated, from the open leather-bound book on her knees. I can remember the colour of the ruddy leather against her pale flowered dress, and the way the fabric hung in bunched-up folds, caught under the book and between her thigh and the hall chair. The mid-afternoon light from the transom above the front door was already weakening, and she looked to me like a fading spectre; her ghostly finger pointed at her place on the luminous page.

"Turn on the light, Frederick," she asked. "I can't see what I'm doing." And it was true, she couldn't.

I think of that night as the pivot point of my last year of high school. Before that night's revelation, everything in my life felt like it was moving me towards perfection, orchestrated by the hand of God, and afterwards everything slid rapidly downwards into an unsounded darkness.

I had scars on my hands because of a gene mutation.

I had never had a twin, not even the little finger of one.

I have always been alone.

PRETTY MUCH RIGHT AFTER FILANDER'S DEATH by *Encyclopedia Britannica*, I decided that seeing God on my bedroom wall was suspect. After I left Annie's, I spent months reading about emotion-induced hallucinations and the meaning of dreams, and by eighteen and a half I'd filed God away in the never-never land of theta waves and rapid eye movements. Twenty years later, I'm not so sure it's that clear-cut. I can't make myself believe or unbelieve things just because I want to.

I look back at everything that happened to me in the first two decades of my life, and it seems such a wandering tune to get me where I am now. Such an inexplicable series of events, C leading to D leading to E leading to F, where all the notes have a pitch that is strange and new and never previously heard by the human ear. How can we know beforehand what the music will sound like? How can we make sense of it afterwards, the notes always discordant and aleatoric? Sometimes I think that all the music I make is simply a confused attempt to create harmony out of an untuned, solo instrument. The piece is already written, libretto and score, and I can only interpret the sounds, sing the words, weigh the silence. An impossible task.

EVERY MORNING I GOT UP one day closer to the wedding and the knot constricted in my stomach, like an over-taut harp string, ready to snap. I slept less and less, and wandered through my music room hearing the silence of the strings and skins. Somehow, I almost always passed them by and ended up at the back of the house; I sang more and more often alone in my kitchen at all hours of the night.

On the morning that there were only twenty-eight days left, I looked at the calendar and noticed that I had arranged to meet Kathleen for supper at the Sea Biscuit. Ed still wasn't showing up regularly in the evenings, and when he did he was more inclined to sit silently than sing, and I had grown a little tired of sitting around waiting for things to get back to normal. I guess I hoped if I just got through all the wedding business as quickly as possible, my life would begin to settle down again. At that point I could still let myself think things would be normal again, one day.

Besides, I didn't know Kathleen from a hole in the ground, and she didn't know me from Adam, and I didn't think that was the best way for us to go to Salvador's wedding. I had finally gotten to the point where it made me weaker in the knees to think about going away with her for the weekend as an unknown entity than to think of getting to know her better before we set off.

I have to reiterate that it was all a matter of degree. On the day of the purported date, I sorted my mail in such a distracted fashion that I did not absorb any of Dave's updates on the kitten's antics. He can talk as he sorts, and I can't, and he knows this, so luckily he failed to notice that I wasn't paying the slightest attention. I walked my route that morning feeling like a sleepwalker, with streets and numbers more mixed up in my hands than they had been since I was a novice postie. The chimes and bells that hung over the Princess Street doors were like an entire fleet of alarm clocks, but none of them were any use, and I couldn't seem to wake up, no matter how many shop doors rang as I went in and out. When I walked up the steps to the Sea Biscuit, with Neil's bills—for fish batter and seafood sauce, presumably—ready in my hand, my muscles felt so weak I could barely get the door open.

"Guess we'll be seeing you tonight," Neil said when I handed him the envelopes, tapping his finger on the reservation book, and I thought my knees would buckle for sure.

Outside, I could smell snow, and I figured perhaps there was a storm coming. The air was damp, and blew in from the lake in a spectacular hurry, like late-breaking news.

After work, I had three voice students, and in every case I found something to criticize with last week's repertoires, so we wouldn't have to go over anything new. When I finished the last one—Becky from the Youth Choir, as it happened—I called Sylvia and sent Ed home early, and then, despite what I'd told him to get him to leave, I locked everything up, turned over the sign on the door, and headed home myself.

I just had to propel myself through a little bit more of the day, I thought. I just had to get through it, and then, miraculously, it would be over. God knows I've been through worse.

I was fresh out of the shower and staring hopelessly into my closet, pants on but belt unbuckled, searching for the right shirt, when the phone rang. There were three rings, and then the machine picked up, but there was no message. I didn't bother to go look at the display, but it rang again almost right away, so I crossed the bedroom with one arm into a grey flannel shirt, had a quick glance, and picked it up.

"Frederick?" It was Kathleen. She said my name after a moment of hesitation, like she couldn't decide whether to talk or hang up.

"Yes," I said. I looked at my watch. The chosen shirt hung from my arm, and I switched hands on the receiver so I could get my other sleeve on as I talked. I don't know why, but I didn't know what was coming. I pretty much never do know, but still, it always surprises me that I don't. Things seem so obvious in retrospect. You'd think even an idiot could figure them out.

"Yeah, well, so," said Kathleen. "I was just going to let you sit at the restaurant for a while, waiting for me. I thought you might even go ahead and order the wine before you figured out I wasn't coming."

"You're not coming?" I asked her. I don't know what I was feeling. It wasn't exactly relief.

"No, Frederick," she said. "I'm not coming."

"Oh." My body hadn't caught up with my brain and I was still frantically trying to do my shirt buttons up, one-handed, thinking I was late. I thought of the day I had just spent, every excruciating minute focused on something that wasn't going to happen—or at least not yet.

"Did something come up?" I asked. "Do you want to reschedule?"

"Why would I let you order the wine if I was going to reschedule?"

"True," I said. "Right." There was a pause. I didn't know how to hang up. "So what happens now?" I finally asked. I laid my forehead against the cold glass of the window.

"What happens now is you cancel the reservation, have a drink in my honour, and reflect on the nature of justice or fairness or equality, or whatever you want to call it."

"How about 'an eye for an eye?'" I suggested. Through the foggy glass I could see Maya's truck pull into her driveway and stop abruptly, too close to the fence.

"Sure," Kathleen said, congenially. "You could call it that."

"So," I said, "Toronto...?"

"No, really Frederick. We can't pull that off at this point, can we?"

"Okay," I said. I couldn't think about anything except getting off the phone, but as soon as I saw Maya get out of her truck and start rearranging those damn pipes, a bizarre impulse started to form in my head.

"When you get back from the wedding," Kathleen's voice said in my ear, "you can call me if you want. Now that we're even."

"Right," I said. I pressed "end" and got the dial tone at the same moment that I finished doing up my last button, just a fraction of a moment before my legs started to move out into the hall and down the stairs. I opened my front door, at the precisely the same moment that Maya's left foot was on her top step, her copper supply clattering under her arm. It was a perfectly timed, totally dumb, completely self-redemptive and face-saving dance. Maya looked over at me and smiled.

"Do you have any plans for dinner?" I asked her.

"SO WAIT A MINUTE," SAID MAYA. "You're telling me this Kathleen woman asked you for a date and you didn't go, and, on the other hand, you've been pining over this *other* woman, this *unattainable* woman, this *married* woman at the library—for *several years* now?"

It wasn't like I had expected a response that would demonstrate her compassion and understanding.

"Freak, Frederick," she continued, "don't you see the pattern here?" She looked at me with triumph. I struggled to focus my brain on this nefarious pattern.

We were drunk on a bottle of Maya's *gallo nero* Chianti and a newly replenished supply of Rickard's Red—I knew Ed wasn't going to be drinking it anymore, but I couldn't stand to see the fridge so bare without it. I'd bought a case of twelve as a kind of place-holder for a vanishing life.

Maya was sitting on the floor between the harp and the piano, her back against the wall and her arms resting on her bent knees. I was leaning on the opposite wall, my legs stretched out along the floor, looking up into the belly of Jiro's second cello, left in my living room much of the time so he didn't have to drive it over every week.

We were surrounded by empty bottles, scattered like ninepins. The case was in the middle of the room, flaps open, almost empty.

Maya burped loudly.

"S'cuse." she said.

"I don't get patterns when it comes to women," I explained. "I'm pattern-impaired."

"I'll explain patterns to you."

"No," I said, "*don't.*"

I tipped the last dregs of a beer into my mouth. I put the empty bottle down carefully beside me and lined my feet up as precisely as possible along the grain of the wood. When I heard Maya start to speak again I closed my eyes.

And then I fell asleep.

WHEN I WOKE UP, I was perpendicular to the grain of the wood. Maya was slumped over, still against the wall, only lying lower down. The sun was well up and streamed into the room, casting weird shadows across our faces from the collected instruments. The phone was face-up on the floor between us, like road kill.

Except it was beeping.

Maya opened her eyes. She looked around the room without moving her head. The beeping stopped.

"Oh," I said, once she stopped looking at the phone and was focused on me, "Did we sleep together?"

"Ha," she said. "Ha. And ha."

"I thought it was pretty funny."

"No doubt it is your finking sense of humour that endears you so much to women."

"Touché," I said.

"Okay," she said. "Let's talk about *funny*."

"No, let's *not*," I said. "My head hurts." I finally looked at my watch. *Shit*," I said. I reached for the phone. After a dozen years with a perfect attendance record, I was late for work. *Really* late.

DESPITE WHAT I'D SAID TO MAYA, my brain, contrary to my wishes, ruminated on patterns and women. There was a week or two when I was completely irrationally sure a message from Kathleen would be waiting for me when I returned home, when I went out sometimes solely in order to be able to come back and look again for that blinking light. No matter where I'd been, or for how long, I thought about patterns as I was turning the key in my stubborn front door lock, as I was pushing the door with my shoulder while pulling the handle towards me, as the bolt clicked open and the door swung inward, as the heat ran out to greet me, licking my face like a dog that's been left alone all day. I checked for messages as soon as I got in, before even taking off my coat or hanging my hat on the hook in the hallway. It almost felt like I made friends with the phone again, or, at least, understood that the phone could bring welcome messages as well as unwelcome ones. Whenever it rang when I was home, I looked at the display with a feeling of vague hopefulness, an elusive longing, an unvoiced wish that I could, for once, be given a second chance and do the right thing. That I could, somehow, make up for having done it wrong the first time. One night, at three in the morning, I got up bleary-eyed from my gnarly bed and made a list of questions on the back of an old Sea Biscuit take-out menu:

How long have you worked at the Grand?
Do you like it?
Do you like music?
What kind of music do you listen to?
Do you have a family?
Tell me about them.

Tell me about them, I thought. I felt a little sick as I looked at what I'd written. *Tell me about it.* It was as simple as that.

THREE WEEKS BEFORE THE WEDDING, Ed and I went for a haphazard getaway in the country, at Sylvia's urging. We go every year in May, and this year she thought if we went early it might shake Ed out of his fugue. I suspected it was more a case of her needing to be rid of him for a few days, so she could think about herself for a change. But the weather was good enough, and the roads were clear, although the snow lay in deep patches among the stark trees in the woods. And maybe I was a little in need of getting away myself.

Our yearly trips are like that male-bonding thing about fishing or hunting, except it's long past hunting season for some things, and long before hunting season for others—and we generally just drive around and sing instead of sit in a camp and drink. Well, in previous years he'd be drinking if I let him, but it's a car, and it's moving, and I'm in it. I think he has a responsibility to drive it safely.

In previous years, we'd be singing together, too, but this year he seemed inclined to let me take care of that part by myself.

We drove north into deer country—to places so overpopulated with *cervidae* that humans there have gardens like the U.S. military has Fort Knox. I have heard that hungry whitetail deer can jump eight or ten feet straight up into the air, and in consequence we saw chicken-wire-roofed garden enclosures still tangled with the remains of last year's harvest—the tips of brown corn stalks poking through the snow. We saw plenty of deer, too, standing in handfuls in the bottomlands of white fields, heads down with the confidence that they had made it through hunting season, and deep winter, and were rounding the corner on almost-spring.

I'm not all that sure what has kept me and Ed amused with each other for so long, stuck in a moving car, though I think that when there's driving going on, it's no longer considered rude not to look at someone when they're talking. I've noticed that you can say a lot more about difficult subjects if everyone's eyes are looking at the road.

Back in the shop there always seems to be business to deal with, the selling of music and our attempts to ward off bankruptcy. In my living room we just made music, loud and half drunk—*his* half—and there's not much stopping for breath to let any words get in the way of our single-minded purpose. But when we're driving, on that weekend once a year, is when I learn, without him taking his eyes from the pavement, how Ed's marriage is sliding around like a bottleneck on a resonator guitar, and how both of them are sick at heart for the children they never had, and it's when he admits that he was drinking too much Red for his own good. It's when he tells me that running an independent music shop is a losing proposition these days, what with YouTube and iPods and all manner of other things he feels too old to keep up with, and that he's thinking about retiring anyway.

"But I'm worried about the Red," he says. "What will I do with myself except just drink even more?"

"You haven't had a beer in ages," I tell him, trying to be reassuring.

"It's only a matter of time," he says, mournfully. "I can feel a tickle in my throat."

And then I sing another couple of songs, and then he asks me, as he always does, how old I am now, and when I remind him, he tells me: "You go get yourself a woman and make some babies together, Frederick, before it's too late."

And for my part that leads into *me* telling *him* all the dates I blew in the past year. I still skirt around the whole issue of making babies, since the notion of fatherhood is about as foreign as a Polynesian nose flute. So this year, in between "The Union Maid" and "I Don't Want Your Millions," I told him about Kathleen and the planked salmon. I told him too about the librarian, though I told the story lightly, as if it hadn't mattered. He shook his head a little at the salmon dinner gone to the dog, but he had a good laugh about my library fines being even worse than they used to be. And it was true that telling him about things made the humiliation tip towards humour.

"But what about that other one?" he said. "Your neighbour? The plumber? Be pretty convenient when you need to go home and find clean clothes in the morning before going to work. Just have to hop over the porch railing."

"I don't think she plays for the same team, Ed," I said.

"I know I'm getting old," he admitted, "but what the hell does *that* mean?"

"Forget it," I told him. "You don't have to keep up with the times on this one."

And then I continued my string of working songs with Merle Travis's "Dark as a Dungeon" as we turned off the suddenly ugly TransCanada into the charming town of heritage Perth, and I directed him through the limestone-lined streets to Abraham and Alistair's houses, duplexed side by side, the pointing faultless and the masonry renovated to perfection. When I got to the end of the song we sat in the car across their street and looked for a while before driving on, as if all we were doing there was admiring the brickwork.

ED AND I STAYED OVERNIGHT WITH FRIENDS of his in Lanark where there was a fine enough Breitmann piano in the living room, and a host of other instruments scattered about the lifelike legs of their Queen Anne furniture like chew toys left for oversized pedigreed dogs. The tastes of his friends, Galen and

Jane, ran from Renaissance to Baroque, and in particular to the transition period between the two, so we spent the evening in instrumental rather than vocal mode.

Ed warmed up slowly. At first, I didn't think he would play at all. Then for a while he would take his hands from the piano keys in the middle of a piece, with no warning, as if his fingertips had been scalded by major and minor chords, and the three of us would hold our collective breath, *pausa*, before he found the notes again. Or, perhaps more accurately, they found him.

But gradually, his rusted fingers were oiled by music's memory. All the melodies we shared that night were interpreted and defined by Ed's sorrow, worn on his sleeves and edging down to his deftly moving fingers. When good music gets made, we can recognize its emotional elements because the notes live in us, like the words of stories. We heard the story of Ed's life that night. At last, bittersweet between despair and hopefulness alive within the same bars and phrases, Ed began to cry—the first time I had ever seen him cry—and as he cried harder, he played harder, stroking the keys one minute as if he were making love, and the next, *appassionato*, as if he were at war and the piano was his enemy. At the *fermatas*, he wiped his nose on his sleeve, but the tears still ran off his cheeks and anointed the ivories.

When Ed cried, Jane cried, feeling sorrow on his behalf. And looking at Jane, Galen's eyes welled with tears. I remained dry-eyed that evening, but after we stopped at three in the morning, I fell onto their pull-out couch with a sense that something piercing, like a hawthorn branch, or perhaps the thin bones of a sixth finger, had worked itself out of me.

IN THE MORNING'S BITING RAIN, Jane and Galen and Ed and I drove down to the restaurant below McDonald's Corners for breakfast—middle of finkin' nowhere, as Maya would say. All four of us seemed to be moving in some kind of dream state, slow with echoes of music, and fuzzy around the edges with lack of sleep. Our server was a young woman with an old-fashioned attitude towards customer service. She took our coats from us at the door and hung them up on a wrought iron hook, and then held her hands out for a second time for our scarves and Jane's umbrella and Ed's multi-coloured felt hat.

"Wet day," she said as she showed us to a table overlooking the lake. "But it's amazing: the lake is already opening up." I followed her overly hopeful gaze outside, where thin sheets of water covered the frozen lake.

"An ice sandwich," Jane observed.

"The lake: my heart," said Ed. Everyone could tell he was drawing an analogy.

When we'd looked at our breakfast choices for a while without any noticeable effect, Ed waved the young waitress over again and told her we'd all like to have whatever the cook recommended, and we gave the menus back with relief, as if a crisis of some kind had been averted.

"I might be too tired to be hungry," said Galen, and it was easy to believe that this might be true, the way gravity was pulling at the skin under his eyes. He hadn't shaved—none of us guys had—and he ran the palm of his hand repeatedly across his emerging whiskers.

"We're getting too old to stay up that late," said Jane, shaking her head. Though we knew the drain of the previous evening hadn't been just about *late*. We all stared bleakly out the window for a while—two cars drove by, and a bundled woman walked by with a dog on a rope, both soaked to the skin—and the three guys a few tables over, the only other folks in the restaurant, talked about taping hockey sticks in energetic voices. A fourth kept getting up from the table and disappearing from view for a while, and when he rejoined them they'd summarize their discussion from the past ten minutes for his benefit.

"It's a happening place," observed Ed.

Our breakfast arrived: four mountainous plates of pancakes, sausages, and beans. Real butter in a flowered dish. Real maple syrup, served in a jar with a ladle. Four steaming coffees—and naturally Ed sent his back to get tea.

"No problem, sir," said the ever-cheerful youth. "Anything else you need while I'm there?"

When it came to down it, we were all hungrier than we'd thought.

"Oh my God, these beans!" Ed said, at his first forkfull.

"Good, eh?" Galen agreed. And then there wasn't any more desultory conversation, but sudden and surprising exclamations about the uplifting power of a good home-cooked breakfast.

"Even if we didn't home-cook it," said Jane.

"No, really, these *beans*," said Ed. "Can you believe these beans? You tell the cook," he called to our smiling waitress. "You tell the cook these are the *best beans* I've ever had."

"You can tell him yourself," she said, and at that the transient man from the other table stood up and walked good-naturedly towards us, revealing the reason for his continuous disappearances.

"You're the cook?" said Ed. "These are the best baked beans I've ever eaten," he repeated.

I looked at Ed, and I had the faintest premonition of a spark in his aging eyes, like when you hear a train whistle a long time before the train appears. A spark birthed, it seemed, by the previous night's music and tears, the lack of sleep, the frozen lake and the melting ice; and midwived most inexplicably, by *beans*, bringing something as yet undefined on the newborn surface of his face. It was like seeing Hope personified, diminutive and clothed in green, after an endless winter. There was a shift in the weight of the air around us.

"Well now, I'm glad you like them," said our cook—who was also, presumably, the restaurant's owner. "I get a lot of compliments about them. I've spent a long time perfecting those beans."

SOMETIMES I THINK WE ARE ALL LIVING out stories of mythic proportion; we are each the heroes, or perhaps anti-heroes, of our own lives. We are called, and we either agree to the trip or refuse to go. There is indeed a pattern to all things. Events are small in number but have large variations, and the patterns repeat themselves like a wheel rolling in the dirt, or a choir singing a simple round with the melody going on indefinitely: love, loss; security, fear; mastery, despair. In every one of our song-stories there are challenges, obstacles, hurdles. At every primordial turn, we ask ourselves moral questions, but the answers are given to us in symbol and archetype; and since we are merely human we cannot decipher what the gods mean to tell us.

On the drive home, Ed was pretty quiet, but it seemed a silence of acceptance rather than sorrow. I didn't sing, either, my head too full of the memories of the previous twenty-four hours, thoughts tumbling in the wheel. When Ed pulled his car up in the dusk assembling in front of my house, I didn't really know what to say to him.

"Come on over tomorrow night," I tried. "It'll be fine, even without the Red." I opened the car door, but he put his hand on my arm and stopped me from getting out.

"I'm going to retire soon," he said then. It was as if he'd just decided that very minute. "I don't suppose you want the shop?" But he asked the question like he already knew the answer.

"Sylvia told me what you're thinking, Ed," I told him. "I don't really think it's feasible."

"Sylvia told me you'd say that," he said, ruefully.

"Do you want the details?" I asked.

"No, I guess I don't need the details," he said. "I can work them out for myself. You have a job already, and the shop doesn't make enough to hire someone else to work there..."

"And the whole Guitar Hero thing," I said.

"And the whole Karaoke thing," he agreed. "Passing for music. *Pffft.*"

"And you've given me enough already," I added. I didn't want him to think I wasn't grateful.

"Oh, don't give me that crap," said Ed forcefully, with sudden anger. "What I've given you seems to be taking you your whole bloody life to get over!" And he let go of my arm and waved me out of the car, and I got my bag from the back seat without thinking of any response.

After he pulled away, I stood on the sidewalk and watched his tail lights come on at every stop sign until he turned left on Montreal Street, a well-lit warning in the ancient language of the gods.

I DIDN'T ASK ED WHAT HE'D MEANT, though I tried to. In the days that followed, when his head was bent over the Gibson, all four fingers of his mottled hand sliding on the strings, tunelessly, I didn't say "Ed, what did you mean by that?" I watched his hand, and I listened to the noise he was making with the guitar, like the distant whistle of a lost bird. When I watched him open the jar of peanut butter in the shop, and mix the jar's contents labouriously, with a knife, plunging it up and down methodically, peanut oil invariably spilling over the sides of the jar and down his fingers, I didn't say, "What am I not getting over?" I just got a dusting rag and wiped up the drips and wiped his shaking fingers, too, like I would a child's—and he let me. When he left the shop in the afternoons, putting his cold hands out thinly and pulling the door closed behind him as one might pull a lover close, for comfort, I didn't run after him and ask, "What am I not dealing with?" I watched him walk away through the wet snow for a few seconds, his shoulders hunched up against the wind, his frame so insubstantial that it seemed he might melt away with the snowflakes, before I picked up the phone to call Sylvia to let her know he was on his way home.

I practised asking him. In my mind, I asked him whenever we were together, the question voiced in my mind almost as regularly as the intake of breath in the dull air of the shop. I tried out different phrasing in front of the mirror in the bathroom, checking my eyes to ensure that they looked as casual as I intended as the quiet words emerged from my dusty throat. I looked around the store room on my way through as if I might find the question hidden there in pieces, waiting to be picked up and assembled in my mouth, a row of teeth ready to bite off anything. In my mind, I even asked him when I came in with the mail, handing over the question as I handed over the small packet of bills and letters. Nothing sounded. I pretended that I didn't want to know; we both knew that I already did.

WE DIDN'T CALL IT BULLYING in those days. We didn't call it anything. We didn't ever once think that what we were saying out loud in the school yard and under our breaths in the cathedral vestry had the power to shift the entire swirling world under our still-growing feet.

The shift occurred three days before the Christmas Concert, near the end of the first semester of our final year.

Kevin put Alex's homework in the office shredder while Mrs. McDermot was out of the room. He'd grabbed it out of Alex's hands in the hallway and run, dodging between the streams of boys moving noisily from classrooms to chapel, and they had passed it back and forth among the senior class as if playing basketball, getting ready to shoot a hoop. Alex had run after them, laughing hollowly. Still trying pathetically to play the game.

It wasn't any regular old homework. It was his only copy—in the days before computers in the schools—of a term paper due that day in music theory, a course whose successful completion was required for his Juilliard audition.

I know because I held my own paper loosely and confidently in my hands, knowing there was no threat to its security.

They got to the end of the hallway, and Mrs. McDermot came out of the office and crossed over to the staff washroom.

"Settle down, boys," she called over her shoulder, but no one paid her any notice.

Somewhere in a twin world, far distant from this one, before any single one of those sheets of paper got anywhere near that terrible machine, a better Frederick lifted his chin like a hero and pointed his slender finger at his friends. He lifted his scarred hand, and shouted, "*Enough!*"

In that other universe, Kevin returned the paper into my outstretched hand, and I, in turn, handed it back to Alex Hughes, since what we did know, after all, despite our still-growing feet, was that some things were just too big to tamper with.

But in this universe, this is what I said: "You *faggot*, Alex."

And it felt good. I enjoyed saying it; the power was all mine. I *knew*—for the length of time those words echoed in my head—that I was omnipotent, and that I could lay waste to the entire world. One of the Madrigal boys, at last. I laughed, and I watched the gang of them in that fateful dance, Alex uselessly leaping to try to rescue his future, held above his head by boys whose voices never could compete with his own, but whose height was, in that moment, worth far more than music. Boys whose savage strength was enough to hold him back in the doorway, flailing his arms like a whirligig, no longer laughing, as his future was stripped of its thin and desperate possibility.

I could have made it be different, then; I know it.

DAYS WENT BY, PUNCTUATED BY unwelcome memory. I delivered the mail and taught voice lessons and after dreaded evenings fell into bed and prayed for dreamless sleep. I never felt rested when I awoke in the mornings. Night after night I lay awake and sometimes half-awake in the dark, surrounded by the scattered fragments of my life. When my alarm went off, my heart was invariably already racing, and I pulled on my Canada Post pants in a kind of torpor, the lethargy of my body in direct contrast to the hazardous speed of my careening mind.

Through those long nights, at first, I was back at St. Mary's: still a boy, still in uniform, still in school. Still living with Annie and singing my heart out in public—at school, in church, at concerts and funerals, in the shower, and on the bus. Those images should have been nothing but comforting: me singing—unrestrained, unselfconscious, utterly free of guilt or remorse. I belted out all my favourite songs, and the world went about its merry business. I remembered how children feel when they first discover Christmas; the way a boy's new love feels at thirteen, when he thinks this miracle is going to last forever; the way a hypothetical Adam must have felt, surrounded by an entire world that had been made for him and his other half by a generous God. Imagine that first spring and summer, when all kinds of curious creatures ran among the fresh green leaves, everything holding such promise that human hearts could admit not even the slightest possibility of future misfortune.

I wanted to linger joyously; it was like lucid dreaming. There can be such peace in dreams, however fleeting.

But suddenly, we open the door of the phone booth and look up to discover a violent storm already underway. It arrives like a lightning bolt. We never saw it coming.

Annie was pinning the holly onto my blazer. She was having a lot of trouble with the procedure. She tried numbers of times, holding the pins in her mouth, her cool hand inside my jacket, holding the lapel away from my skin. She was upset, and I made myself believe she was frustrated with herself for not being able to get it right. She began to cry, and I decided she'd pricked her own finger with the pin. The tears streamed down her face, and I ignored them, wishing they had nothing whatsoever to do with me. I was impatient to be gone. I had a concert to sing: my last St. Mary's Christmas concert.

I had one more semester of high school to sing through. My invitation to audition for Juilliard was stuck to Annie's fridge with a magnet shaped like a treble clef. Even without Juilliard, I had more post-secondary musical options than I could keep track of. Several university scholarships had already been offered. Concert tours were already in the wings. Recording studios were already lined up. I had a future to step into that stretched out before me like all of Eden. Everything I could see was mine.

One night, over and over, Annie was driving me to Massey Hall in her ancient Volvo. She always knew the best way to get somewhere, and we wove through the streets of Toronto relatively unencumbered by traffic. At every stoplight, I watched as the walk signal changed and people crossed in front of the car, or stood at the streetcar stops smoking furiously, as if to warm themselves by inhaling minute amounts of smoky heat, or sat on the curb wrapped in dirty sleeping bags, hoping for enough coins for a cup of coffee. I avoided looking across at Annie. We didn't speak to each other. The holly was pinned to my blazer above my heart, and I had decided not to wear a coat. I held my hands between my knees; keeping warm or praying, I do not remember which.

She dropped me at the stage door, and went to park. I went inside with all the other boys flowing in through the open doors—some singing snippets of carols, warming up their concert voices, some laughing and punching and slapping each other's shoulders, the way boys do—the heat rushing out to meet us and inviting us in. I could feel the heat, but it did not penetrate. I hid my hands under my armpits, as I always did when I was cold.

One night, at last, I was onstage, hearing the opening bars of "Silent Night." A portent, had I but known it. Had I understood but one small thing about myself, or about being human, or about guilt, or about the inexorable end of childhood. How could I have seen it coming? *That* was the end of it, that moment when I moved forward on the stage to sing my last solo—the solo that should have been a duet—at the last Christmas Concert at St. Mary's, during my last, my graduating year. That moment when I opened my mouth to sing, and the music did not come. The moment when I lost my voice, not to puberty, or shyness, but to despair.

The moment when I at last saw myself for what I was, and recoiled.

The moment when God Himself deserted me.

I STOOD IN THE SCHOOL CLOAKROOM and watched the door, as if Alex might come back in and laugh, as if we could still make it into some kind of joke. In my hands, I held a pair of worn gloves, and thought about going after him.

But I didn't.

He'd go to Mary and pray, and then he would come back, I told myself. I waited a long time. He never came back. The side door to the school courtyard stayed closed. There was a clock somewhere; I heard it ticking. But the feeling of power had given way to self-loathing and a growing horror, so it might have been my heart.

I PUT ON MY JACKET, walked over to the shop, and sat around with Ed while he set about tuning every guitar on the racks. There were more E notes oscillating in the air than in an entire symphony. He'd hand-drawn a big sign that read "Closing Sale!" in twelve-inch letters, and there were a fair number of people coming in and out, a little alarmed that a place they'd never before thought to patronize might be going out of business after being an institution of the town for so long. I only went to talk to Ed to keep his spirits up. I also held the instrument he was currently tuning while he went and showed the nice woman the second-hand French horn, and the nice man the rainbow guitar straps, and the nice child the book called *How to Play the Pennywhistle*, all at fifty percent off. On my way home, I stopped in at the bookstore because I couldn't bear to go back to the library, and I spent the evening lying on my bed with a book in my hands. But I found I was reading sentences over and over; after twenty times they still held no meaning.

ON SATURDAY, BOTH MY MUSIC STUDENTS CANCELLED, and I didn't really know what to do with myself. The piano and sundry collections of stringed instruments held no draw; it didn't really seem worthwhile to get dressed. I wandered around the house in my pyjamas and finally settled on the chair in my bedroom to watch the newly awakened Free-for-All and Fly-by-Night on the shelf outside my window, shelling my peanuts and stuffing them into their eager cheeks.

The sky was bright blue, and it seemed like the temperature was climbing, so mid-morning I put one of my kitchen chairs out on the front porch and went outside wrapped in blankets. Spring was no longer a suggestion in the air, but a tangible event. The roads and sidewalks and driveways were clear of snow, and I could see a few crocuses emerging in the bare patch of ground in front of the other side of the porch, the last things planted by Norman before he packed it in and sold his house to Maya.

I heard Luke coming long before I saw him. When he finally rounded the corner, all I could hope was that he'd gotten a good price for the WD-40.

He was so busy scanning the curb that he didn't see me at first; when he did, he made a quick ninety-degree turn with his wheelbarrow and pushed it two steps up my walkway. When the wheel hit my bottom step, a case of empties slid off the top of his pile and landed at my feet.

"You sick?" he asked, perplexed, as if I were the strangest thing he had seen that day.

"Nope," I said. I pushed the empties back. I felt a little self-conscious in my pyjamas, which was ridiculous. I was talking to someone who had been known to wear socks on his hands and underwear on his head.

"Hmmmm," he said. He stood there for a while, thinking. "You got any empties?"

"No," I said, "sorry."

"You got any books you want me to take back to the library?"

"Oh," I said. "No. No books, either."

"Hmmmm," he said.

It finally occurred to me that he might be hungry, and if I got him some crackers maybe he would go away.

"You hungry?" I asked him.

"Yes," he said, and then he looked like he'd had an idea, like he surprised himself with his own idea. "Why don't you come to lunch with me? *I'll* take *you* out to eat for once."

I protested. He argued. I said he really didn't need to do that; he said it would be an honour. I said no really; he said it would make him feel less like a parasite. I said I wasn't dressed; he said that didn't matter. I said it did; he said he would wait, *outside*, while I put some clothes on. He was a pretty stubborn guy for someone whose life had been made infinitely easier because of a discarded wheelbarrow. I finally gave up when he asked me to listen to his stomach rumbling, and went inside to get dressed. By that time my stomach was rumbling too.

As promised, he waited outside, though I had, somewhat against my better judgement, invited him in. When I got back outside, Luke was sitting in my forgotten kitchen chair, reading the Sears flyer.

"Whites are on sale," he grunted.

It was a strange and difficult thing to walk downtown beside Luke and his squalling wheelbarrow. It is one thing to take him to lunch and be in charge of the agenda and the meal. It is another matter entirely to remain calm when everyone was staring at us and I had no idea where we were going.

I thought at first that we would stop at the Sea Biscuit, but instead of turning down Princess Street towards the lake, we crossed over and kept walking, until I thought he had forgotten that I was there, and after a few more blocks I thought he had forgotten all about lunch, and was going instead to his regular pencil and pen gig at the library. But when we got to the library we went past it and continued down towards the lake.

He stopped for good only one and a half blocks later, in front of the Cathedral Church of St. George, home of the very Anglicans who, a quarter of a century earlier, had bartered my voice to the Catholics so my soul could be saved by *somebody*. There was a billboard sign on the cathedral lawn that read "*Lunch by George*, FREE MEAL SERVED Monday to Saturday, All Welcome."

I was embarrassed, but I wanted to laugh, too. I needed to laugh so badly, I forced myself: a weak, knot-in-the-stomach kind of laugh came out of me. Predictably, on the distant dark side of the moon, a ghostly Filander laughed too, though I'm not sure if he was laughing with me or at me.

I WENT TO THE WHOLE NOTE to buy new harp strings at fifty percent off. Actually, I went to the shop to talk to Ed. I was going crazy at home. The harp strings were my excuse.

The small bells hanging on the back of the shop door tinkled as I went in. I stopped halfway through the doorway, pulled the door back and forth in front of me so this tiny, ancient music sounded again, and again. Finally Ed looked up and spoke, his voice a kind of old music in itself, the kind of music that echoes its sadness as it fades.

"It's cold, Frederick," he said.

"I was listening to the door," I said, stepping in and closing it behind me. "One more shop bell bites the dust. You know, when you close. When The Whole Note is gone."

"That whole infra-red electronic chime thing," he grunted. He was making piles on the counter, wobbling towers of strings in thin plastic packages.

"That whole blasted *ding-dong* thing," I agreed. "Whoever buys the building, they'll change this bell."

He shrugged. "Probably," he said. I shook the mist off my coat and hung it on a hook just inside the storeroom. I looked around in there and whistled.

"Jesus, things are starting to clear out," I said. The room was half-empty, the piled boxes only waist-high. There were gaps or clearings in the jungle where all that was left was dust, skid marks on the old asbestos tile, and used staples lying like discarded confetti. It had only been two days since I'd been there. "More stuff is actually going out than is coming in."

"*Nothing*'s coming in," Ed said, looking up from his sorting, nodding at the door. "You can have the bell."

"Thanks, Ed," I said. "I'd like that." I stood there for a while, noted the hesitation in his hands.

"What are you going to do?" I asked him. I leaned on the counter, watching his face. I decided I couldn't wait for the following year, and our next road trip, to ask him. He knew what I meant, didn't pretend otherwise.

"That whole *retirement* thing, you mean."

"Yeah."

"What are you doing here anyway? Do you have a student coming?"

"Aren't you supposed to be the one answering the questions?"

"Answers only lead to more questions."

"Like what?"

"Like, 'Did I blink?'" he asked. "Did I fall asleep while my life went on without me? Did anybody tell me it was going to be like *this*?" One of the piles toppled and he re-stacked them, straightening the square base with the palms of his hands around the right and left edges, just so, and the top and bottom edges, just so. "When you're forty—"

He looked at me intently for the first time since I had arrived.

"When you're *forty*, Death moves into your town; you hear about it on the news, but you don't think too much about it. When you're fifty, you start to notice him in the street occasionally, but mostly you just cross to the other side of the road and let him go by. When you're sixty, you see him in the lineup at the bank or the grocery store. He's breathing down your neck behind the bench you like to sit at in the park. He even comes knocking at your door, fundraising for charity. But then *seventy*.... At *seventy* you realize that there is not one Death, but many deaths, countless deaths. You realize most of the time you just haven't recognized him, he's been in disguise. You realize that all we do all our lives is *meet death everywhere*."

His eyes were old, yellowing, tired.

"What about meeting Life everywhere?" I asked him. "Can't we do that too?" I was desperate for him to say Yes.

"We don't know where to look for Life," he told me. "You might as well be my son. Neither of us knows where in Hell to fucking *look*."

The shop bell jangled, *minacciando*, and we both jumped, but it was just a shopper, searching eagerly for bargains.

THERE ARE A LOT FEWER NEWSPAPERS delivered these days than there used to be, of course, but some neighbourhoods I deliver to are more Luddite than others. It was a dry, cloudless day; the newspapers weren't tunneled into plastic bags, but simply folded into themselves and tossed onto walkways and porches. Old people, shift workers, moms at home with new babies, some of these folks came out as I was passing and tiptoed down the cold concrete to collect their morning news along with their letters.

The geese were overhead, haunting the washed-out sky with their clamouring music. It seemed to me that the noise of their return was different from the noise of their leaving, though perhaps it was simply the energy that changed, their cries *con gioco* rather than *con duolo*. I heard them in wave after wave of sound, sometimes visible but most often out of sight behind the roofs of houses, apartment blocks, or occasional church steeples. It's always a relief to hear the geese. It's like they pull spring along behind them, a reluctant follower of their song of green.

I was pretty busy looking up at the sky, but when I noticed I scooped a few newspapers up on my way and handed them over, unfolded, with the person's mail laid neatly on top. I know the old folks, in particular, have a hard time bending over.

I guess it was just the way I picked up Mrs. J. L. Franklin's paper, and the fact that there was no mail that day for Mrs. J. L. Franklin. I saw her coming down her few front steps in a quilted housecoat and a pair of slip-on sheepskin slippers, and I saw the paper on the brown grass, already unfurled and laying flat.

"Let me get that," I said to her, and she smiled and nodded and stopped with one foot hovering in the air off the bottom step, one hand on the cold wrought-iron railing. I jogged two steps up the path, and bent over to pick up her paper. It was right-side up on the grass and facing me. We can't help reading things in such situations. Our eyes and brains just take care of it without us having any choice in the matter. My eyes and brain read the headline as that paper was lifted between my knees and my belt buckle, even as I heard Mrs. J. L. Franklin say, "Oh thank you, thank you" and the geese cried like dark angels in the clear air.

"*Effects of Bullying Felt Into Adulthood*," it declared.

I handed it over, as if it were burning my hands. But Mrs. J. L. had seen me reading, and turned the paper so she could read the headline, too. I could see her thin lips make the faintest of movements as she took in the words. Her hovering foot made it back to the safety of the step. She had that slight tremor that is common among the old, so that her head bobbed a little as if she were a person in silent agreement with something that had been said. But nothing had been said, I was sure of it. "Terrible, isn't it? All this bullying nowadays?" she asked me, looking up into my face.

My own tremor was the only answer I could make. I tried to smile instead, but the skin of my face was taut.

"Of course, in my day we'd have just said 'fight back', you know. 'Fight back! Don't let those bullies have their way! Don't let them win!' I suppose that wasn't the best thing to say, though, was it? We didn't know about these things then. Everything's different now."

"No mail today. I'm sorry," I managed to say, and Mrs. J. L. Franklin, still musing, turned slowly back towards her wide open front door.

"Everything's so different now," she repeated.

I pulled the next bundle of mail out of my bag and focused on the next house; the mailbox was around to the side. I didn't pick up any more papers. I didn't hear any more geese that day, either, but once I saw a scraggly line of birds in the air, so high above me that I had to squint to see them.

THERE IS A MOMENT WHEN EVERYTHING that has happened in one's past converges. It's like all the disparate things that have happened—all the crazy, totally unrelated, and seemingly meaningless events—come together like an alloy, after a lot of heat, and a chemical reaction fuses discrete substances into a single element. I understand that there are some modern airplane parts that are made up of ten or more different metals: you take a big cauldron and you mix all these random metals, and then you stand back and look, and you realize you've made a big silver wing, and you think, what else could I have made? *Nothing*. All those hot rocks came together and made an airplane wing. *Of course*. I see it now.

It was like that with all the bits of rock from my past, fusing together. The heat was getting turned right up, and everything started to melt. What else could I have thought? Nothing else. All those meaningless events coming together made me think there was such a thing as a universe of intent, such a thing as a guiding hand, such a thing as guardian angels—or that maybe there *was* a God after all.

I don't know why, but I didn't find that reassuring.

"I THINK I'M BEING FOLLOWED," I said to Ed.

"What do you mean, *followed*?" he scoffed. "This isn't a movie."

"I don't mean literally, I mean figuratively. Things are following me around that I thought I'd left behind long ago. And the newspapers—I pick up a newspaper and there's an article on the front page that seems like it was written right *at* me. Why did I see *that* newspaper?"

"Stop reading the newspaper," he said.

Outside the snow had turned to ice pellets and rattled on

the glass of the display windows. My student had cancelled on account of the weather—she lived out of town—and so I had a free hour with nothing to do but stew. Ed was going through the shop marking down prices, but it was a painstaking process that involved first tuning and playing the instrument, and then laying it in his lap to be stroked, and then issuing a series of sighs that finally culminated in the reluctant use of the red pen he held behind his ear: a long drawn-out *arpeggio*. He was driving me crazy.

"It's not just the newspapers!" I didn't want to tell him I felt like I was being followed by memories of Alex.

"Ngh," Ed grunted. "Shit happens."

"But why *now*?" I asked him.

He looked at me accusingly.

"Do you think the world waits for you to be *ready*?" he demanded.

"FREDERICK," SAID ED, suddenly emerging from the storeroom.

"Mmmm?" I was sorting through the stack of last year's receipts, trying to put them in piles according to month, getting ready for tax time.

"What the hell are you going to do about teaching?" He spoke quickly, as if to make sure he got the whole sentence out.

I stopped what I was doing, and looked uncomprehendingly at *Steel Guitar Strings $37.25*. It sounds ridiculous, but the question hadn't occurred to me. I looked over at the soundproof practice room, littered with silent instruments.

"Did you think about *that*," he prodded, "in all your scheming with Sylvia about my retirement?"

"No, I didn't think about it," I admitted.

"Hah!" He cried, triumphantly. "Well?"

"I don't know. I'll—I don't know. But you can't keep the shop open just so I have a place to teach." I put *$37.25* decisively down on the pile marked *July*.

"That wouldn't be the only reason," he said belligerently.

I decided to ignore the tone. "Maybe I'll quit teaching," I said. "Maybe I'll quit delivering mail, too. I'll quit everything and—travel. See the world."

"See the world? You'd get as far as Bath Road!" And he laughed. A good belly laugh, such as I hadn't heard from him in months.

"Naw," I countered. "Halfway to Toronto, at least!" And I joined him, hollowly.

"YOU WANT TO DO *WHAT*?" Aileen said. I had already anticipated that she would think she hadn't heard me correctly, so it wasn't a surprise that I had to repeat myself.

"I want to take my mother out for the weekend," I said. "To Toronto. For my brother's wedding." I added the bit about the wedding because I thought it might make her more sympathetic. I was wrong.

"Are you *crazy*, Frederick?" she exclaimed.

We were sitting at the nursing station on the locked ward, and I was twirling, somewhat belligerently, in my chair. The usual crowd was lined up along the hallway, staring at the floor, their wheelchair backs up against the wall. Louise was coming and going, writing case notes and answering alarm bells and wiping drool.

"Your mother hasn't been anywhere except *around the block* for twenty years!" Aileen said. Her tone suggested she didn't really approve of even that.

Aileen was the head nurse, and, other than the relatively recent business with the wheelchair seatbelt restraint, I've pretty much always respected her judgement. But I realized I'd never really had any reason to come up against her; that she was in charge of my mother's life was something I hadn't previously thought to argue about.

Older than me by a dozen or so years, she had an authority that few tried to circumvent. I don't know what she'd done before she came to minister over the locked ward in her late twenties, but she'd been there long enough to move into that lengthy wasteland called middle age. In general, she was at that stage in life when her eyelids were starting to droop, but at that particular moment there was no sag in evidence and the whites of her eyes were showing profound disbelief. On my way in, I'd spent fifteen minutes with Marilyn watching M.A.S.H. reruns, so I was hyped for battle. I knew I was going to have to fight. I thought it might be an idea to let Aileen run out of a little steam. I continued to twirl, *risoluto*.

"Frederick, I really don't know what you're thinking, but it's *not* a good idea. Your mother would be totally disoriented. She'd have no clue where she was going, or why. We just don't know *what* she'd do in a completely new environment. She has no idea about *weddings*! Do you have any idea what this would mean?"

"What would it mean?" I asked. Over Aileen's left shoulder, I could see Louise give me an incredulous look, whether because I was arguing with the boss or because she'd overheard enough of our conversation to confirm my insanity, I didn't know.

"Well, there's the wheelchair, getting her in and out of cars—you can't do that, you'd need a wheelchair van with a ramp or a lift."

"I'll rent a van," I said. "Surely you can rent one of those vans. I'd need to rent a vehicle anyway."

"You'd need a driver; you need a special licence to drive one." Behind Aileen's left shoulder, Louise was shaking her head emphatically, but I decided not to argue.

"So I'll rent a driver," I said, "if I need a driver."

"And there's all her medications, and special food, and her—her toileting. You can't possibly take care of all that yourself."

"Someone takes care of it here," I pointed out. "Themselves."

"We have RNs and RPNs and PSWs here; they're all *trained* to provide the kind of care your mother needs. And they work in *shifts*. No one person does it around the clock."

"I could have a crash course? It's just one weekend."

"Are you suggesting you could learn everything you need to know about your mother's care in a *crash course*?"

"Enough for a weekend?" I suggested, tentatively.

"Absolutely *not*," she said with finality. She stood up. She thought she was done with me.

Behind her left elbow, Louise was standing with her arms crossed in front of her chest, waiting with some amusement to see what I would do next. I nodded in her direction.

"So, Louise is an RPN, right?" I asked. Aileen looked over at her, and they both nodded. "And she can look after my mother herself? She can do the meds and the feeding and the toileting?" More agreement.

Incredibly, they didn't seem to know where I was headed.

"Then can I rent *Louise*," I said. I stood up. I was done with her.

"WHY DID HE DO IT? Where is the bat? And then along comes the butter. I wish it—"

"Salvador is getting married, and I am going to take you to the wedding with me," I told my mother.

"I never knew the devil did say anything on the ground could be eaten," she said. "But when people get—"

"His fiancée is called Johanna. She seems very nice," I said.

"Can you get poison?" she asked. "There is something fishy here."

"I haven't actually met her, but I've talked to her on the phone."

"Make them up and put them into short, no, shot, no, save, no—"

"It's in Toronto. The wedding."

"We can't find the cat. Please make them get up; there are fish. I put them down *there* where there are those things, *mortars*, when you see—"

"We'll leave on Friday afternoon."

"I wish to have, not, but you can. In the dark. *Please*. You can see that, you can see that, you can *see* that—"

"Louise is going to come with us. You know, *Louise*? She'll be taking care of you."

"You know what I mean. It's never like it is. What I can't be saying. All the tremble, no, the thimble, no, the way I see it—"

"You don't have to worry about anything. Louise and I will make sure everything is all right."

"The drop is a hat. In a plan there is, but it must be. I used to be so, so...." She trailed off, but there was a strange look in her eye, as if, just for a moment, she was aware of her own confusion.

"What?" I asked. "*What?*" I waited for her next words, put my face so close to hers, went in and out of her lungs on the very air she was breathing, my own breath unconsciously held.

"Where is *Frederick?*" she said.

"I'm here," I said. I reached for her papery blue hand; it was as light as a bone flute. She hadn't said my name in many years.

"In the words you can see the bat. Here you never said you would, but all the same, the butter! Think about it. *Please*. On those days I saw it was the thing Jenny said, so many, so many. Where are they all gone?"

The light went out of her eye; I took a breath, continued to hold her warming hand.

"I'm *here*," I whispered. I put my forehead down on the handle of her wheelchair, cold metal against my skin.

THE QUESTION OF MY MOTHER'S CLOTHES had occurred to me on the way out. "Does she have anything she could wear?" I asked Louise. Of course I knew exactly what my mother had in her closet; I had bought all of it at some point over the years. It was really a question of dress codes and protocol. Would anything she already had do for the event?

"It's not like she'll have any sense of that herself," said Louise doubtfully. "She could be wearing anything at all. It wouldn't matter to her."

"It matters to me," I told her.

"Well you'd better go shopping then," she affirmed.

She gave me her advice—both style and likely location, and I set off to find my mother a dress she would be proud to wear to her fourth son's wedding. Even if she no longer knew about pride; even if she didn't understand "wedding;" even if she didn't know Salvador lived in Toronto and was still one of her lost boys.

I'D BOOKED THE ROOMS through one of those internet travel deal sites. I spent a lot of time thinking about whether one or two rooms was appropriate, though in retrospect this seems ridiculous—another one of those *What was I thinking?* moments that seem so common in my life these days. No one would ever believe it acceptable for me to share a room with my mother and Louise, but at the time I was just thinking about giving Louise the message that she was not going to be left totally on her own with my mother. In the end, I booked adjoining double rooms, and told Louise we'd spell each other off. She didn't seem worried about it one bit.

"You *are* paying me," she said. "It'll be just like going to work but with a change of scenery. And maybe I'll get to meet up with my cousin for a short visit at some point?"

"Sure," I said, but I didn't have any premonition of what would happen in the only two hours she was away from her post.

Some people get worked up about the traffic going in to and out of Toronto, but that part doesn't really worry me. I just have to focus on staying in my own lane and trusting that other people are more intent on driving between the lines than in wishing me any deliberate harm. It's a matter of self-protection, like in life itself. Pretty much no one wants to get hurt. So Louise and I stopped talking as the highway widened, and I turned the music on to drown out my mother as the cars and trucks started to rush by in ever greater numbers, buzzing through the early spring grime like out-of-season insects. I emptied my mind and watched the white lines and the white arrows, checked the speedometer and the mirrors in a circular pattern, every few seconds, and sensed more than saw the lanes merging in and out along the route. It's like a meditation. I could still notice the look on my mother's face in the rear-view mirror as a kind of absence, despite the fact that her eyes were flicking back and forth as she watched the four lanes of traffic on the other side of the highway. And although my brain was in many ways empty of everything else but the physicality of driving, I still also had the wordless thought that this was curious: she registers the input but it has no impact. Even a flower responds to its environment by sending its roots to the water and turning its face towards the light.

IT HAD BEEN A LONG TIME, I guess, since Toronto felt familiar and more comfortable than my childhood home. When we got to Queen Street, I got overwhelmed by the city. The lobby and the valet parking are accessed by a hole built into the bottom floor of the hotel, and it took us twenty minutes to pull in and secure a place to park temporarily, and pretty much the whole time the back end of the van was stuck out onto the street, and cars behind us were honking and occasionally even pedestrians thumped the back window as they walked by, in protest of the fact that we were unintentionally blocking the sidewalk. There were more people milling about in the lobby than most Ontario towns can pull together for a classical music concert, and I stood another ten minutes in line at the check-in desk, surrounded by texting accountants and a multitude of Shriners carrying hatboxes. When I got back to where I had parked the van, Louise had lowered the lift and had my mother parked in her wheelchair on the curb, safely boxed in by luggage. She was just handing the keys over to the valet.

"I've left my cat," my mother was saying. "Can't you tell him to stop the floor?" She was getting agitated, and her voice rose with every garbled sentence.

I gave the valet the room number to go with the keys, and he got in the van and started the motor, and then I lost track of where he took it because my mother's voice had risen enough to penetrate past the twenty engines idling under the overhanging building; the valet team yelling instructions; the constant clacking of the revolving doors; the man on my left having a heated discussion with his wife about which bags he was prepared to take out of the car, *again*; the woman on my right having a fight with her daughter about a tattoo; and the roaring, wireless, heavy-breathing over-charged hum of the entire city.

"When the gut is out, send the marmalade!" yelled my mother.

I picked up all the bags, one by one, and started strapping them across my body.

"Inside the white!" she shouted. "Do you have any morning?"

Morning or mourning? I wondered.

I slung the suit bag over my shoulder, the metal hangers cold and weighty against my fingers. There was a bottleneck of people going back through the heavy doors, and Louise couldn't make much headway cutting across the stream of pedestrians to the automatic door we needed to use because of the wheelchair.

"Hide them to blue!" my mother called. People around us were looking, but only in that uncurious and selfish way that people in big cities look, to see if, for safety's sake, they should put a little more distance between themselves and the yelling other.

We moved forward into the small gaps between people's legs. A hurried young man half-tripped on the footrest of my mother's chair and subsequently sent Louise a look that suggested she had better be sure to lock her hotel room door once she got there. Draped with luggage, I tried to move forward so I could carve out a route in front of them.

"I can't snow in the dark! The trees are going hope, but there is no one! Do you see the sofa?"

Louise gripped the handles of the chair and pushed her practised hip up against the metal button.

"Why don't you sing to her?" she said to me as the door opened. "That'll calm her down."

"*Sing*?" I said, surprised. "I can't sing *here*."

"Why not?"

"It's so *public*," I said. I wasn't really thinking about anything except getting us all through the door, and the question confused me.

"Do you think anybody cares what you do?" she asked, a little shortly. "This is *Toronto*."

LOUISE WENT OUT TO MEET HER COUSIN. The door closed behind her, slowly, and landed against the jamb with a decisive click.

The room was quiet except for the background hum that accompanies almost all of our lives these days: the heating system and the mini bar and the water in the plumbing running up to the room next door and the distant traffic. Rather than the room, I guess I should say my mother was quiet. My mother was abnormally quiet. Louise had given her something—I don't know what—and had helped her onto the bed for a nap; she lay on her back on top of the sheets, fully clothed except for her shoes. But her eyes were half open.

She opened and closed her eyelids languidly, as if on the edge of sleep. When they were open, her eyes moved slowly back and forth across the ceiling. I looked up, but there were no cracks in the plaster; whatever she was looking at, it wasn't visible to me.

I sat down beside the bed and looked at the array of medication bottles Louise had set there. I picked them up, one by one, in turn, idly reading the labels. I shook each bottle; they were mostly pretty full. Enough in there to kill a person, I thought.

There are moments in our lives that have a particular energy to them. They are more focused, perhaps, than all the other moments that make up our days and weeks and years. When these moments come—and we can't predict their coming—we view the entire landscape clearly, and realize we are free to walk in any direction, choose any path, take any action.

Enough in there to kill my mother, I thought.

When you have a thought like that, there isn't anything else. The one big thought takes up all the space.

I didn't think about any of the repercussions, whether I would regret it, or whether I would get caught. I held a bottle in my hand and I shook the pills inside in a kind of primal rhythm. Like a heartbeat.

We stayed like that for a long time, me sitting with the bottle in my hand, my mother lying on the bed, looking at *something* on the ceiling. Me listening to the vibrations of the universe. After a while, my mother's eyes closed, and she went to sleep. Even then, the big thought was the only thing I could think: Poison. It was what she'd been asking me to do for twenty years.

PIVOT POINTS. FORKS IN THE ROAD. This hand or that. There are a million such moments, even in the most ordinary life. The seemingly mundane choices, the coincidences of a Godless world, the happenstance, the way the wind blows us forward or pushes us back. The restaurant the old man chooses for lunch; the acquaintance the middle-aged woman meets in the supermarket; the route the child walks to school.

The edges of cliffs, now that's another story. Those times when, looking back, we can easily separate our lives into Before and After. It is almost like we become different people and can hardly recognize any continuity in the world or in ourselves on both sides of the divide. No matter how hard or how long we think, we can't *know* what might have happened otherwise, what other choices we might have made, whatever other accident might have befallen us. But we always seem to think it would be better than the reality.

Before and After the old man chokes on his curried chicken sandwich; Before and After the middle-aged woman begins an affair with a married man; Before and After the child is abducted by someone lurking in the park.

In between Before and After, I said the two words to Alex Hughes that changed the course of both our lives.

These edges of cliffs are irrevocable, though they play and replay in our minds. Awake and asleep, we refashion the outcome through a succession of minuscule choices, finding all the possible ways to change the facts. In our fantasy, we imagine we are in control. We can turn back time. We can choose a different hand. But when we wake up we find we have not managed to change reality in any way. If we pray, we find that God has not managed to do so, either.

The old man still has not chosen a restaurant where someone knows the Heimlich Maneuver; the middle-aged woman has not gone to buy her groceries on Wednesday instead of Tuesday; the child's mother has not walked him to school.

In my mind, I am still a boy in Toronto, and I'm still letting Annie pin the holly leaf onto my school blazer. Alex Hughes, truly the One Best Voice, has not left St. Mary's prematurely, and is there with me to sing "Silent Night" in our fresh tenor voices, the last duet of our final Christmas concert. Or, at the right moment, I realize my own power, see I have a choice about how to use it, and hold out my hand for the stapled sheaf of paper, and for friendship, and for twinhood—I embrace it, even though this changeling twin never looked or behaved the way I expected. I'm perpetually standing on stage at Massey Hall, willing my memory of myself to open my mouth and sing. I've tried and tried, but I can't make anything be different.

I ONLY WOKE UP BECAUSE LOUISE WAS KNOCKING at the adjoining door. Well, pounding, really. I was half awake, with one eye open, but I couldn't seem to move or speak, and after the brief pounding she opened the door and put her head in the crack, and hissed my name:

"Frederick! Your mother! Like, *now*!"

I grunted, she pulled the door closed, and I got my legs over the edge of the bed and pulled on some pants. I went through into the adjoining room, but there was no sign of either Louise or my mother, just two slept-in beds with the comforters slipping onto the floor, the way hotel room bedding always does. I sucked in some air and braced myself before continuing on to the bathroom.

They were both in there. Louise was sitting on the edge of the bathtub with her hand on my mother's shoulder. My mother was sitting in the tub, naked. There wasn't a drop of water to be seen anywhere.

"—told you I could put the cat in. Of all the crazy, no, brazen, no, broken, *no*—"

Louise raised her eyebrows at me apologetically.

"Sorry," she said. "I can't get her out by myself."

"How the hell did she get in?" I asked.

"Did you ever hear the butter on the plate? I am not going to tell, no, telephone, and see *bay lights*, so never mind—" My mother seemed to be talking to her knees. They were, thankfully, bent up in front of her body, hiding most of her nakedness from my view.

"I don't know," said Louise. "I was drying my hair. I took my eyes off her for maybe two minutes."

"Why didn't you tell me it was time to get up?" I demanded.

"Never mind, never mind, never mind, never mind, never—"

"I just thought I'd let you sleep," she said.

"Never mind," I said. "What do you need me to do?"

"When we went to the store the coat was on fire. I didn't know how to eat it."

"I think if you get in behind her and lift her up that way?"

I took another breath, and stepped over the edge of the

tub, facing my mother's back. I bent down and put my arms under hers.

"One, two, three," I said, and lifted.

There is nothing that prepares a man for the sight and feel of his mother's aged body, thin-skinned and soft, white as if all the years of sunlight come to nothing in the end. Her feet and hands seemed suddenly so small in relation to her body. I noticed the myriad dark moles and small skin tags on her back; I was trying to keep my gaze from the rest of her, a difficult undertaking in that room of mirrors. It was not a question of beauty or ugliness. It was a question of vulnerability. It is not nakedness itself, but the lack of awareness of nakedness, that is so piercing. My mother no longer knew what nakedness meant. She did not care a fig leaf about her lack of clothes. Like Eve before the Fall, she did not know that she was naked. She did not care that I was her son, that my naked chest was joined to her naked back, and that I lifted her up so her whole frail and mysterious body could not help but be seen.

"In the dark days, a coat walked. The cat in the hat, hey. No, the cat in the hat. *No*."

That I did know that she was naked—that I knew, that I cared—was my issue, but thankfully I didn't have time to deal with it then.

Louise and I wrapped my mother in a giant bath towel. My mother's skin was cold, and I shivered where she'd touched me. When we'd steadied her on her feet, I went out into the room and cranked up the heat.

I THINK IT'S SAFE TO SAY THAT I HAVE BEEN to many more funerals than the average person, but I've only been to a handful of weddings in my life, and several of them had been held outside, on expansive lawns or breezy hillsides, where the wind blew the vows from the mouths of the bride and groom and tossed them over the hedgerows, out of everyone's earshot. Except for Geoff and Linda's—and they were divorced three years later—I've never actually heard two people repeat marriage vows to each other. And it seems very strange for someone with my childhood familiarity with God, but I'd never been to a wedding in a church.

St. Giles', Toronto, was a large pale-stoned building that could almost hold its own against the shining office towers that surrounded it. I had taken note of the fact that, for Catholics, St. Giles was the Patron Saint of cripples, beggars, lepers, and outcasts—you really can't count on Catholics to keep up with political correctness—and that somehow seemed an appropriate venue for the first Madrigal wedding in a generation. This particular St. Giles was not Catholic, however, but Church of England, and I don't know what, if anything, the shared saint was prepared to do for the Anglicans.

Even though I've never been to one, I know enough about church weddings to know that Salvador and Johanna did it pretty much the way it's supposed to be done.

Except that instead of remaining hidden until the beginning

of that Wagnerian standby, popularized in the past half-century as "Here Comes the Bride," Johanna stood at the head of the receiving line warmly welcoming her and Salvador's many guests.

She was also six or seven months pregnant. She stood at the top of the church steps like a madonna, her white gown flowing over her rounding belly.

WE WERE GOING TO TAKE MY MOTHER in by the side door where there was a ramp, but Abraham and Alistair picked up her wheelchair and swept her up the front steps as if she weighed no more than a child. At the top of the steps, she was installed in a position of honour next to the groom, and solemnly greeted each new arrival with statements like "The cat is in the feather!" and "Staples and marmalade!" I was worried that she'd start to get really worked up, but Louise just shook her head at me.

"She's okay," she said. "Just look at her. She's having the time of her life."

And it was true that she seemed more contented than usual. All the same, I think to mollify me, Louise went and stood as innocuously as possible behind her chair. I was swept up by the flow of people and embraced—"Frederick, I'm *so very* delighted," said Johanna—after which I was clapped on the back and cuffed on the side of the head—"Hey guy, good to see you! You see my lovely girls?" said Salvador, tipping his head at Johanna and her belly—and then I was handed down the line of Madrigal Boys like a mystery gift in the children's game of "pass the parcel." At the end of the line, it was made clear that I was expected to take up the welcoming torch at the tail-end of this boisterous clan, and I stood awkwardly, as if I didn't know that I belonged there and had forgotten how to wag.

After an enormous amount of time and an entire symphony of guests, Samuel, best man, herded Salvador and Johanna into the vestry and the rest of us to the two front rows that had been reserved for family with garlands of white ribbons. My mother's chair was wheeled up the wide centre aisle of the packed church and parked beside Louise and me in the creaking pews.

The ceremony remains a bit of a blur. The priest appeared wearing a white surplice over his cassock and a stole the colour of an unripe pear draped around his neck. When the organ started, the bride and groom walked down the aisle together, hand in hand, side-stepping neatly around the wheelchair.

"Is the hat under the bed?" asked my mother. "Nuts and bolts!"

There was a great deal of speaking by the priest, and some amount of praying. Everyone stood up and sat down quite a number of times. Salvador and Johanna had prepared words to read to each other, and spoke them solemnly. My mother had a lot of things to say, too, but nobody seemed to mind, so I tried to stop being anxious about it.

I sat in my pew and watched Johanna's belly. I watched Samuel, standing beside Salvador; a fraction shorter, a few pounds heavier, but otherwise two identical faces, note by note, built from the same material. All their faces, each a double of one other, but all of them so similar that it seemed impossible to forget the sight of them, lined up, shining a dark light, but still so beautiful.

I NOTICED, FIRST, A PARTICULAR SILENCE, and then saw that my brother and his wife, newly married, were looking expectantly in my direction. I saw how everyone else had followed their gaze. My brothers in the row across from me; all their startling girlfriends and partners, beautiful in yellow and peach and lilac dresses; the family of the bride, the men all wearing bow ties and the women all wearing cardigans; all the heads in the church had turned, and were looking at *me*, Frederick Madrigal, waiting with an inexplicable confidence in my ability to overcome inertia. The organist had moved to a piano, and quietly sounded the first note of a Thomas Morley madrigal I had sung countless times in the lady chapel of St. Mary's. A tune I had heard my mother sing in that tilting kitchen, a lifetime of longing in her golden voice.

The note hung in the air and faded away like my childhood, dream-like and distant. Beside me, my mother struggled up from her wheelchair to stand in the aisle, the centre of attention in the flowered dress I had bought for her. I was afraid she would fall and leaned over to try to get her to sit down again.

Louise elbowed me, hard, in the ribs.

I stood up beside my mother; I had no choice if I wanted to keep her from falling over. I put my arm around her back and tucked my hand into the crook of her elbow. The skin of her arm hung loosely across my scar. The silence surrounding us was full of waiting, but I could not break into it alone.

Louise had surely only heard those words for the first time the day before, through the half-open door adjoining our rooms, as I practised the song over and over. But, brave in ribbons, like a character from Dickens, she stood up beside me and began to sing,

Sing we and chant it
While love doth grant it
All things invite us
Now to delight us.

Her soft voice crackled when she began, a half-note too low. She was forcing the notes, trying to lift her breath into the music. But as she sang the music moved into her chest, and the power of it grew quickly until it had a kind of raw purity that shimmered until all the air of St. Giles' was etched with silver.

And my mother joined in, already standing and waiting for her cue to the lines she still, even then, remembered.

Not long youth lasteth
And old age hasteth
Now is best leisure
To take our pleasure.

What choice did I have? I had been brought to this moment by all the music in the universe, and there was nothing to do but give it back to itself.

Hence, care, be packing
No mirth be lacking
Let spare no treasure
To live in pleasure.

I sang for Johanna and Salvador and their coming baby—my miraculous singleton niece. I sang for their multitude of friends, arranged in pews like memories, as far back as we could remember. I sang for my brothers' identical forms, and for my mother's damaged brain. I sang for my lost boyhood, both my salvation and my fall from grace. I sang for Alex's stolen dreams, and my own, so guiltily discarded. I sang to both innocence and cruelty. In the end, it seems that singing is the only way we can expect to go on.

Then the whole church of witnesses joined in. It was like a hymn to hope.

Fa la la la, la la la, la la la!
Fa la la la, la la la, la la la!

TRUE TO FORM, THE RECEPTION HAD A WILD, Madrigal edge to it, a party *alla zingarese*.

I watched the dancing from a corner of the room; I was exhausted and desperately wanted to be alone.

I hadn't planned it, but after about twenty minutes I told Louise I was going out for a walk to get some air. I put on my hat and coat and went out of the room and down the hall to the curving staircase, where I skirted the lobby, and met the night.

I emerged into a foreign land, but one that has appeared regularly in my dreams. The energy of the city is different once the streetlights come on. There is both a sense of solidarity and a heightened awareness of our own frailty. I felt like an echo of myself, sensed that dull ache in the sternum that makes us feel apart from everything, invisible and unknowable and unworthy.

I wandered aimlessly for a while, turning this way or that when I came to the end of a block. Before I knew it, I found myself in Yonge-Dundas Square.

There were people everywhere. People smoking and skateboarding and drawing on the sidewalk and fighting and handing out leaflets and talking and drinking, but mostly just standing around in the cold, waiting for something to happen. There were a few white open-sided tents set up for some soon-to-be-held event, and there were small groups huddled under their shelter, as if warmth could be made without walls. There were people lying on the ground alongside them, wrapped in dirty sleeping bags, dead or drunk beyond measure, or perhaps merely over-weary of the hardships of their lives and in need of a little time out.

There were people on the move, too. Weaving through the crowds, making deals, running for the subway, sauntering home with an air of nonchalance but clutching the straps of their shoulder bags closely to their chests.

I stood for a while at the corner of Yonge and Dundas, with my back against one of those great pillars near the subway station entrance, half-hidden by shadow. It was still dreamlike and familiar, those night people moving in those night streets. Here and there, music was being made. I could hear the anaemic sounds of a harmonica far to my left, and there was a classical guitar being plucked straight ahead of me on the opposite side of the square. But none of them was near enough for me to hear more than a few faint bars before being interrupted by loud swearing or the blaring of a horn on the street behind me.

I thought of an old Irish folk song, "Wild Mountain Thyme." The song was one of Ed's favourites. I had an image of Ed sitting alone in the shop looking hollow like a thin reed, with no music of his own left, and I could see how wrong that was. I could see that without music, he would die.

I've said that I never thought of Ed as a father figure, but I realized then that that was no longer exactly true. Maybe part of the shift had come about because Ed had suddenly emptied out, and because I've wanted to try to fill him up again, to satisfy some kind of unfillable need. It was the same role I've played with my mother all my adult life. Maybe it's the only way I know how to be a son.

And then I saw a vision of Louise in the crowded doorway of the hotel, the way she'd been that afternoon. I saw the way she held on to the handles of my mother's wheelchair with an unexpected ferocity—for her, taking care of my mother and the other residents was the thing she lived for, her soul, her music.

"Sing for her," the image insisted.

I opened my mouth, and the trembling notes emerged like declarations of first love, soft and uncertain.

My heart was hammering in my throat.

Nobody cares, I thought. As Louise had suggested, there are times when this can indeed be a reassurance.

O the summer time has come
And the trees are sweetly blooming
And wild mountain thyme
Grows around the purple heather.
Will you go, lassie, go?

By the time I got to the end of the first verse, people around me were beginning to turn and look, faces distracted, or curious, or surprised—a few even seemed pleasantly surprised.

The lights from the billboards and the windows of the Eaton Centre and the shop fronts stretching down the street, as well as those of the countless offices and apartments around the square made the dark sky almost inconspicuous, a mere backdrop to life, not even a single faint star visible. But it was a big night all the same, a bigness engineered by human hands. The energy of all those lights and all that noise and all those people made any one thing, any one person, seem profoundly insignificant. And so my voice gathered strength and grew louder.

I will build my love a tower
By yon clear crystal fountain
And on it I will pile
All the flowers of the mountain.
Will you go, lassie, go?

I moved out into the light. I inhaled the whole city. I found my younger self and touched him, lightly, on the outside of his palms. I could sense the graphite on my downy upper lip. I could feel sharp coins under the arches of my feet.

A passing woman dug into her bag and threw some change in my direction, and it scattered along the pavement like lost wishes.

If my true love she'll not come
Then I'll surely find another
To pull wild mountain thyme
All around the purple heather.
Will you go, lassie, go?

In between the final verses I took off my cap and laid it in front of me on the cold pavement. Beside me, my shadow played on the concrete column, and, when I straightened up, I imagined for a minute that Filander smiled.

And we'll all go together
To pull wild mountain thyme
All around the purple heather.
Will you go, lassie, go?

I MEANT TO GO BACK THE WAY I HAD COME. But I was disoriented, trying to put the lights and the buzz and tangle of traffic noise behind me. Somehow I ended up at the other end of the block.

I walked along, brushing shoulders with myriad men and women, both broken and whole and in transition. I travelled only a few blocks before turning off into a much quieter and more familiar street. I stood in the middle of the block and leaned against the wrought iron gates, and the strange silence and stillness stretched around me like a dark cocoon. The cathedral, the school building, nothing had changed. I zigzagged up the street, and my shoes on the pavement sounded as if from a closed room.

In front of the cathedral, the statue of Mary still held out her stone hand, as if beckoning, asking, begging for my return. Her stone face was fine-featured, and her stone gaze was filled with compassion. She was looking right through me.

"Hail Mary, full of grace," I began. "The Lord is with thee. Blessed art thou amongst women, and blessed is the fruit of thy womb, Jesus. Holy Mary, Mother of God, pray for us sinners, now and at the hour of our death, Amen."

I remembered the words to the prayer as easily as I did the lyrics to any song, the way we remember the songs and poems and prayers of our childhood, one word tumbling out after the other, the stream of words taking us by surprise, coming from a distant place in our minds so rarely touched and almost completely buried.

"Hail Mary, full of grace," I repeated. Most of my brain was watching the sentences line up, word following word, without paying any attention to their meaning. I might almost have been reciting my Social Insurance Number or my bank card number or my address. "Blessed art thou amongst women."

Even if we speak only by rote, calling into the darkness invokes a mystery more profound than our own solitary mind. Even if we have no belief in the summons, we begin to feel a Presence.

The shift was almost imperceptible. At the edges of my field of vision I began to see dust motes sparkling in the dark. The statue looked a little less stone-like; her hand stretched out a little farther towards me. It was impossible not to want to reach out my own hand. I ached for it.

I thought of my own mother, how she'd been hovering for twenty years between life and death, without the comforts of either: not the strength of communication, not the sympathy of the void. But with a blessing, too: she'd lived those twenty years without guilt.

"Holy Mary, Mother of God, pray for us sinners, now and at the hour of our death."

I noticed I had kneeled before I realized I was praying.

THE CLOAKROOM DOOR SWUNG SHUT behind Alex, and I did not go after him. I held tightly to the gloves he had left behind, limp and hollow versions of his fine hands. I offered them to the closed door, as if I could pull him back by such insubstantial means. He did not come back. Not then.

In that terrible moment, he ran away from me, and he kept running until he had cut himself loose from shadowy twinhood. He cut himself loose, literally, with a disposable double-edged razor blade carefully removed from his foster father's Gillette. And then I ran from him, my own hands already scarred by the loss of Filander, and now somehow doubly scarred by the loss of a second-chance twin.

Every life has its defining moments, even if we cannot see until much later where those moments begin and end, how they get sewn together to make the fabric of our lives, or how they get ripped apart to make scraps and offcuts that don't make a quilt, no matter how many times the pieces are turned. What I said, and then what I didn't say, to Alex, has unwound and unravelled my life for over twenty years. It has unravelled both of us. Nothing fit together neatly after that. The edges of the present overlap. The holes in the past persist.

Alex did not come back then. And when he did come to find me again, the following year—when he sought me out despite what I had done to him, and to myself—he was fortified by drink, which I mistook for cowardice rather than a bolster to courage. Twenty years passed before he gave me another chance to hand back those gloves, and do the right thing. Even though I was still unforgiving, he came again, perfectly sober, as if, unlike me, he had grown strong enough, at last, to imagine alternatives to a life without song.

I did not then think of Alex as my twin, more real even than Filander, and I have not allowed myself to consciously think it since; but on some deep level I have always felt it, and conscious of it or not, in the moment when he ran I felt the full impact of the loss. When I ran, it was because I was unable to lose any more of myself, even if I was sure he did not look like me at all.

WHEN I WAS A CHILD, I thought that everyone had melody the way I did, that it was for all of us an automatic part of human existence like breathing or blinking. Music is our first home after all. What we hear in the womb—our mother's heartbeat, the rushing river of her blood, the tuning of her bowels, the vibration of her vocal chords—prepares us for the time when percussion, strings, brass, and woodwinds combine to create a life. When I walked, I marched to a tune that came into being with the slap of my shoes on the sidewalk and the stretch of my tendons and the pumping of my own small heart and the rush of my blood. If I started to run when I caught sight of Dougie Fairweather waiting for me after school, lurking behind a lilac bush, the tempo changed of its own accord, keeping time with my thrice-worn sneakers as easily as a professional symphony responds to the conductor's baton. When I read the words in a book or turned its pages, there grew organically a song about books and reading, full of cadence and flutter and the cymbal crash of the last word. When I bathed, I did so with a liquid melody punctuated by dripping scales. When people talked around me, I heard a euphony in their words that I assumed was part of speech itself, like fragments of birdsong strung along a melody line. If the music inside me met with music externally—in a shop or an elevator, or in our kitchen at home late at night—there was a seamless merging of notes, strung together in a perfect medley. When I got to St. Mary's, my assumptions were confirmed. Everything in the world was guided by music, accompanied by music, created by music, note and tone and timbre. I assumed we were all Aborigines calling the world into life with our songlines.

I believed everyone had music; I only wondered how it didn't show in some people, how it didn't come out of them, how it was contained inside. It wasn't easy to suppress, this I knew. How could one suppress breathing or blinking? I'd tried it myself, lying in my bedroom at Annie's, staring at the ceiling with my eyes wide open until they ached with the effort. I conceded defeat time after time and closed my lids slowly across my dried-out pupils, the lullaby playing, the mystery unsolved.

It wasn't until After that I realized that not everyone had music inside them. I only figured it out because the music in my own head and heart and body suddenly stopped. What had been constant, familiar, companionable, and inherent disappeared like songbirds in September. It was like I forgot how to breathe. It was like I lived without breathing for years.

TWO DAYS BEFORE MY FINAL CHRISTMAS CONCERT at St. Mary's, the phone rang at Annie's house, and I watched her cross the dining room, her heels clicking on the oak floors, *giusto*, to answer it in the kitchen.

I was sitting on the sofa in old sweat pants and a brand new red flannel shirt—a recent birthday present sent from Ed and Sylvia—with my bare feet up on the coffee table, the floor around me littered with sheet music. We'd been discussing my audition piece for Juilliard, with Annie at the piano ready to play whatever I handed her, reaching out easily for the sheets of paper, outstretched hand to outstretched hand.

"Hello," she said, in her telephone voice.

Her back was facing me, but as soon as the person at the

other end began to talk she turned and looked at me intently through the glass in the French door, her forehead tight, and her face growing pale. So I knew right away it was something to do with me.

She mostly listened. Whoever it was had a lot to say, so there were long spaces of silence for me in that living room, listening for clues. I don't think I had any inkling of what it was about—how could I?—but I know I stopped humming and put down the piece I was holding in my hand. I just sat and waited with an anxious twist in my stomach that wouldn't let the notes out.

"Yes," she said. "I see."

"Yes."

"How did it happen?"

"No, no. That won't be necessary."

"I think so, yes."

Finally, the conversation seemed to be coming to a close. I remember thinking how interesting it was that I could be aware of that, could accurately read all the little non-verbal clues that had to do with timing and cadence, could know, too, that there was something else Annie hesitated to say. But in the end, she did.

"Will he be *all right*?" she asked, and there was praying in her voice.

She got her answer, her head leaning against the side of the refrigerator.

"Of course," she said, "of course," and the call ended. She turned slowly to put the receiver back in its cradle, and when she turned around again she did not look at me.

"Who was that?" I asked, clearing my throat.

"The headmaster."

"What is it?"

There was a length of time when her mouth opened and closed, *piangendo*, but no words emerged.

"Alex Hughes won't be singing with you on Saturday," she

said, finally. "He tried to kill himself. They think he's going to be all right, but he—" She waved one open palm over the upturned wrist of her other hand. It seemed she could not look at me.

There was a silence that had nothing to do with music. There was a hollowness in my ears so profound that I felt I had gone stone deaf.

The silence lasted a long time. It might have been twenty minutes; it might have been an hour. Annie sat on the sofa, leaning forward with her elbows on her knees, and did nothing but stare at the carpet.

I did nothing but stare at the top of her bent head.

ANNIE'S HEAD STAYED BENT; when I left her for the last time, she was shrunken, like a distant shadow. She moved around—she cooked, drove the car, swept the snow off the steps—but something that had been holding her life up had been bent or broken.

My heart ached, and I couldn't bring myself to go to school. I sat in my room in Annie's house for days, staring at nothing and chewing my cheeks raw. I was praying. I prayed for some miracle to save me from St. Mary's, from my teachers and friends, from the statue of the Virgin I would have to pass as I made my way toward the school gate. I was praying to God, but the Devil was the one who heard me.

Annie brought me sandwiches that I didn't touch. Unseen, the crusts dried and curled and shrunk. Everything shrunk. Nothing mattered. She stood stooped in the doorway, over and over, and tried her best:

"Do you want me to drive you to the hospital?"

"No."

"I can. I can swing by there on my way to the library."

"*No thank you.*"

"I just think it would be easier than taking the bus."

"I'm not *going* to the hospital." The truth was, I could walk if I wanted to. The hospital where Alex lay with slashed wrists was in East York, and so just across the Danforth.

"You're his *friend*, Frederick. Don't you think—"

"No," I said. "*No*. Leave me alone. I'm not going." And she would leave me alone for a little while. But eventually there would be another sandwich, and another attempt.

"Call, then," she said, placing a fresh plate on my desk. "Just call him on the telephone. I'll get the room number for you."

"I'm not calling," I told her. My teeth ached with the effort. It was my last word on the subject, to anyone.

MY MOTHER AND LOUISE AND I ARRIVED HOME in the dark. I parked the van in the fire lane, and we got my mother's chair—with her asleep in it—strapped into the hydraulic lift and lowered onto the walkway in front of the care facility. I left the van there while we wheeled her upstairs to her room, where I helped Louise lift her into bed. I pulled her shoes off, and Louise unsnapped the back of her dress and pulled it away from her body. It came away like she was shedding a skin.

She'd slept the entire way home. Louise said she'd sung the whole way through the reception with every song the DJ played that she knew. She had exhausted herself with music.

I started to pull the blankets up around my mother's shoulders, but Louise stopped me.

"I should probably change her diaper first," she told me. It was said gently, as if she understood full well what it is to hear that said of one's mother.

"Oh," I said. "Perhaps I'll get going then?" I had been pierced enough for one day.

"Right," she agreed. "You need sleep too." I think we were both relieved. I went to go, but it didn't seem right to just leave.

So I said, "*Thank you*, Louise—" hesitating then, because that was both not nearly enough and at the same time all I could say.

She came around the bed to where I was standing. "Good

night," she said. And she kissed me gently on the cheek, her lips leaving the faintest trace of her leftover courage on my skin.

I COULDN'T IMAGINE SLEEPING. I lay in the too-soft bed thinking about my mother, her brain, singing in the street, the wedding. Thinking about Louise, and, rather alarmingly, about how her lips looked when she called for me to sing. Thinking about Salvador getting married. Thinking about all of my brothers, the lack of infant Madrigals, my mother's brain. One of those round and round kind of nights, when you think you have finally freed yourself of a particular train of thought, only to find that the divergent ideas led you right back to the place you started, like a snake swallowing its tail. I went through it all again and again and again.

THE DOORBELL RANG AT ANNIE'S. I went to answer it in my bare feet, feeling the hardwood beneath me as if I were made of stone. There was no glass in the door, nor any sidelights, so when I looked out at the two men on her front step, I was taken so much by surprise that I didn't immediately realize that they were two of my brothers. If they had not been twins I would hardly have recognized them. Though they were only in their early twenties then, they were big men, fully grown. In my head, I can see them as I would if I looked back now, heartbreakingly young. But as a teenager, they looked to me as if they were ancient oracles of familiar and potent power. I was afraid, but then it seemed I had already been filled with fear, even before they arrived at Annie's door.

I held the door open so long that Annie came up behind me. I could feel her presence behind my left shoulder, as if there were something otherworldly there, hollow and wounded. Alistair introduced himself and Abraham, and Annie, called into action by middle-class training, invited them in, shutting the door firmly behind them. Alistair, who was always just a little more socially adept than the others, removed his boots in the hallway, and so Abraham followed suit. Although there were enough seats in the living room to easily accommodate the four of us, I stood in the doorway with one frozen foot in the hall.

In their sock feet, my brothers' discomfort was more palpable. I could see them fingering the arms of the leather furniture and sizing up the grand piano.

Annie offered coffee, but they refused almost in unison, as if the refusal of refreshment had been something they had previously agreed upon.

"It's not really a social call," Alistair explained, a line I had always believed belonged only in movies. There was twitching, and throat clearing, and eyes sliding, a wave that rippled across their twin faces, still rough and browned from the sun, even in December.

"Well," said Annie, into the vacancy of conversation, attempting to force a lightness into her voice that she was clearly unable to feel. "Perhaps you'd like tea?" It seemed an ineffectual way to incite them to state their business, since business was what they'd come for.

"We have some bad news," said Alistair.

"More bad news?" said Annie weakly. She put out a trembling hand, but it patted the air uselessly in front of her.

"We came to tell Fred." My brothers both looked at me then, and Annie suggested she would leave for a few minutes, to give us some privacy. I think really she could not bear any more and she half got up out of her chair. They hurried to assure her that that was not what they'd meant at all. She sat reluctantly down again, putting her hand on the arm of the chair for support.

Then there was some more delay, and rearrangement of legs and arms, and Annie asking impatiently for me to come and sit down, and me refusing. We all waited, wondering who would speak to break this ominous spell.

It was Abraham who told me.

The scene became more dreamlike. Faces float in and out of focus. Points of time were replayed and reversed and replayed again. I watched the whole scene from the outside: how I gripped the doorframe, how my knees locked my legs into an upright position, how everyone watched me so closely, how my face felt like it was made of flesh-coloured stone.

How I felt, initially, nothing at all, and then a wave of shame for that nothingness briefly flushed my face. But it passed quickly, and I was conscious of controlling the muscles of my cheeks, hardening my eyes, holding my breath. I made myself into stone. For the next feeling was relief, and it overpowered the shame like a deluge. Relief, like a hymn to creation sung by a hundred angels. Like a miracle of music, as if music could be sung with such cowardly feeling.

How I hid that so well from them all, my brothers and Annie. How they continued to look at me with concern.

How I said: "We're going to be late for the concert." As if I could still think about a musical future.

How everyone got up, and my brothers and Annie said things that I didn't understand; they must have been talking another language, the way people do in dreams, a language our sleeping mind invents when things are simply too big to be properly understood.

"Are you sure you still want to do this, Frederick?" Annie asked me, and that one sentence is like an island that I could recognize in fogbound waters. I noticed then that she had finally given way to crying.

How I somehow communicated my impatience. How my brothers left Annie's house, putting their boots on a hundred times in the hallway, tying their laces over and over again. How they promised to try to come to the concert. How they would wait in the lobby after the show. How Annie told them whom to call to see if there were any last-minute tickets. How she explained that they should say they are my brothers, as family members have priority seating.

All that was the lead up to my last solo—or so the programme's last-minute insert falsely announced. For a solo must be sung in order to come into existence.

There was nothing but a void.

In the void was my mother, speechless, lying unconscious and on life support in the ICU of the General Hospital in my home town.

I hadn't been home in four and a half years. I hadn't seen her even once in all that time. I'd written letters with resentment.

And she was my out, my escape, my excuse. Her catastrophe was my salvation. I could leave St. Mary's. I could leave everything behind me.

Scene by scene, night after night, that terrible evening replayed in vivid detail, meting out these events minute by minute, line by line, bar by bar, note by note. The thing that is the most painful for me to remember was that, when I was standing upon that stage with my voiceless mouth open, two of my brothers and Annie and half the elite of Toronto in the audience, I looked around desperately for Alex, Second Best Voice. As if, in my moment of greatest need, he might grant forgiveness and be a stand-in for God, or for Filander, however imperfect, and come to my musical rescue. But in reality, he was gone from me, gone from St. Mary's, and already lost to singing.

I WAS ON THE STAGE AT MASSEY HALL, wearing my St. Mary's navy blazer and my best maroon tie. Annie had pinned a sprig of holly onto my lapel. It had a green smell and a brightness that shone out like a spirit light. I looked down to see evidence of snow still on my shoes, and small gritty puddles forming on the long boards of the stage. When I looked up again, the house lights were inexplicably up, and I could see the hall was packed with people, floor and balcony and gallery. Annie was sitting in the front row, with my brothers sitting awkwardly beside her, but on the other side of her there was an empty seat, and for a minute I was sure she was waiting for my mother. For a minute, I felt such relief, for if Annie was waiting for her arrival I knew she could not be in the hospital. She could not be ill; hadn't my brothers always been liars? And if their news was false, perhaps my world was full of falsehood. There had been no shredded paper, no name-calling, no running away, no not-following. It was going to be all right.

I heard the first few bars of "Silent Night" in my head. I opened my mouth. I could feel how my teeth came together for a fraction of a second, how my tongue touched the bottom of my lower incisors, how the "S" sound waited there for the right note, but the note did not get sung. Instead, the tune circled around to the beginning again, the orchestra conductor, our music teacher, looking at me intently. I inhaled again, ready to sing. No G note, but once again the opening bars of the song. Behind the music there was not the kind of quiet that is customary in concert halls when a performer is about to begin, the quiet of anticipation and good manners. People's mouths were moving, their heads turning up and back, their hands gesturing as if engaged in animated conversation. I couldn't hear anything except the opening bars of "Silent Night," and then a musical circle so we could come once more to the beginning.

I fell in and out of sleep, but whenever I woke up "Silent Night" was being played by the orchestra all the way through, as if it had always been intended as an instrumental interlude in the evening's programme.

I DON'T REMEMBER MUCH about the rest of the concert. I don't remember at all how I got myself off the stage. Perhaps I was helped off, but I have no memory left of that time. I know the next day there was some discussion about me going home with my brothers, but Annie, in a last wise decision related to my care, refused to allow this, on the grounds that I needed something—or somebody—more familiar to me than they were. They took their fading tans and their monochrome tattoos and their steel-toed boots, packed themselves into a rusted-out and dented car, and drove off into the snow-struck day without any evidence of affront. I expect that they were as relieved as I was. They both slapped my back and shoulders before they went, in a classic display of masculine solicitude.

Annie looked out at her car sitting in the driveway dozens of times, listened to the weather report, looked at her boots on the mat, picked up her keys and put them down again.

In the end, Ed came to get me, closing the shop early three hours away and driving all the way to Annie's without even stopping there for a cup of tea before he turned around and went back again with me in the passenger seat. I remember the snow blew diagonally across the highway, riding the wind, and for an hour or more we drove in the wake of a hulking snow plow. I think I was fixated on that flashing light, so much so that all other thought became blessedly impossible. I remember Ed spoke to me rather earnestly during the trip home, but I have no idea what he said. Knowing Ed, I expect he offered up his usual mix of eclectic philosophies and grim pronouncements; I do know he was trying to be comforting. I was spared any more back-slapping, at least.

He took me right to the hospital. He asked me if I'd eaten, knowing I hadn't, and suggested we stop in the cafeteria for a sandwich, but when a meat and mustard concoction was placed in front of me, on that ubiquitous plastic orange tray, I found myself unable to swallow.

We went up to the ICU. When we got there, AA came out so that I could go in— there was a rule about only two family members allowed in at one time. They were the only pair of brothers available for such a visit, since the others were either hospitalized, incarcerated, or in semi-hiding Down Under.

Up until then, Ed had been beside me on this journey, but he hesitated in the doorway, unsure of his place. I could feel that, but I didn't turn and encourage him, so he stayed where he was and let me go in alone. Long afterwards, he told me that my brothers, perhaps making the most of their singular freedom, soon evaporated into the elevator, and he himself sat indecisively in the waiting room for hours, contemplating questions of biology.

The unit was pretty full, unused curtains pulled back between occupied beds, so all the patients could be seen at once, in a long line of human catastrophe, held together with tubing and kept alive by machinery. I had never seen so much distorted and damaged flesh in my life.

I went at once to sit at my mother's bedside. In many ways, I suppose I have never left.

MY MOTHER'S CONTORTED FACE WAS A HORROR I couldn't bear to look at, nor could I bear to look away. I was caught there, looking and looking away, believing and denying. I did not pray. I knew my voice had gone to hell with my mother, and there was, after such an irretrievable loss, no such thing as divine intervention.

After I'd sat with my mother for a while, a doctor came and asked to talk to me. He had a form on a clipboard that he wanted me to sign. He offered me a pen. He put the clipboard on my knee.

"My brothers are in the waiting room," I said. "They're just out there. They're older than I am."

"They're not there," he said. He put the pen in my loose hand.

I SLEPT AT ED AND SYLVIA'S PLACE on my first night away from Annie's, but the next day, perhaps to give me something to do aside from waiting for news of my mother, Ed took me over to my mother's apartment. She had moved from my many-bedroomed childhood home, without my knowing anything much about it aside from her new address, into a small apartment provided by the city, at a fixed rent, to people in receipt of Social Assistance. Public Housing, they call it. And it's a fitting name, as it seems that living in Public Housing gives Joe and Josephine Public the right to ask the tenants and their kin personal questions about their secret lives. Only some of us, it seems, are allowed to keep our secrets to ourselves.

Ed was not related to the Publics. He sat at my childhood kitchen table and hummed to himself for two hours while I wandered through the apartment like a caged animal and rifled through drawers and shelves like a thief. He never once asked me what I had found, what I was looking at, or what I was reading. He hummed away, "Ain't No Sunshine" and "Down on the Corner" and "Spirit in the Sky," and had no idea that I desperately needed him to ask, waited for him to ask, prayed that he would ask. It was my last prayer, and it went unheeded.

My mother's secrets were in a shoebox in her kitchen cupboard, lodged between Courtney Glass' undefended dissertation on The Madrigal Twins and a set of six chipped egg cups, with feet that looked like yellow chickens. The box was faded, the design outdated, and the shoe size—boy's 7—revealing its age. In it I found the few historical documents my mother had considered important enough to file, weighted down by a cowrie shell that read *Aloha from Big Island* on its polished pink surface.

These documents included a marriage contract, Winchester to Madrigal, and three sets of birth certificates naming our father, and one—mine—that did not. There was a small handful of baby pictures of each of us, and the negative of one of all of my brothers together that I recognized from one of the twin books. There was a red and white social insurance card. There was a letter that included her social assistance file number, circled in blue pen. There was an old receipt for bail paid for Nathaniel Madrigal, pending a charge of Theft Under $5000. There was a small and haphazard collection of elementary school report cards. There was a copy of each of the Christmas concert programmes while I'd been at St. Mary's, with my mother's name written along the top in Annie's fine handwriting. There were ten or more years' worth of pocket calendars, with lines scratched cryptically through some of the dates—perhaps two or three a month—with double-digit amounts written in the narrow margins.

There were no divorce papers. There were no bank books. There were no answers.

I did locate a stack of twin books underneath the bathroom sink.

Over the next few days, I had to meet with social workers, fill out forms, and have copies signed by doctors in triplicate. I had no idea what any of it meant; I had only just passed my eighteenth birthday the month before, and it was clear that I'd been living a sheltered life. I just kept signing whatever they put in front of me. My brothers had disappeared into air as thin as the line my mother then walked between staying put in her damaged body or leaving it.

My mother's social worker was Ms. Public personified. What, exactly, were my mother's assets? Had I come across any evidence that there had ever been a man staying in the house? Did I know if there were bedbugs, cockroaches, or mice? How soon could her belongings be moved?

My mother's apartment needed to be vacated to make room for someone else. Even though she had survived the brain surgery, there was a general consensus that she would no longer be needing her home. I packed up some of her clothes to take to the hospital and left the furniture for the next tenant. I didn't want any of her things except the pile of twin books and a handful of relevant papers. I threw out the rest—the bail receipt, the report cards, the calendars.

At least, I thought, she had gotten clean away from the slum landlord.

And, I thought, I had gotten clean away from my guilt.

WE CAN TELL OURSELVES WHATEVER WE LIKE, but our bodies don't lie. I lost over twenty pounds that winter—quite a feat for a teenaged boy. Annie wrote to me, care of Ed, long fervent letters inviting me back to her house in the Beaches to finish the term out, reminding me that God-given gifts carry an obligation to be shared. "You are not to blame," she wrote. When I didn't reply, she forwarded all my mail to Ed and Sylvia's—all of it related to an evaporated future of auditions, entrance requirements, an official mark of Incomplete, and other lost causes. I think she hoped that these letters might persuade me, when she could not. All of it failed; it was a year of failure. I didn't go back to St. Mary's Choir School, or to Annie's house in the Beaches. I enrolled myself in the local high school and graduated in the spring. Despite Ed and Sylvia's urging, I did not join the Honour Choir or the school band.

I got a part-time job as a bicycle delivery boy, bicycle provided, and rented a minute flat above a laundromat in the student district. I lived for the next three and a half years in a rising fog of detergent dust and dryer lint. When all the machines were running, my bed migrated across the sloping floor. I fell asleep to the sound of their vibrations and routinely woke up on the opposite side of the room. I kept my head down and managed to produce a decent enough average to get accepted into Commerce at Queens. It wasn't as hard to get into in those days as it is now.

Not too long afterwards,the Ns came home from Australia, Salvador got out of jail, and Samuel got out of rehab. In the early years, my brothers came by occasionally, but never stayed long. I was always happy when they were gone.

Every Sunday, as penance, I went to see my mother.

She got better slowly, over the course of weeks and months and years. By "better" I mean she came off life support and breathed with her own lung power. She moved from being perpetually flat on her back, to sitting up in a chair without her head lolling. She re-learned to stand, and to take shuffling steps forward, but she had no sense of destination. She was moved from the hospital to the most attentive level of care available in a nursing home. She regained something of language, but nothing of meaning.

I IMAGINE THAT MOST PEOPLE FEEL, at times, that their lives have been co-opted by forces beyond their control. Who gets to choose what happens? We are never safe from blameless accident, from misguided goodwill—nor yet from careless stupidity and unintentional evil. And even sometimes, from jealousy, anger, vengeance, greed, and brutality—the rawest and basest of all human experiences. I am not exceptional in having lived some of these things; my small story fades into nothing, *a niente*, compared to that of countless others. So why tell it? I suppose because making peace with a small story is as important as making peace with a large one. For most of us, the tragedies are not absolute. We get up and go on, in some deep way transmuted from our former selves, but usually not visibly so. And then we spend the rest of our lives trying to answer the question: What the hell *happened*?

I WENT BACK TO WORK AFTER THE WEDDING, and I delivered letters for two days without consciously thinking about much of anything. There was too much to think about; instead, I sang to myself in the streets, quietly, my feet keeping time on the walkways and driveways and front lawns of my mail route.

When we anticipate something for a very long time, its arrival inevitably generates a different scenario from the million and one responses we've practised in our heads. For many years, I'd expected to feel a mixture of loss and relief—but mostly relief. When the nursing home called at 4:53 a.m., I answered the phone from a deep sinkhole of sleep, as if my waking life had been worn down to sand and washed into the sea. I tried to say "hello," but my voice had been eroded by breathing underground, and a sound came out that was not related to speech, but to music.

"Frederick? It's Aileen. Are you awake? I'm sorry. Are you awake now? Your mother's passed away."

I appreciated that there was no beating around the bush. I put the receiver down carefully, and I curled myself around my bony knees like a cannonball diving champion, and I left my body there on the bed. I floated upwards until I was touching the ceiling, and I watched as I wept fiercely like a father losing his only child. I could feel the shadow of a knife in my chest where my heart was, down below on the bed, a fierce, piercing point of sharpness.

There are some times in life when there is nothing but wracking sobs and snot, and at those times there is no *time* at all; there is just the pain, and its slow release. When I stopped, finally—and I think I only stopped because any more sobbing and my ribs would have cracked from it—the sun was bright in a bitter sky and Free-for-all was tapping impatiently on the windowpane, and I was back inside my body, and my head throbbed and my eyes were swollen almost shut. I wiped the salt and the snot away with the edge of my sheet, and I wondered, as if it were the most important question in the world, what the hell I would find to do with my Sunday afternoons.

I CALLED IN TO WORK, MUCH TOO LATE, and let them know I wouldn't be in. I went downstairs in my bare feet, found the peanut butter, put some out on the windowsill in an old yellow bowl, and watched, for a good while, as my twin squirrel friends nibbled the bowl clean until the intricate pattern of cracks in the ceramic were once again visible. I got dressed slowly, putting on socks and underwear like *I* was the stroke victim, and searched way at the back of my closet for my second clean white shirt in a week.

I didn't eat, or drink any coffee. I thought about my stash of Ed's Rickard's Red, but it was a kind of a joke thought, and I noticed how the right corner of my mouth turned up just a little, like half of me recognized it as funny. When I was finally ready to go see my mother, I opened the front door and stepped out into a new kind of orphaned day.

Maya was sitting on the rail that divided the front porches of our two houses, but her feet were on my side of the decking. She looked like she had been sitting there a long time—probably, in fact, since she had heard the phone ring through the too-thin walls in the pre-dawn, and then heard what came after. There was no sign of her orange coveralls or of the piles of pipe that normally accompany her on a working day.

"Is it your mother? I'll drive you," she said. Instead of pipe, she had a box of Kleenex tucked under her arm.

We went down the short pathway together and crossed over to her truck. I had to move a rusty tub faucet off the passenger seat before I got in. The shocks in her truck were shot, and it was a bumpy ride.

She didn't speak at all during the short trip, for which I was very grateful.

MY FIRST LIFE—MY BIRTHRIGHT—was taken from me on the day I opened my mouth to sing where others could hear me, in dark downtown streets crowded with revellers, my cap open on the ground to catch the coins of passersby. How carefully I placed that cap; how well I watched those streets for signs of the second coming. With those nickels and dimes, I set the stage myself for all that came after. Didn't I want to be found there? Hadn't I desperately hoped my voice would call to someone, *anyone*, to bring me out of my prison? And hadn't I gone into that borrowed life with such a feeling of joy and power—a kind of musical intoxication—and never once truly looked back at what I had left? What was there to look back at? An over-crowded kitchen with a filthy, slanting floor. A torn flag hanging limply in my open bedroom doorway, the joists rotting behind the wallboard. My mother making sure she could afford to feed us, and the police ringing the doorbell repeatedly for my brothers, her Madrigal boys. The drips and the creaks and the dirty spoons and the boots on the stairs and the bell made up the only symphony I ever wanted to leave at intermission.

I was obliged by a miracle, swept from that improvised music to notes planned and executed with precision. Suddenly, light was everywhere. Light streaming in through the living room windows like radiant energy, touching everything, settling on Annie's exquisite piano like dust from God's long-handled broom. More rooms to sleep in or sit in than people, and a bathroom all to myself. A kind of hush over everything that waited only for the most pleasing of notes to sound. That expertly tuned piano. Annie's fine voice. My own.

But in its turn, the life given to me by my benefactors was derailed in an instant between absolute power and crippling remorse, between the opening of my mouth to sing, St. Mary's One Best Voice, and the terrible silence that followed.

I often think now about the irony of being taken from one mother into the arms of another, more saintly perhaps, yet even more remote. Mary, mother of God, patron saint of mothers. Would *you* have traded your body to feed and shelter your child?

Hail Mary, full of grace, hear my sins.

There are some things in my life that I haven't done well. I deserted my past, as if it were possible to create an opus without the overture. I was too much a child, even when I should have been becoming a man. When I had my chance to be a hero, I behaved like a coward, and have been a coward ever since. I believed too much in my own salvation, yet I turned away from The Call. I wholeheartedly believed those who told me that I was the One Best Voice.

I was never the One Best Voice.

Hail Mary, patron saint of mothers, including my own.

What started as a cowardly retreat to safety became, in time, a different kind of gift: in the last quarter of my mother's life, though too late for her to know it, I was a good son.

MY MOTHER, IT SEEMS, DIED SINGING the Thomas Morley madrigal we'd sung together at Salvador's wedding. She got up in the middle of the night, got out of bed, and took off all her clothes. She did all this very quietly, and Aileen, who was on duty that night, heard nothing until the singing started. "At first, I thought someone down the hall had turned on a radio," she told me afterwards. "It was faint, like the volume was turned down, and the music kept cutting in and out like the dial wasn't quite on the station."

"Well, that part was maybe right," I said, and it seemed possible. The idea of my mother's voice as a garbled radio signal was somehow comforting. It meant that somewhere, for some people, her song was coming in loud and true; somewhere, nearer the radio tower, someone could have reached their hand out and laid it on the console—my mother's heart—and would have heard clearly all that it contained.

Aileen went down the hall to investigate and found my mother standing naked, facing away from the door, holding herself up by singing, with one hand on the headboard of her bed and the other waving the air in front of her in time to a trembling beat unrelated to her voice. The bed sheets were trailing on the floor, and her clothes and diaper were jumbled around her feet.

"I tried to get her to lie back down, Frederick," said Aileen, "but she really resisted me. I didn't want to force her. She just seemed so determined to keep singing."

"It's okay, Aileen. I'm glad you let her sing." I know she was feeling badly about it all. Even with all the endings nursing home staff experience, Guilt can still follow Death in through any open doorway.

"I was just worried she would be cold. But I didn't really have any choice. It was like there was someone else in the room she was singing to. Her eyes were focused, and she didn't turn her head from the window. Not once. I don't know what she thought was there."

"It's all right, Aileen. She thought *someone* was there. That's all that matters."

"Do you think so?" she asked me, doubtfully.

"I am sure of it," I said. It seems that it's often the job of those who are most bereaved to offer comfort to others.

But I don't know what or who my mother saw at the window. I like to think she had an audience at the end, even one of her own imagining. I often think now of who it might have been: me, or my brothers, or perhaps my father or her own long-departed parents, or even God himself. I don't think it matters who, as long as, in her demented mind, someone heard those final wavering notes and understood at last what she was singing about.

When Aileen couldn't get her to lie down, she pushed the button beside my mother's bed for help. What she didn't know then was that in the next ward over, a man named Clarence McKinley was having a noisy heart attack, so all the ward staff—her emergency backup—were already focused on the bed where Clarence lay. She didn't know then that, after a time, he died there, clutching his chest and inhaling, the air like a rasp across his throat.

So Aileen waited with my mother, but no one came.

"She got to the end of the song, Frederick, and then she started singing it again from the beginning."

Aileen figures she heard the whole song right through at

least five or six times, sitting right next to my mother on the edge of the bed with her arms stretched out to catch her if she fell. She tried draping the sheet around my mother's bare shoulders, but my mother tossed it off without once looking at her.

And after a time—perhaps on the seventh round of the song—my mother died there, standing and looking towards the window, her last note falling from her lips like a leaf from a tree. And Aileen did catch her as she fell, and held that frail and naked body to her chest as the note fluttered to the floor. When it landed, so lightly, she told me, my mother's heart had stopped beating.

I don't know where my mother is now. I sometimes try to think of her as an angel or a star or a mote of cosmic dust or a slip of energy that cannot be destroyed, to see if any of these visions feels more right and true than any other. The truth is I don't know what I believe about what happens when we die. The truth is I can't imagine my mother dead at all.

Like Saint Cecilia, who is said by some to have died singing, my mother's very existence is a kind of martyrdom to song. And while Cecilia, patron saint of musicians, was beatified, my mother will be almost entirely forgotten by the official record once the retention guidelines allow for the destruction of her medical and social assistance files. I don't mean to suggest that I think my mother in any way saintly, only that she too had something of the spirit in her voice. As we all do.

I CALLED SALVADOR FIRST, honeymooning in Sicily. We agreed that there was no rush for the funeral, and I assured him that I had no expectation that they would cut their holiday short. There would only be family, Ed and Sylvia, the Four Consonants, Louise—and perhaps a few of the other nursing home staff—in attendance; there were no friendships that had survived her twenty years of dementia.

And then I called the rest of my brothers, Nick-Nat-Sam-

Abe-Al, one by one, and told them that, at last, our mother had died.

Jiro lent me his van. He offered to drive me, but I told him it wasn't necessary. I went to pick up the urn and came home with it tucked carefully under my arm. I stood in my living room doorway for quite a while, imagining placing it on top of the piano or at the foot of the harp I'd traded my car for.

In the end, I took it through to the kitchen, and cleared away the twin books from the shelf. It looks fine there, and it feels as if this is where my mother's voice belongs.

COMPARED TO MANY THINGS IN LIFE, delivering the mail is profoundly simple. You show up at the sorting station, put bits of folded paper in numerical and geographic order, and then walk around getting rid of it all—an envelope here, a package there. At the end of the day, it's all gone. The load has been lifted. The mailbag is empty. There are no regrets hidden in the folds, nor any guilt trapped under the ever-lightening straps.

I went back to work two days after my mother died and read those scribbled addresses like I was reading a holy book, full of reverence. I watched Dave put letter-mail into his slots at breakneck speed, and the artfulness of his precise movements impressed me as much as any music.

"How're those kittens?" I asked him. I was wrapping bundles in red and blue and yellow elastic bands, the jewelry of our storied profession.

"Oh, they're great," he said. "Always up to *something*. Last night one of 'em ran up the living room curtains and got stuck behind the flat screen," he said over his shoulder on his way out. "Had to unplug everything to get the little bugger out."

I followed pretty quickly on his heels. Outside, I walked my route like I was visiting the stations of the cross.

AFTER WORK THAT FIRST DAY BACK, there was another kind of shrine to contemplate: Maya had decorated early for Easter.

There was a big pink cardboard rabbit taped to her front door, and garish purple and yellow plastic garlands were woven in and out of the balustrade in a continuous stream from her house to mine.

It wasn't until I walked up my steps that I saw the basket. It had an exuberant sky-blue bow on the handle and a nest made out of crinkly paper. There was nothing in it except a note.

Come right on over and eat, the note said. *I've got a pot of baked beans in the oven, and I'll tell you, I make the best dang finking beans.*

But I went home first, to change out of my uniform.

EVER SINCE ED AND I GOT BACK from our weekend away, I'd catch myself thinking about that little restaurant in the middle of nowhere, overlooking a lake in the middle of nowhere. In particular, I'd been thinking a lot about those beans. Although I've never baked them myself, I understand it's possible to use any of a wide variety of types of beans as a starting point—navy beans or black turtle beans or great northern beans—or even to mix two or more varieties together. Then, Ed tells me, there is the matter of onions or no onions, pork fat or no pork fat, mustard or no mustard, and decisions about whether to use molasses, brown sugar, maple syrup, tomato sauce, or ketchup, and in what quantities. There are a lot of choices to make with beans; more than you might think.

One of the main decisions—perhaps the primary decision, although we may not even be conscious of it—has to do with why we are cooking in the first place. Is it merely that we're hungry and sick of steak? Do we want to feed our families, our friends, our customers? Do we want them to enjoy their food, or are we only concerned with nutrients, fibre, or flatulence? Are we for some reason deeply concerned with *perfecting* our offering of beans? Are we motivated to bring a maximum of pleasure to others, in our own small bean-baking realm?

Somehow I know all this has something important to do with me.

A FEW DAYS LATER, I walked over to Ed and Sylvia's, meaning to get there at lunch time, though I set out pretty early. At the end of my short walkway, before I really got going, I turned and looked back to admire the shingle newly placed inside my front window: *THE HALF NOTE*, it read, in beautiful large block letters, and, on the line underneath, slightly smaller, *Voice Lessons*. And then my name and phone number. It was perfectly visible from the curb. I smiled, one of those bittersweet smiles that turns up the corner of only one side of the mouth.

Then I took a bit of a long route, sightseeing, you might say, on the way. It was a fine day—that day in spring when you absolutely *know* that there'll be no more snow; the day when miracles are commonplace: purple crocuses in bloom, buds swelling on branches, myriad tiny sparrows and chickadees collecting shreds of dried grass to build nests, the way they do every year, over and over as if there was no other point to life. It was that hallowed day that those of us who are atheist can almost concede that we might be wrong.

I started out with my jacket on, but I took it off after only a few blocks and carried it under my arm, my hands in my pockets. I passed Ruth-Ann doing my route, and for a moment it was like being in a dream where everything is backwards. But I didn't try to duck out of the way and hide or anything.

"Hey Ruth-Ann," I called out. "How's it going?"

"Frederick?" she said, one hand on a bundle of envelopes and a multi-coloured elastic bracelet around her wrist. "Thought you were supposed to be sick?"

"Mental health day," I explained.

"Good for you," she said, smiling. "Soon as I get on permanent, I'm going to take one of those every month!" I laughed and watched her go up the street with my mail, watched her go up the path to the Evans' house, noticed that their front step still hadn't been repaired. I should have put a warning card in their slot long ago, but I knew they didn't have the money to fix it.

"Watch your step!" I called. She waved the packet of mail in my direction by way of acknowledgment, and went blithely up to the Evans' door.

I went around the corner and stood for a while in front of the house of my childhood, transformed by one enterprising young couple and now inhabited by another. The elderberry bush had been gone for a long time, but there was a hole freshly dug in the narrow rectangle of dirt beside the door, as if the new owners were about to plant something. As I stood there, the front door opened, and a young woman came out and peered intently down into the hole. If only she could see what was buried there, I thought. I moved on.

I walked through downtown, going south an extra block so I could pass the shop window, The Whole Note sign taken down and the windows papered over with wax paper. I tried to peer through the translucent glass but could see little of the work taking place within. I suppose that is the way it should be. The change that happens inside unseen and secret until opening day, to emerge with a great fanfare, re-named and renovated.

There was no ribbon cutting for me. I was being transformed, but I just kept walking.

I MADE IT TO ED AND SYLVIA'S HOUSE. I stood on the front step and noticed how the paint was peeling off the front porch and falling into the dormant flower beds, like seeds with no hope of sprouting. I rang the bell.

Sylvia came to the door. I could see her silhouette travel up the hallway, behind the etched glass. She moved the way she always had, precisely and with purpose. How curious, I thought then, how we can continue to answer doors as if nothing is different. And also, how we can continue to stand on doorsteps and ask to be let in. As if nothing is different.

Sylvia opened the door wide and let me in, along with a rush of damp spring air.

"Frederick," she said. "How lovely to see you." She was smiling, and the smile came from almost all of her.

I leaned forward and kissed her on the cheek. "I thought I'd come see if Ed wanted to go out for lunch," I told her, in case Ed was within earshot, though she herself knew very well that I was coming.

"I'm sure he'd love to—wouldn't you, Ed?" she called into the living room behind her. She looked back at me and winked.

I had come over the day before while Ed was out getting his hair cut, and helped Luke load Ed's spare keyboard and its stand into his wheelbarrow, wrapped in a blanket. We had wheeled it downtown slowly, with Luke driving, and me walking in front with my hand above the squealing axle in case the whole thing started to tip.

Ed appeared in the doorway in his sock feet, with the day's newspaper in his hand, folded over to the sudoku.

"Come on, bro," I said. "Let's go out to eat."

I didn't tell him that Luke and the recently-transported keyboard—and in fact the entire crowd of the town's low-income diners—were already waiting for us at Lunch by George.

MORE FANFARE, ANOTHER SEPARATION SURGERY. The twins were joined at the head. *Craniopagus*. The operation was expected to take over twenty-four hours, but everything went so well it only lasted a quarter of that time. The team of doctors is ebullient. A photographer has captured an image of the crowd in the operating room—the two babies on opposite sides of the frame—to emphasize the novel fact that now there can be such a thing as distance between them.

"It's a miracle," the lead doctor is quoted as saying. "These two beautiful boys will now be able to lead normal lives."

I got the scissors from the drawer and the scrapbook from the shelf. I always do a review of the clippings first, start at the beginning, flip through the pages, *affettuoso*, until I get caught up to the present. The pages are stiff with dried glue, and the oldest clippings at the beginning of the book have begun to yellow. It is my libretto, and the story it describes is my separated life. The pages make music as they turn, crackling and sighing: a song about history, dust, longing, remorse, and, above all, solitude.

Hassan and Hussein; Trishna and Krishna; Crystal and Cristina; Alex and Angel; Lianjia and Lianyi; Regina and Renata; Panwad and Pantawan; Sherrie and Sharise; Moni and Mukta; Deneth and Denuwan; Abigail and Isabelle; Ahmed and Mohamed; Catherine and Caroline; Iyad and Ziyad; Macy and Mackenzie; Zareen and Aafreen; Sita and Geeta; Hope and Faith.

Frederick and Filander.

Normal lives, I think to myself. I try to imagine what that could mean.

The article suggested that not all conjoined twins are difficult to separate. It depends, of course, on how they are joined, and whether any major organs or parts of the brain are shared. I picked up the scissors and then put them down. I did that several times, as if I was split down the middle and couldn't decide what to do.

Frederick Madrigal and Alex Hughes.

Finally, I threw the uncut newspaper into the recycling bin and got up from the table, *forzando*.

MUSIC HAS CHARMED LOVERS and inspired mystics and led armies into battle. It is both wedding and funeral march, selling agent and propaganda tool, jealous cry and lullaby. Music may be Robert Burton's "sovereign remedy," but it is also *Die Fahne Hoch* and the wavering sound of the bagpipes dying out over Culloden Field. Extremes of musical expression are only a reflection of the extremes of human nature. These days it's easy to forget that music is a force for both good and evil, the way we all are in our lives, the way our hearts and minds and spirits are swept up in a river of countless melodies, watching the banks rush by, grabbing at strings of notes as they serve our own purposes. Playing or not playing out the tunes of our destinies, before we drown.

In my life, music has both saved me and destroyed me. Over and over, I am built up and torn down by singing, composing one day and standing naked on the walls of Jericho the next. It's impossible to separate out parts of oneself. Asking myself who I would be without music is like asking who I would be without a voice to sing with or without my particular elusive mother. There are some tunes it is inconceivable to untangle, since their roots descend into the rich darkness of pre-history, among the humus and the worms. That first flute, that first drum. That first voice.

I know that I've deliberately chosen to continue on in a smaller life than I might have had. I wonder sometimes, if there had been two of me—if I had had Filander for real—whether I would have had the courage for any number of lives that called me out of everything I knew. I didn't go. How could I? There was my mother, and Ed, and my voice students, and the choristers, and, of course, the mail to deliver. What could be more important than that?

SUNDAY. I WOKE SLOWLY, my brain emerging from its sleeping state with fragments of floating thoughts riding on a familiar melody. I listened in a detached kind of way, my eyes only half open, for a long time. The sun was playing through the branches outside, rippling the light in the room into a folk tune with an ancient history. After a while, Free-for-all and Fly-by-night began to tap on my window, adding a percussive element to the morning's song.

I got up and put a handful of peanuts out on the shelf, and then I had breakfast: a poached egg on toast, a banana, and a very small glass of orange juice. I had told Ed I'd walk over and meet him at his place for lunch, to help him get his gear ready for our gig at the care facility at two o'clock, so I only had the one thing on the agenda for the morning.

I waited until a decent hour. To pass the time I got out a couple of rags and a bucket of water and the Murphy's Oil Soap, and I dusted and mopped and oiled until it looked as if music had just been invented, right in my own living room. Finally, I took my new portable phone into the kitchen and pushed the dirty dishes aside with my elbows so I could lean on the counter underneath the back window. Behind me, my mother's voice sat mutely on the shelf. In front of me, Maya's tree, still leaning stoically, was getting ready to welcome spring. I'd gone through my phone's call log and found the number for A HUGHES. I held the scrap of paper in the dancing light with a shaking hand, *tremolando*, and, with only the slightest hesitation, I dialled. As the phone began to ring at the other end, the year's first robin landed on a branch directly in front of me, his tail feathers a little ruffled, but his chest the deepest and smoothest russet. I couldn't hear anything at all from outside because the window was closed against the cool spring air, but still, even though I'd never sung it myself, I knew every note of that joyful tune.

ACKNOWLEDGEMENTS

FOR THIS BOOK:
Heartfelt thanks to readers Ann Archer, Zella Baran, Frances Boyle, Peggy Campbell, Wynn Quon, Cheryl Sutherland, and Mary Thomson, who provided valuable feedback when this story was in its infancy. Thanks also to Gillian Rodgerson, Donna Truesdale, and Rita Wilson for reading at least one version of the completed manuscript and encouraging me to keep working.

Thanks especially to Deb Harvey for reading and reading and reading, and never faltering. She is the kind of reader every writer wants, and the kind of friend everyone deserves.

Thanks beyond words to my best and most favourite editor, Ceilidh Auger-Day, who spent many hours, days, and weeks helping me flesh out, cut, tighten, and rearrange, all for the love of me—and of Frederick. Without her all these words would not have made a book.

Thanks to Katherine Knight and Carter Pryor for appearing from the heavens and making the cover of *The Madrigal* such a fine one.

Thanks to the folks at the Silvania Lodge in McDonalds Corners for taking such care with their baked beans—and for all those who do their jobs with love, and who work to bring pleasure to others, however fleeting it may seem.

I am deeply grateful to the City of Ottawa, and especially to Arts Nova Scotia for providing the subsistence funding that helped support the creation of this novel.

I know a lot about music's power, but less about its technicalities. If I have made errors, please forgive me; it is Frederick who is the musician. I did the best I could in telling his story.

Some readers may notice that a few organizations and institutions that appear in these pages approximate actual places. Please know that any shadows cast by the buildings in this novel are entirely fictional.

AND BEYOND:
Thanks beyond measure to one of my most exuberant fans, my publisher, Luciana Ricciutelli, for having such absolute faith in me and my writing.

Thanks to another of my most exuberant fans, Patrick Gibson, for sending my previous book, *The Clock of Heaven*, all over the world, and for making sure everybody he knows is waiting for this one

Thanks and thanks and thanks to Tove Morigan and Nik Craik for raising little people—Kaia, Silas, and Freya—who understand the joy, solace, companionship, excitement, and salvation of a good story.

Thanks from the deepest part of my heart to Andrea Rallo, for the continued practical support and emotional generosity that allows me the time and space to write. Without her I could make no books at all.

Photo: Universal Portrait Studios

Dian Day is the author of the award-winning novel, *The Clock of Heaven*. She lives in rural Nova Scotia.